PRAISE FOR THE NOVELS OF

Whiskey and Water

"The many varied plots skillfully and subtly interweave into a finale with serious punch. Elizabeth Bear's writing style is as dense, complex, and subtle as her plots and characters. The style reminds me a little of Tolkien. This is definitely not a book to sit down to for a light, fluffy read. But if you immerse yourself in this rich, dark world, you will be rewarded with characters with layers of motivation and relationships that weave through the world's destiny like an intricate spider's web."   —SFRevu

"[*Whiskey and Water*] reaffirms [Bear's] skill at creating memorable — and memorably flawed — characters as well as her sure hand at blending together the modern world with the world of the Fae. Her elegant storytelling should appeal to fans of Charles de Lint, Jim Butcher, and other cross-world and urban fantasy authors."   —*Library Journal*

"Bear brings a new level of detail to the subject, and her magical creatures are an interesting mix of familiar and unfamiliar traits."
                              —Don D'Ammasa, Critical Mass

"Bear succeeds in crafting a rich world. . . . It's a book that I couldn't put down, with a world in which I found myself easily enthralled and enchanted, not necessarily by Faerie, but by Bear's poetic expression and knife-sharp narrative."   —Rambles

" 'Intrigued' and 'delighted' sum up my reaction to *Whiskey and Water* as a whole. Don't think of it as a sequel, because it's not: It's the next part of the story, and just as rich, magical, and poetic as its predecessor. . . . I'm hoping for another one."   —The Green Man Review

continued . . .

"The wonderful Promethean Age series just keeps getting better. Bear has a knack for writing beautifully damaged characters, who manage to be both alien and sympathetic at the same time, and then putting them in situations where they have no choice but to go through the fire. The result is glorious." —*Romantic Times* (Top Pick)

"Cleverly designed and well written . . . a delightful tale filled with all sorts of otherworldly species." —Alternative Worlds

Blood and Iron

"*Blood and Iron* takes everything you think you know about Faerie and twists it until it bleeds." —Sarah Monette, author of *The Mirador*

"Bear works out her background with the detail orientation of a science fiction writer, spins her prose like a veil-dancing fantasist, and never forgets to keep an iron fist in that velvet glove." —The Agony Column

"Complex and nuanced. . . . Bear does a fantastic job with integrating these centuries-old elements into a thoroughly modern tale of transformation, love, and courage." —*Romantic Times*

"Bear overturns the usual vision of Faerie, revealing the compelling beauty and darkness only glimpsed in old ballads and stories like 'Tam Lin.' " —*Publishers Weekly*

"This is excellent work. Bear confronts Faerie head-on, including the dangerous and ugly bits, and doesn't shield the reader with reassuring happily-ever-after vibes. . . . She also writes a few brilliant scenes and set pieces, the most memorable for me being . . . the beautifully handled (and beautifully explained) Tolkien homage near the climax. . . . I'm looking forward to spending more time in this world." —Eyrie

LOOK FOR THE NEXT NOVEL OF THE PROMETHEAN AGE
Hell and Earth

Novels of the Promethean Age

Blood and Iron
Whiskey and Water
Ink and Steel (7/08)
Hell and Earth (8/08)

Ink and Steel

The Stratford Man, Volume I

A Novel of the Promethean Age

Elizabeth Bear

A ROC BOOK

ROC
Published by New American Library, a division of
Penguin Group (USA) Inc., 375 Hudson Street,
New York, New York 10014, USA
Penguin Group (Canada), 90 Eglinton Avenue East, Suite 700, Toronto,
Ontario M4P 2Y3, Canada (a division of Pearson Penguin Canada Inc.)
Penguin Books Ltd., 80 Strand, London WC2R 0RL, England
Penguin Ireland, 25 St. Stephen's Green, Dublin 2,
Ireland (a division of Penguin Books Ltd.)
Penguin Group (Australia), 250 Camberwell Road, Camberwell, Victoria 3124,
Australia (a division of Pearson Australia Group Pty. Ltd.)
Penguin Books India Pvt. Ltd., 11 Community Centre, Panchsheel Park,
New Delhi - 110 017, India
Penguin Group (NZ), 67 Apollo Drive, Rosedale, North Shore 0632,
New Zealand (a division of Pearson New Zealand Ltd.)
Penguin Books (South Africa) (Pty.) Ltd., 24 Sturdee Avenue,
Rosebank, Johannesburg 2196, South Africa

Penguin Books Ltd., Registered Offices:
80 Strand, London WC2R 0RL, England

First published by Roc, an imprint of New American Library,
a division of Penguin Group (USA) Inc.

First Printing, July 2008
1 3 5 7 9 10 8 6 4 2

ROC REGISTERED TRADEMARK — MARCA REGISTRADA

LIBRARY OF CONGRESS CATALOGING-IN-PUBLICATION DATA
Bear, Elizabeth.
    Ink and steel : a novel of the Promethean Age / Elizabeth Bear.
        p. cm.
    ISBN: 978-0-451-46209-1
    1. Prometheus Club (Fictitious characters) — Fiction. 2. Secret societies — Fiction.
    3. Magicians — Fiction. 4. Fairies — Fiction. 5. Imaginary wars and battles — Fiction.
    6. Dramatists — Crimes against — Fiction. 7. Shakespeare, William, 1564–1616 — Fiction.
    8. Great Britain — History — Elizabeth, 1558–1603 — Fiction. I. Title.
                        PS3602.E2475I55 2008
    813'.6 — dc22   2008000746

Set in Cochin
Designed by Spring Hoteling

Printed in the United States of America

PUBLISHER'S NOTE
This is a work of fiction. Names, characters, places, and incidents either are the product of the
author's imagination or are used fictitiously, and any resemblance to actual persons, living or
dead, business establishments, events, or locales is entirely coincidental.
    The publisher does not have any control over and does not assume any responsibility for au-
thor or third-party Web sites or their content.

Principal Players in Ink and Steel

combined with a selection of historical and
literary figures as may be convenient to the reader.

Alleyn, Edward: (Ned) A player. Principal Tragedian of the Lord
  Admiral's Men.

Amaranth: A lamia

Arthur: A King of Britain. Mostly dead.

Baines, Richard: An intelligencer and Promethean

Bassano Lanyer, Aemilia: England's first professional woman poet.
  Mistress of Henry Carey. Sadly, not appearing in this book
  because I did not have room for her.

Bassano, Augustine: Court musician to Elizabeth, Venetian Jew, fa-
  ther to Aemilia, and intimate of Roderigo Lopez. Also not ap-
  pearing in this volume, but I promise you, he and Aemilia and
  Roderigo and Alfonso had many interesting adventures that
  Will never found out about. Someday I will write the Jews of
  Elizabeth's Court book and you can find out all about it.

Bradley, William: Stabbed by Thomas Watson in Bankside. Dead.

Brahe, Tycho: An Astronomer

Burbage, Cuthbert: Brother to Richard Burbage

Burbage, James: Father to Richard Burbage. Owner of the Theatre
  in Bankside.

Burbage, Richard: A player. A Promethean. Principal Tragedian of
  Lord Strange's Men, the Lord Chamberlain's Men, and the
  King's Men. Eventual Shareholder at the Globe.

Burghley, Baron: (William Cecil) Lord Treasurer. A Promethean. Member of the Privy Council. Father to Robert Cecil.

Cairbre: A bard, the Master Harper of the Daoine Sidhe

Cecil, Anne: Wife to Edward De Vere, daughter to William Cecil, sister to Robert Cecil

Cecil, Robert: Secretary of State. A Promethean. Member of the Privy Council. Later, the Earl of Salisbury.

Catesby, Robert: A Catholic recusant

Chapman, George: a playmaker and poet

Cobham: Briefly, Lord Chamberlain

Coquo, Oratio: Edward de Vere's catamite, a former choirboy. I am not making that up.

Corinna: The love object in Ovid's fifth elegy, and a character in *Tamburlaine*

Davenant, Jenet Shepherd and John: Innkeepers along the road to Stratford

Dee, Doctor John: An astrologer

Drake, Sir Francis: A privateer

Ede, Richard: A keeper at the Marshalsea prison

Edward: A player. A member of the company of Lord Strange's Men.

Essex, Earl of: (Robert Devereaux) A Promethean

Faustus: A Scholar

Fawkes, Guido: A Catholic recusant

Findabair: A princess of Faerie. Dead.

Fletcher, John: A vile playmaker

Forman, Simon: A physician of sorts

Frazier, Ingrim: A servant to Thomas Walsingham

Ganymede: Jove's cupbearer. Euphemistically speaking, a term for a catamite.

A gardener

Gardner, William: Justice of the Peace for Southwark
Gaveston, Sir Piers: Leman to Edward II, formerly King of England
Geoffrey: A Faerie, with the head of a stag
Green, Robert: A vile playmaker and pamphleteer

Henslowe, Philip: Owner of the Swan Theatre
Holinshed: A historian, of sorts
Hunsdon, Lord: (George Carey) Lord Chamberlain. A Promethean.
    Member of the Privy Council.
Hunsdon, Lord: (Henry Carey) Lord Chamberlain. A Promethean.
    Member of the Privy Council. Father to George Carey.

John: A carriageman
Jonson, Ben: A vile playmaker, son of a bricklayer, educated at West-
    minster. Formerly a soldier in the low countries.

Kemp, Will: A player. Clown for the Lord Chamberlain's Men
Kyd, Thomas: A vile playmaker

Langley, Francis: A moneylender
Lanyer, Alfonso: A court musician, and husband to Aemilia Bassano.
    Sadly, also not appearing in this volume.
Lavinia: A victim of rape and dismemberment in Titus Andronicus
Lopez, Doctor Roderigo: A Promethean. Queen's Physician and Am-
    bassador from Antonio, pretender to the throne of Portugal.
    Of Jewish descent.
Lucifer Morningstar: An Angel, once, and most dearly loved of God.
    Gave Ned Alleyn rather a bad turn, on one occasion.

A mare
Marley, Christofer: (Kit; Christopher Marlowe; Sir Christofer) A
    Promethean. The dead shepherd. A playmaker and intelli-
    gencer. Dead (to begin with).
Marley, John: Father to Christofer Marley, a Master Cobbler of
    Canterbury
Marley, Tom: Brother to Christofer Marley

Mathews, Mistress: Landlord of the Groaning Sergeant
Mebd, the: A Queen of Faerie
Mehiel: An Angel of the Lord
Mephostophilis: A demon of Hell
Merlin: A legendary bard
Monteagle, Baron: William Parker, a cousin of William Shakespeare
Morgan le Fey: The half sister to Arthur, King of England. The Queen
     of Air and Darkness. And, formerly, Cornwall and/or Gore.
Murchaud: Morgan's son, a Prince of Faerie

Nashe, Tom: A vile playmaker
Northampton, Earl of: A friend to Sir Walter Raleigh
Nottingham, Earl of: The Lord Admiral, a patron of players.

Orpheus: A legendary musician who sought to rescue his love from
     Hell
Oxford, Seventeenth Earl of: (Edward de Vere) A Promethean, al-
     leging himself a poet

de Parma, Fray Xalbadore: A Promethean. An Inquisitor.
Plantagenet, Edward: (Edward II of England) A historic king, the
     title character of *Edward II* by Christopher Marlowe
Peaseblossom: A Faerie
Poley, Mary: Sister to Thomas Watson, estranged wife to Robert
     Poley, mother of Robin Poley
Poley, Robin: Son of Mary Poley
Poley, Robert: A Promethean. A moneylender and intelligencer.
     Eventually, a Yeoman Warder of the Tower.

Raleigh, Sir Walter: A sea captain, sympathetic to the Prometheans
A lame raven
Robin Goodfellow (aka Puck): A Faerie
Rosalind, also Ganymede: The heroine of *As You Like It*

Sackerson: A bear.
Shakespeare, Anne: (Annie) Wife to William Shakespeare
Shakespeare, Edmund: Brother to William Shakespeare

Shakespeare, Gilbert: Brother to William Shakespeare

Shakespeare, Hamnet: Son to William Shakespeare

Shakespeare, Joan: (Joan Hart) Sister to William Shakespeare

Shakespeare, John: Father to William Shakespeare. A glover of Stratford-upon-Avon.

Shakespeare, Judith: Daughter to William Shakespeare

Shakespeare, Mary: Mother to William Shakespeare

Shakespeare, Richard: Brother to William Shakespeare

Shakespeare, Susanna: Daughter to William Shakespeare

Shakespeare, William: A vile playmaker. Principal player of Lord Strange's Men, the Lord Chamberlain's Men, and the King's Men. Eventual Shareholder at the Globe.

Sidney, Sir Philip: A respected poet. Husband to Frances Walsingham. Dead.

Skeres, Nicholas: An intelligencer

Sly, Will: A principal player with the Lord Chamberlain's Men

A sorrel gelding

Southampton, Earl of: (Henry Wriothesly) Patron to William Shakespeare, Promethean

Spencer, Gabriel: A player

Spenser, Edmund: A respected poet

Strange, Lord: (Ferdinando Stanley) A Promethean, and patron to players

Stuart, James: (James VI, James I): King of Scotland and eventually England

Stuart, Mary: (Mary, Queen of Scots) Mother to James VI of Scotland. Dead.

Stubbs, Philip: A Puritan, dismembered for treasonous writings

Taliesin: A legendary bard

Tam Lin: A legendary nobleman kidnapped by Faeries

Thomas the Rhymer: A legendary bard

Topcliffe: The Queen's torturer

Tresham, Francis: A Catholic recusant

A troll

Tudor, Elizabeth: (Elizabeth I, Bess, Gloriana) The Queen of England, or perhaps Pretender to its throne

Tudor, Henry: (Henry VIII of England, Great Harry) Dead

de Vere, Elizabeth: Daughter of the seventeenth Earl of Oxford

Wade, William: The Queen's other torturer, clerk of the Privy
     Council

Walsingham, Etheldreda (Audrey): Wife to Thomas

Walsingham, Frances: (Frances Sidney, Frances Devereaux) Daugh-
     ter to Sir Francis, widow of Sir Philip Sidney, wife of the Earl
     of Essex

Walsingham, Sir Francis: A Promethean. Spymaster to the Queen.
     Formerly, her Secretary of State.

Walsingham, Thomas: Cousin to Sir Francis, Patron to Christofer
     Marley

Watson, Thomas: A poet and intelligencer. A Promethean. Dead.

*Divers demons, ifriti, faeries, prentices, goodwives, publicans, recusants, damned
souls etc as required.*

And since we all have suck'd one wholesome air,
And with the same proportion of Elements
Resolve, I hope we are resembled,
Vowing our loves to equal death and life.

—CHRISTOPHER MARLOWE,
Tamburlaine the Great, Part 1, Act II, scene vi

Ink and Steel

Prologue

And since my mind, my wit, my head, my voice and tongue are weak,
To utter, move, devise, conceive, sound forth, declare and speak,
Such piercing plaints as answer might, or would my woeful case,
Help crave I must, and crave I will, with tears upon my face,
Of all that may in heaven or hell, in earth or air be found,
To wail with me this loss of mine, as of these griefs the ground.

—EDWARD DE VERE, 17TH EARL OF OXFORD, "Loss of Good Name"

Christofer Marley died as he was born: on the bank of a river, within the sound and stench of slaughterhouses. The news reached London before the red sun ebbed, while alleys fell into straitened darkness under rooftops still stained bright.

It was a bloody end to the penultimate day of May, in the thirty-fifth year of the reign of the excommunicate Elizabeth.

The nave of the Queen's chapel at Westminster lay shadowed when, at the secluded entrance of a secret room, the seventeenth Earl of Oxford hesitated. Edward de Vere pushed his hood back from fine hair and wiped one ringed hand across his mouth. The panel slid open at his touch, releasing the redolence of oil. The sputter of candles along the walls reassured him that he was not the first.

Four men waited within the stifling chamber.

"Marley is dead in Deptford." Oxford tossed the words on the table like a poacher's take. "Stabbed above the eye by *your* cousin's man, Sir Francis. And we are lost with him: have you so thoughtlessly betrayed your Sovereign?"

"Marley dead?" Sir Francis Walsingham's chair skittered on stone as Elizabeth's hollow-cheeked spymaster lurched upright.

Seated beside Walsingham was Henry Carey, Lord Hunsdon—the Lord Chamberlain—who blanched white enough that it showed in uncertain candlelight. Beyond him was the Queen's physician—and Walsingham's—Doctor Rodrigo Lopez. A final man stood by the wall—round, short, but of undeniable presence: the player Richard Burbage, famous already at twenty-six.

"Not on my orders," Walsingham said. "Is't certain?"

"We are undone." Oxford pulled a chair forth from the table and sat heavily, a dark metal ring on his thumb clicking. "The magic—we can perhaps manage that without Kit. I taught him what he knew, and it was not all I learned at Dee's left hand." Oxford concealed a tight smile; that learning ranged from the science of astrology to the arts of summoning succubae.

Lopez, a swarthy Portugall and well-known a Jew, whatever his protests of conversion, leaned forward over folded hands. He stared at Walsingham with significance and said, "This is not the first attempt on one of our number—"

"Our aims may have diverged," Walsingham answered, "but the others have not forgotten our names."

"And there's plague in the city," Lopez said. "Think you 'tis unrelated to those *other* Prometheans?"

"Can *you* discern a native plague from a conjured one, Physician?"

"Some would argue there are no native plagues, but only devil's work—"

Oxford cleared his throat and his memories. "But with Marley, we lose the Lord Admiral's Men, leaving us without a company—"

"There is my company," Burbage put in, but Oxford's voice rose over the player's effortlessly.

"—and without a playmaker under whose name to perform our works. Never mind Kit's ear for a verse."

Walsingham extended a long, knotty hand, bony wrist protruding from dusty velvet, skin translucent as silk over gnarled blue veins. "Oxford—"

But Oxford shook his head. "I have not Kit's grasp on an audience, Sir Francis."

Hunsdon's hands lay flat on the scarred tabletop. He closed his eyes. "It risks Elizabeth."

Walsingham's chin jerked sharply. "We'll find another way."

He stared down at his hands until his attention was drawn outward again when Burbage coughed.

"What is it, then?"

Burbage drew himself up. "I know a man."

Act I, scene i

*O God, that men should put an enemy in their
mouths to steal away their brains!*

—WILLIAM SHAKESPEARE, *Othello*

"Will."

"What?" The leather-bound planken door swung open; the playmaker lifted his head from the cradle of his fingers. He cursed as the hastily cut quill snagged lank strands, spattering brown-black irongall across his hand, his cuff, and the scribbled page. "Richard, you come hand in hand with fortune tonight. You did perchance bring wine?"

"No such luck." Burbage shut the door, then hooked a battered stool from beside Will's unmade bedstead with one booted toe and perched without waiting to be asked. He grunted as he leaned forward, elbow on knee, and tugged his doublet straight. " 'Tis early for wine, and I'm in no mood for a public house and ale with my bread. So"—he thumped a pottery bottle on the trestle—"it'll have to be spirits."

"Morning?" Will set down the handkerchief with which he'd been dabbing his sleeve and looked up at a shuttered window. Beside his elbow, a fat candle guttered, and his commonplace book was propped open before it.

"Morning. You've worked the night through. And your chamber-mate . . ." . . . *won't be returning.*

Will shrugged. He hadn't noticed the hour, though the absence weighed on him. Or not the absence—Kit was often at the beck of patrons or conquests—but the irrevocability of it.

Burbage accepted his silence. "Have you cups?"

Will stood and moved to a livery cupboard, patched shoe scuffing rough boards. "What ails you, friend?" He turned with two leather tankards in his hand and came around the front of the table.

Burbage dragged the cork from the bottle with his thumbs and poured. "To Kit."

Will lifted the second cup and held it, wincing, below his nose. "To Kit." He closed his eyes on an image of a man smug as a preening cat and soaked in his own red blood. Will drank, leaning a hip against the table as if it were too much effort to reclaim his chair. "You'll have heard the rumors he was working for the Papists, or the Crown."

"I would not hazard myself to hazard a guess," Burbage replied, hooking a bootheel over a rung. "It's noised about that it was a drunken brawl, and Kit's been in his cups of late, as poets sometimes go when they've had a little triumph. . . ." Jokingly, he reached as if to pull the tankard from Will's hand, and Will shielded it deftly. "But," Burbage continued, "Kyd gave evidence against him, and Kit was still at liberty, as Kit seemed to stay no matter the charge levied against him. So there's something there. What's the manuscript?"

"*Titus Andronicus.*"

"Still? The plague will have us closed into winter, Will. It's five thousand dead already. And *Titus* a terrible story. We need comedy, not blood. If we ever see a stage again."

"It's not the story," Will answered. Burbage was a shareholder in the troupe—Lord Strange's Men—and as such he was half Will's employer. The brandy tingled on the back of Will's throat and his tongue felt thick. Still, he reckoned even harsh spirits a more welcome mouthful than blood. *Kit killed. Would he risk everything . . . ?* But Kit had been rash. And brilliant, and outrageous, and flamboyant. And young. Two months older than Will, who was just barely twenty-nine. He sipped again. "They can't all be genius."

Burbage laughed and tipped his mug. "Did you ever pause to wonder why not?"

Oh, the brandy was making Will honest. "Heady stuff," he commented. "If my skill were equal mine ambition, Richard—" Will shook his head. "What will we do for money if the playhouses can't open? How long will Lord Strange champion players who cannot play? Anne and my children must eat." He'd picked up the quill. He turned it over, admiring the way candlelight caught in its ink-spotted vanes.

Burbage waved the bottle between his nose and the pen. "Have another drink, Will."

"I've a play to write—"

"Which opens tomorrow, doubtless? And poor Kit undeserving of a wake?"

"Unfair!" But Will lifted the tankard and breathed the smoky fumes deep, feeling as though they seared his brain. "Poor Kit. . . ."

"Indeed. Would serve your Queen so, Will?"

"Serve her to the death?" That brought him up short. "Is that what poor Marley did? Not stabbed for treason, or murdered by his conspirators before he could name their names. Nor killed for his"—Will lowered his voice—"atheism, and the talk of . . ." He drank again, but held his hand over his cup when Burbage would have filled it. "I can't write."

"Drink will fix it."

Will did not uncover his tankard. "Drink fixes little, and what it doth fix can oft be not unfixed again."

"Ah." Burbage shifted his attention to his own cup as Will stood and paced. "In vino veritas. Is a Queen worth risking your life for, Will?"

"Why ask you these things of me?" Splinters curled from the wainscot shelf. Years of dry heat and creeping chill had cracked the wood long and deep between cheap plaster. Will picked spindled wood with one inkstained fingernail. He'd papered the walls with broadsheets, which also peeled. "A Queen. The *idea* of a Queen. . . ."

"The reality not worth your time?" Burbage leaned on the wall, brandy-sharp breath hot on Will's cheek. He thrust Will's cup into his hand; Will took it by reflex. "It's her got Kit killed, isn't it? Blood and a knife in the face. That's what Queens get you."

"Treason," Will whispered. Burbage's face was flushed, his cheeks hot, red-blond hair straggled down in his too-bright eyes. Like a man fevered. Like a man mad. "You speak treason."

His hands were numb. The tankard slipped out of his fingers, and the brandy made a stream that glistened in the candlelight like liquid amber as it fell. The stink filled his room, sharp as the bile rising up Will's throat. "That's treason, man!"

"Treason or truth? A ragged old slattern, belike. Bastard, excommunicate daughter of a fat pig of a glutton, a man who might have invented lust and greed he liked them so well—"

Will's hand acted before his mind got behind it; he struck Burbage across the face, a spinning slack-handed blow. Drunker than he'd thought, he overreached; the fallen tankard dented under his knee as he landed on it. "Fie!" Brandy soaked his stocking. At least he thought it brandy, and not blood. "Get from me!" Will pointed at the door with a trembling hand, though the player towered over him. "I'll find another company an those are your sentiments!"

But Burbage, pink-cheeked from the blow, extended his own hand to help Will to his feet. Will could only stare at it. "Your eloquence does desert you when you're drunk enough. On your feet, man. You've passed the test."

"Test?" Will wobbled up, one hand on the wall, refusing Burbage's aid. "You've maligned the Queen."

Burbage winked stagily, while Will limped to his abandoned stool. "Her Majesty would smile on it. Come."

"I'll go nowhere with you until you make yourself plain." A burning sting told Will the brandy *had* found a cut under his stocking. "You've bloodied me."

"I'll pay the danegeld," Burbage answered. "I can't *tell* you, Will. You have to come meet them."

"Who?" Blood soaked through light-colored wool, but only a drop. Will winced and picked cloth away from the cut.

"Your coconspirators."

Will looked up as Burbage rested a heavy hand on his shoulder. "Didst not hear me say—"

"I heard thee clear," Burbage answered. "Since thou'rt so loyal then, come on with me and find why Marley was killed. The rumors are true, Will: he was a Queen's Man, sure."

Will blinked. His skull was still thick with drink, though the pain cut through it somewhat. "What do you need me for?"

Burbage smiled, and Will thought he saw the edge of pity in it. "Will. To take his place."

Will followed Burbage into a cool, overcast morning. The gutters hadn't yet begun to stink, but Burbage picked his way fastidiously, one arm linked through Will's to steer the still-unsteady playmaker across a maze of slick cobbles and night soil. "Why not go home to Stratford-upon-Avon?" he asked. "Go back to merchanting. Look at this place: half the shops shuttered, the playhouses closed."

"I'm a player. And a playmaker. Besides—" They passed a hurrying woman in russet homespun, her skirts kilted up and a basket over her arm. She clutched a clove-studded lemon to her nose, and Burbage snorted as she shied away from them. "I have a wife and children in Stratford."

"A player? Might as well be a leper, for all the respect they give us," Burbage pointed out companionably, turning to watch the servant or goodwife pass. Her shoulders stiffened and she walked faster. Burbage looked down and grinned, then tilted his face up at Will.

"I'd die there. Suffocate under dry goods."

"You'll suffocate under vermin here." Burbage tugged him out of the path of a trio of rangy yellow and fawn dogs in low-tailed pursuit of a sleek, scurrying rat. "If the money concerns you, go home."

"I need this, Richard. Your father's a playhouse owner. You've grown up with it. For me—"

"It's worth abandoning wealth and family?"

"I support them," Will answered, ignoring the twist of guilt his friend's words brought. Slops spattered down behind them, and Will stepped into the shelter of an overhang, Burbage following with an arm still linked. "I'll bring them to London once I make a success."

"Bring them to this?" Burbage dropped Will's arm, his gesture expansive. Will admired how Burbage framed himself against the darkness of a brown-painted door in a pale facade, sweeping his arm up beside his hat, every inch the unconscious professional. Will shook his head. Burbage was younger. Younger, but raised to the theatre and knowing in his bones things Will struggled to learn. "Keep them

home, Will. Away from the plague and the filth. I'd go back to Stratford myself, if I could."

"I cannot see you without London as a backdrop. As I cannot see
myself on any other stage. And I need to write, Richard. The stories
press me."

"Then you're stuck." Burbage led him out of the narrower streets
of Southwark, toward a more open lane where a few trees straggled
between massive houses. Will blinked as sunlight abraded his eyes.

"Well and truly. Where are you taking me?"

"To solve all your small problems and grant you large ones." Burbage produced a heavy key and unlocked a round-topped wooden
gate in the garden wall of a mortared brick dwelling.

Will glimpsed green leaves and blossoms beyond; a sweet scent
put him in mind of a haymow. "This is Francis Langley's house. The
owner of the Swan. The moneylender."

Burbage ignored the comment, holding the gate to let Will pass.
"You'll need to find a way to make it appear that the money comes
from legitimate sources, and not be seen to be wealthier than the run
of playmakers, at least here in London. Can your Annie run a business
as well as a household?"

"Money? My Annie can run—*my lords!*" The grass was wet with
nighttime rain under his knee as his bow turned into a stagger and he
swept his hat from his head. Will put a hand down and tried to make it
look intentional. Burbage laughed behind him as he closed and locked
the gate.

"Oh, that was unkind of me, Will," Burbage said as a heavy hand
fell on Will's shoulder.

Will angled his head. The hand wasn't Burbage's. Neither was the
following voice. "On your feet, William Shakespeare: we speak as the
Knights of the Round Table here. In defense of their Sovereign, all
men are equal. And that's a little excessive even if we weren't."

"My lord." But Will got to his feet and looked into the downturned
eyes of Edward de Vere. Over his left shoulder, William Cecil, the
Baron Burghley and the Lord Treasurer, bulked large in embroidered
brocade, side by side with the Lord Chamberlain, Lord Hunsdon.
Doctor Lopez, the Queen's Physician, loomed sallow and cadaverous
a little behind them. And—

Sir Francis Walsingham stood narrow and ascetic on the right, leaning against the wall among the espaliered branches of a fruit tree. Heavy dark sleeves dripped from bony wrists; he tossed a lemon idly in one hand.

Will's jaw slackened, words tumbling from his tongue as he rose to his feet, looked to Burbage for reassurance. "A ghost—"

"Merely," the Queen's dead spymaster and Secretary of State replied, wry sympathy informing his tone, "a startling resemblance to one, Master William Shakespeare. I'm both Walsingham and quick, I assure you. And lucky to be. I've been in hiding these three years past, that my Queen's enemies may think they succeeded in removing me. But Lopez here preserved my life."

The doctor bowed, a heavy ruby ring glinting on his hand, while Walsingham drew a breath. Before Will could speak, the spymaster made a shift of direction quick and forked as lightning. "You know that Marley studied with John Dee, the astronomer."

"There are rumors."

"There frequently are." Oxford stepped away as Walsingham came closer. Burghley, a massive shape in rustling brocade, folded his hands before his ample belly. Will felt their eyes running questions up and down his frame. "The rumors are true. Marley was— well, no magician. But a playmaker with an art for it, and a loyalty to Britannia."

"I had heard he was associated with the Catholics—"

"Where a man goes, and what a man seems to do, are not always the truest indications of a man's loyalties."

"You want an apologist," Will said on a rush of breath he hadn't known he held. "I can do that, in service to Gloriana."

"Ah," Burghley answered. "Would it were so meet and simple. Aye, that's half what we need of you. The other half is a sort of science, or philosophy—" Will saw the deaf old man's eyes trained on his lips as he waited for Will to answer.

"Black Art? You can't be seriously . . . My Lord Treasurer," Will finished, suddenly aware that the nobleman was eyeing him quite seriously indeed, a small smile rounding Burghley's cheeks under the white carpet of his beard. Will raised a hand to press to his breast, realized his action half completed, and let the hand fall again.

"Oh, I can," Burghley responded. "And not Black at all. Just the gentle art of persuasion, my shake-spear."

A sharp scent of citron filled the walled garden, a drift of coolness brushing Will's hand. Citrus oil: Walsingham had driven a thumbnail sharp as a knife into the rind of the lemon. He tugged, revealing white pith and bright pulp. The pearls of oil in the rind burst and misted, hanging on the soft moist air. "Like persuading lemons to fruit in May," Walsingham said, offering half the rent fruit to Will.

Will took it numbly. The skin was still warm with the touch of Walsingham's hand, and Will followed the gesture of that hand toward the espaliered tree. He blinked.

Lemons hung along one branch in late-summer profusion, olives on another. The third grew heavy with limes. "Just an art," Walsingham said. "Like grafting and gardening. In London, you can make surprising things grow."

"You want me to hide spells in my plays? As Marley is said to have done in *Faustus*?"

"We want you to change hearts and raise the rabble to the old tales of kings and princes and ladies fair. To show the danger of damnéd ambition, and the virtue of keeping one's troth. As Kit did."

"I cannot write as Kit did."

"You will," Lord Hunsdon promised. "You've a gift in you, man — in your *Comedy of Errors*, and your *Henry VI*. You'll write as Kit did, and better."

"And wind up like Kit as well, no doubt, with a knife in the eye." *Henry was half Marley's*, Will thought, but didn't correct the Lord Chamberlain. Juice dripped over Will's hand, but Will did not raise the fruit to his mouth.

"There is that risk," Oxford allowed. A light wind ruffled his fine hair as the day brightened and warmed. A dove greeted the sunlight with cooing, and starlings fluttered on the grass.

"We have enemies." Lopez's accent was less than Will had imagined. He tucked his hands inside the drooping sleeves of his black robe, posture imperious, expression cold. "Mistake it not. Our society was quite infested by traitors, loyal to Spanish Philip or to themselves. We've picked them from the ranks, but Kit is not the first of our number to fall to their machinations."

Perhaps it was the chill in Lopez's manner, the dismissal. But Will rallied against it, when he might have bent under greater sympathy. "It's whispered in the kitchens, Doctor, that your swarthy hand was behind the poisoning of Walsingham."

"Aye," said Lopez. "And who spreads the whispers, playmender?"

"Will," Burbage whispered.

"Won't."

Burbage took a step back. Will felt six men lean toward him. "Won't wind up like Kit," he amended. "I mean to die in mine own bed, warm and comforted. There's no way out of this once I've accepted, is there?"

"There's no way out of it now," Walsingham said kindly. "I won't lie to you: we stand only for Elizabeth, and nothing else. No Church or love of God or man may come between us and the love of our Queen. Our enemies stand against us with weapons fouler than a knife in the eye."

"What? Cannon? Sedition? Gunpowder?"

"Plague," Hunsdon answered. "Poison. Sorcery. Politics. The wiles of men who should be removed from secular things; the Catholic and Puritan factions who plot against the Queen are their dupes."

"Puritans and Sorcery? Odd bedmates indeed."

"I've seen odder," Walsingham replied, a shadow darkening his brow. "They are puppeted by shadowy hands. Including, it seems, hands I have trusted in the past." Walsingham's gaze dropped to the lemon in his hand. He raised it to his mouth, lips pursing tight when he tasted the juice.

Will contemplated his own half fruit. "And all I must do is write plays?"

"All you must do," Burbage answered when no one else would, "is write plays. And love Gloriana. Welcome to the Prometheus Club, Master Shakespeare."

"Long live the Queen." When he bit down, Will tasted shocking sour and bitterness, and the salt of Walsingham's hand.

Act I, scene ii

*Hell hath no limits, nor is circumscribed
In one self place. But where we are is hell,
And where hell is there must we ever be.*

—CHRISTOPHER MARLOWE, *Faustus*

Kit awoke in darkness, confirming his suspicions. Secretly relieved
not to find himself in a lake of fire, he would never have admitted
it to a theologian.

It was dark, aye, and the right side of his face felt—

Tom. Tom, how could you have betrayed me?

Oh. "Oh," he said and tried to sit. Nausea and vertigo swept him
supine again. He groaned; cool hands pressed a cloth across his eyes.
Long hands and calloused with work, but tapered: a woman's, redolent of rare herbs and roses.

"In faith, Rosemary," he said, so he would not hiss in pain. "I hope
I'm not dead. I thought death was meant to be an end to worldly cares,
and here I find rather less release than might be hoped from a knife in
the eye. Tell me then, be I dead, or in Cheapside?"

"Neither dead nor in Cheapside, sir knight," an amused voice answered. "And you'll find the legend of your wit precedes you. Drink, if
you'll risk it." The cool fingers touched his lips, and water dripped into

his mouth. Water? No, some tisane, sweet with honey and tart with lemons. Rosehips and catmint. "Better?"

"No knight," he answered. "But a playmaker. Yes, better by far than the taste of my oversleeping. Was I fevered?" He put a hand up to cover hers, but his trembled and hers was strong.

"Bards are honored as much as knights here," she answered. "And you're a Queen's Man, which makes you more a servant of the crown than many entitled to a *Sir*. You are lucky to be alive."

That did open his eyes—his eye, as the right one seemed swollen shut. He remembered a knife in the hand of his master's man— Poultice or no, he sat, pulling the wet cloth aside. His ring was missing, the gold-and-iron ring Edward had given him. "Where did you hear such deviltry, woman?"

She was tall. Hair black and coarse as wire, gray at the temples, strong and fine of feature with an aristocratic nose. If she'd not had her hair twisted into a simple straight braid and been dressed in gray-green linsey-woolsey, he might have said she was like enough his Queen to be Elizabeth's own cousin.

"From Gloriana," she replied, straightening her spine like a Queen herself. "And before you ask why you live, Kit Marley, Queen's Man— call it a favor from one Queen to another."

She plucked the cloth from his hand, and he winced to realize that it was daubed with clotted blood and a few red streaks that were fresher. And that he was shirtless as well, and the skin of his chest was damp. His head pounded at the assault of the light. Kit decided he'd as well err on the side of caution. "Beg pardon, my lady—"

"Head wounds are bloody," she said, turning away. "Art pardoned. What?"

"Your name, that I may repay this service?"

She stopped with a fresh soaked cloth in her hand. And smiled. "May a man serve two Queens?"

He opened his mouth to answer, but she waved him still. "You'd know me as Fata Morgana." She held out her cloth. He took it, and she turned away again. "But you may call me Morgan. Welcome to the Blesséd Isle, Christofer Marley, like many a bard stolen before you."

He blinked, and his head felt so much better for closed eyes that he kept them that way. "You speak a fair modern tongue for a wench a thousand years dead."

"One strives to be current." Her hands on his again, and a smell of wine as she pressed a goblet on him. "Drink."

"And have you drug me?"

"Would have done it with the tisane, Sir Kit, had I mind."

"Again you sir me, Rosemary. Or is your name Rue?" he said, but he drank. It was black currant wine, or perhaps elderberry: sweeter than the grape, and more potent. He tasted herbs in it, and sandal-wood and myrrh. "Yppocras."

"To strengthen your blood. You were hurt. Stabbed and left for dead. And buried without a wake."

"How badly?" He opened his left eye. "May I see a glass?"

The chamber was homely, despite rich furnishings that did not match the plainness of her gown or hairdressing. He judged it hers, though, by the dress laid across the clothespress and the comfortable way she moved about, barefoot over golden flagstones and heavy pat-terned carpets in place of rushes—an enormous luxury. A cool breeze blew in, the shutters standing open to the night. It did not feel like May. "We've no steel," she answered. "But here."

From her belt she drew a silver blade, a dagger twice the length of his hand, polished like a looking glass. She held it up; he tilted his head to get the lamplight at a likely angle.

The right side of his face was seamed with dried blood, for all the lady's bathing, and as ugly a cut as he'd seen laid bone plain from brow to a cheekbone almost lost in a welter of puffed flesh and purpling bruises.

" 'Sblood, I can see why they left me for dead." He frowned when she flinched at the oath. "Pardon, my lady." She might be mad, but she had been kind.

"It's not the cursing. It's the oath."

"Your pardon in any matter," he answered as prettily as he could. "For if I have your pardon, it cannot matter what fault enjoined it, and if I have not your pardon, then I shall have to facet my flaws to the light until you find one that sparkles prettily enough for forgiving."

She snorted. "Not a knight indeed." Ferret-quick, she lifted the poignard in her hand. Before he could flinch, she slapped him hard with the flat on each shoulder, numbing his left arm from shoulder to wrist. "There. That's done it. I dub you Sir Christofer. I'd make you a Knight of the Table Round, but if my brother ever wakes I'd hear of it. So you'll have to settle for Cornwall and Orkney and Gore. 'Twill serve?" She studied his face intently, birdlike. " 'Twill serve."

He made as if to stand, sliding his legs over the edge of her bed. She'd left his breeches where they belonged, at least, but her frank appraisal as she drew the curtain aside pulled a blush across his cheeks and made his swollen face ache. *With a smile like that, were I less hurt, I'd try my luck with her. No blushing maiden, this.* "My lady —"

"It will scar," she replied, as if he'd asked the whole question. "And badly. But a Queen's Man's the better for a few of those, earned with honor."

He flinched again. *So much for any secrecy I might have been left. But I can't fault her herbwifery. And at least she hasn't mentioned blasphemy. Or sedition.*

Or sodomy.

He wondered if she might be one of Queen Elizabeth's rumored bastards. The longer he looked, the stronger the likeness grew. "Will I keep the eye?"

"No," she said flatly. "Not a chance. You could let it scar closed, but there's less chance it will take a taint and kill you if you wash with clean boiled water and let it drain."

"Oh." He sat back against the bed, his bare feet flat on her carpeted floor. "Sir Kit One-eye." She spiked him a frown, and he grinned in return, although it stung. *Oh, Tom. After everything —* It was an ache in his chest as if cold fingers closed over his heart, stopped his breath. He laughed past it. "Could have been Kit-in-his-Coffin, though."

"By the breadth of a finger. Finish your wine. When you're dressed, if you can walk, you'll see the Queen."

The Queen, he thought, and breathed out in relief as he raised the cup.

Morgan showed him a white-painted wooden tub behind a screen, with flannels and cakes of scented soap attending steaming water. The screen was a delicate lacework of pale stone. "Soapstone," she said when she saw him running curious fingers over it. "From the Orient. You have clever hands, Sir Christofer." She caught one and studied it, then lifted direct gray eyes. "How many have you killed with them?"

Despite the silver in her hair, her face was no older than his; her thumb traced circles on his palm. Every sentence from her lips was a fresh assault on his practiced masks, and he swayed between stepping forward and stepping back. "More than I wanted." His plain tone was its own surprise. "Fewer than I should. I must get a message to Walsingham."

She touched his face lightly before letting her hand trail across his collarbone and the bruise her dagger had left. "Your murderers know not that the corpse they planted was but glamourie, and gone by sunrise of the day following—and in a year, who could find the grave? They buried you in a winding sheet, without a marking stone. They said you died blaspheming. Not the first knight to fall so."

"I did? I remember Ingrim, the great oaf, slinging me about by a hand in my hair, and with a dagger in his other. And Poley and Skeres—" *Held me down.* There were other memories in that, old ones Kit wanted not, though they came up anyway on a spasm like bating wings. "Then pain, and great blackness. Blaspheming? No truth in the accusation, but vilest contumely! I do attract it: my wit and good looks." He touched his ruined face lightly, came away with gummy blood on his fingertips. "Can you get a message to Walsingham?"

" 'Twas Walsingham's men did this to you."

Kit shook his head and regretted it. "Sir Francis, not that book-chewing rat of a Thomas, who had the gall to call himself a friend to me." He wondered if she could hear the grief in his tone. From the way her head cocked, birdlike, she did. "I must advise Sir Francis that I live." Sensation was returning to the right side of his face. It would have hurt less if it had been carved clean away.

"He's dead himself, Kit. Hast the blow to thy head addled thee? Gone from thy Queen's service these five years, and gone to his reward these three. However Queen's spymasters are rewarded. Unjustly, if earth models heaven." She stepped away, leaving his flesh burning where her hand had pressed it.

So she doesn't know all my secrets. Lacrima Christi. He let his breath trickle out, relieved and enflamed. *The Privy Council, the Queen must have interceded, to bring me here and under care.*

At least I've the proof I give good service.

Morgan's black braid flagged against her shoulder like a banner. "You'll want to scrub that wound with soap once you're in the water."

"Is that wise?"

Her hem whispered over stone as she vanished around the screen. "It's all that could save you. If the wound goes bad—so close to the brain—well, it's not as if we can amputate. Soap will cleanse the wound."

"And hurt."

"Not so much as when I sew and poultice it. As I'll have to if you want a neat, straight scar and not a mess of proud flesh." He winced at the thought, then unlaced his breeches and tested the water on his wrist.

"Do you care for a man in an eyepatch, my lady?" No answer, but he thought he heard a chuckle. The water came to his chin and was hot enough to make his heart pound once he settled in. A deep ache spread across his back, thighs, and shoulders as tight muscles considered relaxation. He leaned against the carved headboard and stretched his toes to meet the foot.

"Scrub," she reminded. He sighed and picked up the soap.

When he was half dressed again, she washed the cut with liquor until white, clean pain streamed tears down his face. But it throbbed less after, and his head felt cooler. The stitching was worse, for all she fed him brandy before. The needle scraped bone as she tugged his scalp together and sewed it tight; he whined like a kicked pup before she finished.

"Brave Sir Kit," she whispered when she'd tied the final knot. He leaned spent against a bedpost. "Braver than Lance was over his wounds, when I dressed them. He spat and swatted like a cat." She gave him more brandy and bound a poultice across the right side of his face. When he set the cup aside she leaned down and licked the last sweet drop from the corner of his mouth.

He startled, gasping, but regretted it when she leaned back, eyes narrowed at the corners with her smile. "My lady, I am not at my best." And then he worried at the knot in his gut, the fascination with which he followed her. *This is not like me.*

Anything to think of, but Tom.

"Welcome to Hy Bréàsil, poet." She balled up the cream silk hanging on the pale oaken bedpost and threw it against his chest. "Put your shirt and doublet on. It pleases the Queen to greet you."

He dressed in haste: the shirt was finer stuff than he'd worn, and the dark velvet doublet stitched with black pearls and pale threads of gold, sleeves slashed with silk the color of blued steel. "What royal palace is this?" he asked as she helped him button the fourteen pearls at each wrist.

"The Queen's."

"They're all the Queen's. Westminster or Hampton Court? White-hall? Placentia?" He scrubbed golden flagstones with a toe and noticed that someone had polished his riding boots until they shone like his shirt. The pressure of bandages across his face calmed the pain; he hazarded a smile.

"Call it Underhill." She tugged his collar straight. "Or Oversea, and you won't be far wrong. Names aren't much matter, unless they're the right name. There." She stepped back to admire her work. "Fair."

"Art my mirror, then?"

"The only mirror you'll get but a blade." She'd changed her dress while he was bathing and wore gray moiré: no less plain than the green dress, but of finer stuff and stitched with a tight small hand. Slippers of white fur peeked under the hem, and he stole a second glance to be sure.

Ermine. He was glad he hadn't taken advantage of what the mad-woman offered, and resolved not to absentmindedly thee her again. "Her Majesty does me honor."

Morgan offered him her arm. He held the door open as she gathered her skirts. "She has an eye for a well-turned calf."

"I've an eye as well," Kit admitted. "Only one anymore, alas. But it serves to notice a fair turn of ankle still—" His voice faltered as they came through the doorway. His knees and his bowels went to water, as they hadn't when Morgan showed him the gaping wound across his face. As they hadn't when she kissed his mouth.

The door opened on a narrow railed walkway over a gallery that yearned heavenward like the vault of a church. The whole structure was translucent golden stone, carved in arches airier than any gothic-work, the struts blending overhead like twining branches. Between those branches sparkled the largest panes of glass he'd seen. Beyond the glass roof, through it, shone a full moon attended by her company of stars. People moved in eddies on the stone-tiled floor several lofty stories below; they passed through a guarded, carven double door two stories from threshold to lintel. Even from this vantage Kit could see not all were human. Their wings and tails and horns were not the artifice of a masque.

He licked his lips and tasted herbs and brandy, and a kiss.

"Fairy wine," he said, half-breathless with awe and loss and betrayal. "I drank fairy wine. I cannot leave."

Morgan le Fey stepped closer on his blind side, resting her strong hand in the curve of his elbow. "I warned you about the tisane. And as long as you're tricked already, we may as well see this ended so we can get dinner. Come along, poet. Your new Queen waits."

Act I, scene iii

Touchstone: *When a man's verses cannot be understood, nor a man's good wit seconded with the forward child Understanding, it strikes a man more dead than a great reckoning in a little room. Truly, I would the gods had made thee poetical.*
Audrey: *I do not know what "poetical" is. Is it honest in deed and word? Is it a true thing?*
Touchstone: *No, truly, for the truest poetry is the most feigning; and lovers are given to poetry, and what they swear in poetry may be said as lovers they do feign.*

—WILLIAM SHAKESPEARE, *As You Like It*

May became June, and Burbage's prophecy held: the plague carried off another thousand souls, rat- and cat-catchers roamed the streets with their poles of corpses and their narrow-eyed terriers, and the playhouses stayed closed. Will's new lodgings were over the tavern Richard Burbage favored, north of the River and closer to James Burbage's Theatre. They were considerably more luxurious, possessing a window with north light for working by and a bed all to Will's own use. But *Titus* grew a scant few manuscript pages, and Will swore to Burbage that they might as well have been written in his own dark blood.

Will sat picking at a supper of mutton and ale in the coolest corner of the common room, his trencher shoved to one side and *Titus* spread on the table, the ink drying in his pen. The food held no savor, but he set pen in inkbottle anyway and worried at the meat with his knife so he wouldn't sit there only staring at the mottled page. How long did one go without writing before one stopped calling oneself a playmaker?

It wouldn't be so bad if the *pressure* to have the stories out would relent. Instead of nagging after him like a lusty husband at a wife just delivered of the *last* babe.

The image made him smile, and then it made him frown. *How long since you've seen Annie last? If you can't write plays, you could go home and watch your son grow.*

He picked the pen up, and a fat drop of irongall splattered a page folded in four for convenience of writing. But his grimace of irritation was interrupted when Burbage walked out of the warm summer twilight, crossing to Will's table after a quick examination of the room. A taller man might have had to duck the thick beams—Edward Alleyn would have been stooped just crossing—but Burbage strutted through clots and eddies of drinkers like a rooster through the henyard. A flurry of conversation followed as the custom recognized London's second-most-famous player. Will gestured Burbage to the bench.

"Good even, Will. I'll not sit: had your fill of mutton?"

"Since what you have to say will no doubt rob mine appetite." Burbage shrugged, so Will smiled to take some of the sting from his words. "Whither?"

"We'll to Oxford." Burbage offered Will a handclasp. This time, Shakespeare took it to stand.

"A long walk," he said, though Burbage's grin alerted him.

"Just across London Bridge," the player continued, softening his voice. "We're stayed for at the Elephant, Cousin. Step quick!"

Will gulped the last of his ale and hung the tankard at his belt, then gave the landlord's son a ha'penny to run his papers and pen up to his room. The leftover mutton and trencher would be given as alms to the poor or—more likely—go into the stewpot. He wiped moisture from his palms onto the front of his breeches and took Burbage's arm. "I feel as if I'm summoned by a patron, and I shall have to confess so little done on *Titus*—"

"*Titus* this and *Titus* that." Burbage led him north. "Vex me not with *Titus*. What thorn is in your paw on that damned play?"

The houses and shops lining London Bridge came into view. Will checked his stride as the foot traffic clotted, keeping one hand on his purse. Stones clattered under hooves and boots. Will squared his shoulders, hooked thumbs in his belt, and charged forward so abruptly that Burbage struggled to pace him, bobbing like a bubble in an eddy in his wake.

"Will!"

Will shook his head as Burbage caught his elbow.

"Will, what is it?"

Will jerked his chin upward, and Burbage's eyes followed the motion. The Great Stone Gate loomed over them, cutting a dark silhouette across a sky pink and gray with twilight. The last light of a rare clear sunset stained the Gate—and all its grisly trophies—crimson, and dyed too the elegant wings of wheeling kites and the black pinions of the Tower ravens.

"If Kit hadn't been murdered in an alehouse," he said low, steps slowing, "his head could be up there among the traitors."

"What heard you about the Privy Council proceedings?"

"I heard that Kyd and that other fellow—Richard Baines—named him as the author of heretical documents. That he stood accused of atheism, sodomy, and worse."

"Kyd under torture," Burbage amended, tugging Will's arm. "Baines—someday I'll tell you about Baines."

Will had almost to be dragged several shuffling steps before he was walking on his own. "I've writ not a good word since."

It was Burbage's turn to stumble. "Will."

Will rested a hand on Richard's shoulder. "What?"

"You know what Kit was charged with. Sayst thou you know something of the truth of those allegations?"

Will knew his eyes must be big as the paving stones underfoot, his face red as the sunset painting the Gate. "Regarding Kit's alleged sins, I'll not doubt it. But no, I'm not likely to be charged the same. We shared the room for prudence's sake."

"Then what?"

A shrug and a sigh. "We were friends. His hand was on my *Henry*

VI, thou knowest, and mine in his *Edward III*. If he can come to such an end, whose Muse dripped inspiration upon his brow as the jewels of a crown drip light—what does that bode for poorer talents?"

"Poorer talents?" They were swept up in the tide of pedestrians before they had gone three steps, in the stench of the Thames, in the rattle of coach-wheels and the blurred notes of poorly fingered music: the sprawl and brawl of London. "Not so, Will. You've an ear on you for cleverness and character better than Kit's. And you're funnier."

"I can't match his technique. Or his passion."

"No. But technique can be learned, and you won't, perchance, end your life drunken and leaking out your brains on some table in a supperhouse. If Kit had the patience and sense of a Will—" He raised his hand to forestall Will's retort.

Will's shoulders fell as the air seeped from his lungs. "I listen, Master Burbage."

They came out of the shadow of the Gate and its burden. "The Privy Council would have cleared him, Master Shakespeare. As it's done every time before: with a wave of the hand, words behind closed doors, and a writ signed by five or seven of the Queen's best men, Kit Marley goes free where another man would go to Tyburn. How many men charged with heresy and sedition are free to rent a mare and ride to Deptford, and not on a rack in the Tower? And you'll be afforded the same protection."

"And the same enemies." But it wasn't just the danger of his own position, or the unwritten things twisting in his brain. He plainly missed Kit.

"You'll make enemies any way you slice it, with your talent. Ah, here we are." Burbage pointed to the scarred sign hanging over a green-painted door, and then led Will down a dim, stinking alley toward the back, where a wobbling wooden stair brought them to the second story. Will clutched the whitewashed railing convulsively, despite the prodding splinters. Although, if the whole precarious construction tumbled down, a death grip on the banister couldn't save him.

A door at the top of the stair stood open to catch what breeze there was. Burbage paused at the landing and softly hailed Oxford within, while Will stood two steps below.

"Enter, Master Players." Edward de Vere did not stand to meet them, but he did gesture them to sit. Stools and benches ranged about the blemished table, and the small room was dark and confining despite the open door: it did not seem the sort of chamber an Earl would frequent. Incense-strong tobacco hung on the air in ribbons, the sharp, musty tang pleasing after the stench of the streets.

"Lord Oxford, as you've summoned us," Burbage said, taking a stool. Will doffed his hat, reseated it, and sank onto a bench and stretched his legs.

Oxford nodded to the player, but turned his bright eyes to Will. "How comes the play, gentle William?"

The question he'd been dreading, and Will twisted his hands inside the cuffs of his doublet, folding his arms. He almost laughed as he recognized Kit's habitual pose, defensive and smiling, but kept his demeanor serious for the Earl.

An Earl who studied him also seriously, frowning, until Will opened his hands and shrugged. "Not well, my lord. The story's all in my head, but—"

"Times being as they are."

"Yes."

"I understand thou hast tried thy hand at some poetry. A manuscript called *Venus and Adonis* has been commended to me. Compared to our Marley's"—Oxford's nostrils flared momentarily, as if he fought some emotion—"unfinished work. I'd see it read."

Heat rose in Will's cheeks as he glanced down at his shoes. "You'd see my poor scribblings gone to press, my lord?"

"I would. And command some sonnets. Canst write sonnets?"

Oh, that stiffened his spine and brought his hands down to tighten on his knees. Burbage shifted beside him, and Will took the warning. "I've been known to turn a rhyme," Will answered, when he thought he had his tongue under control.

"I need a son-in-law wooed," Oxford said. He stood and poured wine into three unmatched cups. Will raised an eyebrow when the Earl set the cups before Burbage and himself. *More than mere politeness, that.* "Henry Wriothesley, Earl of Southampton: I'd see him married to my daughter Elizabeth, where I can perhaps keep him from trouble. He's close to Essex *and* to Raleigh, no mean trick. Kit'd befriended

Sir Walter's lot—their School of Night, so-called—and learned a few tricks by me of the philosopher Dee. It's trouble waiting to happen: too many of the Queen's favorites in one place and rivalries will brew."

Will's eyebrow went even higher at the familiar form of Marley's name. "And you wish me to—"

"Dedicate thy book of poems to Southampton. As if thou didst seek his patronage. Afflict him with sonnets bidding him marry. Raleigh is an enigma: there's no witting which way he might turn in the end. Essex is trouble, though."

"Though the Queen love him?" Burbage said, when Will could not find his tongue.

Robert Devereaux, the second Earl of Essex, was thought by many a dashing young man, one of Elizabeth's rival favorites and a rising star of the court. But her affections were divided, the third part each given to the explorers Sir Walter Raleigh and Sir Francis Drake. And there was something disingenuous in the look Oxford drew across them both, just then; Will was player enough to recognize bad playing.

Sonnets. Sonnets, and I couldn't write a good word to spare myself the chopping block—

"Gloriana," Oxford said, toying with his wine, "is a shrewd and coy Queen, equal to the title *King of England* which she has once or twice claimed. Despite her sex. Ah, would that she had been a man."

That tripped Will's tongue. "Do you suppose she mouths those same words, when she feels herself alone?"

Oxford tilted his head as if he had not considered it. "Master Shakespeare, I would not disbelieve should I hear her Maid of Honor mutter such gossip to the bees." He stared past his guests to the smoky vista beyond the open door. "So. Thou wilt write me these poems? Or write Southampton these poems? And bring me the manuscript for *Venus and Adonis*, that the ages might know it?"

"Will you see *Hero and Leander* published as well?" Will hesitated at the cloud that passed Oxford's face. *He liked Kit as well.* And then Will smiled. Kit had had that about him, the ability to inspire black rage or blind joy.

"It's fine work, isn't it?" Oxford didn't wait for Will's nod. He knocked the dottle from his pipe and began to pack the bowl again.

"Chapman—another of Raleigh's group—proposes to complete it and see it registered. In Kit's name, not his own."

"Decent." Burbage rocked back in his stool, rattling the legs on the floor. "My lord, you'll put Will in a place where, if Southampton is flattered, they may become friends—"

"Even if the courtship fails, we'll have an eye in Southampton's camp. There've been a dozen attempts on Queen Elizabeth's life in as many years: your Kit's sharp wit helped foil two of them, and he was friendly with Essex's rival, Sir Walter. Now we have neither a hand close to Essex, nor one close to Sir Walter. Intolerable, should what I fear come to fruition. Essex has links to the—" He stopped himself.

Will observed calculation in that pause. "What you fear, my lord, or what fears Walsingham?"

Surprise and then a smile. "The two are not so misaligned. We were one group, the Prometheus Club, not too long since. All of us in service of the Queen. But Essex and his partisans are more interested in their own advancement than in Britannia. So, Will. Wilt woo for me, and win for my daughter?"

Will swallowed, shifting on the hard bench. "I was to write you plays, my lord. And you would show me how to put a force in them to keep Elizabeth's subjects content and make all well. I was not to spy for you—"

Oxford tapped a beringed finger on the table. "I'm not asking thee to spy, sirrah. Merely to write."

"Not plays—"

"No. The playhouses are closed, Will, and they'll be closed through the New Year. We'll try our hand there again, fear not: but in the current hour, the enemy has the upper hand."

"The enemy. This plot against the Queen. Closing the playhouses is—a sort of a skirmish? An unseen one?"

Oxford smiled then softly. "*You* begin to understand. They know what we can do with a playhouse. Art is their enemy."

"Puritans."

"Naught but a symptom. Walsingham and Burghley are ours, after all—" Oxford drained his cup. "I offer you a poet's respect. Nothing is so transient as a play and a playmaker's fame. Except a player's."

Will looked at Burbage, who sat with his hands folded between his knees, thumbs rubbing circles over his striped silk hose. Burbage tilted his head, eyes glistening. 'Twas true.

"The poem's the thing, then," Will said, when he thought he'd considered enough. "Give unto me what you would impart, and I will wreak it into beauty with my pen."

Oxford twisted his palm together, fingers arched as if to ease a writer's cramp. "Excellent." Another intentional hesitation. "Your play."

"*Titus Andronicus.*"

"Send it me. I fancied myself something of a poet in my youth. Perhaps I can be of some small aid."

"My lord," Will answered, covering discomfort. "I shall."

Act I, scene iv

Was this the face that launch'd a thousand ships,
And burnt the topless towers of Ilium?
Sweet Helen, make me immortal with a kiss. —
Her lips suck forth my soul; see, where it flies! —

—CHRISTOPHER MARLOWE, *Faustus*

Kit's heartbeat rattled his ribs inside his skin. He clutched the balustrade in his left hand, Morgan steadying him on his blind side as she led him down the sweeping marble stair and into the midst of creatures diabolic and divine. His riding boots clattered on the risers: inappropriate to an audience with the Queen of Faeries, he thought inanely. But it was homely and reassuring that they hadn't had time to make him boots and that the doublet, for all its fineness, bound across his shoulders.

"Breathe," the ancient Queen whispered in his ear. "You'll need your wits about you, Sir Kit, for I can offer thee but small protection, and my sister the Queen is devious."

He turned his head to glimpse her; the movement brought a twisting sharpness to the savaged muscles of his neck and shoulder, which were stiffening again. Morgan must have seen him wince, for her fingers tightened. "Thou'rt hurting."

"Fair face of a witch you are," he answered with a stab at good humor. "Without herbs or simples better than brandy to dull a man's pain."

She paused on the landing above the place where the stair began to sweep down and made a show of fussing right-handed with her skirts. He leaned on the rail and on her other arm while the pale gold-veined stairs reeled.

"I'd dull your pain," she answered, glancing at him before ducking her head to flick the soft moiré one last time. "And thick your tongue, and set your head to reeling. Which canst ill afford when you go before the Mebd, Sir Poet."

Her hair moved against the back of her neck, a few strands escaping the braid. He stopped his hand before it could brush them aside. A blade of guilt dissected him at the impulse, and he embraced the pain, gnawed at it. He had nothing left to be unfaithful to, save Elizabeth, now that his sweet Tom had discarded him. Kit welcomed the cold, the distance that came with the thought. *Nothing like ice for an ache.*

She's very like Elizabeth would be, had she leave to be a woman and not a King. "Queen Mab?"

"The Mebd," Morgan corrected, steadying his arm again. Below, faces turned up like flowers opening to the sun. "Queen of the Daoine Sidhe." She pronounced the name *maeve*, the kingdom *theeneh shee*. "She has a wit about her— Ah! Sir Kit. Come and meet my son."

"Mordred?" Kit asked, putting the smile he couldn't quite force onto his lips into his voice.

"Dead at Camlann," Morgan answered. "He was fair. Fair as thou art, ashen of hair and red of beard. A handsome alliance. Come and meet Murchaud the Black, my younger."

Something in her tone made him expect a lad of thirteen, fifteen years. But the man who met them at the foot of the stairs, a pair of delicate goblets in his hand, was taller than Kit by handspans, his curled black hair oiled into a tail adorned with a crimson ribbon, his beard clipped tighter and neater than the London style against the porcelain skin of his face. Kit's palms tickled with sweat as he met the man's almost colorless eyes, saw how the broad span of his neck sloped, thick with muscle, into wide shoulders. It was a different thing from the inexplicable warmth he felt for Morgan. More raw, and less unsettling. He'd like to see those black curls ruffled.

"Mother," the lovely man said, extending a crimson glass of wine. His voice was smooth, at odds with the power in his frame.

She unwound her hand from Kit's elbow, but let her fingers trail down his arm before she stepped away. Her son pressed the second goblet into his hand, taking a moment to curl Kit's fingers about the delicate stem. The touch lingered, and Kit almost forgot his pain. "Your reputation precedes you, Master Poet."

"Sir Poet," Morgan corrected. "I knighted him while no one was looking."

"You did? Mother, bravely done!"

She laid a possessive hand on his shoulder. Kit looked after her in confusion, and she gave him only a smile. "Things are different in Faerie," she told him, and dusted his cheek, below the bandage, with a kiss. "Now drink your wine and go ye through those doors — and court and win a Queen."

"You're not coming with me?"

"Kit. Show them strength, not a cripple leaning on a woman's arm."

He met her loden eyes, then nodded, tossed back the wine, and set aside the glass. Rolling his shoulders under the too-tight doublet, he stepped into the rivulet of courtiers threading toward what must be the Presence Chamber.

Frank stares prickled Kit's skin as he followed the crowd, conscious of the antlers and fox-heads, the huge luminescent eyes and the moss-dripping armor of those who moved around him. *Masques*, he told himself, and didn't permit himself at first to return the curious glances. Hooves clattered on the floor on his blind side: he flinched and turned to look, and a naked satyr caught his eye and bowed from the waist.

Kit blushed and stepped back, looking at the floor. *As if I had an idea of precedence here.* The rose-and-green tiled floor rolled under his boots like the rising, falling deck of a ship. He hesitated and put a hand on the paneled wall. A woman brushed his arm, elegantly human except that the diaphanous robes which stroked her swaying hips and breasts seemed to grow from her shoulders like drooping iris petals. Then his attention was drawn by an antlered stag, richly robed in velvet green as glass, resting one cloven hoof on the jeweled hilt of a rapier and walking upright like a man.

Kit's pulse drummed in his temples and throat. *Adrift,* he thought, and raised his right hand and touched the silk handkerchief binding his bandage. The fingertips of his other hand curled into detail carved upon the wainscoting. "I don't know what to do." *A novelty. I wot a knife in the eye does change one or two things.*

"Follow me." A sharp voice dripping wryness. Kit looked down, putting it to a wizened man who seemed all elbows and legs like a grasshopper. He came to Kit's belt; his long ears waggled under a fool's cap. "Before Her Majesty waxes vexed."

"Waxes vexed, and wanes kind?" Kit pushed against the wall. "Dizziness, Master Fool. You know me?"

"Your plays have a wide circulation." The little man grimaced: it crinkled his face so oddly that Kit at first did not recognize a smile. "Art Marley, and I'm Goodfellow, but mayst call me Robin if I may call thee Kit. We're fools both, after all, and of an estate."

"I'll not dispute it." Kit pressed the heel of his hand to his injured eye, as if the pressure could ease the throbbing that filled his brain. "I've the belly to make a go of it if you'll steady me, Master Fool."

"One fool hand in hand with another. A Puck for a puck. You've the belly for many things, I hear."

"I'm notorious." The banter was tonic to a flagging confidence. A tall man with four horns and the notched ears of a bull swept past, wearing a breastplate of beaten gold and trailing a cloak of burned blue velvet and vair. A circlet crossed the man's fair brow, just under the horns, and Kit returned his stare. *I am notorious.*

The bull-horned man turned his head, maintaining the eye contact, and almost stumbled over a side table. Kit wished he had a rapier to rest his hand on; a heady rush he liked better than wounded dizziness filling his breast. As if air filled his lungs again after a blow to the gut. *I'm Kit Marley.*

I'm Kit Marley. He curled his lips into a grin and stiffened his shoulders, put a cocky sparkle in his eye. Flickering torchlight picked out the river of Fae, limned them like the demons of *Faustus,* and the heat of it stroked Kit's cheek. The bull-horned man turned suddenly to watch his feet. *Marley the poet. Christofer Marley the playmaker. Marley the duelist. Marley the player, the lover, the intelligencer. I've the honeyed tongue to seduce wives from husbands and husbands from wives, secrets from seditionists and plots from traitors. I'm Christofer Marley, by Christ!*

I can do this thing.

He tasted a breath, and then another one. *For Good Queen Bess. For Elizabeth. I can do this thing and any other.*

"Lead on, Merry Robin," he said without letting the grin slide down his face, though it tugged his stitches and filled his mouth with musky blood. "And show me your merry men."

" 'Tis not the men that need concern you. 'Tis the maid stands at their head." Twiglike fingers encircled Kit's wrist and the elf tugged him forward, creeping on many-jointed toes.

Kit had a brief, swirling impression of heavy paneled doors worked in bas-relief with masterful artistry, designs more Celtic than Roman. The throne room was longer than it was broad, the floor tiled in patterned marble of rose and green, the dark windows hung with rippling silk and open to the night. The Fae moved freely, clumping in knots of whispered conversation, calling witticisms across the table set with glasses and wine. Kit's head throbbed with the scent of rosemary and mint, strewn with flower petals underfoot. Robin Goodfellow tugged his fingers, and Kit turned his head slowly so he would not miss a detail on his blind side.

No hush fell when he entered, but the conversation flagged for half an instant before Robin led him forward. On the far end of the hall, raised on a dais, the Queen lifted her head. Kit would have gasped if he'd had any wonder left in him.

She curled in a beaten gold chair, languid as a lioness. A cloth of estate stretched over her head, and as Kit approached—uncouth nails ringing on the paving stones—she raised eyes that struck him through the heart. It wouldn't have taken much to send him to his knees, true, but Robin was there, and made the stumble look a genuflection. Kit didn't look up, but the image of the Queen's golden hair knotted in braided ropes stayed with him, and the haunting perfection of eyes that caught the light and glimmered one moment green, one moment violet, like orient jade. *That most perfect creature under heaven,* he thought, *the moon full in the arms of restless night.*

She moved an arm, by the sound of it. Stretched in leonine grace. Unfeeling of the hard, cold stone he knelt on, he imagined the purple silk of her mantle drifting from a wrist as white and smooth as a willow branch. He imagined the perfect pale mask of her face marked with a rosebud smile, and shivered deep in his soul. Her voice was furred like catkins, soft as the wind brushing his hair, and he heard a rustle of slick cloth and a jingle of bells, as if she stood, or stretched, or danced a step and stopped.

His breath froze in his belly when she said his name. *She's just a wench,* he thought desperately. *She's ensorcelled me. This is sorcery. Glamourie.*

"Gentle Christofer." Another whisper of bells. Robin got up and shuffled aside. He didn't dare raise his eyes. "You grace our court with your presence. We have seen your work. It pleases us, and we know of your other duties before your Queen, and Gloriana pleases us as well."

Somewhere, he found a voice, although it didn't sound like his own. "You are gracious, Your Majesty."

"Look upon us," she said, and his chin lifted without his conscious will. *I am bewitched,* he thought, and then realized how close she had somehow drifted, silent as a thistledown. She reached out with soft fingertips, laced them through his hair, and traced the outline of his ear as if exploring a flower petal. He whimpered low in his throat, an anxious whine, and gritted his teeth as a low, amused chuckle swept the room.

They knew what she was doing to him. His breath came like a runner's around the fire in his chest, but he managed to answer in pleasant tones. "Yes, Your Highness."

Like velvet stroked along his spine, like a hand in the hollow of his back, her voice kept on. "I'd grant you a place in my court, Master Poet. Your old life is lost to you. Will you play for my pleasure, sir?" A little ripple of delight colored her tone at her own double meaning.

"I'm sworn to another—" he began.

The hardest words he could imagine speaking then, but the Mebd cut him short with a wave of her lily-white hand. Pearls and diamonds slid about her wrist when she moved, and emeralds and amethysts sparkled on her fingers. "Hath been our royal pleasure to assist our

sovereign sister Elizabeth in maintenance of her realm, whether she
wits it or not. She'll not grudge us your service, Master Poet—"

"Sir Poet." A voice like the yowl of a cat after the Mebd's silken
perfection. A voice from his blind side.

Kit turned his head. Morgan stood beside him and a few steps
back, her hands loose by her sides as she dropped a brief curtsey to
the Queen. "I've knighted him, sister dear."

"Ah." The Queen let her fingers trail across Kit's neck. "Stand,
then, Sir Poet."

Her voice said she smiled, but her eyes didn't show it, and Kit
struggled but didn't have to take Morgan's subtly offered hand. "A
man cannot serve two Queens, Your Highness," Kit said softly, against
the pressure within that told him to throw himself down and kiss this
woman's slipper, the perfect hem of her perfect gown. "Much as it may
pain him." He shook his head, in pain. "Oh, thou art fairer than the
evening air / Clad in the beauty of a thousand stars; / Brighter art thou
than flaming Jupiter / When he appear'd to hapless Semele: / More
lovely than the monarch of the sky / In wanton Arethusa's azured
arms . . ."

"Your *Faustus*," she said, but she seemed well pleased. She stepped
back, a silver slipper gliding through the rose petals curling on the tile,
and Kit felt something *snap* in the air between them as cleanly as if he'd
broken a glass rod between his hands. "We know it." She settled back
on her chair. "Thou canst never go home, Christofer Marley. Art dead
unto them."

Kit swallowed around the dryness in his throat. The dream was
broken, the moment of perfection fled like the touch of the Queen's
soft hand. His belly ached, his chest, his ballocks, his face; he trembled,
and only half with exhaustion. "Your Highness," he said, and his voice
was again his own, if raw as the cawing of crows. "I crave a boon."

"A boon?" She leaned forward in a tinkle of bells. "We shall consider it. What offer you in return?"

His luck had been running. Let it run a mile longer. He stepped
away from Morgan, nearer the throne, dropping his voice. "A bit of information, Your Highness. You have an interest in Elizabeth's court?"

She smiled. Oh yes, he'd guessed right, from the fragments of information gleaned from her speech and Morgan's.

"Sir Francis Walsingham, Queen Elizabeth's spymaster? He lives, in hiding."

"As do you," she answered, with a slight, ironic smile. "It signifies. What wish you in return?"

"Let me speak to him but once. I have information I can give no other, and it is vital to the protection of the realm. If Elizabeth's reign means something to your Royal Highness—and I can see your sister Queen is dear to you—I beg you. On bended knee. Let me make my report."

"And?"

"And secure my release from service." For all his practiced manner, he could hear the forlorn edge in his own voice, and imagine the mockery in Elizabeth's. *Am I so easy to set aside then, Master Marley?*

The Mebd watched him as he suited action to words, bowing his head, sinking on the stone steps of the dais though they cut his knee like dull knives. The queen sighed; Morgan shifted from foot to foot behind him. At last, he heard the sibilance of her mantle as she nodded, and her voice, stripped now of glamourie. "Let me see your wounds, Sir Christofer," she answered, not cruelly. "Draw off your bandages."

His fingers fumbled when he tried. The room spun, and he laid his palm flat on the edge of the steps to keep from tumbling down them. Morgan came up beside him and lifted the coils of linen with gentle fingers, and the Faerie Queen sucked air between her teeth like any woman would at what she saw.

"Hist, let me lay hands on thee," she said, leaning forward on her throne to probe with cool fingers. "I cannot heal the scar or give you back your vision, poet. But I can seal the cut. Have I consent?"

"Yea," he answered. Morgan's hand on his shoulder, only, kept him upright. The Queen stroked the wound again, and the pain ebbed, and the floor and the walls blurred and spun. She muttered a word or two he did not hear. *Well,* Kit thought when she leaned back, *I've benefited from sorcery and had dealing with the fair folk. If there's a hell after all, no chance of avoiding it now.* He thought of Faustus and managed a smile as Morgan and someone on his other side—Murchaud—helped him rise.

"Art dismissed." The Mebd turned her attention away.

To complete Kit's disgrace, Murchaud had to carry him back up the stairs to Morgan's chamber. The knight took his leave, and Morgan stripped Kit over feeble protests and placed him in bed. Sometime before morning, she drew the hangings back and crawled under the coverlet, and he found to his delight that a little rest had restored him more than he'd expected.

There was something to be said for living after all, and for being alive, and the simple joy of a woman who threaded strong hands through his hair and touched the seamed white scar across his face as if it were merely another thing to be caressed—like his nose, his ears, the lower lip she nibbled into silence when he would have whispered fair words in her ear.

She left again by dawn, wriggling from under his arm, and though he lifted his head to see her slip through the door, he did not turn when the door reopened and he thought she returned. A warm body slid beside him as he drowsed. He startled from sleep to wakefulness in a moment, stifling a cry; the hands on his shoulders were dry and calloused with bladeplay, big enough to close a circle around his upper arm, and the lips that touched his throat and the teeth that caught at his skin were framed with a tickling rasp of beard.

A flutter of breath trickled through his teeth. He forced the words to follow it. "I'm unfit for wrestling, Sir Knight—"

Murchaud chuckled, his mouth growing bolder as his long hands tightened on Kit's shoulders, around Kit's chest. "Come, come, Sir Poet," he answered. "I'm understanding of your plight. Needs do nothing but sigh just like that, and I shall see your sighs well answered on this morn."

Act I, scene v

Mercutio: *Thou art like one of those fellows that when he enters the confines of a tavern claps me his sword upon the table and says "God send me no need of thee!" and by the operation of the second cup draws it on the drawer, when indeed there is no need.*

—WILLIAM SHAKESPEARE, *Romeo and Juliet*

June stretched through the heat of summer into August, until Will leaned against the wall beyond Oxford's patterned study door, a sheaf of poems clutched in his hand, and fumed. Oxford's words rang in Will's head. *Walsingham has* Titus. *It's good for what you have of it. Pray for an end to the plague, and write me an end to the play.*

I didn't give the play to Walsingham, Will fumed. *I gave it you for comment, good my lord —*

He bit his tongue against a curse and realized his hands were bending the paper his poems were scribbled on. Hastily, he smoothed them against his knee, and eyed Oxford's penmanship on the page — tidier than his own spiraling squiggles when his brain outran his hand.

Will folded the papers once in his hand. "God send me no worse patron than a frustrated poet," he murmured, and headed out. A housemaid opened the side door for Will. Satisfied that the ink had dried, he tucked the pages into his doublet, rubbing his eyes against brightness as he stepped into the street.

He bought a pasty from a market stall and ate it standing in the lee of a half-timbered house, beside the garden wall. A ribsprung calico peered at him from a roof angle and dared to mew. "The plague chasers will be on thee," Will observed. "Mind you hide your face, Malken, or your kits will starve without a mother." He worried a bit of mutton loose from his lunch and tossed it to the tiles beside her paws: she flinched, expecting a stone, then grabbed the morsel and was gone.

"Kits and kits," Will whispered, cramming the rest of the pasty into his cheek and dusting the crumbs into the gutter. Errant rays of sunshine stroked his face. He raised a hand as if he could catch and hold them. Paper crinkled between his doublet and his shirt. "Marley, if your ghost can hear me, I bid you good grace. Whatever you may have done—" He stopped and cocked an ear, but heard only a distant mewing that might have been the calico's kittens. He tried again to picture the scene at Eleanor Bull's house, a drunken Kit drawing Ingrim Frazier's dagger, attacking the other man, without warning, from the rear—

—and failing to kill him. Failing so miserably that Frazier took the knife out of his hand and drove it without further ado into Kit's eye. While Robert Poley and Nick Skeres stood by helpless to intervene? *Is it that it's too pitiful and crass a dying for a man like that? But great men die in pitiful ways—*

No, he decided, as the pasty settled into his gut like a kick. *It's that if Kit were to stab a man, he'd look him in the eye when he did it.*

And he wouldn't miss. Will nodded, chewing his knuckle, unaware that he'd begun walking again until a curse and a blow alerted him to the horseman who had nearly run him down.

Will needed to know what about Kit's plays had cost him his life. That had his name dragged through the streets as a traitor and a criminal, and the Queen herself covering his murder. He needs must know his enemies. Before he wound up with a knife in his own eye. Ignoring for the moment that the Queen didn't want it cleared, Will wondered if he might redeem Kit's name.

He brightened as he turned toward the river and the looming

presence of the Great Stone Gate. Southwark, and home. If Oxford wouldn't answer his need, then perhaps Lord Hunsdon would.

But in the meantime—

—*I think I'd like to speak to Master Robert Poley.*

Poley frequented a tavern near his house on Winding Lane, where Will had played at tables with Kit once or twice. He glanced at the shadows lying across the street: just time for a man to be thirsty for a bit of ale and hungry for a bit of bread and cheese. He wondered if Poley would recognize him.

He wondered if the man might be encouraged to drink—

—*Her Majesty has signed a writ forbidding all inquiry into the events in Deptford on 30th May, 1593.* But, Will reasoned, she hadn't forbidden the buying of drinks for Master Robert Poley. He whistled as he swung out, each nail-studded boot landing square on the cobblestones, strides clattering.

The public house was called the Groaning Sergeant. Will stopped inside the door to let his eyes adjust, although the shutters stood open. The Sergeant bustled with a dinnertime crowd—only a few benches open closest the fire, where it would be uncomfortably hot. But the aroma of beer and baking bread enticed, and he smiled into his beard as his gaze swept the common room and he saw Robert Poley's blond head bent toward a darker man's in the quietest corner.

Poley, like Langley, was a moneylender, and a far less scrupulous one. He was well known as a cheat and an informer, and he was one of the three men who had been witness, in the little room where Kit was murdered.

Will resettled the rustling pages under his doublet and took the uncomfortable seat by the fire. As the evening cooled, the benches would fill in around him, and in the meantime he'd keep an eye on Poley and use the firelight for working on his sonnets. But first— He hailed the tavern's sturdy gray-haired mistress, who brought him small beer and warm wheat bread smeared thickly with sweet butter—and a pot of ink and a quill that wasn't too badly cut, on loan for a penny more.

Will mopped the table with his sleeve and spread his crumpled sheets on soft wood where they would catch most of the light. A breeze riffled the fine hairs on his neck as he ate the last bite of bread. He drank the beer leaning backward so the drops from sloppy drawing would fall onto his breeches and not the poems, and he did what he thought was a passable job of not looking like he was watching Poley.

Poley, who was drinking wine without water and eating beef like a man of prosperity. And who seemed to have set up shop in that particular corner of the Sergeant, given the number of men who came and went near him in ones and twos and sometimes threes. Some sat for a game of tables or draughts or diced a bit, while some merely quaffed a drink and spent a few moments in quiet conversation. Will wasn't sure quite when, but after the third or fourth visit, he started jotting descriptions and the one or two names he knew—*Gardner, Justice of the Peace for Southwark. Oh, really?*—on the reverse of a sonnet that began *Is it for fear to wet a widow's eye.* He kept another sheet handy to drag across the paper.

He and Kit had run in different circles, away from their connection to the theatre and the financial straits that had occasioned sharing lodgings and companies—the Admiral's Men and Lord Strange's Men—for whom they both wrote plays. Will didn't know most of Poley's associates. But Poley was one of the men who had been in that small room where Kit had died.

Poley never passed more than a glance in his direction in the brief gaps between guests. Will noticed that such patrons as did not seek Poley avoided him; he surmised that this was as much to do with Poley's own reputation as the company he kept. The visitors seemed to come and go at regulated intervals. As the sun set and the moon rose, Will gathered up his courage and took a single deep breath.

He spindled his poems lengthwise preparatory to tucking them back inside his doublet. That accomplished, he was making his way to the landlady to purchase ale for himself and wine for Poley when he saw a face he *did* recognize, and froze.

Richard Baines. A tall, fair man with a saddler's forearms, a cleric's smile, and a poison pen. Blessing his dull brown doublet and the darkness of his hair, Will stepped back into the shadows beside the bar, watching as Poley rose to meet his newest guest—which Will had not seen him do before—until the two heads leaned together, fair and fair. They embraced, and Will saw the glitter of a band on Baines' thumb, a gold circle surrounding an inset of some darker metal, like the one

Oxford wore. The flash of it drew Will's eye to an odd-shaped scar on the base of the thumb, a string of pale knots like pearls.

Baines, Will knew through Kit and Thomas Kyd, and Baines *would* recognize him. But the men weren't looking, so Will turned as if watching the landlady go shutter the windows, ducked to swing his hair across his profile, and started for the door.

Why is Robert Poley, who stood by when a knife went in Kit's eye, talking to Richard Baines, who puts a knife to his reputation now that the man is dead? For it was Baines who had written a note to the Privy Council that might have seen Kit hanged for heresy.

Salty sourness filled Will's mouth, and he hesitated a moment and stole one final glance, thinking it safe enough with Baines' back to the room. But he found himself staring directly into Poley's eyes, as if the man had been tracking his motion across the room.

Will froze like a doe at the crack of a twig as Poley's hand went out to rest on Baines' thick forearm. Baines turned, and both men began to stand, and Will took one more hasty step toward the door before Baines' mocking baritone arrested his motion like a bullwhip flicked at his nose.

"Well, well." The big man swung a leg over his bench as he turned and stood. "William Shake-scene. Come sniffing after better company now that your fancy-boy's dead?"

Will stepped diagonally toward the door. "I was after supper," he said, wishing himself better armed than with a handspan beltknife. "And I've had it. Good even to you, Master Baines, and I'll thank you not to idly insult me." Some impulse made him step forward and add, "Or slander my friends, sirrah."

Benches scraped on planks as the Sergeant's custom recognized a brewing fight.

"Friends," Baines answered with a sneer. "That's not what they call it that I ever heard. What will you do for a living now, you poor excuse of a playmaker? Without that drunken sodomite Marley to doctor your work and bugger—"

Will opened his mouth to interrupt, but a determined, feminine voice overrode the first rumble of his retort. "Master Poley." The landlady stepped between Will and Baines, ample hands on her ample hips, and tilted her head to glare around Baines' broad shoulder at

Poley. "You will control your friend. I'll not have any man driving off custom."

"Mistress Mathews," Poley said, and he laid a hand on Baines' arm. "As you wish it." But his eyes met Will's quite plainly, and the glare that followed Will to the door said, *And don't come back.*

Well, Will thought later, barring the door of his own room behind him before tossing his much-battered sheaf of sonnets on the table, *that could have ended much worse.*

Act I, scene vi

> **Bernardine:** *"Thou hast committed—"*
> **Barabas:** *"—Fornication.*
> *But that was in another country,*
> *And besides, the wench is dead."*

—CHRISTOPHER MARLOWE, *The Jew of Malta*

A better awakening than the last, though Kit was surprised to sleep so deeply in a stranger's bed, with a stranger's arm around him. His right cheek pressed a pillow that smelled of Morgan's rosemary, and he remembered before he opened his eye that it should hurt. It didn't. He remembered as well Morgan snipping and pulling bloody stitches after the Mebd had healed it, and her lips and body drawing out the agony the Faerie Queen's sorcery had darted in him. But it wasn't Morgan's arm around his waist, her hand splayed possessively across his belly—though the dark hair drifting across his face in un-braided waves did not belong to Murchaud.

Kit, thou hast outdone thyself. He couldn't recall Morgan returning, which frightened him: a man with enemies didn't live long if he slept too heavily to hear an opening door.

But Morgan le Fey probably had her own ways of moving quietly. And Kit couldn't remember when he had last wakened with this silence still in him, the clamor of fear and rage and duty and bitterness and memory stilled.

"Usually," Kit murmured, when the hand that clipped him slid down to stroke his flank, "men whisper the delights of bedding sisters. Or mother and daughter."

"Art anyway satisfied?" Murchaud answered, cuddling closer.

Kit turned to see him— " 'Twill serve." —and Morgan chuckled on his blind side. "Your Highness." She rose into his field of view, hair spilled across her face. The break in his vision was worse than he'd expected, especially close in.

She stopped his lips with a finger, eye corners crinkling, then touched his scar. It felt as if she stroked a bit of leather laid on his skin. "Aren't we beyond that, my lord? Does this pain you still?"

"Only my heart," he answered. "But if I may look upon a sight as fair as you with but one eye, I'll count the other well lost. What—what did she do to me? Your Mebd?"

"Always the flatterer," Morgan answered. "And my Mebd she isn't, and what she did on thee was old sorcery, deep glamourie, to turn a man into a mindless, rutting stag."

Her fingers caressed his throat, and a low moan followed.

"I've used it myself," she admitted. "You feel it still."

"Yes."

Murchaud's hands tightened on his hips; Murchaud's teeth closed on the nape of his neck like a stallion conquering a mare. He cried out, but Morgan's mouth muffled the sound. "You're wondering," she whispered, her cheek pressed by his cheek as her son pulled him close, "when I'll give thee a mirror to see how the Mebd healed thee. You're wondering how she realized it, and you're wondering that she englamoured thee of an evening, and at how you strode through sorcery where another would have been lost. And why I have taken an interest in you. Art not?"

Murchaud nibbled the place where Kit's neck ran into his shoulder, and his hands were adventurers. "Aye," Kit whispered against Morgan's lips. His fingers brushed breasts like heavy velvet, skin like petals. She pressed close, guiding his hands to her waist and the abutting curves. Her fingertips traced an old scar on his chest, another on his belly, a third along the inside of his thigh. They were puckered and white, old burns that he tried not to think on.

"Time here answers the will of the Queen," Morgan said. "She took a few months from your wound, is all: their passage dizzied and drained you. If thou hadst not been so brave in the cleaning, it would not have gone so well for thee."

"Lye soap. I should thank you."

"There's one mirror in all the Blesséd Isle," Murchaud said. "You've bought the use of it, although releasing the secret Walsingham's undeath might prove a high price."

Morgan's lips moved on Kit's. "Meanwhile, consider how you might repay me for returning your wits, that you might bandy words with the Mebd."

Remembering the white flame the Mebd had kindled in him with a mere smile and a turn of her hand, Kit shivered. "Anything, so long as it is mine to give, the lady may claim as her own. Only—how did you protect me, madam?"

"Your boots," she murmured, wickedly, "have iron nails."

He stopped. And then he laughed, delighted at the simplicity of it, and stretched against her as he took her in his arms. She wrapped him in silk, and Murchaud enfolded him in steel, and he could have wept at the silence they gave him, and the forgetting, that when they drew him down between them nothing whispered *remember*.

Instead, the whisperer was Morgan, speaking against his ear: "Things are different in Faerie."

Christofer Marley closed tight his eye.

The mirror was not hidden in a private chamber or guarded under lock and key. Rather, it stood at the end of a blind corridor, in an oval frame of tarnished silver—tall as a door—wrought with lilies and spirals. The stand was swathed in velvet. The polished glass could have been obsidian.

"It's called the Darkling Glass," Murchaud said when Kit hesitated.

He stepped closer, laid one hand on cool crystal polished without a ripple. His palm left no print; his reflection was more a matte sheen than an image. "And I—"

"Step through it." Morgan came up beside him. A tall white candle he did not recollect having seen her light burned in her right hand. She raised it beside his face, illuminating the dark band of his new eyepatch

crossing a pale seam of scar. Flecks of blood and scab showed where
Morgan had pulled stitches free, but the ridged white line was straight
from his hairline to where it vanished under the eyepatch.

Morgan touched a finger to his mouth and he dressed it in a kiss.
His lips had been called voluptuous by men and women both, his dark
eyes enormous, exotic with the fairness of his hair. The heavy diagonal
of eyepatch exaggerated the softness of his mouth. Not as good as an
eye in his head, and he knew he'd have work to make up the lack, but
it had a rakish dignity.

And it might win him Walsingham's sympathy.

Morgan leaned against his shoulder. He caught a pale glimmer
like the moon over his left shoulder: Murchaud's reflection, further
back. "Step through any mirror to return. I put that power in thee.
And there's something you need to know."

"I've tasted the food of Faerie."

Her gown gapped at the collar when she inclined her head. "It
will draw you back. A few days, a week. A passing of the moon. It is
impossible to predict."

"And if I do not come?"

Her cool cheek brushed his ear; her dark hair spread across the
black velvet of his doublet. "You will suffer, Christofer Marley," she
said with a luxurious smile. "And when you have suffered more than
you can imagine, you will die. Look—there is your Walsingham now.
Dost see him?"

The old spymaster's accustomed image swam into the glass. He
bent over his desk examining a document with a lens held between
bony fingers. Light streamed over Walsingham's shoulder in a swirl
of dust motes, limning his hair and beard silver-gilt like a cloud. "Now
we know he lives, we can find him," Morgan whispered. "Have a
care."

Kit opened his mouth to reply, but a firm hand pressed the small
of his back. He stepped forward and tripped through the mirror, and
fell with ill grace into a stunned silence and Sir Francis Walsingham's
arms.

That silence lasted moments, as Walsingham studied him, and
turned as if to see what door in the air he'd fallen from, and then studied him again. And then knotted fingers like ribbons of steel in his hair

and turned his face up and kissed him hard, as a brother might. Before jerking back suddenly and stepping away, the long sleeves of his robe falling across his knuckles.

"Marley," he said, touching his lips and speaking between the fingers. "Not a ghost, I wot. Hell threw you out?"

"Hell wants me back when you've done with me, Sir Francis." The smile came up from somewhere under Kit's breastbone, and it bubbled through his chest and throat until his lips could not contain it. "But I have secured a visitation."

Walsingham turned away, shuffling his papers into a pile and weighting them with the lens. He stole a glance across his shoulder, and Kit tried the smile again. "Sir Francis. You're fussing."

"Kit—thine eye." He turned again as Kit came forward, his right hand rising to touch the terrible scar. "Plucked out?"

"Cut through." Kit looked down. "Your cousin Tom had a hand in it, I'll grant. How am I living? Do you know?"

Walsingham crossed to the arched window and shuttered it; he crossed again, and barred the door. "Will you drink wine with me, Christofer? Thomas and the Queen's Coroner identified your body. I've broken with Thomas over it. He maintains his men were innocent, your death the result of some unhappy double-dealing you revealed in the course of the conversation that day—but what were you doing in Deptford, and where have you *been* the past four months and more?" *Why did you leave me thinking you dead?* It wasn't said, but Kit could taste the betrayal.

"Four months?" He put a hand on the desk to steady himself as his belly contracted. "Four months and a night."

"Long enough for that to heal." Walsingham touched his face again. "Oh, that grieves me, Kit. But not so much as the thought of your body cold in an unmarked grave. I'd have pricked thee out for a lover, not a fighter."

"Cannot a man be both?"

"And a poet as well. Where have you been?"

"Stolen away by Faeries. I have—what day is't, Francis?"

"Then don't answer me, man. October the third."

"Good Christ!"

"Your wound is well healed." Walsingham poured the wine after all, though Kit had never answered him, and let Kit choose his glass. "And you stepped into my rooms as if from thin air —"

"I told thee. Stolen by Faeries. Would I lie?" Kit tasted the wine, rolled it on his tongue. He set the glass down by the papers, and the handwriting drew his eye. An angled look, a gesture for permission, and Walsingham's nod, and Kit reached across the sand tray and took up the sheaf. "Will's improving. But then this is Oxford's hand . . . Oh, Francis. Not Will."

Walsingham covered his eyes with his hand, the other one — with the glass in it — dropping to his side. "We needed someone."

"Will's —" Kit set the papers back on the desk and weighted them with his now-empty wineglass. "Naive."

"Will's as old as you. Older than when you came to me —"

Kit turned to regard Walsingham square from his one good eye. "Francis, the man has children."

Which was a body blow. He'd never married, and Walsingham knew why. He wiped the taste of wine from his mouth. Never married. Now he never would.

Too much to risk. To much to fear for. Too much to give up for a nuptial bed.

"Kit, so do I." Walsingham shook his head. "Something's altered in you —"

"A knife in the eye will change your perspective."

Kit, cruel. Walsingham's face went white, and his mouth worked, and Kit saw him as if for the first time: *old.* "I would have protected you," he said, and then quoted words that might have broken Kit's heart in his chest. " 'Wouldst thou be loved and feared? Receive my seal, save or condemn, and in our name command, what so thy mind affects or fancy likes —' "

"Nay!" A hiss, not a shout. Kit's hand stinging flat on the polished desk, cupped to explode the air beneath it, and Walsingham leapt at the sound and the rattle of the ink pot. *Edward II*, and Kit couldn't bear it. "Nay, sweet Francis. I wrote those words not for thee, and I'll not have you filthy your mouth on them!"

"Not to me? To an age, surely. It's put about that you were killed for them, by Essex's men, or those who took them as an affront to Scottish James, a satire on his love for his exiled minion Lennox."

"No," Kit answered, drawing breath to slow his racing pulse. "Him they were writ to knows it. Sweet Walsingham, who else should I trust with this? I must be—" Another breath, a calmer one. "I must be released of mine oath. To the Queen."

Kit would have gambled that the old man's face could grow no whiter behind the gray in his beard. He would have lost the bet. "Kit, why?"

A tilt of the head to bring his scar into the light. "The Faerie Queen who rescued me demands it."

Walsingham held his gaze a long minute, then shook it off like a workworn old stallion shaking away a fly. "Kit. I cannot release thee. You must plead with your Queen."

Kit had known. He nodded, lightheaded and cold. Eleven years, that oath had held him. And now it could be gone on a breath.

Like his life.

"Arrange it, Sir Francis. Will not thy Queen hear thee?"

"My Queen," Walsingham answered, "has never forgiven me her royal cousin's death. But, aye. She will hear me if I ask. What will you tell her?"

"That by her own coroner's hand, I am dead. And a dead man can give no service to a living Queen." He ignored the irony in Walsingham's quick smile. "You will care for her in my name?"

"Kit." Just his name, and all the answer he needed.

"There is another thing. More vital."

Walsingham caught the tone, and long acquaintance made him nod, gaze level, and come so close that Kit could taste the wine on his breath. The spymaster didn't speak, but he bent his head to listen. *Such trust,* Kit thought, shocking even himself. *I could have a knife in that belly before he drew another breath.*

As Frazier put a knife in your eye, Christofer Marley?

"No one knew where to find me but our little conclave of play-makers. I was staying with Tom—and his wife."

"I know your arrangement—"

Kit ignored the disapproval. "Not Raleigh's people— And the message summoning me to Deptford came under Burghley's seal, phrased as a Royal command."

Walsingham had not become Walsingham because he couldn't follow a trail. "We were betrayed from within."

"Yea. Verily. More than by Tom. By someone who knew who could summon me, and make me run—" Kit put enough dry irony in it to make Walsingham laugh, but laughing made him cough.

Kit went to Walsingham and laid a hand on his shoulder, but the older man shook him away until the fit ended. Then Walsingham raised too-bright eyes and continued as if uninterrupted, "Who do you think betrayed you?"

"The orders came from Her Majesty, under Burghley's seal. But there are forgers aplenty."

"And if it's Her Majesty's hand ordered your death? Going to her for succor were dangerous—"

Kit let the implication slide off with a ripple of his neck and shoulder. "My life was ever hers to dispose of. I make no exception for my death. When the Queen says go-and-die—"

Walsingham shifted on his feet.

Kit glanced at the crack of light between the shutters. "Francis, may I look at Will's play again? I think Oxford's made some poor suggestions, and it is some hours yet until dark. And I think I cannot well go abroad by day."

Walsingham laughed. "There's more wine. I'll have a fair copy made before I show it to Will."

"Wine would be welcome. And then I'll tell you of the Faerie Court and its Queen."

Walsingham stopped with the wine bottle in his hand, staring at Kit as Kit appropriated his chair. The ink was fresh, the pen well cut.

"You're serious."

"As treason."

"Huh." Walsingham came closer, to peer over his shoulder. "And even now, you can't resist a manuscript?"

Kit shrugged and dipped the pen. "What poet could?"

Act I, scene vii

Moore: If that be called deceit, I will be honest.

—WILLIAM SHAKESPEARE, *Titus Andronicus*

L ord Hunsdon never answered Will's request, but on the fifth of October, very early, a note was delivered to Will's lodgings, inscribed to *Mr. W.S.* It directed him to the home of Francis Langley, and it was signed—*F.W. Come at once. Titus needs you.*

Does that mean unseemly *haste,* Will wondered, shrugging a brown woolen doublet over his shirt and tending to the lacings, *or just all due speed? Titus needs you.*

At least Walsingham has a sense of humor. An anticipatory tickle of dread pressed his breastbone like a thumb. It had been so long. There was no telling what horrors they'd wreaked on Will's poor words. Will stomped his boots down, jarring puffs of dust from between the floorboards. At the door he paused, casting a final eye around his chamber to find all in order. Behind him, he tugged the panel tight.

It was a fine autumn morning, sharp and cool, still pink with sunrise. The moneylender's house was close. Will hesitated by the garden gate—the only door he had been shown through—and rattled it testingly.

It was unlatched.

He glanced over his shoulder. The street lay empty, and Will shrugged and lifted the handle. *Not cut out for espionage.* He blushed as he remembered his confrontation with Baines. The rumors about Kit had only grown more scurrilous since, and he suspected Baines and Poley were behind them. He slipped through the gate, aware that any observer would have seen a drably clad skulker with no right to be there.

The lemons and olives were long over, yellowed leaves drifting from the grafted tree espaliered to the gray garden wall. Will shrugged his doublet higher on his shoulders and kept on, hoping he didn't surprise a maidservant whiling away the early morning hours with a cellarer.

As it was, the gardener dropped his pail as Will rounded a curve in the gravel path. "Master Shakespeare!" He must have leapt almost out of his boots, because he staggered in the spilled manure, and then whipped his cap off, covered his face with it, and laughed. "Oh, you startled me. Sir Francis is expecting you. He's had breakfast laid. Shall I tell the steward you've arrived?"

"By all means, Master Gardener."

Walsingham was already seated in an armchair before a long hearth banked to embers. The spymaster gestured Will seated and handed him a toasting-fork, indicating a plate of crompid cakes. "I shan't stand on ceremony," the old man said, waving one hand as if to include the wainscoted walls and the chambered ceiling in his invitation.

"Isn't this Francis Langley's house, Sir Francis?"

That smile turned the corners of Walsingham's eyes up. "The front half. Closed for the winter now, and Langley has never hesitated to earn a few crowns in whatever closemouthed way he can. Pay no mind to the details of my subterfuge—Oxford gave me your work, with some scribblings on it. I took the liberty of making a clean copy"—he gestured to a pile of papers neatly sorted in the basket between the chairs—"and I was hoping you'd consent to look it over."

Will retrieved his breakfast from the banked embers and inspected it, knowing it couldn't be nearly warm yet. He set it on the dish and picked up the pages so quickly that Walsingham chuckled, "One poet is very like another."

It was not the manuscript he had given to Oxford, so that Oxford could doctor it with his magic scenes. Not Will's own looping, hurried script, but a fine university italic, formal as the Queen's. His own text in a center column, neat as if ruled, and running down the right margin notes and suggestions.

A corner of his lip curled as he recognized Oxford's overwrought phrasing. A suggestion *here* was better though, a sharp-ended pun and an enjambed line that ran a ragged stanza smooth. It almost, Will thought, captured a rhythm of normal speech, but left the formal power of the blank verse intact—

His mouth went parched and he reached without thinking for the cup of cider next to the dish, feeling Walsingham's eyes upon him. "Some of this," he said, when he had wet his tongue enough to free it from his palate, "is very helpful, Sir Francis. You have a good ear: I know this is not Oxford's doing, this radical line."

"Nor mine. A poetical friend."

"Indeed," Will answered. He dropped the pages on his knees and picked up the crumpet. Walsingham had applied butter, but the pastry wasn't warmed enough to melt it. He bit into it anyway, at pains not to scatter crumbs. "He has a lovely hand, your secretary. It was your secretary who transcribed this for you?"

Walsingham smiled at him around the rim of his glass. "He said we couldn't fool you," he said, setting his cider down.

Will closed his eyes. "If Walsingham lives, why should not Marley? Oh, tell me I am not dreaming, Sir Francis. Tell me where he is, that I may rest mine own eyes on him."

"Here," Kit said through the doorway. Will stood up, pages scattering unheeded by his feet, and crossed the richly tiled floor, and pushed the panel open on its hinges, and took Marley by the wrists, and pulled him into the parlor and the light.

Will regarded Kit for a moment—a compact man with a pouting lip and fine fair hair, wearing a tomcat strut—and tilted his head, and finally, carefully, he smiled. "Not unscathed after all, then, Christofer."

"No," Kit answered, crossing the sitting room. "Not unscathed at all." He knelt, the plume on his hat bobbing over his shoulder, and began shuffling the scattered pages of manuscript together. "Ah, all this work just to conceal my hand. I told you he'd catch us out," Kit continued, speaking to Walsingham, who impaled another cake on his toasting-fork.

Will sniffed, then leaned against the wall. "This smells pleasant enough for a room inhabited by two dead men."

Kit laughed, stood, and set the pages of *Titus* on the mantelpiece, weighing them down with a thick stump of candle on a gilded dish. A wry and wicked grin. "Die? I have died most verily, and two or three times since I bespoke thee last."

"An you're alive, then, what need have these of me?" Will looked at Walsingham guiltily, but the old man seemed not to hear. Instead, he closed spidery fingers on one arm of his chair and struggled to stand for a moment, the toasting-fork still in his other hand. Kit crossed to him without thinking and lifted him to his feet, a strong hand on Walsingham's knobby wrist, and then he blushed and stepped back as if in apology.

Sir Francis snorted and handed Kit the toasting-fork and its burden. "I know I'm old. You won't offend me." He looked from Will to Kit, and settled his robes with a shrug. "Kit, you could explain better to Will what we need of him than I."

"Aye, Sir Francis." Will wasn't sure he understood the look that passed between the other two. A moment of silent understanding, and then Kit twisted his lips in a slow, arrogant smile. "I can educate him well, I warrant."

> *Love me little, love me long.*
> —CHRISTOPHER MARLOWE, *The Jew of Malta*

The door closed tight behind Walsingham, and Kit let his head roll down to rest against his chest. Another borrowed shirt, though this one fit him better. He propped the toasting-fork, cake and all, back in the rack and returned to Will. Will, his dark hair oiled in curls and his blue eyes brilliant over handsome cheekbones, his dogged nose wrinkled in consternation, his neatly trimmed beard not thick and not obscuring the line of his jaw.

Will, who looked gutted and hung in the silence that followed the click of the latch, but Kit knew him enough to see he'd find his feet in a moment.

Not Will. Kit glanced at the manuscript on the mantel, the earnest eyes of the man confronting him. There was brandywine on the sideboard, and hand-blown glasses from Cornwall—which might have made Kit laugh, if he had been in a laughing mood. "Did you want that cake?"

"I want answers, Kit."

Ah, there it was. The spike of stubborn under the man's quiet demeanor. This time, Kit did smile, and crossed the room to raise the decanter. Delicate glasses, with a soft blue spiral design, the bottom center rising like a whirlpool in reverse. Homely and humble, compared to Faerie's crystal bubbles. He slid his palm around one while it filled.

"I'm drinking," Kit said, watching Will in a looking glass hung on the wall. His hand trembled and his eye was unsure. Brandywine the rich gold of amber splashed the marble of the sideboard. Kit turned with the glass in his hand. "Art thou?"

"Will I have need of it?"

"Yes."

"Then no." Will winked; he'd scored in the familiar game.

I might have overfilled the glass. But no. Kit didn't spill any more. "Come on," Kit said. "We're going to the kitchen. Sir Francis takes little breakfast and almost nothing at dinner, and keeps no cook. The servants will likely be done with their repast and gone about their duties."

"The kitchen?"

"I've something to show thee." Kit held the door for Will. He led them through Walsingham's well-appointed hallways and down a half flight on the servant's stair, near blind in the darkness, careful not to stumble.

They came into a room that was both close and dark. "Hold my glass," he said, and found the latch. There were always secret ways in Walsingham's houses, and before Francis had survived the poison that had left him so ill he had chosen to pretend he had died of it, Kit had known most of them. "Voila. The kitchen."

As predicted, the room was deserted, dark, and close. A banked fire glowed on the hearth; the yeasty thickness of rising bread spread under oiled cloths made him sneeze. A homely place. For now.

He retrieved his glass and noticed that the level had dropped. "Ah, Will."

"What?"

"It's like *Faustus*, isn't it? The scent of charred flesh. The heat of the ovens of Hell." A table along one wall held heavy knives and kitchen axes, a chopping block and hooks for fowl and roasts. An unfortunate hen graced the center peg. Destined for soup: Walsingham could manage little else.

"Kit, what are you about?"

But he didn't answer. The taste of the liquor nauseated him, but he swallowed anyway. A fat hen on a hook. *Not Will.*

Will cleared his throat. "I need to know how to do what you did. How to write plays that—"

"Change things?"

"Aye. I do not think my teacher understands what he says he understands. Know you the Earl of Oxford?"

"Edward," Kit said. The firelight made the room dim, but he could see the ripples shaking through his glass. "Aye, we are—acquainted. That is to say, he is beknownst to me, and I to him." He glanced over his shoulder—the long turn for his missing eye—to make sure Will took his meaning. "Have you noticed how he treats his wife?"

"I have not—had occasion."

"Ah." Kit turned and leaned against the table beside the chopping block, the hard edge pressing his back. The sensation quickened his breath in memory. "Her name is also Annie. She's Burghley's daughter: Oxford was raised Burghley's ward, as was Essex. Essex, who is not fond of Sir Walter." Kit brushed the black silk of his breeches, knowing Will would take his meaning: the habitual black of Raleigh's disciples, matching the doublet Walsingham loaned him, which Kit had left in his room.

The School of Night. Sir Walter Raleigh's group of freethinkers and tobacco-smokers, opposed to Essex's group as the men each sought favor with the Queen. To which Kit had been associated. "The alliances are complex."

"Oxford wishes his daughter married to Southampton, Essex's friend," Will said quietly. "Your little conspiracy has members on both sides of the game, then. The Prometheus Club, I gather, is us—"

"The Prometheus Club is both factions," Kit said. "It was one conspiracy, now sundered at the root."

"One conspiracy of the Queen's favorites? Sir Walter and Essex?"

"Oh, older than that. From the earliest days of her reign, before you or I were even conceived of, sweet William. The schism came later, and there are those in the other faction who place their own advancement above the Queen's—or England's—well-being. I believe myself that Good Queen Bess takes some pleasure in playing Essex and Raleigh for rivals—and I wonder a bit if it was Essex who saw fit to have me removed, as I was Sir Walter's friend."

"I'faith, Kit, is there any man in Elizabeth's court you haven't let bugger you?"

"There's a few I've buggered instead." Kit waited for the chuckle. Will did not fail him. "Will. I said, *friend*. In any case, Oxford and Burghley have not been on good terms since Oxford decided that Anne was not to his liking."

"Your doing."

"Edward's doing. Anne was blameless as poor Isabella, and kept her blamelessness better. And I'm not Gaveston. 'Tis not meet a good woman should suffer for no greater crime than a bad marriage—" He felt Will's eyes on his face, and forced himself to match the gaze. " 'Tis true."

"I believe you," Will answered.

Tremendous tension came out of Kit with the breath he had been painfully holding.

"Thank you."

"But then—why art thou dead, or playing at it? And why have you concealed yourself these months?" Will was angry, and the thought warmed Kit. *How few true friends have you had since you entered this life? Only Walsingham.*

" 'Tis a complicated story, but it suffices that all thought me dead, except perhaps Her Majesty, and I might have been dead indeed. All but Sir Francis still believe it." He put a hand out, pleased with its steadiness, and clapped Will on the shoulder. "Art a true friend to me, Will. How it pleases my heart, I hope you know."

Will's lips thinned around a smile. "Is there some message I could pass your parents in Canterbury?"

"My . . . No. Since I left Cambridge to become a vile playmaker, they've regarded me as a cuckoo's egg. Better leave me dead."

"I must tell you—"

"That is?"

"I ran afoul of Poley and Baines at the Sergeant."

Despite the warmth in his belly, Kit's mouth ached around the words he couldn't quite say. *Oh, not Will. Not Will.* "Poley. And Baines together. Did they see you?"

"They threatened me."

"Ah, no. Will, you have to break with Oxford and Walsingham now. Burbage too—"

"Now that you're returned, they can do without me. But I am pleased to defend my Queen, and if you teach me what you know, the art of your plays—"

"Don't choose sides in this." Kit wanted to take the other man by the shoulders and shake him, but he gave him pleading instead. "Flee. Take your Annie and get away. I'm not returned, man. I'm dead, and you'll be dead with me if you stay." He caught himself worrying his eyepatch, and forced his hand down. Put it on Will's arm, instead, and clutched the broadcloth of his sleeve. "Some one of us is a traitor. Some one of us betrayed me, and will betray you. I trust only Walsingham. You cannot choose sides, Will: they'll eat you."

Will looked at him for a long moment, and then shook his hand off and moved away, close to a broken-backed chair pushed up beside the hearthstone. "Run if they've broken you—"

"*Broken* me!"

"—I'll not be called a coward."

It stung as much as if Will had spoken the accusation plain, and Kit flinched and looked down.

In the dark kitchen that was very like the dungeon that Kit had come here to remember, William Shakespeare shook his head. "I mean to choose the side that's right."

> **Tamora:** *So should I rob my sweet sons of their fee;*
> *No, let them satisfy their lust on thee.*
> —WILLIAM SHAKESPEARE, *Titus Andronicus*

Langley's kitchen grew hot and close while Will leaned against the arm of a broken chair and listened to embers crack on the grate. It was a long time before Kit answered. " 'Tis not what side is right. 'Tis what side you're *on*."

"Elizabeth and the Protestant Church—"

"The third or fourth time you're raped by a priest, you may start to regard the Church's moral pronouncements with a jaundiced eye." Kit turned away, still cupping that glass, and ran the other fingers over the scarred wood of the block.

"Kit, from you of all people—" Will left the chair, came close enough to lower his voice and murmur through tightness. "Sodomy's accounted a sin worse than any."

"What? What two men do willing is a sin worse than rape or usury? Than murder? Than denying God? I know Church doctrine—" A deprecating tilt of his head to show how well he knew it.

Uncomfortable words through a stiff throat. "Equal to witchcraft, they say."

"Then burn me for a witch and a playmaker. I thought better of you. *The unspeakable Christofer Marley, may he rot in Hell, and he got less worse than he deserved.* Say it if you think it! It's what the Puritans will write. Although—by their own doctrine, and I understand it aright, I've as good a chance of 'election' to Heaven as any of them, for if all our acts and our salvation are predetermined, how can you condemn any man?"

Will had no answer. It was different, to know generally enough for coarse laughter what men and boys did in small rooms and shared beds, and to look into the face of his friend and see a rough, kind sort of honesty that begged him to *understand* it. He moved some steps as if Kit's sin could taint him.

Kit picked at the mortar between stones with a fingernail, eyes downcast. "More get at it than you might imagine, Will. Some hypocrites touch and kiss and clip—and never call it what it is. But I am a lover of discourse, good William, and as I have said before, I would liefer lose my life than my liberty of speech." A pause, and Kit chuckled. "And as I prophesied it, so it has come true."

"No. But I would hear you say you've never enjoyed the pleasures of a beardless boy, who cries rape now."

"Never one who took no enjoyment in return." Kit met Will's gaze a moment, then turned his head and spat upon the floor. "Oh, unfair, Shakespeare. What do you take your Marley for?"

The cellar stone was cool as Will pressed his hand against it. He thought of his friend's beautiful hands and lips turned to acts his stomach coiled to think on, and struck out savagely to deny the image. "Is that why you refused holy orders? Because you couldn't trust yourself around boys?"

Kit half turned back. He shrugged, and Will saw the bitter edge of a smile, as if Kit had expected no less. "Call it an unwillingness to practice hypocrisy, and another unwillingness to abandon the plea- sures of the flesh. I should not expect anyone to understand who does not know for himself—and there was Rheims. Richard Baines was at Rheims."

"Rheims? Where the Romish seminary is?"

"I went to France for Walsingham and Burghley, and made pre- tence to study among the Papists while they plotted. It almost got me barred from my Master of Arts at Cambridge, but the Privy Council interceded. They knew what I had done to preserve our Gloriana. I did not tell them all I suffered—"

"This same Baines who has slandered you since your death?"

A transparent attempt to turn him aside, but Kit was inexorable. " 'Tis not surprising. Gloriana has said that she would rather a loyal Catholic than a Puritan: our Queen is a freethinker, for all Burghley and his son Robert Cecil would like to see every Catholic hanged." Kit looked up, folding one hand into the crook of his elbow as he lifted his glass to his lips. "Some of them are Prometheans. Ours, theirs. Does Baines accuse me of atheism and sodomy? Of blaspheming and railing?"

"He does, and puts about the word that you died drunken, cursing God after a knife-fight in some filthy alley."

"Would that I were drunken at Rheims, when they put the irons to my skin. There's an art to it, did you know? You burn a little, and a little more. A finger's breadth at a time, and never so deep as to numb sensation." Kit's voice was level and soft as a tutor's, his eye unfocused. "And sodomy? Aye, and five men by turns, and one an Inquisitor. As for cursing God? Baines should know how I blasphemed in Rheims, before Baines stopped my mouth with a black scold's bridle. Baines was there, also acting as an agent for the Crown. I could never prove treason against him, though I professed it: he swore he thought I was the Pope's own man and not the Queen's when he betrayed me. All lies. He belongs to *them*, though he pretends service to the Queen — but what man cares that outrages are perpetrated against a catamite, or a heretic, or a poet?"

Kit scratched his wrist, half idly, a cat attending to its paw. And Will tasted bile. He wished he could stop his ears with his fingers, but he swallowed and stepped toward his friend. "Sayst thou he knew of this? An Englishman?!"

"Oh, Will." Marley worried his eyepatch with nervous fingers. "Will, he held me down."

A dark, too-knowing eye. A sliver of an earnest smile. Will looked down, looked away. Anywhere but at his friend. "Kit —"

"It wasn't so much different than Cambridge, all in all. I have been told I was a lovely boy."

"Oh, sweet Christofer." Will's knees folded and he sat down on the floor. One hand landed on the edge of the half-mended chair. He hauled himself into it, shaking.

Kit squared his shoulders, leaning against the wall, one hand circling in the dim room like a white moth near a flame. "So, three times now I've escaped him and his masters. In Rheims, when he referred me to the Catholic plotters — though I have some satisfaction in knowing that truer Papists caught him out before he left France, and they put *him* to the question in the strappado. Then in the Low Countries, when he forged a charge of counterfeiting upon me. And in England, now, and a knife in a hand I thought a friend's."

"Can you prove it was Baines?"

"I can prove it was Thomas Walsingham. And Baines will do as a sop to my rage, can I not find the grace to beard his master. But yet the Crown sees in them both loyal men. I must have proof, or his death. Elizabeth can lack stomach for blood." Kit stopped as if his voice ran dry. "But I see I shock you."

Will unclenched his hands from the chair arms and stood. "No. Tell me more. Tell me about these shadows we oppose. Tell me how you escaped."

Kit threw his brandy back like a man intending to get drunk, and quickly. Glancing at the glass in his hand as if he meant to hurl it into the hearth, he shook his head and after three quick steps set the fragile thing lightly on the mantel. He crouched before the fire and held his hands out. "You're expecting the story of a daring escape."

Will nodded. Close heat made his beard itch.

"I swore Bess and the Church of England blue and bloody. I vowed I'd see her headless corpse dragged through the London gutter. I vowed— I made them think they had broken me. Hell, they did break me. I would have crawled, and gladly, but I hid my loyalty to our Queen—" A sound almost like a hiccup, so Will averted his gaze. "It doesn't matter. I lied. And I lived. And later a few were hanged. Hast seen a Tyburn hanging?"

God help Will, he had. Slow strangulation, but not to the death. With the criminal cut down living, disemboweled living, emasculated living, hacked into bloody chunks.

God have mercy, by then almost certainly dead.

"That's what a Queen's Man is, Will. It isn't for you."

Will raised his hand from Kit's shoulder, brushed his fluff of hair aside. He half expected a flinch, but Kit turned the long way 'round to look upon him square. "Christofer—"

"How plainly can I tell you? *Get out.* This is not for you."

"How old were you?"

"How—? I was twenty-three. It wasn't so long ago."

"You survived."

"Lucky me. Unlucky Edward the Second. Or"—with an airy wave of his hand—"that Gaulish or Saxon commander. Whatever his name was. The one the Romans cut slits in, so more could go at him at once. Or was he a Roman raped by Gauls? Still, an Inquisitor. I'm tempted to count it some species of honor."

He's drunk after all, Will realized, and almost laughed that the only reason he had known it was that Kit couldn't remember the name of an obscure historical figure. "Not the tactics the Inquisition normally approves."

A tilt of Kit's head, and that fleeting smile, shy as a girl's. "It does seem a touch unprofessional, doesn't it? These Catholics at Rheims were no true Catholics. They did not seem overly concerned with what the Church bids or unbids. I can't but say I agree, somewhat: had God not wished us to savor meat and enjoy drink, he would have given us tongues too numb for tasting. Had he not intended us to enjoy companionship, would he have given us tongues so facile for conversation . . . or such a taste for it? The Church is not God."

"Kit, that's heresy."

A smile bent around his scars. "I died for it."

Will opened his mouth. Embers in the banked hearth popped.

Kit rested his hands on Will's shoulders, leaned his forehead against the bridge of Will's nose. "These are very bad people, Will. Get out. Go to the Continent. Join a nunnery. Save yourself."

Will set him back at arm's length and studied his face. Flushed, maybe, but his gaze was sharp and he stood steady on his feet. "You haven't run."

"I'm Kit Marley."

"And I'm Will Shakespeare. Dammit, Marley, an you'd ward me, tell me truth!"

"The truth?"

Will took a breath. "Aye."

Kit gestured to the chair and hooked a peeling stool over with the toe of his boot. "If you can't be dissuaded," he said, "then by what's holy, Will, sit down."

You must be proud, bold, pleasant, resolute —
And now and then stab, as occasion serves
— CHRISTOPHER MARLOWE, *Edward II*

The fire burned low. Kit found a black iron poker beside the hearth — a long bit of rodstock with a looped handle, the tip spiraling to a point like some black unicorn's horn — and poked the coals idly, knocking sparks and cinders up the chimney. An orange flame licked in the crevices, and Kit wedged the poker there, resting the loop on his knee.

Will coughed once against the back of his wrist. Kit at last folded his arms one over the other and smiled. "You're tangled over *Titus*."

"I'm horrified," Will answered with a shrug. "I've got to Lavinia — mutilated, ravished — and next I must have the Moor's treachery to

Titus, and I find myself as tongueless as Lavinia, and as bottled full
of tales. Hands cut off, tongue torn out. How does a man make that
real?"

"You haven't her rage to put in it."

Will nodded. "Her rage and her hurt. 'Tis not something that can
be set right in an act."

" 'Tis not something that can be set right. That's what makes it a
tragedy." The coals had gone dark near the poker's tip. Kit leaned forward and puffed air until they flared blue and orange, casting disconcerting heat across his face. "The plays—your plays—have the power
to make people believe. Some of it—this craft—lies in what I did to
Titus. Some of it is in your own vision and tongue. Oxford writes some
scenes and words, but he only knows what I taught him. It's Plato's
magic; you make an ideal thing, and if the people *believe* that thing, the
world itself must be beaten to the form."

"Plato. Like love, then."

"Aye," Kit said dryly. "If you believe in love. And then the performance. Alleyn was good enough to carry the spell. Burbage and Kemp
are strong as well." He twisted the poker in the fire, one boot propped
on the hearthstone. "There's an art to that too: to giving the audience
belief in a dream as real as the touch of hand. The Senecan structure
won't work for it, and blank verse is too static. Fourteeners are a loss,
too formal—"

"A Platonic ideal."

"—and people will live for it. It seems too simple, doesn't it?"
Kit looked away from the embers. The loop of the poker grew warm
against his knee. He shifted its resting place from his stocking to his
breeches. "But give them men who could grasp heaven, and who turn
away through willfulness and greed. Give them strong kings, or give
them the truth of what happens when kings are not strong. Make
them grieve for men they would hate—but it must be fresh, not styl-
ized: words spoken trippingly on the tongue. Reality *is* drama." He
paused, and watched Will chew his mustache. "Like that lemon tree of
Sir Francis'. If you can convince enough eyes they've seen a thing—if
you can convince a man or a beast he *is* a thing—better than he is,
more loyal, more true—that thing holds."

"I have often thought," Will said carefully, for this was a heresy too, "that a man given half a chance might act morally. Because he knows what morality is."

"Not Robert Poley."

"No. But another man."

"What man?"

"Myself. You. Her Majesty. You don't believe in God. And yet you were never but kind to me."

"Oh," Kit said. "I believe in God well enough. It's the Church I take issue with."

"But who would believe Kit Marley, monarchist?"

"A King we must have. A man might prefer a strong woman who temporizes to a weak man who beheads." Kit looked at his nails.

Will cleared his throat after a time. "And . . . you say *Titus* is formal."

"And finish it formal. You've an ear for a scansion and a fair eye for an image, and there's this in you: thou fearest not to own the myth. But now you must put the *fire* in it, and not shy away, and bring them under the spell of your words. You've played my *Jew*."

"I have." Will smiled. " 'Tis strong. But the third act—"

"I know." It wasn't all the play he would have had it be. "Write thy plays about *people*. You've a way of spinning height and depth I envy. All I'm fit for is making light in darkness, and spreading blood and bitter farce across the planks."

"Foolishness, Kit. I've read your *Leander*."

"Pretty, isn't it? I'm partial to *Tamburlaine* myself: still my best work, I think."

Will choked, and laughed, and turned back on himself nimble as a ferret. "Where's this danger?"

"The danger's in the men who don't want the plays written. Men like Baines, and Sir Walter's rival, the Earl of Essex."

"Raleigh is an ally?"

"Raleigh is someone I cultivated a bit, but he is not one of ours. Robert Devereaux, though—Essex—is one of theirs. Though both sides still use the same name, and trade alliances like chessmen."

"What do *they* want?"

Kit marshaled half-drunken thoughts. "As I think it? Elizabeth off the throne, for one thing. A ruler in her place without such—

personality. Gloriana is the Faerie Queene. The other Prometheans, their goal is the elevation of man."

"Admirable."

"They want safety and an end to poetry, Will. An end to greatness of spirit, and all men made equal. They want to own God, and use him to make all men subject. I should liefer lose my life than my liberty of thought."

"And our half?"

"*Our* half, is it still? Elizabeth and England, we stand for. 'Tis rough work. Even for a rogue like myself, whose works drip with gore, unacquainted with gentle thoughts."

"Can the man who wrote *Hero and Leander* claim to be unacquainted with gentle thoughts?"

"Acquainted and yet unacquainted." Kit shifted before the iron could scorch his leg. The tip was not yet glowing. " 'Tis a quaint small thing, a poem about passion —"

"Kit, it's a poem about Leander's arse."

The iron slipped: Kit caught it right-handed and hissed, juggling a twist of sleeve around the metal to shield his hand. " 'How smooth his breast was, and how white his belly, / And whose immortal fingers did imprint, / That heavenly path, with many a curious dint, / That runs along his back, but my rude pen —' "

" 'Can hardly blazon forth the loves of men.' " Will's long nose dented sideways with the twisting mouth. "I'faith, I think betimes you purpose to shock. You underestimate the wit in your pen, rude as it may be — or so I've heard tell. From those with more interest in the loves of men than I."

"Rude enough for most purposes." It was his last chance to impress upon the man the severity of his choices. "Is this pen enough to write with?" He lifted the poker until the smoking end hovered a finger's width from Shakespeare's eye. *Will. Move not.*

"Kit, what are you about —" There was a little squeal in Will's voice, good. And a tremor under it as Will pressed his head back hard against the wall. Ah, there was a red glow at the tip after all, like a pen dipped in blood.

Excellent.

"Look on it well," he said, watching Will's shoulders rise as if that could protect his face from the cherry-hot iron. Kit swallowed bitterness when it rose up his throat one more time, but couldn't quite get the taste down. A thunder in his chest like beating wings prevented it. Will's eye was gray-blue and looked very soft; he didn't blink, and the dark pupil swelled as if it would encompass the whole of the iris in velvet black. Will's eyelashes curled from the iron's heat; Kit drew it back a little. "That could be thy final vision. Imagine it. Can you imagine? Image yourself unhanded like Stubbs, or racked like Kyd, or branded and blinded like me. Damn you, William Shakespeare. *See it.*"

The apple in Will's throat bobbled. He dared not nod.

"Tell me once more you mean to do this, and I'll let it lie."

Will's mouth worked. "I mean to do this thing."

"Bloody hell." But Kit said it tiredly, and turned and strode to the table, and drew back his arm. The poker was heavier than a rapier, but he managed well enough to be pleased: the strength wasn't out of his shoulder.

A *thump* first, and close on its heel a sizzle. Kit thrust the fireplace poker through the body of the unfortunate hen—off-center, his aim untrue with his missing eye—and into the mortar of the wall. It didn't hold: he stepped back from the clatter as it fell. "Damn you to hell, William Shakespeare."

"Oh." Will stood. "I can probably manage that for myself." He came and threw an arm over Kit's shoulder, and Kit dropped an arm around his waist. "I knew you wouldn't put my eye out."

Kit heard an edge of hysteria in his own laugh, and wished he could afford to get drunker. Clearheadedness was the last thing he wanted. "I wouldn't rely on that *knowing* too much, my friend."

Act I, scene viii

Hark, countrymen! either renew the fight,
Or tear the lions out of England's coat . . .

—WILLIAM SHAKESPEARE, First Part of *King Henry the Sixth*

Will itched with the sensation of words filling his brain, like a pressure behind his eyes. Kit saw it: Will could tell from the sly way the other poet abandoned him in the drawing room amid cider and staling crumpets, beside a leather-surfaced secretary fitted with every tool for writing a man could want. Will fetched another cup of cider and settled himself with his back to a window so light could fall over his shoulder. He proceeded to deface first one and then another sheet with his cramped looping hand. Fewer mark-outs this time, fewer words scratched through.

It was well that Kit walked into the edge of the door frame on his way back into the room, or Will might have upset the ink pot in startlement. Will glanced up. The light had changed and he'd turned in his chair to follow it without noticing, and he'd covered half a score of folded leaves with notes and lines of dialogue, scanned lines sketched here and there with a double-underlined blank, waiting for the perfect word.

"Christus lacrimavit," Kit growled, rubbing his shoulder. He'd changed to a shirt of cobweb lawn, this one without scorches on the sleeve; a doublet of black silk taffeta, slashed crimson, was slung unbuttoned around his shoulders. "Walsingham is resting. How comes it?"

"It comes." Will pushed the pages across the desk, waving Kit an invitation. "I don't remember you so clumsy, even drunk."

"If I were still drunken, I'd have something to answer for. 'Tis noon. Didst not hear the bell?" Kit riffled pages until he found the first. "I've been tripping on nothings since . . ." He tapped a knuckle on the eyepatch without looking up.

"Not yet accustomed?"

"It seems only an hour gone by when I had two good eyes to see with. Will, that any mortal man can write such verse so quickly is an affront to angels. This exchange betwixt Marcus and Titus—with Titus unhanded, and his sons beheaded, and his daughter dismembered— *'Why dost thou laugh? it fits not with this hour.' 'Why, I have not another tear to shed.'* That's good, I warrant. It does sing true: to read it, you can see the man smile, and it is terrible." Crisp pages rustled; Kit held each up, opened along the folds to read slowly, tasting the words.

Learning them, Will thought. *Is he truly so blind to the irony?* He found himself looking at his friend's face for a shadow of pain, and saw only a player's concentration, a thin line etched between Kit's dark brows.

Will went to the window. He rested a hand on the glass and stood looking over the garden, watching yellowing leaves twist in a soft October breeze. "If you mean to go about London unnoticed, you might dress less like Christofer Marley and more like a cobbler's son. I can bring a false beard from the Theatre, and a bit of gum. No one will see aught but that and the eyepatch, an you play the role."

"A cobbler's son." Amusement in that. "Only a man who dresses like a glover's son would say so."

One more rustle, then silence as the pages stopped turning.

"We've come from close places, haven't we, Will? And worn very different roads to the same end: poetry and service."

"*Your* father saw the value of an education."

"As yours did not. I may have to teach you Latin."

Shakespeare snorted.

Another leaf tugged loose of a pear twig before Kit spoke again. "I shan't be in London long."

"Where will you go?"

"I cannot tell."

"Where can I write to you?"

"I do not know."

Will paused. "You'll be on some mission for Her Majesty," he said, considering. "I understand."

"No," Kit answered. "I go tonight, under cover of darkness, to beg my service back from Gloriana, in point of fact. I have been offered refuge by a foreign monarch, that I might live."

"That you might live?" Will set his rump on the window ledge. Kit still stared at the pages, but his eye no longer scanned the lines. "What mean you?"

"I am —" A breath, and a sigh. Kit's shoulders rose and fell as he stepped back from the desk, scrubbing his nails on his doublet. The motion arrested; he plucked at the material, pulling it into the light to examine. "It is a little Kit Marley, isn't it? No matter. I'm poisoned, Will, with a slow poison, and the cure lies in a foreign land. If I do not return I shall die." He ruffled paper. "Horribly, I am assured."

Which was truth, Will decided, watching Kit. Or as much of a truth as anyone was like to get from Marley. "I shall worry."

"And I for thee. You'll be in more danger. But I shall discover how a letter may find me, if a letter *may* find me, and send you word on the means."

"I may take a month in Stratford come Christmastime. If the plague stays in London. If the playhouses stay closed. If you send a letter." Will resumed his chair and reached for a fresh sheet. He could feel Kit's smile resting on him.

"Annie is speaking to you again."

"Annie thinks I should see my children, as she had Susanna write me, 'before we're grown and gone.' I'll be sleeping in the third-best bed with Hamnet, I imagine. And she's yet a better wife than I deserve, Kit: there's few enough women who would even *pretend* to understand why a man might leave kith and kin to crawl through the gutters of strange cities, all for the grace of a poem."

"There's few enough men who understand it," Kit replied. "And, here or in Stratford, I may be capable to make a visit, now and again."

"From overseas?"

"Not so much overseas as under them," Kit said cryptically. He glanced at the window, measuring the light, and fanned the folded sheets upon the desk. "Shall we work on these a little, before I must disguise myself for Her Majesty?"

"Will Sir Francis loan you a cloak? A hood should suffice in a carriage. Keep the doublet: you'll want to look pretty for the Queen. Otherwise she won't believe you're Marley."

"At least I don't dress like a Puritan," Kit answered, with a scornful glance for Will's brown broadcloth, and reached across the desk for a pen.

Act I, scene ix

*Y*ou'll want to look pretty for the Queen. Kit caught himself examining his fingernails in the light of the candles burning on a gilt wooden table, and let his hands fall to his sides. There was ink along the knuckle of his forefinger, but that was nothing unusual, and at least he was tidier than Shakespeare. Will took no pride in his appearance — or his scribing — whatsoever.

And writing lines such as his, he does not need false pride. Anyway, 'tis Sir Walter's duty to look pretty for his Queen, and not mine. Queens will just have to take me as they find me.

Gallant thoughts, for a man alone in a small white marble room with no escape, when anything could be coming down the narrow passageway he'd entered through. A long table and a few narrow windows dominated the room, lit between flickering shadows by a rack of candles like stag's antlers. He wondered if he were quartered in a priest's closet, or some stranger appurtenance — and how riddled the walls of Winchester might be.

Walsingham had led Kit through a secret passage within a chapel at Winchester Palace, and then taken Kit's dagger and abandoned him. Kit wasn't sure what garden the small, tight window looked over, but it admitted a breath of air, and over the flowers he could smell the river.

At least it wasn't an abattoir, as in Deptford.

The Queen was letting him cool his heels. He examined the ink stain on his fingertip again: it resembled a map of Italy. He pressed back a mousy handful of hair. At last, soft footsteps sounded beyond the panel, and Kit turned with a question on his lips, hoping it would be Walsingham come to retrieve him but fearing it could be another sort of visitor altogether—one armed with sharp steel and a quarrel.

The panel slid open, and Kit stepped forward. And met, open-mouthed, the masterful gaze of his Elizabeth. Alone and without escort.

"Highness!" he stuttered, and bent a knee somewhat credibly, for all his head-kicked foolishness. His breath hurt his throat, but he held it and kept his eyes on her shoes. Gold cloth, sewn with pearls. Toepointed slippers clicked daintily on the marble as she stepped forward, her hem so stiff with lace that it made a sound brushing the threshold like a curry down a horse's back. The scent of herbs and musk as she hesitated, and Kit wondered for a moment if she might strike him. She was not unknown to lay her wrath on those who displeased her.

"Sir Christofer Marley," she said, after a while. He choked on that held breath and looked up at her despite himself. Into a prescient smile under the crimson tower of her wig and eyes wide with mockery and amusement. "Yes, we know something of your adventures. Stand up straight, lad: even Queens tire of bended necks when they haven't an axe to hand."

He stood. "Your Highness is well-informed."

"We pay a great deal for the privilege," she answered. "In gold and coin, and in the flesh and blood of our loyal subjects. Has she claimed thee?"

"Your Highness?"

"The Queen of Faerie," she said, with a lift of her chin. She shut the panel behind herself and claimed the center of the narrow chamber. Kit's pulse fluttered in his throat: a different sort of awe than what the Faerie Queen produced. This was the awe of temporal power, of strength and age and a wit equal to any man's. *She is the pillar the sky is hung from.* "The beautiful pitiless lady. Has she claimed you?"

"She wishes to, madam," he answered. "But her sister, called Queen Morgan, was the one who knighted me."

"And bedded you? Oh, don't blush like that. For all 'tis engaging. We know something of the ways of the Fae. So. Stolen by Faeries, Queen's Man. And yet you seek an audience with your Sovereign, and we are disposed to grant it. Speak."

"Your Highness." Her eyebrow arched under its paint as he sought for words. *Do women always fluster you so badly, Kit?*

Only when they're Queens. He genuflected again, straightening hastily when she coughed.

"Sir Poet," she said, not unkindly. "We are pleased that our subtleties have preserved you, and well-pleased are we to see you well. But now our good Walsingham tells us you beg release of your oaths of service. Your Queen would know why, and what adventures befell you. Our intimate Spirit, Burghley, had you buried, and those were of a certainment not our orders."

"My Queen." He would have gone to one knee again, but her worn, irritated fingers caught his elbow and held him on his feet. He couldn't look Gloriana in the eye, though she put her fingers under his chin and tilted his face like a maiden aunt with a wayward boy. "What choice is left me?"

He saw her lips purse under the masque of her paint, smelled the marjoram and ambergris and civet that clothed her. She tilted her head to examine his eyepatch and the scar that ran beneath it. "What befell thee, Queen's Man?"

"Your Highness knows—"

"Your own words, man, and be quick about it."

"A dagger in the eye, Your Highness." He choked. "Thomas Walsingham's men—"

"Your death was to be an illusion, Christofer Marley," she said, seeming not to notice when her words rode over his. "A false body put in your place, and you spirited overseas. As was arranged in the letter you should have had under our seal. You have given much, and demanded little. We thought to make recompense."

"It was not so, Your Highness."

"We see." Her hand left a trace of scent on his skin as she stepped away, her gaze steady on his scar. "I've witnessed worse, but it is not pretty. And earned in our service. You are a poet," she continued without a breath. "Give us a poem."

That was a challenge. She smiled when he drew himself up. "And yet before I yield my fainting breath, I quite the killer, though I blame the kind," Kit whispered, amazed at his own audacity. "You kill unkind, I die, and yet am true, For at your sight, my wound doth bleed anew—"

"Falsely said, but pretty. Like all sentiments of poesy. As a poet myself, I'll forgive it. Our subterfuge—Burghley's, Thomas Walsingham's, and mine—was to have saved you."

Kit nodded. A cramp knotted his stomach; he had to brace his knees or they would have failed. *Dead men are hard-pressed to die again.* "My Queen. I knew you could not prove false to me, for all you are a Prince, you are a woman as true as any woman, and the mother of a son."

She stepped back as if stung, and then shook her head in admiration and rue. "Hist! Kit Marley, you've got a tongue in you. Wilt convert me to atheism now?"

She leaned close, voice confidential. "You are privileged in your loss this once and once alone. Unmarried Queens do not have children, sir."

"Your Highness. As I am bid—"

She smiled then, gentled. "We are given to understand that we owe you life and reign twice over, Sir Poet. We meant to reward you with your life, but it seems you have that in spite of us. What would complete thee?"

"Do you know, Your Highness, of Thomas Walsingham's faithlessness?"

"Not unlike his cousin," she said, "whose trickery painted me to a stand where I must have my royal cousin executed. The men who support me are true to my reign, but they *will* work at cross-purposes. We believe he is upright in his conviction that your death was warranted—

for all he was misled to that conclusion. Do not ask yourself revenged on him."

"I would not. Does Your Highness wish our task ended?"

A tilt of her head under the weight of pearls and hair. A subtle smile. "We are," she said, "very fond of plays. You were about to answer my question."

I should ask for Ingrim's head roasted and brought in on a platter with an apple in his mouth, and bits of boiled egg to make the eyes. "I was a guest of that same Thomas Walsingham when your summons found me," Kit said carefully. "There were papers. Manuscripts. Poems, part of a play—"

"I am sorry." He believed her. "He has burned them."

"Better my life lost than my words, Your Highness," Kit said. "There is nothing else I will be remembered by."

She stared down her nose. "You will be remembered as a sodomite, a heretic, and a mediocre playmender who died in a cluttered tavern through a tawdry brawl over some free-looking young man's favors. We pardoned your Ingrim Frazier, and we have buried your name, and we have saved your body and perhaps your immortal soul. Our Spirit's cousin, the estimable Widow Bull, will be tarred as a feckless tavern wench, and all that will be known of Marley is that he was a shoemaker's son who came to a sad and ugly end." And then that smile, and a negligent wave of a jeweled hand. "You may save your thank-yous."

Every word a blow, and yet the logic galled like a spur against his skin. "Widow Bull is Baron Burghley's cousin? Your Highness! I did not know that."

"She is also a distant cousin of the Queen of Faerie's court musician." Elizabeth's smile broadened. " 'Twas she saved your life, sweet poet." Her delight was a schoolgirl's, and Kit could almost smell stolen flowers when he met her eyes.

"Thank you, Your Highness," he murmured, and she laughed like a very young woman indeed.

"I knew it should come. Now beg your boon. The hour grows late, and old women kept from their beds wax querulous."

She'd used and discarded him like a street-corner lightskirt, and still he permitted her to charm him.

As if permission had anything to do with it. "Your Highness. If it suits you, would you share what you know of the Mebd, your sister Queen?"

Elizabeth's eyes widened: her only indication of surprise. "A fair and clever question, Sir Christofer," she answered. "And one I cannot answer with the rectitude that it deserves—but I will send you as well armed into Faerie as I may, and hope you will remember your old Queen with fondness." Her smile grew pensive under white lead paint and carmine. Dizziness spun him. "I have been ever too fond with you greedy, extravagant boys.

"Our reign reinforces the Mebd's, and so in subtle ways she supports it. The tricks you wreak with your plays have a greater place there than here, for her land is wove of the stuff of ballads and legendry. A strong Queen in England means a strong Queen of the Blesséd Isle, and she is old enough to know it. Old enough to remember Boudicca and Guenevere.

"But you have a problem, Sir Christofer." She paced, pausing at last by the candelabra, and passed her hand through flames as if she caressed a lover's face. "Because it wasn't the Queen of Faerie who knighted you and bedded you and took you into her service, was it? And when we release you, it is not to her service you will go. And she is dangerous when thwarted, that one, and ambitious to a fault."

"Morgan," he said, understanding, as another spasm wracked him. *Was the soup poisoned?* "Does she want her sister's crown?"

Elizabeth shrugged, and her eyes grew dark before she turned away. "Who can say what one Queen wants of another?"

"Who can say, indeed. I will never—" He stopped, and then found his voice again. "Great Queen—"

"Do not flatter me, Christofer. 'Tis boring."

"Your Highness. You release me from your service."

"We do."

He bowed around the hollowness that filled his throat, though pain grew in his belly like a flame. *I must return to Morgan,* he thought, realizing the source of the agony suddenly. "Service is what I have borne you, Your Highness, for I have not known you. And now that I bear you no service, I find I do know you. And my Queen, for what a playmaker's word is worth, I have traded that colder thing for a warmer thing, and with your permission, I will say now that I bear you love."

"So many masks, Sir Christofer." She raised one hand to her face. "We have that in common." Her eyes narrowed as he broke, leaned forward, a cold sweat dewing his forehead.

"Your Highness—" he apologized, and she waved him silent. .

"Gone too long from Faerie already," she sniffed. "There's a mirror in my chambers that will serve. Come, then. Lean on mine arm."

"Your Highness. It is beneath—" *your dignity.* But a bubble of pain silenced him.

Elizabeth jerked her chin, dismissing his protest with a gesture. "I am old and a Queen, and you shall do as you are bid. I will not have your life on my conscience after so much contrivance to preserve it!"

"Your Highness," Kit answered. And for the last time in a short mortal life, obeyed an order from his Queen.

She handed him through the mirror, an old woman's exquisite fingers steadying him. The glass' surface clutched like bread dough, then snapped away before it could tear; he tumbled through, striking his knees and hands on stone. When he pushed himself up he thought the Queen's long hands had come with him.

But no, it was a rasping voice, jingle of bells in flicking ears, a strong small figure propping him up. "Sir Poet?"

"Puck." Kit struggled to a crouch, the agony in his gut receding. And didn't understand why his next words were, "Where is Morgan?"

And whence the twist of worry and *lust* that almost sent him back to his knees a moment after he'd toiled up off them?

"Oh, about her tasks, I imagine. Or in her rooms. The Mebd set me to watch for you. She thought you might need assistance."

"I did," Kit said, "but I found it. Morgan's rooms—does Murchaud keep quarters here?"

The Puck's lips compressed as if Kit had said something unwittingly funny, but there was—concern? sorrow?—in the droop of the little man's ears and the set of his eyes. "Aye," he said. "I'll show you Morgan's rooms. And Prince Murchaud's. And the ones that will be your own."

"Mine own?" It was a pressure. The beat of a wave. As if being gone from Morgan's side had pooled behind a dam, and now all struck him suddenly. *Gone? Kit, you* bedded *her not two days since.* But *gone* was the word, and *gone* stayed with him.

"Aye," Puck said. "The Mebd's given you an apartment. Would you like to—"

"Morgan," Kit said, and it came out a whimper. *God, what has she done to me, Christ, what has she done—*

"As you wish it." Puck reached up to take Kit by the elbow. Kit thought he heard pity in the little Fae's voice, but it might have been only the jingle of his bells. "The gallery over the Great Hall is by way of these stairs—"

Kit lurched up them half at a run, aware that Robin fell behind on purpose and watched him go, bells jingling. Kit found Morgan's door as much by luck as memory, tried the latch, slipped within breathing like a racehorse.

Morgan.

She sat before the window, embroidering. Her golden hands moved over and under the frame, chasing a silver needle, dragging threads of colors Kit could barely comprehend through linen white as doves. She glanced up, pushed her stool back from the frame, and stood.

"Safe home," she said, and he hurried across the floor to her, the iron nails in his boots ringing immunity. She met him halfway, sleeves rolled back from the linen of her kirtle, clad in a gown so antique Kit had only seen the style on statues and in tapestries. "Sir Kit."

He hadn't words. *Something* screamed betrayal in his belly. *Christ. Christ.* He couldn't name it. She brought her arms up, laced them about his neck when he froze, suddenly, aching. Craving. "My Queen—"

She laughed, mocking, her black hair tossed over her shoulder, braided into a rope to bind his soul. "Long and long since I heard *those* words," she said. "Speak more."

But words abandoned him again. He fumbled at the knots on her gown, tore cloth. *Never like this* and *this is not me* but she was lovely, oh, skin gleaming in the light that streamed through the window, thighs like pillars revealing a flash of Heaven's gate as she stepped neatly from discarded clothing. He had no words. For the first time in his life, he had no *words.*

He couldn't kiss her mouth. Couldn't bear that intimacy. He dragged her into an embrace, teeth against her throat, half sensible that he first crushed her, scratched her against the embroidery and jeweled fixtures of his doublet and then slammed her to the wall, cold stone against his knuckles, her naked body twisting in his grip, her hair knotted in his fist. *Christ.*

It *hurt.* He bloodied his hand on the rough stone dragging it from behind her, fumbled the points on his breeches, the warmth of her sex against his scraped flesh like a siren song. *What am I doing?*

What —

No, he was a juggernaut. Automaton. She whimpered as he tore at her shoulder with his teeth, tasted the salt of her tears, his tears, remembered a mouth full of more blood than this and the pain of torture, rape, confession. He strangled on a scream he couldn't quite voice, unlaced an erection he thought might just burst — *Christ, she's pliant —* and end his suffering, pinned her to the wall as she squirmed against the velvet and silk and rough decoration of his clothes.

No. No. No.

"Christofer." A murmur. One hand, light on his collar.

God. Almost a whisper. More of a groan. His hand cupped her sex. He might have been a statue. "Morgan."

"Not yet."

"What?" He ached, twitched. Writhed toward her warmth —

"I'm not ready."

Oh.

He stroked her breasts with bloodied hands. Caressed the curve of her belly, the amplification of her thighs. Fell down on his knees before her. Kissed the arch of her hips, the black-forested delta below. She tasted of vinegar, rosemary, honey.

He wept. He made her scream and knot *her* hands in his hair, pulling until heat seared his scalp. When she gave consent at last, he took her — there, on the floor by the window, her naked body arching against his black-velvet-clad one — and she licked hot tears from his cheeks and laughed.

Act I, scene x

Malvolio: . . . Thy Fates open
their hands; let thy blood and spirit embrace them;
and, to inure thyself to what thou art like to be,
cast thy humble slough and appear fresh.

—WILLIAM SHAKESPEARE, *Twelfth Night*

For once, Burbage knocked before he entered. Or possibly, he tried the handle and found it latched. A new habit.

Will rose from his seat against the chimney—his room had no hearth, but the heat from the ground floor's giant fireplaces kept the corner nearest the bed tolerably warm except in the coldest hours of morning—and carefully laid his quill aside before crossing the wide floorboards to answer. His fingerless gloves made his grip on the wooden doorpull uncertain, but he fumbled it open after a moment's struggle.

December cold flushed Burbage's cheeks as he came into Will's drafty single room. He unwound and dropped his muffler on the table next to Will's squat lamp and the papers, where it shed a few flakes of snow. "Will, I have word from the Lord Chamberlain. He's spoken to Lord Strange, and the playhouses will open in January. We'll start rehearsals for *Titus*, and see if we can break the plague once and for all."

Will leaned back against the wall, stretching limbs stiff from too long hunched over his writing. "Will it suffice?"

"I don't know." Burbage laid his hands against the chimney bricks, warming fingers tinged white. "There's more. The Queen requests a comedy for Twelfth Night. The word through Burghley is that she wishes to see weddings and beddings in no particular order. Have you something?"

Will handed Burbage the first two or three of the folded sheets scattered across his table. "Almost the last words I heard from poor Kit Marley were that I should not short myself for comedy."

"Katharine, eh? A likely name. Why Padua?"

"In the cold months, a man likes to dream of warm places." Will shrugged. "She's a shrew no man will marry, and—well, 'tis a metaphor. As a wise and gentle woman respects her lord, so must a land bow to its sovereign. I'll finish it in time for Oxford and Walsingham to dig the nibs of their spells between its lines, and then for mine own hand to correct their scansion."

Will picked up the page he had been working on, judged it dry, and held it closer to the poor light. "Thy husband is thy lord, thy life, thy keeper, / Thy head, thy sovereign; one that cares for thee, / And for thy maintenance commits his body / To painful labor both by sea and land, / To watch the night in storms, the day in cold, / Whilst thou liest warm at home, secure and safe; / And craves no other tribute at thy hands / But love, fair looks, and true obedience; / Too little payment for so great a debt. / Such duty as the subject owes the prince, / Even such a woman oweth to her husband—"

Will glanced up. Burbage was smiling.

" 'Twill serve?"

" 'Twill please the Queen: she has little use for women."

" 'Tis a trick I had from Kit—"

"Will." Burbage shook his head. "You know Strange won't hear Marley spoken of, and has forbidden us to rehearse his plays. It is a risk to so often speak his name. He's dead, man, and there's little you can do to stem the tide of scandal now."

"He was your friend, Richard."

"Aye, and dead, I say again. And you are my friend as well, and quick. Do you hear me?"

"I hear you," Will answered, but rebellion soaked his heart. *Not so dead after all,* he wanted to retort. But he remembered Kit's words: *One among us is a traitor.*

It could be Burbage.

It could be anyone. A chill settled into Will's bones. He tossed the scribbled leaf upon his table and stepped back beside Burbage, against the warmth of the chimney wall. "Twelfth Night —" and then he paused, another dread setting in. "I promised Annie I would come to Stratford for Christmas. I was to leave on Monday morn."

Richard tugged his mittens back on. "Send her a letter. Bid her to London: quote those lines you just quoted to me. Surely they will stir a woman's heart to understanding. Are these ready for Oxford?" A gesture indicated the pages on the table.

"They are." Will edged one sheet a little farther from the lamp with a forefinger. Oil from his fingertip glistened on the paper. "Take them from my sight."

"Will."

"What?"

"I had supper with Ned Alleyn at the Mermaid last night. Most of the players — Lord Strange's Men and the Admiral's Men — have been whiling away an idle hour there now and again while the playhouses are shuttered. It wouldn't do you any harm to be seen more often: you're missed, and some wonder if you're well. But aside from that" — Burbage raised a hand to forestall Will's interruption — "Ned said if I saw you, to tell you this: *Robert Poley's been looking for our Will, and in the company of a great oaf of a tradesman, blond as a Dane.*"

Burbage mimicked Alleyn's sonorous tones perfectly. Will would have laughed if he hadn't recognized the description. *Baines.* "Looking for me? Did Poley say why?"

"As it was Poley, I assumed you owed him money and he'd come to take it out of your back in one-inch strips. Chapman's still in debt to the usurious bastard —"

"No. It's not money. Thank you, Richard, and I'll come by the Mermaid tonight and thank Ned myself."

"Ned said the second man was near as big as Ned himself." Burbage's voice fell. "There's more on Strange, as well. Burghley — as it happens, Lord Strange was contacted by a Catholic conspiracy. They wished to see him as pretender to the Throne, and Elizabeth . . . done with."

"Strange? Accused of treason?" Will's voice too dropped to a murmur, as he thought of skulls painted red by the afternoon sun. "Surely not—"

"No, he reported the conspiracy to Burghley, and Burghley—who has no fondness for Catholics of any stripe—will use the information as best befits the Queen. All is well."

What of the loyal Catholics who will be punished as well as the guilty? But Will didn't say it, although he counted the silence more of a betrayal than failing to defend Kit. There was no way to raise Kit's supposition that the Catholic enemy were not Catholic at all, not at their deepest roots. Because the man was, as far as Burbage knew, six months dead. Will comforted himself that Walsingham should know it, if Burbage didn't.

"But by that action," Burbage continued, "Strange has made of himself an obstacle to the plotters. Have a care, Will, and keep an ear to the wall." He tapped the boards.

"Oh." Will ordered the pages before he handed them to Burbage. "I will."

Flakes of paint came away on Will's fingertips as he pushed the Mermaid's peeling plank door open. Edmund Spenser's pointed visage and dull brown beard greeted Will's eye, framed in a lace-tipped falling collar. *And what does Spenser in London?* Will had heard he was in Ireland, avoiding Lord Burghley's wrath. But no one man in London could keep track of the politics that attended his *own* name—unless that name were Walsingham—never mind the ones that trailed like cloaks and hat-plumes about the shoulders of every man who was any man at all.

A coterie had gathered around England's greatest poet. Spenser held forth, one hand curled around the base of his wine cup and the other moving through the air as if he drew strands of wool for spinning. Will paused, not to interrupt the tale, but he did not miss the broad-shouldered gentleman beside Spenser, greased black hair hanging over his untied ruff, slumming it amidst base players and poets and pamphleteers.

It was not a usual thing for a patron to move among his servants in the theatre. The customary arrangement was for him to loan out his livery for whatever status or notoriety the players could provide; in exchange, the players were not classed masterless men, criminals, but servants to a lord.

Ferdinando Stanley, Lord Strange, turned only slightly as Will entered, offering the playmaker bare acknowledgement. But his dark eyes drifted past Ned Alleyn, big as a chalk giant, who had taken up the thread of conversation now, bony hands moving like angel's wings. Will followed Strange's glance and nodded, skirting the crowd— wooly-faced Chapman jostled his elbow in silent greeting—and went to fetch a bench.

Will kicked rushes aside so they wouldn't snag under the wooden legs when he dragged his prize back. The other men gave him room to sit beside his patron. Strange himself waved for the wine, never disrupting the flow of Ned's monologue.

"My lord." Will poured two cups as the door swung open on a frigid blast. The breeze blew Kemp and two Burbages—Richard and his brother Cuthbert—into the room; Cuthbert shut the door firmly. " 'Tis an unusual pleasure to see you here."

"You are to perform for the Queen." Strange leaned so close Will could smell his hair pomade. A stout man, Strange, and soft around the middle despite bad teeth—but his hands showed tendon. The right one moved in a manner Will memorized as a character detail, turning like a leaf moored to the stem.

"We are."

Strange hid his mouth behind the rim of his cup, the interior belling back his voice. "Thou knowest Southampton is the enemy's dupe."

It was only a player's presence of mind that kept Will's startlement from his face. He was glad attention was focused on Richard Burbage and Ned Alleyn, circling one another like a terrier and a mastiff who might decide to be friends and who also might not.

"The enemy, my lord?" Will sipped his wine.

"Don't blanch so. I would not be Burbage's and thy master if I did not know *some* things." Strange's slick hair broke in locks as he turned a lopsided smile on Will. "Have a care. I may not be able to protect thee, but Burghley will. As long as thou dost remain useful to him."

"Burghley? Not Oxford?"

Strange lifted one shoulder eloquently, appearing to watch the verbal sparring between rival players ride the edge between wit and acrimony. "Oxford was a mistake—"

"Oxford thinks Southampton can be convinced."

"Thou wouldst get better odds on Raleigh."

"Noble rivalries, my lord?" Burbage had caught Alleyn's elbow and drew him away from the fire. The taller man bent his head to hear the smaller's arguments. The cross Alleyn had worn ever since a particularly disastrous performance of *Faustus* dangled from its cord as he leaned down.

"If you like." Fingers against the table, a nervous, rilling tap. "Don't trust Edward de Vere, Master Shakespeare. And don't trust too much in the patronage of Southampton, for all thou dost flatter him with thy poetry. He's a boughten man."

"You know this, my lord?" Will noticed the dark line furrowed between Strange's dark eyes. "Aye. You know it."

"I know too much." Strange finished his wine. He inverted his cup and pushed himself to his feet; the other men at the table jumped up as a Lord stood. "I am expected home to sup. Finish the bottle, Master Shakespeare."

Strange threw coins on the table. His tired smile struck Will hard. There was too much resignation in it. "Don't give up hope on your poor players, my lord," Will said, hoping that Strange would hear both his words and the meaning under them. "The playhouses will be open soon."

Lord Strange turned back from the door and smiled. "See that you make me proud, Master Shakespeare. Masters Burbage, Master Kemp." And with that, Ferdinando Stanley collected his hat from the peg by the door, and went.

Will's letter to Annie—dispatched the following morning—netted only a stony silence in reply. He meant to send a second one a week after the first, but good intentions were lost in the whirl of rehearsal and rewrite and frenzied preparation of two plays at once: the tragedy *Titus Andronicus*, for which Will need not only learn his roles but also face down Oxford in a series of hour-murdering meetings; and a lighthearted comedy which was finally, after much argument, entitled *The Taming of the Shrew*. The clownish Will Kemp was appointed Lord of Misrule—chief of Christmas festivities—for Lord Strange's Men, thus ensuring that drunkenness and disorder would ride sovereign over the frantic preparations for the Twelfth Night play. And between a tailor's visit or three, rehearsals all day and all night (and drinking at the Mermaid), occasional church services and the Twelve Days festivities, the first time Will had a moment's silence between his own ears was on January 5. And only because a thin-lipped, towering Ned Alleyn, who—plied by Burbage with liquor and conversation—would perform with Lord Strange's Men this once, threw the entire company out of the Mermaid Tavern and into the street to *go home, the lot, and rest your heads so as not to lose them before Her Majesty!*

Will's stomach had been too sour for much drinking, and now, as he lay in his bed against the warmth of the chimney, it was too sour for much sleeping. *Perform before the Queen.*

He sat up in bed and let the bedclothes slip aside. A draft came between the floorboards as he set his feet down; he stood anyway, shivering with his coverlet wrapped around his shoulders, and crossed to light a candle. After unrelieved darkness, the glow warmed him as much as a fire. *Perform before the Queen and her rival favorites, and remind them that their duty is to their sovereign, and not to their quarrels.*

Oh, I wish Annie were here to see this. He set the candle on the sideboard and opened an oaken cupboard, drawing out the soft wine red velvet drape of his new doublet. Kit would have loved it: it fit like a second skin, snug at the waist and broad at the shoulders, slashed in peach taffeta and buttoned with knotted gilt. Kit would have been much calmer, Will thought, as he picked up a clothesbrush and polished the nap of the already spotless velvet. The steady rasp of the brush on the cloth helped him think: his racing, exhausted thoughts rocked instead of spinning, and Will forced himself to breathe and contemplate.

Put on the role, and play it. Turn a trembling hand into a swordsman's confidence, and quivering voice into an arrogant sneer. I'm a player, if I'm not a Burbage. I can manage a role indifferent well. So tomorrow I'll be a role—

And then the day after tomorrow, I will write to Annie, and see if she'll have me home for Lent.

———

January the sixth—Twelfth Night—dawned with a cold that settled
over London like the locking of a chest, but even in winter of a plague
year, festivity could be found. A solemn sort of merriment fought with
nausea as Will peered through a gap in the draperies, amazed at the
splendor of Westminster Palace bannered in holly and ivy and ablaze
with more candles than a church. The great Gothic hall echoed with
the busy footsteps of players and tirers, servants flitting like shadows
through the bustle on any pretext to get a glimpse of the great Richard Burbage, of the famous Edward Alleyn. Alleyn was easy enough
to mark: broad-shouldered as a monolith, his lips moving silently as
he reviewed his cues. Burbage vanished twice for not above half an
hour each time, and each time Will noticed a serving girl went missing
simultaneously. One sweet dark-haired lass caught his own eye, and if
it hadn't been for fear of rumpling his doublet, he might have sought
a kiss. *Just for luck.*

But it was past time for that, and time to be tending to paint, red-
dening boys' lips with carmine and lacing them into their corsetry. A
black wig for "Katharine" and a blond wig for "Bianca." Will swallowed his own fear: the younger boy, also named Edward, was trembling as Will made a mirror for his paint.

" 'Tis only a Queen you perform for," Will said in the boy's ear,
tidying his kohled eye with a cloth. "Surely that's happened before."
Edward giggled, for all his cheeks stayed white as a bride's.

Will patted Edward on the shoulder above his bodice before walking away. "At least your name's not under the title."

He went to have Burbage mend his own painting. And found the
round little player pacing five short steps, back and forth and back
again. Richard considered. "Too much on the lips."

Too much indeed, Will thought, standing—what seemed a moment
later—just out of the audience's view. There was the Queen, her chair
surrounded by her admirers. Sir Walter Raleigh, glossy in his black,
leaned to murmur in Her Majesty's ear. Her hand came up to brush
his shoulder, and the loosely sewn pearls on his doublet scattered at
the snap of a thread. Will could plainly see the Queen's condescend-
ing amusement at her favorite's expensive conceit. On her other side,
ferret-faced Henry Wriothesley—Southampton—frowned at the dash-

ing Earl of Essex in his white-and-gold, who frowned more deeply still at Raleigh while Raleigh affected not to notice. Will noticed for all their posturing that it was Burghley's son, Robert Cecil, to whom the Queen most often bent, and spoke, and smiled.

All fell silent as the prologue began. *What would Marley do?* The expected confidence did not burgeon Will, although Burbage stepped close enough to bolster him with a shoulder.

But Marley was dead, or as good as: Will on his own, and—

— *"boy: let me come and kindly"*—

— *There's my cue.*

Will swallowed a painful bubble, let his hands fall relaxed to his sides, and stepped out on stage amid a swirl of trumpets, half convinced his voice would fail him. "Huntsman, I charge thee, tender well my hounds. Broach Merriman—the poor cur is embossed, and couple Clowder with the deep-mouthed brach."

This is the stupidest thing I have ever written. She'll have me whipped around town for stepping above my station. A nothing part, a pompous Lord, and Will had been playing on stage six years now. Still, his hand shook. *The Queen. I am no Richard Burbage, to collect hearts like so many butterflies.*

"Sawst thou not, boy, how Silver made it good at the hedge corner, in the coldest fault? I would not lose that dog for twenty pound."

But the Queen was leaning forward in her chair, the last three fingers of her left hand moving in a faint, dismissive gesture when Essex tried to draw her attention. The Earl looked down sulkily, fiddling something in his lap. Over his shoulder, Lord Burghley— standing near to his son and a little further from the Queen—caught Will's eye.

The boards creaked under Will's foot. He upstaged the huntsman, forcing him to turn so Will could follow Burghley's gaze and catch a glimpse of Essex's task. The Earl riffled the pages of a little book, an octavio, of a size for tucking in a sleeve or a pocket. He couldn't be reading the playscript; it wasn't published. And Southampton was leaning forward over Essex's shoulder, his lips moving.

Interesting.

"Thou art a *fool*," Will said. "If Echo were as fleet—" There was something, a pressure. Almost as if a stiff wind sprang up. But the Queen was laughing, and Will leaned on that, camped his dialogue, airy turn of a sleeve to offset a pompous thundering. The scene was almost all his, and he carried it.

The prologue ended, and Will beat his retreat with a glance across the audience. Engaged. Alive, at least. He gulped ale through a tight throat and leaned against a pillar, listening. *It was a mistake to recruit Alleyn—he's too overblown for comedy—no, he's managing it. Oh, this may work—*

He fretted his hands, one over the other, *feeling* the power rise up in opposition to his work. Feeling the play itself, its rhythms and stresses, the *connection* between player and playgoer. The surge of emotion and thought that bound the audience to the performance, and the energy that ran between them, like lovers giving one another all.

I should have taken out the jokes about tongues and tails. Not before Her Majesty.

But Elizabeth laughed again, a provoked and provoking sound that carried over the sedate chuckles of her courtiers, and Will grinned despite himself.

'Tis no different before the Queen.

But there's a power here.

It was a heady thing, and he finished the ale and straightened against the wall as he grasped it. *This is what Kit was trying to show me.*

This. This power. This consensus.

This is the thing we manipulate.

I can do this thing.

Will toweled the paint from his face, tossing the spotted cloth onto a pile. Someone thrust a cup into his hand. He quaffed it, choked when he found wine instead of ale, and turned to Burbage's grin. "You're a success."

"We're a success." Will embraced Richard. His own shirt was transparent with sweat when he stripped it over his head, and he wet a cloth and wiped the salt from his chest. Burbage, of course, looked pressed and dapper. "Hand me my clean shirt, wouldst thou? We must go be charming and earn our bread."

"As long as 'tis Kemp singing for his supper, not thee."

"What? I am a very nightingale—" Will tucked the shirt into his breeches and pulled his doublet on.

"In that thou shouldst sing only after dark, when they cannot see

thy face to hunt thee, aye." Burbage clipped Will about the shoulders
while Will was still fussing with laces, and steered him back out into
the hall. The Queen had risen from her chair to lead a galliard. Will let
his gaze sweep the room, wondering if he could catch the eye of that
dark-haired girl again, but instead found Essex's gaze. Will bowed to
the Earl, who affected a habit of white silk that contrasted sharply
with Raleigh's glossy black. Burbage, still holding Will's elbow, caught
the bow and echoed it in unison, making Will smile.

Richard was many things. And the best at most of them.

The players straightened as the Earl turned away, his brow thundering, his arms crossed as if he slipped something into a sleeve pocket.
"He does not approve," Will murmured.

"More intrigues. He's of the other camp, and I no longer doubt it.
Did you mark his ring?"

"Nay—"

"Some of the Prometheans wear them. But then again, so too do
some mere mortals who meddle with magics. An iron ring on the finger, or steel in the ear."

"Who is that he spoke to?"

Burbage arched his neck, as if searching the crowd. "The tall fellow with the lovely hair?"

"In gold pinked with white. The very one."

"The one coming toward us? Why Will," Burbage said, "that's
Master Thomas Walsingham."

A glance aside to Burbage, and Will swore under his breath. Burbage's color was high—Will noticed a drinker's vein or two blossom-
ing on his cheeks, that hadn't been there a year before—and his smile
set. "Kit's . . . patron."

"Kit's betrayer, and ours, as I have it from Oxford. But yes, they
shared a house and rumor says that isn't all, though Master Walsingham a married man. That's his wife, Etheldreda—they call her *Audrey*,
there. The gingery one."

The lady was breathtaking in a rose-colored gown, cut low across
her bosom, a mass of hair Will thought was probably nearly all her own
tired high. He shifted his attention back to Tom Walsingham, whose
progression toward the players was slow but inexorable. "Waste of a
fine old Saxon name."

"She rather looks like a Saxon Queen, doesn't she? Ah," Burbage said. "Will you have wine?"

"You're leaving me to *his* tender mercies?"

"He wants you. I'm only in the way. Drag him for information if you may: he's got his hooks in Chapman too, and has a taste for poets, I've heard."

"*Chapman?*" Will blinked to clear the unlikely vision from his head. "Oh, you mean his patronage."

Burbage laughed and clapped Will on the shoulder as he moved away. "Just don't mention Marley and you can't go far wrong. I'm going to collect our payment from the steward."

Will swallowed the last acid taste of the wine and pretended engagement with the dance. Gloriana's grace was legend, her long oval hands raised high as she let her partners move her. Even in her sixtieth year, she moved as if the mass of her skirts and jewels and her gold-red jeweled tire weighed nothing. She dined alone by habit, Will knew, and imagined it was as much to conceal the unladylike appetite her exertions must give her as for fear of poison.

"Master William Shakespeare?"

It was a smooth voice, a touch of Kent in it, and Will turned and met Thomas Walsingham's querying gaze. Will had to lift his chin; Tom had a hand on him at least in height and half that across the shoulders, and might have been wearing heeled shoes for court. "Master Walsingham."

"An excellent performance." Walsingham lifted a glass; the wine it held was clear dark yellow in torchlight. "I'm sorry we haven't met. I've seen one or two of your plays from the galleries, and been impressed. Master Marley first commended you to mine attention, and after him George. You know Chapman—"

"Very well," Will answered, glad he hadn't a glass of his own, lest he choke on the contents. —*and you can't go far wrong. Oh, excellent advice, Richard.*

Excellent advice.

"Master Marley? Of a truth?"

Walsingham's lips seemed to vanish for a moment. "Though he was never a one to cast broad credit."

"No," Will said, and thought *interesting* again. "I had understood you ended on bad terms."

"Aye," Walsingham answered, "in that he ended badly. But 'tis not a topic I wish to dwell on overmuch. That was a fine play, by a fine group of players performed."

"I will convey your compliments—"

"Convey more than that." Walsingham reached out, and Will almost flinched from his calloused, elegant hand. Will studied it, Burbage's comments on rings fresh in his mind, but contrary to fashion Walsingham didn't affect any. Instead he slipped a paper into Will's doublet, smoothing the nap of the velvet before drawing away. "Convey that note to mine exchequer. He'll see your company rewarded for lightening the Queen's burden."

"It is our joy and duty, and we are already well compensated, Master Walsingham." The galliard ended; the dancers made courtesy to the musicians and called for drink. Will joined the polite applause.

"So I understand." Walsingham smiled; it rounded the angle of his cheek and turned him from handsome courtier into dashing rogue. Even forewarned, Will felt himself charmed. "But a man should be of a mind to make friends where he may, and players are fair friends to have. Sometimes. And summer is coming, and my house at Chislehurst is not too far from London for a play."

"Ah," Will said. "Yes," he said. "Carefully made friends are a good thing to have, if they return the care."

Walsingham's eyes darkened. "An excellent play. May you write many more, and be as careful in your friends. Sometimes their care can have an—unexpected source. Do contact me. Oh, here is Doctor Lopez. Do wish to counsel this fine playmaker on his health, good Doctor?"

"A moment of his time, if you can spare it," Lopez said in his accented voice. Walsingham, nodding, withdrew. "Master Shakespeare, I wish to congratulate you on the success of your work tonight."

He did not mean the play. As Will turned to him, he was as certain of that as he was of the mockery behind Lopez's arch expression. "The Ambassador honors my poor efforts," he said.

Lopez rubbed the tip of his nose. "Honor puts no beef on the table," he said, and dropped a clinking purse in the rushes at Will's feet, where Will would need to stoop to retrieve it. "I've a word from Burghley. The word is 'well done.' "

"Thank you, Doctor," Will said.

Lopez patted him on the arm, a ruby ring worn over his glove glittering with the motion. "You're more biddable than the last one," he said, as he turned away. "That can only bode well."

Will's shoulders tightened; his arms hung numb. Five heartbeats later he took a breath, and ducked down to retrieve the purse. However callously offered, a shilling was a shilling, and the purse had clinked like a great many of them.

It had the aspect of a dance, he thought, as he stood and found himself facing Essex. "My lord," he said, and bowed low.

"Take your ease," Essex answered. He was alone, for a wonder, with neither courtiers nor the simpering Southampton in attendance.

Will relaxed incrementally. "What is my lord's pleasure?"

"A word of warning," Essex said. "Have a care in handling the coin of a poisoner, Master Shakespeare. You know that damned Portugall was Sir Francis Walsingham's doctor when Sir Francis breathed his last, in agony."

"I have heard it so bandied, my lord," Will agreed.

"Hmph." Essex regarded Will down the length of his nose, expectantly, and Will cringed like a bumpkin. There was something to be said for having the face for comic parts. "Moreover," said Essex, "it's well-known that Sir Francis' papers vanished from his chamber at his death, and Lopez was among the few with access to the same."

And you so upset by it, my lord, for you would have wrested control of his agents after his death? "I shall be entirely cautious, my lord."

"See you are." And now Essex in turn was withdrawing, after a short glance over Will's shoulder. "Lopez is a traitor, and I do not doubt he'll hang. It would be a shame to hang a poet with him. Good day, sirrah."

"Good day, my lord."

Will counted three, and turned from Essex's receding back—and into the orbit of Her Majesty, the Queen. Her gown was figured silk, white on white, her mantle thick with ermine against the January cold that even the press of bodies couldn't drive from the hall. Sir Walter

Raleigh in his black hung at her shoulder, a raven to Elizabeth's ger-falcon, all devilish beard and tilted cap, eyes sharp as a mink's over his impressive nose, an air of pipe-tobacco and dissolution on his shoulders in place of a cloak. Robert Devereaux, the Earl of Essex—*God is merciful*—was now nowhere in evidence.

"You—Your Majesty." Will dropped a hasty bow, wondering if his face would tumble to the floor and shatter like a mask if *all* the blood really did drain from it.

"At your ease, Master Shakespeare," she said.

Raleigh stayed a step behind and to her left. He caught Will's eye as Will stood, sure he was about to faint, and he winked. Her Majesty never saw it, but the slight gesture calmed Will enough to get a breath, and as the air filled him the panic retreated. "Your Majesty is very kind—"

"Rarely." Her gray eyes crinkled at the corners, irises dark in the alabaster of her paint; it was the only trace of her smile. By her breath, her teeth were rotten, and Will pitied her that. "And only when it suits me. Do you serve England, Will?"

"With a will, where I may—" he said daringly, remembering that she had laughed at his dirtiest jokes. Raleigh's nose twitched. "—an it please Your Majesty."

"Clever lad," she said. "You'll do well, if you play the games of court as well as you played your art tonight. Of which art speaking, I understand we have common friends."

"Surely, I could not claim equal to the title of friend to any who Your Majesty might grace with that station."

She turned to Raleigh, amused. "He's got a courtly tongue in him, at least. Sir Walter—"

"Your gracious Majesty." The pearls on his doublet glimmered like moonlight as he bowed under her attention.

"What think you of this one, stepping into the place he must fill?"

"Walsingham likes him. That's never a good sign." But it was said wryly, one black eyebrow arched, and Raleigh's eyes held Will's as he spoke.

"So long as Robin of Essex doesn't like him as well. Tell me, young William, what factions do you favor in our petty dickering?" A direct, bright question, her voice mild and interested, the turn of her neck like one of her swans within the elaborate serpentine of her ruff.

Oh, that is one question that is many questions, Madam. "The Earl of Southampton is my patron, Your Majesty, and Lord Strange the patron of my company. But my loyalty is given to my Prince, and she alone may command my heart." She seemed to wait expectantly, and he permitted himself a bold bit of a grin. "That portion my good wife permits me the use of, in any case."

Gloriana laughed, showing the powdered curve of her throat, and stopped as abruptly. "Don't teach this one to smoke, Sir Walter. 'Tis a filthy habit. Master Shakespeare, good evening."

"Your Majesty. Sir Walter." Will bowed, watching jeweled skirts soar away. A firm hand clapped him on the shoulder and he glanced up, into Raleigh's glittering presence. "Sir Walter."

"Good to show her spunk, William." That wink again, before he too took his leave. "We'll see you at court again, I expect."

Will stood shivering as they left him, and almost jumped out of his clicking court shoes when Burbage appeared beside him, holding a cup of wine. "I see I danced away just in time. How was your pas de deux with Her Majesty?"

"More a pas de trois, I think. A game was just played over me, Richard, and I do not know the name of it."

"As long as you didn't lose," Burbage said, and thrust the cup into his hand. Will took it, fingers half insensate. *Tom Walsingham likes me?*

I thought he just made a threat on my life.

Intra-act: Chorus

Two weeks later, the playhouses opened as scheduled, and a letter arrived at Will's lodging house, forwarded without comment by Annie from Stratford.

Mr. Will. Shakspere
Stratford-upon-Avon
Warwickshire

My dearest countryman & fellow:

Please that this find you well, I have prevailed upon one Robin of my present company to deliver unto you this letter & my fondest remembrances, that all passeth well with you & the fair Anne your wife & that you me recollect fondly as you serve our fair Prince. It is to me as my days creep by that, gone as I am from England, England is almost near enough to touch: a great frustration to an exile.

But even as my spirit sometimes flags, I find I am come home, & am given to hope perhaps my necessary & permanent absence will not prove so onerous as fear'd. I have an eye for you, my dear Will, & will be of assistance as I may find opportunity. I beg you trust me safe, if in politics, & well-occupied with many pleasures and problems.

A letter may reach me through unusual channels, although perhaps not privily: FW knows the path. I hope you will forward your Adonis, & whatever other works you think may interest me. I would

*send gold to afford the purchase of books but it would not outlast the
sunset as other than dross, & having been taken once for coining I'll
not will that adventure on you. So if you seek to do me this kindness I
fear you shall have no recompense but mine unending affection.*

    I am closer than you imagine.

This 14th day of January 1593 (as I think it)
I remain yrs affectionately & in
good hope of our eventual re-acquaintance
your most distant friend

    Postscript:
Yr Shrew *was an outstanding success. I will be observing your
future career with some interest.*

Act II, scene i

All: God forbid!
Faust: God forbade it indeed; but Faustus hath done it.

—CHRISTOPHER MARLOWE, *Doctor Faustus*

Murchaud had reach on Kit, and two good eyes, and Kit was not used to fencing with a surrounding audience hampering his movement. But Kit sidestepped as the pale sunlight of Faerie flashed along the spirals decorating Murchaud's rapier. Despite the unkempt grass tugging his boots, a little spatter of dignified applause followed the gesture of his main gauche as it knocked his opponent's foiled blade off line.

Foiled, but still razor-sharp along the edge: the blade brushed Kit's shirtsleeve in passing, parting the linen as easily as the skin of a peach. Kit stepped in to take advantage of the break in Murchaud's guard, ducked a thrust of the main gauche, and—extended along the line of his blind eye—lunged. Murchaud barely twisted aside, Kit's rapier stroking the brown leather jerkin over his muscled belly, and his riposte fell short as Kit skittered back, swearing breathlessly, sweat trickling between his shoulders. The onlookers shifted, a murmuring riot of colored costumes against the sweep of green lawn, the gardens of heartsease and forget-me-nots, the high golden walls of the palace.

Kit forced his attention away from the audience as Murchaud advanced, teeth white in the angle between his lips, lips coral pink against the black of his beard. *Stop looking at his smile, Kit you ruddy fool. Watch his chest, his eyes — hah! as if that will keep you from distraction!* A thrust, a flurry of parry, riposte, bind — Murchaud's breath on his face as he pressed with all his greater weight and the strength of his arm. Kit locked his elbow, holding against the press, went for Murchaud's belly with the main gauche and felt his hand knocked wide. Murchaud bent a knee, bulled and lifted, hilt ringing on hilt, shoving Kit's rapier high and wide. Kit scrambled aside, sucking his belly against his spine and out of the path of the blade, feeling through the shifts of Murchaud's weight for where the main gauche would be. Somewhere on his blind side, and Kit's hand was out of line. He ducked backward, wove, dipped a knee as he parried another lunge and felt the edge part not just shirt but skin, the hotter trickle of blood joining the drip of sweat down his forearms —

—and froze at the needle prick of Murchaud's eighteen-inch dagger in the curve of his jaw where the pulse ran close. A slow, thick thread of blood curved down his throat, delicately as the pad of a thumb dragged over skin, and he shivered. Murchaud smiled in earnest now, and Kit tilted his head away from the knife and closed his eye as the applause swelled. "Yield?"

"Yield." Kit forced clenched fingers to unwind from the grip of his rapier. The blade rasped on Murchaud's and thumped pommel-first into the grass. He waited for the knifepoint to ease away from the red-hot dimple it wore. Instead, the blade caressed his throat, came to rest in the hollow of his collarbone, pressed just sharply enough to sting as Murchaud covered Kit's mouth with a kiss as claiming as any bridegroom's.

The applause for *that* was more than a polite ripple.

It could have been an hour later or a dozen, although sunlight still streamed between the bedcurtains to stain Murchaud's pale skin tawny. Kit pillowed his head on the man's ridged belly and sighed, idly picking at the clean wrap of linen covering the scratch on his arm. Murchaud wound a few of the long fair strands of Kit's hair around his fingers like a girl playing with her ribbons. "That was better."

Wryness twisted Kit's mouth into something only a fool would call a smile. "What? The fencing, or the—fencing?"

"Thy swordsmanship is improving," Murchaud continued blithely. "And the strength of thine arm."

"Exercise is the best remedy for a weak arm, I'm told." Kit still tasted that public, thrilling kiss. Still heard the roar of approving laughter that had followed.

Now, Murchaud's laughter trailed into thoughtfulness. "We'll make a warrior of thee yet, Sir Christofer. How long hast been among us? Four days? Five?"

"Time passes quickly with thee by my side." He'd expected from his previous visit that by the time a month passed in Faerie, the world of London would be thirty years gone. Not so: perhaps the difference changed with the whim of the Mebd, but the once or twice Kit had found an unattended moment in which to prowl through the palace's golden corridors and peer into the Darkling Glass, it seemed only a few hours had passed for Will and Sir Francis. He had sought the Pro-metheans behind his murder, as well, but the glass shied from them, as if he would pick up ice with an oiled hand.

Kit didn't feel himself *guarded*, precisely. Or watched. But he was seldom left alone, waking or sleeping. *Of course Morgan can watch me if she wishes. And no doubt the Mebd can, as well.*

Murchaud continued, "Thou wilt need learn something of the fac-tions, if thou art to be ours. I'll presume a certain comfort on thy part with politics, given thy career—"

"—fair enough." Murchaud's fingers tugged Kit's hair as Kit turned his head to kiss the Elf-knight's belly. "There is thee and thy mother," Kit continued. "By whom I read I have been claimed. But I know not yet what task you mean to set me to."

"We've uses for poets. Not unlike the uses to which thou hast set thyself, in thine old Queen's court."

"Commission thy poem," Kit answered. "I could pen a sonnet on the arch of ev'ry rib, passage of verse on thine eyes, and lay a very pastoral over field and fallow of thy flank and loin. 'I'll hang a golden tongue about thy throat—'" Murchaud's sweat was bitter and sweet; a droplet of Kit's own blood had dried on his breast, and Kit kissed it away.

Murchaud pressed fingertips to the hollow of Kit's throat. "It should have sealed by now."

"Like any corpse, I bleed at the touch of my murderer—"

"There is Faerie and there is Hell," Murchaud interrupted, with the air of one reciting a catechism. "They are allied under a contract drawn up long ago, when the Christian, now Romish, church first came into its glory. Portions of that Romish church are under the sway of those who oppose science, poetry, freedom of thought, and liberty of speech. Those same men have their fingers in the puppet Puritans too—"

"I know this," Kit answered. "The secret underbelly of the Prometheus Club. The claims and counterclaims as to who has honest right to the name are too complex for me to follow, but as I understand it, once—"

"Hush," Murchaud interrupted. "Faerie pays a tithe to Hell for Hell's wardenship. My mother, Morgan, wishes to see the tithe ended, and Faerie to stand on its own." The Elf-knight's calloused fingertips traced the curve of Kit's ear. They played languidly on even as Murchaud's next words froze Kit's breath into stone. "What didst thou intend, when I overheard thee to tell Shakespeare that thou wert no Gaveston?"

Kit sat back out of the bedclothes, tugging his hair out of Murchaud's grasp and squinting against the sunlight to meet his eyes. "You watched me."

"In the Glass. Aye: we stayed to ward you, should someone take your reappearance amiss."

Kit swallowed the self-loathing that filled his mouth. *You've gotten careless, Marley. Careless and unbalanced, and it will have you dead twice over if you don't find your feet among these stones.* "Sir Piers Gaveston," Kit said calmly, "was the leman of Edward the Second. For whom Edward abandoned a loyal wife and peers who would have supported him, neglected his Kingdom, and paid with his freedom and eventually his life—and Gaveston's life, now that I think on it. For all Edward was a selfish spoiled boy more than he was a King, he died quite terribly for his sins. There's a story about an impalement—"

"I know it," Murchaud answered. "But that does not play fair with my question, sweet Kit."

"I bethink myself," Kit said carefully, "that in such case the beloved
is as much at fault as the unfaithful lover. I knew a man—a man enough
like Edward to share his name." Kit closed his eye so he wouldn't see
the name Murchaud's lips shaped, questioningly. *Oxford?*

Kit continued, "I cared for him. I did not much care for how he
used his wife. I wrote a play to let him know it, and mayhap change
his ways."

"Success?"

"None to speak of."

Murchaud chuckled. "Is now the wrong moment to tell you that I
am also a married man?"

"Married?" Kit shrugged, forcing his expression to blandness.
"Most men are. Most women as well. I had thought myself, one day—"
He paused at Murchaud's smile, recognizing amusement and anticipa-
tion. "Where is your wife?"

"She sits on Faerie's throne," the Elf-knight answered.

"The Mebd. Is your wife."

" 'Tis less impressive when you consider my parentage," Murchaud
said dryly, taking Kit by the wrist and drawing him down among the
bedclothes. "And things are different here."

"Yes," Kit said against the pillow. "I've noticed."

Kit woke uneasy in waning light. The wound in the valley of his throat
stung, and beneath the door he heard the footsteps of servants, a rattling scratch. He drew the sheets up to cover his shame and called a
welcome once he rubbed enough grit from his eye to be assured Murchaud was no longer in the chamber.

A brownie entered bearing a taper twice his own height. He was
a wee man clad in tattered brown trousers, braces strapped over his
teacup belly. "Sir Christofer?"

And the whole castle knows to find me in the Prince-Consort's bed. Kit
touched his lips, remembering a kiss; the aching hollowness that
lately emptied him when he was away from Morgan gnawed his belly.
"Awake. More or less."

"I've brought hot water and your dinner clothes." The brownie
gestured with his taper, and other candles about the room flared to
life. Kit wondered how someone so small would tote water, but steam

rose from a silver ewer beside the wash-basin, and Kit saw a black
doublet and breeches and smallclothes laid out on Murchaud's clothes
chest.

"Thank you," Kit said. In London, he would have offered a tip.
Here, he'd been given to understand, gratuities would be perceived
an insult.

"Anything else?"

"Soap and some tooth powder?"

"Seen to," the brownie replied with what might have been a grimace or a grin. "You've the three-quarters of an hour before dinner is
laid."

"Where is Murchaud?"

"With—" The candle flickered, and that *was* disapproval, even in
the half-light. "—his royal wife."

The door shut between them. Kit let the sheets fall aside to release
their perfume of sweat and almond oil as he stood. *Disapproval of me?
Or of Murchaud? Or of the Queen?* He ached with the battering, but it was
pleasant enough.

Unlike what gnawed his belly. *Kit, this is obsession.* He cleaned
himself at the basin, scrubbed his hair with the rose-scented soap,
and wished he had someone to pour the rinse water for him, but
managed.

The shirt was silk again, and wrought with pearls about the bands:
he wouldn't have been permitted that in London, but here he was a
knight. *I wonder if Faerie has sumptuary laws.* The doublet was new. It
wasn't black after all, he saw when he held it up to the light, but a deep
undulled green no mortal dye could match. The slashes were lined
with silk of a paler green, and the embroidery and the buttons shone
in some oil green peridots. There were clean white hose, a cap and
gloves, the silver sword he'd practiced with that afternoon, its same
plain, functional hilt adorned by a much finer belt and scabbard. And
there were shoes with jeweled buckles, which gave him pause.

*Well, I can't very well wear the one pair of riding boots every day for eter-
nity.* "Even my father's nailing won't stand up to that," he said out loud,
with a little bitterness behind it. John Marley had not been kindly
disposed to Kit's choice to leave Corpus Christi without taking holy
orders. A priest in the family . . . There had been five other mouths to

feed, and a man might hope his eldest son would be in a position to provide for his dotage. A poet living on the largesse of other men was unlikely to manage that. Or respectability either.

You said you had a calling —

Father, I did. Which had been half the problem. Kit dressed carefully, combed his damp hair, buttoned his buttons, laced his points. He wished he had a mirror to check the effect, although he didn't mind that the shoes gave him an extra inch of height.

He squared his shoulders, tucked his hair behind his ears, and went downstairs to meet his fate.

The great hall bustled. Kit moved through Fae both less and more familiar, already missing the click of bootnails on marble floors and the protection of forged iron. He paused at the doorway, but the herald saw and announced him, and as he moved forward, looking for a place below the salt, his eye was drawn by a jaunty wave from the high table. Robin Goodfellow, the Puck, who sat beside what must by its chair and cushions be the Mebd's chair of estate, held open a position on his left. Kit strode toward him, conscious of how recently he'd made a spectacle of himself in this very hall, more conscious of the ripple of hushed conversation that followed. Murchaud sat at the Queen's right hand, his mother further right, and Kit's stomach clenched and twisted with unkind recollection.

But Morgan looked up at him and smiled as he walked before her. He returned the nod, and knew he blushed crimson when she stood to reach across the table and caress the velvet of his sleeve. "A lovely color on you," she said. "Is the fit well?"

"My lady," he answered, with a nod that mayhap concealed his desire to catch her black hair in both hands and scour his face with it. "Your gift?"

"You can't go about clad in castoffs," she said. "We'll see about a wardrobe tomorrow. And outfitting your chambers —"

"My lady is too kind." He searched for the marks of violence on her skin, near the deep narrow neckline of her gown. There might have been a bruise, powdered over, but he wasn't absolute. The looking left him sick, and he could not look away.

"Your lady is not kind enough. Go, take your place."

"Will I —" *See you tonight?*

Her smile was the flex of a mayfly's wings. "Perhaps," she said, and froze him with her dismissal. Murchaud said nothing, but acknowledged him with a wink. He went to take his place between the fool and another Fae whose name he did not know.

"Sir Kit."

"Master Robin."

"Ah. You remember my name better, then—"

"I apologize," Kit said, and stood beside his chair rather than trouble himself to sit only to rise and sit again. "I was overwrought."

"It is understandable. How fared you in the mortal lands?"

"Miserably," Kit said, which was an answer. One cut short by the flare of trumpets. The Mebd entered, and was made courtesy to, and took her chair. She did not seem to notice Kit, though her long sleeves and her mantle of pure white silk brushed his leg as she passed. Kit seated himself as Robin did, and invisible footmen attended their chairs.

"I'm bid to tell you," Puck said, "you'll be called upon when the meal is done. There's poetry in your future."

"Something new?"

"Impress us, is the word."

Kit bit his knuckle, thinking. *I could manage a stanza or two of blank verse between then and now.* There was an oiled cloth on the table, and he sketched a few letters in it with the hilt of his blade. He'd had a thought before—*That most perfect creature under heaven, The moon full in the arms of restless night*—but the second line limped, and he wasn't sure this was a time for pretty flattery and praising one lady over another. He smiled. *Proserpine and Hades. Oh, can I get away with it?*

Kit stole a glance at the Mebd and past her to his master and his mistress. Morgan saw him; he raised his brows in question. Her eyes sparkled as she tilted her head. *Yes. They delight in being shocked. The question is, can I manage more than a half-dozen lines by the time the subtlety's presented?*

He leaned toward the Puck as the meats were passed, and the Mebd made her selections. "Why am I seated at the high table, Master Robin?"

Robin's bells jangled, a scent of peppermint arising. "Because it amuses someone to see you here." Twig-fingers tapped the back of

Kit's hand as the poet broke his bread into tidbits. "Your manners are dainty for someone who is not accustomed to eating with nobility."

"Not unaccustomed to it," Kit answered. "I've done my share of dining above my station—"

"And what is your station, Sir Poet?"

Kit stopped, a buttered morsel of bread to his lips. There was more to the question than the obvious: the glitter in the Puck's huge soft eyes, wide and wicked as a goat's, made that plain. "It varies with the weather," he said at last, picking up a cup he had no taste for just to feel the wine swirl within it. "Cobbler, preacher, poet, spy. Which would you have me?"

The Puck chewed noisily, dipping greasy fingers in a bowl of rose-water after setting a leg of swan aside. He swallowed, enough of a mouthful that his throat distended. "Lover, killer, playmaker, thief—"

"Never a thief."

"But all the others, if that's the one that stings."

"Only a vile playmaker in the end," Kit answered, with a shrug he himself wasn't sure was acknowledgement.

"What turns a cobbler into preacher, Kit?"

"Or a preacher into a Queen's Man?"

"That too."

Kit opened his mouth on a glib lie and shut it. He glanced over Robin's shoulder, where the Mebd sat, and beyond her, her husband, and beyond her black Morgan le Fey. "When I was thirteen," he said, "my father beat his apprentice so badly he was fined by the Guild. I thought I'd rather a scholar's beatings than a prentice's. I entered King's School at fifteen." The words came quietly, and he was proud of that. "I was too old. They took me anyway. I went to Cambridge on a scholar-ship. My family were proud. Some years later, I came to find that the vocation I thought I had was a lie, for the Church's God was no God of mine. Or if it was true, then I was called by mistake. If God makes that sort of mistake."

Kit stopped and sat back in his chair. The Puck slid a bit of roast meat before him. Kit lifted his dagger and poked at it, but did not eat.

"And then?"

"And then it was live by my wits or live not at all. 'Tis easy to starve in London. And unlike the Church, the only thing Gloriana asks of her servants is that they love her above breath and fortune. Why am I telling you this?"

The Puck laughed. "Because you need a friend, Sir Kit."

Kit looked up. He set his knife aside. "Do I?"

"Aye."

"Well, then I wot I do."

"Eat," Puck said. "You'll need strength when you tell your poetry."

Act II, scene ii

Mercutio: Oh, then, I see Queen Mab hath been with you.

—WILLIAM SHAKESPEARE, *Romeo and Juliet*

The second letter arrived in cold, wet April a week or two before Will's christening-day, after the playhouses were reopened from a Lent that Will had hoped—and failed—to spend in Stratford. It was in Kit's hand, or a clever forgery, and written with some care: no words were scratched out or blotted, and the ink was black as jet on creamy parchment. The tone was much as the first letter.

Gold to dross, Will thought, refolding the letter and examining the seal once more though he was growing late for his meeting with Lord Hunsdon. The seal was of brittle green wax, imprinted with an image of a goose feather. All carefully chosen to lead Will to an inevitable conclusion.

Gold to dross.

Will Shakespeare had been a country lad, where the reek of frank-incense and superstition—of Papism—still clung. Even if he hadn't seen in manuscript a few cantos of Spenser's poem in praise of England's own Faerie Queene, he would have known the signs as well as any man, although a rational—a properly *Protestant*—mind might reject them.

Kit's with the Faeries. Or he's mad: there's always that. But he somehow knows mine acts almost as soon as I perform them. And he repeats his plea that I inform him, through Walsingham, of politics and players, and anything else that might befall.

Easily enough done, and no more risky than reporting to Walsingham himself. Which Will still intended. But—

I should burn this letter.

But it would be noticeable to carry it downstairs and slip it into the fire, and there was no hearth in Will's room. After some consideration and a few false starts, he lifted the ticking off the bed and tucked the letter between the ropes and the frame, where it stuck quite nicely. Completely concealed, even with the ticking off: Will crawled under the frame to be sure. Then he got his arms around the rustling ticking and wrestled it back into place, poking the flannel to settle the straw inside the bag. He sneezed at the dust, wiped watering eyes on his sleeve, and twitched the bedclothes smooth.

Mid-April was still sharp enough that Will layered a leather jerkin over his doublet. He hurried through the streets, mindful of slush in the gutters, and crossed London Bridge with the sun still high in the sky. There was no concealment of this meeting: Will reported to the scowling gray Tower itself. He presented himself to the Yeoman Warder at the main gate, struggling to hide the uncertainty of his glances toward the prison while assuring the guards that he was expected. After showing his letter from the Lord Chamberlain, he was ushered through, and walked down the long, rule-straight lane within. The inside of the massive knobbed stone walls was no more comforting than the exterior had been, and he considered uneasily what the murders and covenants of ravens along the edges of the rooftops dined upon. Legend claimed that should the ravens leave the Tower, England's fall would not be far behind.

Will was not expecting the Lord Chamberlain and the Lord Treasurer to be waiting for him, apparently at their leisure, a half-played game of chess set on a small cherrywood table between their chairs along with wine and glasses. The footman who opened the door did not accompany Will into the opulent little chamber.

A hearth blazed, and a brazier as well—the room dryly hot in deference to old men's bones. Will spared a glance for the figured leather

on the walls as the door clicked shut behind him. Burghley and Hunsdon looked up in unison; Burghley turned a chesspiece, a white rook,
in one crabbed hand.

"My lords." Will bowed with a player's flourish.

"Master Shakespeare," Burghley said, flicking Will upright with
irritable fingers. The hand that pinched the ivory castle indicated a
third chair. "Drag that over, won't you?"

Will obeyed, and sat where he was bid to be seated: a little back
from the table, well within the cone of warmth from the hearth. He
tugged his mittens off, an excuse to look down at his hands. "My lords.
From the summons, I had expected we should all be present for this
interview."

"Ah, yes." Burghley returned the rook to the little army of white
pieces haunting his side of the table. The only indication of Burghley's
deafness was by how close he watched Will's lips, and a slight tinny
loudness when he spoke. "We will speak to Master Burbage individu-
ally. Master Shakespeare—"

The hesitation in his voice was all the warning Will needed. "My
lord," Will said. "Not the Earl of Oxford?"

"No." Hunsdon leaned forward and picked up his goblet. He re-
filled it from the bottle, then extended the cup as if not noticing the
dignity he did Will. Will accepted it and sipped.

It could be poisoned, he thought, too late, as heady fumes filled his
senses. The wine was red and sharp, not sweet, but with a tannic richness that made him bold. "If your lordship would have pity—"

"Shakespeare," Hunsdon said. "Your master, Ferdinando Stanley,
Lord Strange, is dead."

It was as well that Will had finished the wine in the cup, for it tumbled from his nerveless fingers and bounced off a rich hand-knotted
carpet, spilling a few red drops on the dark red wool. "Dead."

"By poison," Burghley answered. "Or, some say, sorcery. Ten days
to die, in terrible agony—"

"Will."

Hunsdon's voice, his given name. Will blinked and realized he was
standing, his hands knotted on the relief that covered the gilded arms
of his chair. "My lords."

"Master Shakespeare, sit."

Will sat. "Good my lords—"

"There is more."

Will leaned forward to hear Burghley's weary voice more clearly. "Our Queen is threatened, Master Shakespeare. I have ordered the Irish aliens to present themselves and make explanation of their presence in England. And Essex has accused the Queen's own physician of treason and conspiring to poison her—"

"Lopez," Will said. And then quoted sardonically, "The vile Jew."

"Lies," Burghley said flatly. "Essex's machinations. More and more, I believe Essex—and Southampton—dupes of the enemy. If anything other than the black half of the Prometheus Club, it was a Papist plot. But Lopez has confessed."

"Confessed? Topcliffe?" It was the name of the Queen's torturer, the man who had broken Thomas Kyd, and Will spoke it softly.

"William Wade." Hunsdon breathed out softly through his nose. "Clerk of the Privy Council. Instrumental in bringing low Mary, Queen of Scots, and exposing her treachery. He . . . showed Lopez the instruments."

"Ah." Will gulped, remembering the sear of a red-hot iron by his face.

"My son Robert attended the hearing," Burgley said. "He and Essex have been dueling in the Queen's favor for Lopez for months, you understand. We had a hope of saving Lopez until Strange died. Eight times Essex pressed her to sign the writ, and eight times she refused. But now . . . Essex will prevail, and Lopez will die. Would that Gloriana were a man, and not turned by a pretty man's face—" He stopped, as if hearing himself on the brink of treason. "Lopez has been a valued ally, and preserved Sir Francis when we had thought all hope lost. But it may be that now we must sacrifice him."

"Like Kit," Will said.

If he had intended the words to cut Burghley, they were futile. The old man only nodded. "After a fashion."

Will coughed against his hand. "How may I serve Her Majesty?"

He thought Burghley smiled behind his beard. "We'll have Richard revive *The Jew of Malta*—"

"Is Kit not out of favor?"

"Favor or not, we have no other play that may distract the masses and offer a channel to their wrath. Until you write one."

"My lord?"

"Master Shakespeare. Give me a play about a Jew. Before there are riots in London. Essex's plot will see innocent persons lynched, and there is naught we can do to prevent it." Hunsdon covered his mouth with his hand. "I am not a Jew-lover, but it is not they who must be blamed for this outrage."

Burghley tapped the edge of the chessboard in exasperation. "Put your damned hand down, Carey, if you want me to understand what you say."

"My lord," Will said. "I have never known a Jew."

"I have one for you," Burghley answered. "I must warn you. Like Marley's"—and Will noticed no reluctance in Burghley's naming of the forbidden poet's name—"your Zionist may not be charming: the groundlings I think would not understand it, were he. But neither must his enemies be."

Lord Strange dead.

Murdered.

And Lopez to hang for it.

"As my lord wishes," Will said, and bent to pick his fallen goblet off the floor.

Act II, scene iii

Love is not full of pity (as men say)
But deaf and cruel, where he means to prey.

—CHRISTOPHER MARLOWE, *Hero and Leander*

Summer bled to autumn, autumn to winter, winter to the first cold
trickle of spring—and then through summer until the cycle repeated itself. The seasons in Faerie did not proceed quite as Kit was
used to them, but rather each one smoothly into the next without fits
and starts, each day a sort of idealized *image* of what a day in summer,
or autumn, or winter should be. He concealed his iron-nailed boots in
the bottom of his clothespress in the spacious quarters he was given,
and he soon found himself moving through the court, at first as a curiosity and then as a fixture. And while he saw the Mebd often enough
at court functions, he was not again summoned before her, or given to
understand any purpose in his presence at her court.

Murchaud kept him at arms practice—outside, in the slick scattered leaves of the beech wood behind the palace and then in courtyard snow; then in the Great Hall and the armory when that snow
drifted over their knees. Kit filled the time between as best he could.
He was not accustomed to idleness, and he chafed, and paced, and
read—and wrote when he had the patience, though all his words

seemed hollow—and he woke alone most mornings. Some of those mornings, the shape of Murchaud's or Morgan's body lay already cold in his bed, an ache filling his belly and a hopelessness behind it. He never lost himself again, as he had after his visit to Sir Francis, but the threat of it hung over him always like black wings. He took to courting Morgan with a practiced distance that seemed to please her very well, while the Elf-knights and ladies treated him as some exotic pet. *Like Elizabeth's wizened little devil monkey on its chain.*

One cold February morning, Kit lay against his pillows and watched a dry snow coil and blow beyond the diamond-paned windows. He turned on his side, blew a jet-black hair and days barren of scent from the other pillow. The coverlet of silk and down on his bare skin, the fur-trimmed tapestries on the bed, the transparent diamond panes themselves were luxuries lost on him as he stood and went to the window. He didn't notice the cold, and only half noticed that the glass did not lay his reflection over the snow. He was leaner and harder, for all of Faerie's rich food. Murchaud drove him hard.

Kit's breath frosted the glass. *You should have known when you swore off love that you would only tempt fate to bind you in her wicked chains.*

Still—he reached out and idly drew a lance-pierced heart in the misted window, amused by the obvious symbolism, then glanced over his shoulder as if someone might have seen him. When he raised a guilty hand to wipe it clear, he saw the flurry was tapering away, and saw as well a silhouette wrapped in a figured cloak making her way across the drifts below. Ebony locks rustled unbound across her shoulders; something whiter than the snow fluttered in her milk-white hand. His flinch caught Morgan's eye; she looked up. Even from this distance he could see her smile and the movement of her hair across tapestry brocade.

He imagined what he looked like framed naked in the window, lust stirring as he recollected the scent of her, and stepped to one side, his face burning. *She'll be here in a moment,* he thought, and considered for an instant meeting her naked and shameless at the door. She'd laugh—

If his blushes wouldn't set him on fire.

Kit, he admonished. *For a brazen libertine, an adulterer, a sodomite, an atheist, a fornicator, rakehell, heretic, godless playmaker and debaucher of*

innocents, you're a sorry state of affairs. Self-mockery turned his mouth
awry as he found a clean shirt, the yoke wrought with whitework,
and the green breeches and pale gray woolen stockings that matched
a green and silver velvet doublet. Morgan's favorite colors. He judged
it would take her a quarter hour or so to come inside, shed her cloak,
and make her way through the palace, but he was still running a hurried comb across his hair when a tap rattled the door.

He opened it a moment later, surprised to find not Morgan waiting beyond the door, but a broad-shouldered, black-bearded man: the
Mebd's bard Cairbre, snow still clotting the tops of his boots. "I happened to chance upon your mistress in the Great Hall," the bard said
abruptly. "As I was on my way to my rooms, she asked me to bid you
come to hers."

Kit straightened the lacings on his doublet, pulled his swordbelt
from the rack, and stepped into the corridor. "Thank you, Master
Harper."

"Think nothing of it." The bard's cheek crinkled beside his eye, his
lopsided smile disappearing into his beard. "When are you going to
show me your poetry?"

Kit's fingers slipped on slick black leather and he looked up from
adjusting the rapier carriage at his left hip. "A year ago, had I known
your interest. I had thought —"

A raised eyebrow to go with that angled grin. "A poet likes a poet's
company, Sir Kit. And it seems to me that you have lovers aplenty, but
perhaps could use a friend or two. In any case, your lady awaits." The
bard stepped back, meltwater marking his footsteps on the rose and
gold flagstones. "Stood I in your boots, I should hurry."

When Kit looked back, Cairbre was still staring after, a bemused
expression shadowing his face.

A few minutes later, Kit stopped in the open doorway of Morgan's
room and raised a hand as if to knock on the doorjamb, then paused
when he saw her settled on a bench, her skirts hiked above the knee
in heavy folds as she struggled with fur-lined boots. *Her* bedroom
window stood open, and a cool, moist breeze blew through it, carrying
up a scent at odds with the midsummer colors of her window box of
violet-gold heartsease. "My lady."

"Kit. Your assistance, sir?" She extended a leg, and he knelt before her, taking the soft leather heel cap into the palm of his right hand and sliding the fingers of his left between the furred edge and the silk of her hose. The boot slipped into his hand, dripping melting snow between his fingers, and he turned her leg to kiss above the ankle bone, nubs of knit silk catching softly on dry lips.

She cleared her throat, and he smiled and removed her other boot. There was a practiced trick to standing with a sword at one's belt; he managed it neatly enough. She drew a fistful of skirt into the light to examine the water stains along the hem. She showed him a little more leg than she had to when she swung the skirts into place and stood.

"You summoned me," he said, following her to the window. The vista was not so different from his, although overlooking the lawn and not the beech wood, and from a higher vantage. But the breeze that flowed through the open panes was a spring breeze, not a winter one, and her window box riotous in bloom.

"I've a letter for you," she said, stroking a pansy with one fingertip as if oblivious to his consternation. "I intercepted it before your friend the Puck could get his hands on it. You and your friend have things yet to learn about keeping your confidences from the notice of the Queen."

She wouldn't look up. He caught the damp wool of her sleeve and turned her toward him. "My lady. A letter? Have you read it?" It was more emotion than he'd managed in months.

"Don't flutter so—" She lifted her fingers to the collar of his shirt and let them trail up his cheek. Her eyes shifted again—gray to green, this time, and drifting into hazel—as she closed his left eye with a touch of her fingertips and kissed him softly. "Your secrets are safe with me."

Despite his effort to stay stern, a smile moved under her kiss. She drew her fingers down his face, and when he opened his eye his breath knotted in his chest, a ragged silken scarf. He let his hand slide down her sleeve, grasped her wrist, raised her fingers to his mouth, lowered them quickly when the gesture brought a memory of tearing cloth. "Don't tease me."

"No," she said, studying his expression as she stepped away, their hands for a moment making a falling bridge between them. "It would be unkind to tease, would it not? Like taunting a tame falcon in a mews."

A little prick with the dagger of her tongue, and a twist to make the blood flow. It stopped him, when he might have heeled her across the room again. He'd had a sharp tongue of his own once, he recalled, but he couldn't seem to find it after her kisses. "Lady, but give me a purpose, and I will be a falcon on the wing, answering only to your glove. A man is not a toy—"

"No?" But she smiled, and came back with a folded letter in her hand. The seal looked untouched, but he knew well the ways around that. It told him more that the creases were crisp and sharp, a splintered edge still showing where the sheet had cracked. The hand was Will's untidy abomination—the scrawl of a man who wrote frequently, and hastily—and it bore no name or address beyond *C. M.*

"Thank you," he said, and tucked it into the pocket in his sleeve, ignoring Morgan's arch expression.

She tapped a knuckle against her lips and turned back to her window garden, pinching dead pansies away. Mint and melissa grew between the blossoms; her fingernails met like snips, filling the room with lemony aromas. "You wish a purpose, Sir Kit? Poetry and pleasing your lady suffice not?"

"A man gets used to living by his wits. I was never merely a poet, madam."

She pinched another pansy—a just-opening bud, this time—and brushed it against his cheek. "There are roles for you to play," she said, tucking the stem into a pink on the breast of the doublet. "But best perhaps if you play them innocent, Queen's Man. I have your love?"

"Oh, a little," he lied. "Love is ever increasing or ever decreasing, they say. So better a little love grow great than a great love grow little."

"Or be lost." He startled at the softness in her voice as she knotted her hands in her skirts and lifted them to step back. "For what mortal flesh can bear the true heat of an immortal love?"

There's pain there. With the thought came the urge to go to her. He pressed his palms against his thighs instead. "You expect me to be courted by your enemies."

"Ah," she said. "The boy is clever. And that green looks well on thee: we'll make an Elf-knight of thee yet."

"When mine ears come to a point, or horns sprout on my forehead. Then, perhaps."

"Horns, sweet Kit? Or antlers?" But she smiled and blew a kiss. "A task. Very well. When thou dost write thy William in return, see thou if canst encourage him to weave a few tales of his country youth into his plays."

"Arthur and Guenevere?" Kit asked, letting a little of the irony filling his mouth soak the words.

"By the white hart, never!" Morgan laughed and shook her hair over her shoulder. "We'll have enough of that from Spenser, I warrant. Although chance and legend alter us: I was as fair as Anne and Arthur, *once upon a time*." She raised a fistful of hair black as sorcery and shook it in the light. "Gloriana does like to play on the Faeries, and it strengthens us to be spoken of—so I think it should please Master Shakespeare's Queen and thine as well."

"Madam." A little task. But something. "Your wish is—"

"Oh," she interrupted, giving him an airy wave at odds with her earthy grin. "And a play for Beltane, I think. Something we can see performed for Her Majesty the Mebd."

"Beltane—" He tasted it. Short notice, but he'd had shorter. "Ten weeks. Have you a subject?"

"Intrigue." She straightened the blossom on his breast. "And passion. Mayhap one of those great lost loves of which we spoke. Drystan and Yseult. Something ill-starred would suit us both, and Her Majesty. But mind that thou lookst wistful and sigh and fret while thou'rt composing, and see who chooses to speak with thee. And on what matters."

"My lady." *Drystan and Yseult. No, Orpheus, I think.* But he was smiling as she took his elbow and led him to her door, her stockinged feet whisking against the flagstones like a cat's white paws. *A stalking horse.*

I've played that role before.

Dearest & most-esteemed Leander:
Your letter does indeed find me very well, if exceeding busy. I fear I have not had occasion to converse with my wife since our last encounter

but I shall pass your felicitations when I may. The subject is complex, but suffice to say I have hopes for rapprochement.

I am attending your request for books & broadsides: they will follow under separate cover. You will be amused to read that, following hard on the discovery of a poisoning plot against the Queen of which you will no doubt have heard, plays about Jews are once again popular in London, & we are becoming reacquainted with some names that languished in danger of loss.

I hope these humble words find you well. In any case, thinking of you I am moved to remember Sir Francis & a certain incident with a lemon bush. I wonder if my predecessor had such a sour experience of his own.

> *April y 29th, year of our Lord 1594*
> *Your true and honest friend*
> *Wm.*

. . . incident with a lemon bush. Kit set the letter down on a marble-topped table below the window, and smiled. *Clever William. How I miss thee, and wrangling late into the night on scansion and wordplay and line.*

Lighting a taper at the hearth, Kit remembered Cairbre's invitation. *Poets are so often thought solitary. But we need the society of our fellows as much as any tradesman.*

The taper lit a clever lamp, which burned a blue spirit flame, and this Kit bore to the table beside Will's letter. It would cost him the seal, but that little mattered. What mattered were the pale words, written painstakingly in invisible lemon juice, that slowly caramelized into visibility as he toasted the letter a few inches above the flame, holding his breath lest it flicker and the edge of the paper catch light.

When the words burned dark enough to read, Kit laid the letter in the light from the window and leaned forward to blow out the flame. He tucked a few strands of hair behind his ear and closed his eye for a moment, then—reluctant, frowning—bent forward.

And read.

And blasphemed.

And read it once again.

Act II, scene iv

Beatrice: Speak, cousin; or, if you cannot, stop his mouth with a kiss, and let not him speak neither.

—WILLIAM SHAKESPEARE, *Much Ado About Nothing*

My beloved Adonis—

I read with disquiet your words & the implication that unsavory individuals have taken an interest in your activities. In pursuance, I would consider it a great kindness if you should contact Mary Poley in Winding Lane. She is the abandoned wife of one Robert Poley, with whom you are acquainted, but more to the point she was the sister of the late Dr. Thomas Watson, the poet, who was long a friend to me—& her husband is greatly unfelicitous to her, & to her son. You need have no fear that she will expose you to him, and she may be a great source of intelligence as to his actions.

Will tilted the letter into the light of the candle which he had used to scorch the concealed words from between lines more innocuous and manifest. The heated lemon juice was only pale brown against the cream-colored paper, but Kit's precise hand was easy to discern.

Poley will not see to their maintenance & so, in Tricky Tom's memory & out of mine own friendship with the lady, I have been of what assistance I could to her in the past, & so I believe she should be grateful for a kind word or two, even from a stranger who mentioned my name as the name of a friend. She may be of assistance in warding yourself from that same Robert, her husband; Mistress Poley is a good woman, & much concerned with the future prospects of her son—a likely lad.

Will's nose wrinkled in amusement. "*Her* son. Kit. Are you insinuating the lad is your bastard?" And then he frowned, and nibbled the edge of an ink-stained thumbnail, uncertain why the thought made him so uneasy.

My mistress has asked that I bid thee, my beloved friend & only begetter of whatever joy is afforded me, remember the pastoral fancies of thy callow years & find ways to set them into verse. I am minded of county ballads & old tales I imagine you too are conversant with, of Nimue, & the Irish & Welsh stories & those of Yorkshire & Scotland: Finvarra & Oonagh & their kin.

"You want me to tell fairy tales to the Queen, sweet Kit?" *He sounds lonely.*

You should sound lonely, exiled from home and friendships, and worried about the ones you've left behind.

Will closed his eyes. When he opened them, he read more quickly, and without pause.

Have a care for Poley, Will. If he & his have realized that you are my replacement, you may find yourself with dangerous enemies: have a care not to be associated too plainly with Hunsdon, Burghley, Oxford & their friends. I will dare declare Robert Poley & Thomas Walsingham scions of the enemy, & ask you be wary of them.

It is of import that you acquaint yourself with the politics, if you have not already done so: Essex's group do support the Queen, although they are more interested in their own advancement than the stability of the crown. Raleigh is a little better: I can like the man for his ideals, at least, which are intellectual & inquisitive, but he is a popinjay. (Those are not sentiments to be repeated, sweet Will, lest you withal blacken my name further than mine enemies have already.)

More dangerous are Poley & Baines (& I now think Thomas Walsingham), who have made themselves so seeming indispensable that their word be taken even over mine, & I have proven my worth to Gloriana in great extremis.

I read with great delight the pages of yr. Merchant you included with the books, & have returned some suggestions along with mine own current project. Also, I am quite engaged with your character of Beatrice—she reflects your Annie, does she not?—but feel Hero could be stronger or mayhap more delicate of constitution; her speeches now show nowt but woman scorned, & women (even scorned) are no force to be trifled with. You may wish if you can so contrive to seek Her Majesty's approval. Gloriana fancies herself something of a poet, & was of infinite service making that infamous she-wolf Isabella more a breathing woman than the Dragon of legendry. Further—

It went on for a page and a half, line-by-line comments on the play, ending wryly,

—have enclosed some notes for the play or more like masque my mistress has commissioned of me, something of an orgy & something of a revel, & I am feared only half-suited to my poor talents. I wish you would examine them with some haste, & return post to me through the usual channels.

I think on thee & London daily. With all love & affection, your dear friend—

Leander.

Will read the letter over again, permitting himself a few more smiles. *Very well then, if Her Majesty will sully her hand with playmaking, I will offer her mine own poor words to dirty herself on.* He stopped, and frowned, and looked up at the darkened window. And then he fetched quills—the stained one for the irongall, and the white one for the invisible ink—and sat down at the table and composed himself to write.

Beloved companion of mine art—

Will stopped, brushing the nub of vane that lingered on his quill against his upper lip. He glanced at the stack of pages beside his elbow, the ink on Kit's manuscript so black it gleamed, and frowned.

Have a care not to be associated too plainly with Hunsdon, Burghley, Oxford &
—Kit, how do I write to tell thee that Lord Hunsdon has claimed Burbage, Kemp and I withal into an playing company, now that Strange is dead? That we are become the Lord Chamberlain's Men?

He ran a hand through his hair, streaking it—for once—with lemon juice instead of ink. And then he pulled a fresh sheet of paper toward himself, and wrote *Dearest Annie* instead.

Three days later, Will and Burbage trudged through a cloying summer rain to the Spread Eagle, a tavern near the bearbaiting pits that could be forgiven a certain lack of charm for the virtue of its pies, although for safety's sake Will wouldn't drink anything weaker than ale. A filthy floor and walls dark with smoke and grease did nothing to brighten its face, but Will had forgotten to eat through the afternoon, and his stomach grumbled painfully when the wench—another attraction of the Eagle—slid his supper under his nose.

Burbage looked up at the sound and laughed, pushing bread through bloody juices, then stuffing the soaked sops into his mouth. "You'll waste away to a ghost," he said.

Will broke the pie open and scooped aromatic meat and onions to his mouth. Gravy trickled into his beard; he wiped it on the back of his hand. "Oxford's help isn't help," he said in a low voice. "If I suspected he were competent, I'd believe he meant to impede rather than assist. At least *Jew* and *Merchant* are showing a success, for all I'm hard-put to believe we staged them so swiftly as we did. Has there been word of Lopez?"

Burbage, chewing thoughtfully, only turned his head from side to side. "He'll hang, for all Burghley can do. We may be lucky enough that our work will fend off riots and worse, however. And the hunt is on for Papists. I marked a dozen recusants in stocks today. 'Tis a time to keep your hand in your sleeve, methinks."

"Mayhap." Will busied himself with pie and ale, unwilling to meet Burbage's eye. Rain still rattled the shutters, and all London smelled of damp. All summer, the rain had barely lifted long enough for a man to wring the water from his cloak before descending again. "I've a play in mind that might catch Her Majesty's fancy. A tale of two warring houses. Another tragedy."

"We could use a comedy for the Theatre. Now that the plague has lifted—"

"—that we've lifted the plague—"

"—aye, well, yes. People want happy things. Can you write me a comedy by All Saint's Day, Will?"

"I wot."

A shadow fell across the table as a stocky figure, cloak dripping rain, passed between Will and Burbage and the light. "William Shakespeare." A sonorous voice spoke in educated tones. "You're going bald on top, Will."

"The heat of a well-used brain," Will replied. "I see you have experienced the like."

"Not I," Burbage interjected. "I keep mine too well greased with ale to rub and burn. Sit down, George."

"Since you've invited—" The poet George Chapman unwound his cloak from under his beard. Will shuffled the bench away from the trestle, and Chapman sat heavily. "I've a letter from Spenser." Chapman slapped the table to draw the wench's attention. "He's back in County Cork, would you believe it? Master of the Queen's Justice, in Ireland. Sad days when the greatest poet in a generation must politic for his bread—"

Will choked on piecrust and reached for his ale, spilling half of it across his lap when Chapman thumped him between the shoulders. Burbage glared, lips compressed, though Will thought he had recovered nicely. He pulled a kerchief from his sleeve and dabbed at his breeches. "He's completed his *Faerie Queene*?"

"A canto or two." The girl came over; Chapman refused ale or wine and ordered instead small beer and stew. Will wondered if his famous temperance was distaste for drunkenness, some Puritan bent, or merely the caution of a man with no head for liquor. "Will you grace us with another play this summer, Will?"

"One or two." Will wrung his sopping kerchief onto the boards and spread it across the trestle to dry. "A tragedy first, and Dick Burbage wants a comedy to warm a heart or two. I may write him half a dozen this year, if he stays unwary. I've been reading the Italians, and my lord Southampton wishes me to come spend some weeks in residence with him before the summer's out, and write him poetry—"

"May God ha' mercy on this house," Chapman said.

"A plague upon you, then," Will answered with rare good humor, considering his breeches were sticking to his hose. "And yourself, George? What have you been working at?"

"Master Marley's *Hero and Leander*," Chapman replied. "I still mean to finish it. Don't flinch like a girl, Master Burbage. For all his excesses and a tawdry end, our Kit deserves to be remembered for his gifts as well. And with his *Jew* in production again, I can see no better time to press the issue. Kit would have wanted to be recollected."

Will shrugged. "Isn't that what poets crave?"

Chapman's stew arrived. He busied himself for a moment buttering bread with absolute attention, and then looked up—first at Burbage, and then turning his broad contemplative face to study Will. "No, William." He set the bread down on the boards beside his dinner. "I think you've something more to prove than skill, to select an example. I think you are a man who is afraid to be alone. After your death, if the ages forget your name, so be it . . . so long as we know you today, and tomorrow, and touch on your wit."

Will swallowed ale to wet his throat. "That may be, George. At least I've a wit to touch on, yes?"

"At least," Chapman answered, and turned his concentration on his board, bench creaking. "I'll show you what I've got of *Hero* if you'd like it—"

"Exceedingly."

"Done, then," Burbage said, suddenly rising. "Will, if you would walk with me? You had wished to speak to my father about buying shares in the Chamberlain's Men—"

Will stood, leaving the crumbs of his dinner on the trestle. "Richard, I have intentions to visit a woman tonight. Perhaps tomorrow?" Burbage nodded, and Will continued, "George, I shall see you at church."

"Indeed you will. Or Friday at the Hogshead. Or are we meeting at the Mermaid, on Bread Street?"

"On Bread Street. That's where all the rogues and scoundrels have gone."

"In your company I'll find them."

Will paused, hearing the smile in the older poet's voice. He scooped the ale-soaked rag from the end of the table and—without turning—threw it over his shoulder. He didn't wait to find out if it wrapped itself around Chapman's head as satisfactorily as the wet *thwack* of cloth hitting flesh suggested; instead he broke for the door, trusting Chapman's dignity to be too great for a really rollicking pursuit.

Will's first impression of Mary Poley was of a bright, sudden eye, half occluded by a tangled spiral of brown-black hair, gleaming through the crack in a door she gripped so tightly her knuckles went white along the edge. "Who is it?" Her sodden skirts shifted: she leaned a knee with her weight behind it on the door, in case he tried to push through.

"William Shakespeare," he said. "The playmaker. Are you Mistress Poley?"

"I am." She didn't relax her grip on the door, and that jet-shiny eye ran up him from boot to beard and back down without meeting his gaze. "Are ye looking for a washingwoman?"

Her tones were educated—not surprising, given her family. Will lowered his voice. He'd expected—more genteel poverty, somehow. "I'm looking for Master Kit Marley's friend."

That hand flew to her mouth and she stepped back involuntarily. Will didn't waste a gesture; he pressed the flat of his hand against the timbers and shoved the door open, careful not to strike Mistress Poley in the face. He slipped through sideways and pushed it shut behind, standing back against the wall as she cringed away.

"Mistress Poley—"

"Shh!" A jerk of a gesture over her shoulder. "My boy's asleep. Finally. He has terrors—"

"Poor lad." Will lowered his voice. "Mistress—"

"What d'ye know of Kit Marley? And why d'ye trouble my house?" *House*, she said, drawing all fourteen hands of herself up like a stretched-taut string, as if the rotten, spotless little chamber with its two sad pallets on the floor and its peeling plaster were a manse.

"Kit Marley was—" Will stopped, and frowned at the little woman trembling with rage, a banty hen defending the nest. *She'd be perfect for Burbage*, he thought. *No wonder Kit liked her.* And then she shoved a hand through her unkempt hair, tilted her head back to glare at him, and sniffed.

Will sat down on the floor, his back against the door. "—my friend. And he cared for you, so I know he would have wished mine assistance to you, if you will so kindly accept it." He reached into his pocket and tossed a little felt bag clinking on the bare boards between her feet. She glanced down, but didn't step back or stoop to pick up the coin.

Will drew a long breath through his nose, closed his eyes, and finished, still mindfully soft. "And your husband had a hand in killing him, and I'm interested in learning why."

She glanced over her shoulder: the small form curled on one of the pallets still lay unmoving, and she turned her wary, wild-animal expression back on Will. She probed the bag with her toe—barefoot, Will saw—and seemed to consider for a second before she stooped down like some wise little monkey and made the coins vanish beneath her apron into the stained folds of her skirt. "On a darker day," she said, crouching and resting her back against the wall, but not sitting, "I might give ye that Kit was killed for *my* sins." She balled fists reddened with scrubbing against her eyes, whipcord muscle flexing across skinny forearms.

"But it wasn't Robert wielding the dagger." Will suddenly felt very tired, as if the space of a few feet across the floor between himself and Mistress Poley were a rushing river that must be swum. "Do you see your husband often, Mistress?"

She pulled her hands down. "Never an I can cross the street in time. But there might be yet a thing or two I may aid you with, Master Shakespeare." She nodded, a sage oscillation of her head, and then she grinned. Will blinked in the dazzle of her smile as she squared her shoulders and rose against the wall without setting a hand on the floor, realizing that she was no older than he. *Not that you're quite the beardless boy any more.* "Aye, Will Shakespeare, then. A friend of Kit Marley's is a friend of mine."

Act II, scene v

Barabas: Some Jews are wicked, as all Christians are.

—CHRISTOPHER MARLOWE, *The Jew of Malta*

Kit's eye never shifted from the unrippled surface of the Darkling Glass, his fingertips hooked under the lip of the carved flower petals marking the frame. So long as his hand rested among the cold, sculptured blossoms, he heard the words of the players clearly: Burbage's metered, resonant voice declaiming, "He jests at scars that never felt a wound—"

Burbage—and Kemp, and Will, and the rest of the company— moved about the shaded stage before an empty house, on an early autumn afternoon. Sunlight glared on the packed earth of the yard, outlining a not-quite-perfect circle with the bite of the stage taken from it, its margins defined by the gallery roofs. Kit leaned closer, tracing the action behind the mirror, where small forms moved sharp and crisp in the cold, polished blackness of the glass.

But it *was* cold. Cold as a scene viewed through a rippled casement. Kit drew his brown woolen cloak tighter, tugging the hood up to hide his hair and the black band of the eyepatch crossing his face. He settled his sword at his belt with his left hand, hiding it under a fall of cloth, glanced over his shoulder, and—finding himself unobserved—

thought very carefully about a dark corner of the Theatre's second gallery, in the private boxes above and behind the stage. It came into view, a familiar concealed corner behind a pillar and a bench where lovers might steal a kiss—

—Or where a cloaked man might linger and in his own person overhear the voice of Richard Burbage speaking beautiful words: "By a name, I know not how to tell thee who I am: My name, dear Saint, is hateful to my self, because it is an enemy to thee. Had I it written, I would tear the word—"

A warm breeze brought Kit the scent of the streets and the distant barking of a dog, and the contrast to Faerie's cool air and birdsong came home with a pang. He sweated in his cloak, and saw that the players sweated as much in their costumes, and thought, *how much I miss this* only a few moments before he realized that he could not, in fact, step back to Faerie as simply as he'd stepped away.

I'll need to find a looking glass. He wasn't worried: he thought he might have two or three days before the pain set in, and if he couldn't visit Will—because Will would be watched—there were other errands Kit could busy himself upon.

Once night fell.

In the meanwhile, he crouched against the wall in a garishly painted box at James Burbage's Theatre, first to be so named, and concealed his face, and watched men who had been friends rehearse a play. Several of his own poor scribblings had made their mark upon these boards—those sanded scorches were from an overturned firepot during a miscarriage of *Faustus*, some years since—and by this current rehearsal, Kit judged that Will Shakespeare had made a fair mark of his own.

The play progressed. The shadows slid, and Kit slid with them, his eye stinging and a smile on his lips. He sighed and settled down on the floor cross-legged, peering around a bench, his left arm going numb from elbow to wrist while he leaned his chin on his arm. He didn't dare blow his nose, and so sniffled quietly—and uncomfortably—into the rough wool of his cloak.

And then the truth of what he was seeing sank in, and he sat back against the wall, rapier sticking out to the side like a stiff, unwieldy tale. *Two warring houses and their children lost—coming to their senses too late, uniting when the future they might have defended is lost to them. Not Catholics and Protestants, but Capulets and Montagues.* Kit bit down on his finger to keep from laughing out loud.

I'd almost forgotten. His family is Catholic.

Injustice and undue accusations — your simpering Hero and her slander, your stern Beatrice and your clever Benedick united over all their own protestations — You'll work our trickery even on the Queen, won't you? And Burghley and the rest can go to Hell with their persecutions and their factions and— Kit's grin turned downward and he tapped a thumb on his lip, only half aware of the excited babble of the players on the stage below.

Kit sat up straighter and then scrunched into the darkness as a tall, beskirted figure, her gray-streaked hair—almost the same mousy shade as Kit's—bound up on her head and her dress sagging at the bindings as if it had been worn for hard travel. She scanned the galleries imperiously; he caught a breath in his teeth and held it, didn't let it slip until her eye was past.

One last voice—Will's—rose above the abruptly stilling clamor from the stage. *He must have his back to the yard.* But Kit didn't drop his eyes from Annie Shakespeare's face to see Will turn. Didn't look away from the Amazon's form as she set her heel and laid each palm softly on the curve of a hip. Tilting her head, the smile in her eyes never touching her lips.

Will must be looking by now, by the utter silence in the stage and yard. By the way Annie angled her chin up, to command a glance across the packed earth and cinders and up the five-foot lift of the stage. She drew a breath—Kit saw her shoulders settle as her bosom rose—and opened her mouth—and never got a word into the air, as a whooping Will Shakespeare piled off the stage and swept her off her feet and spun her up in the air.

And that's as good a distraction as I'm like to get, Kit thought, and slipped away down the stair into the drawing twilight, whistling to himself when his elf-booted foot met the dusty cobbles of the road.

Some hours later, footsore and sweltering, he stepped back into the doorway of a shuttered cookshop across the alley from a tavern he'd stay away from if he had any sense at all: the Groaning Sergeant, Mistress Mathews' sole domain. He leaned into the shadows, trusting the cloak to hide the outline of his body against the brown wood of the door, lifting the pommel of his sword to tip the scabbard straight so it wouldn't tap the wall.

He sighed. *Francis could help me. If I had the wit to go to his house from Faerie, and speak to him straightaway. I'll never find my way in now.*

But then I wouldn't have seen the play.

Men came and went. Kit stretched against the wall as the hours drifted by, keeping himself awake through force of will and force of habit. Traffic was steady; the Sergeant's clientele stayed awake late. When the lights within flickered out—longer after curfew than the law, speaking strictly, allowed—and the custom left, he did permit himself to slide down against the door frame and doze. But no more than doze; even if no enemy found him, it would profit him little to be taken and jailed as a vagrant, a masterless man.

Toward morning, he crept from his vantage and forced the cellar on a house which had been boarded up for the summer, abandoned to the threat of plague as the residents guested with some relative or country friend. He stole a meager supper from a few forgotten pots of preserves, and slept. Curfew found him again lurking in the shadows with a clear view of the Sergeant.

Kit's patience was rewarded sometime in the blessedly cool hours before matins, as he shifted the cloak and his sweat-lank hair off his neck. The smells of morning baking filled the air, and his stomach grumbled. *'Tis been too long since you went hungry, Marley. You're soft.*

But then a figure emerged from the alleyway beside the Sergeant and—with an unconcerned glance at the apparent derelict in the door-way opposite—slipped inside. A tall man, hair platinum in the pre-dawn, hands broad even for his frame.

Richard Baines.

Kit unwound his fingers from the hilt of his rapier. He checked the sky, cocking an ear for church bells, and decided discretion might serve better than boldness. At least clouds were gathering: a not-unexpected stroke of luck, given the chill wetness of the summer, but it would make his cloak less unlikely and Baines easier to shadow.

Kit emerged from the doorway, tipping his rapier straight again so the outline wouldn't show, and staggered around the corner to the alley. It didn't take as much effort to move drunkenly as he would have preferred: two nights propped in a doorway left his neck and back complaining, the muscles of his thighs stiff as if they'd been nights in the saddle.

Thunder crackled; Kit skulked behind empty barrels under a second-story overhang. He kicked a dead starling aside and settled himself to wait, but a few moments later the sky pissed rain like a drunken Jove. He tugged the hood of his cloak higher, wet wool slicing his limited vision in half. Inside the cookshop, pots clattered, onions browned. *Christ wept. Never trust to luck.*

In a quarter hour, Baines—cloakless, ears hunched into his collar—left the Sergeant. Poley walked alongside, better equipped for the rain in a gray oiled cloak and high boots. Kit swung in behind them, fifty feet or more. Baines' shoulders, clad in a brown leather jerkin that grew slowly darker with the rain, bobbed through a crowd, and Kit for once was glad of the other man's height.

The men wended north. The grit between his soles and the cobbles turned to mud, but Kit's feet stayed snug in Faerie boots and he never slipped. Poley and Baines led him down alleys and through mires more wallow than highway. A bloated rat corpse swept down the gutter. Pedestrians ducked into taverns and doorways, but Baines and Poley continued. And Kit followed. Baines never looked back. Poley did, but Kit was careful to vary his distance and his walk, and one shrouded, sodden figure looked much like another. He got lucky: they took the Bridge rather than a wherry south across the Thames.

The two men stepped down another side street and into an intersection. Kit recognized their destination: a well-favored establishment known as the Elephant, a Southwark tavern whose sign peeled artistically rather than from simple neglect.

Kit checked his step as they continued around the building to where, he knew, a ramshackle stairway led to a warm and comfortably appointed room. He stepped under an overhang and leaned into the corner by the garden wall, gasping like a hooked fish. His stomach clenched on emptiness, but he forced himself to straighten and walk silently through the rain.

His hand itched on his swordhilt. Not his left hand, to keep the blade tucked under his cloak, but his right, ready to draw the blade whickering into the air and cast that cloak aside, to run Baines and

Poley down, shouting. To run them through before they could climb those stairs —

Where's Nick Skeres? he thought, picking his way over litter and startling a feral pig nosing through garbage. It fled in a clatter of trotters, and Kit held his breath lest the sound should bring investigators. But the rain probably covered it.

Where's Frazier? The name brought a twist of coldness into his belly, and kept him from thinking about who might be already waiting in that room. He released the rapier's hilt and thrust the lank strands of hair out of his eye. They stuck to his cheeks and forehead; he stifled a sneeze and swore. *Morgan will put me in a hot bath again.* It was her cure for everything, insane as it sounded, but it hadn't killed him yet.

Baines and Poley had just reached the landing as Kit glided around the corner and slipped beneath the whitewashed frame of the stair. They did not shut the door. Kit looked up at the timbers and sighed, knowing from experience that the landing and much of the stair were visible through that entryway. *Perhaps —*

I can't make the climb in a cloak. The sword would be enough trouble, but he wasn't leaving that behind. He circled through puddles, using a few wan flickers of lightning to get an idea of the strength of the crossbracing holding the stairs, wishing he had a bit of leather to bind his hair. It drifted again into his eye and mouth as he lifted his face. He drank in the unclean savor of London rain, blinked a particle of soot away. A pang of hunger left him dizzy for a moment; he sighed and took hold of the thickest timber. *Quickly, Kit, or you'll miss what you've come to hear. You don't know who's in that room.*

All you have is a very nasty suspicion indeed.

And one that could mean a great deal of danger to Will, especially if his friend's secret plan to undermine the ill-feeling between Protestants and Papists came to light.

Kit dropped his cloak in the driest corner and ran each hand up opposite sides of the rough-hewn timber, glad the edges had not been planed to corners and the bark was only haphazardly smoothed away. He grabbed as high as he could, locked fist around wrist, and half hopped, half pulled himself into the air. He wrapped his legs around the pillar, the rough surface burning skin through clothes —*so much for these hose* —and breathed.

One. He reached as high as he could, coiled his arms around the pillar, and dragged himself a few inches, cursing rain and splinters. Something stabbed his thigh, working deeper as he shimmied up. He kept his grip and pressed the scarred side of his face against the timber.

Another flicker, and a halfhearted growl of thunder. Kit struck his head on a crossbrace and flinched, but held on. The stars he saw were brighter than the lightning. A slow hot trickle winding through his hair was soon lost in all the swift, cold trickles; he hoped the thump would be as lost in the sound of the storm. The voices he strained to hear almost vanished under the pattering of droplets; Kit chased them, hoisting himself onto that crossbrace and straddling it. His arms and legs trembled. The crossbrace dug into his back, and the splinter burned in his thigh.

Good work, Marley. And how get you down? He wiped his hair out of his face again and saw dilute blood on his fingers, though the bump on his head seemed superficial.

He closed his eye and listened through the rain: first to the commonplaces of intelligencers in the tones of Baines and of Poley, reports of Catholics and Puritans Kit dismissed as no longer relevant to his service. Until—

"... no, I haven't seen Nick today, but he intended to attend. He must have been delayed at some trouble, my lord. I can tell you until he gets here that your Shakespeare's been well behaved," Poley said in his sharp, sardonic tones. "He spent the night in his room with his wife. Had supper sent up, and the candle went out shortly after. Not a peep: he seems apt to take the Queen's penny and write his plays as he's told."

And then the third voice. Precise, a little pinched. As pompous as his peascod doublets: the voice of Edward de Vere, the Earl of Oxford. Kit covered his face with his forearm, blocking the incessant drip. "Have your men see he stays under control, Master Poley. I'd not waste another playmaker.

"Though so long as he seems biddable, there should be no danger; Lord Burghley relies on me to guide his production, and there have been no incidents such as those that provoked us to deal so harshly with Master Marley."

Kit almost lost his grip on the beam.

"Have you aught else to report? Anything of Thomas Walsingham?"

Baines' voice, the first part lost under the rumble of the thunder and the sudden agony of Kit's throat constricting. *You broke it off, Kit. You were young. You learned. You never—*

—meant a thing to him.

Edward.

". . . Thomas Walsingham's trust is secure. I've made evidence that Marley was involved with enemies of the Queen, and Thomas has accepted Master Poley's judgement. With some tearing of the hair. I gather they were—bosom friends."

Kit straightened his arms against the beam overhead. Cold water dripped onto his forehead and ran down his arms as he let his head loll back. It mingled with slow heat leaking down his cheek, dripped burning against the back of his throat. He tasted salt and didn't lower a hand to wipe it dry.

"Edward," he mouthed. "Oh, unhappy Marley." He'd blamed poor Thomas for his murder all unfairly, and it was fickle Edward all along.

Baines said, "Walsingham suspects nothing, my lord."

"—Excellent. What news from the Continent?"

A band of heavier rain swept the alley, and Kit couldn't bear in any case to listen longer. The pang that wracked his belly was the final consideration: he couldn't be sure if it was hunger, or the doom that would drive him back to Faerie, but he didn't dare stay wedged under the stair. He slung a leg over the crossbrace and locked his ankles around the timber again, thinking, *At least going down will be easier than coming up.*

Except his hand slipped on slimy wood as he shifted his hip off the crossbrace, and he grabbed wildly for the timber and got a slick handful of rain-soaked bark that peeled free.

He wasn't sure how he remembered not to shout as he skidded two feet, asmear with whitewash and crumbs of wood, that splinter lodged so deeply now he thought he'd die of it, his eyepatch tearing loose a knot of hair as it went into the gulf underneath. His sword stayed blessedly fast in its scabbard, though, and for a long moment

Kit hugged the timber and just *breathed*—long, slow rattling breaths that hurt more coming out than going in.

Somehow he made it to the ground and stood against the timber, shaking more with his realization about Oxford than with the terror of the climb. He knew the length of such reports to the minute, and Poley and Baines would be emerging soon. *What's another betrayal? I already knew what he was—*

—At least I've confirmation Edward II *stung him. Although perhaps more than I intended.* And then a bright flare of hope, quickly doused. *It wasn't Tom.*

And so what if it wasn't? The thought that must concern me is whether Edward is our only traitor.

Kit pulled himself away from the timber and bent to retrieve his cloak. He couldn't find his eyepatch; the rainwater felt odd trickling over the drooping eyelid and the scar on his blind side. But at least with the cloak too sodden to wear, it was unlikely anyone would look past the whitewash daubing his form, the blood and mess and the long-healed wound to recognize a dead man's profile.

He needed Morgan. He needed to get another message to Francis, that his cousin was innocent and Oxford the man not to be trusted. *We—*

We.

Kit, there is no we *any more. You serve a different Queen.*

He would have laughed if he'd dared: first the sinking horror of betrayal and then relief that left him giddy. *Edward, not Thomas. Why is it so much better to be betrayed by one former lover than another?*

Because it is better to have a vile impression of someone once cared for reinforced, than to have one's heart shown irreparably flawed.

He picked his way out into the steadier traffic of the street, too weary and pained to keep to the shadows though passersby were offering his bloody, whitewashed, rain-streaked visage curious stares and wide berths. There was a rain barrel up on bricks a half block further on, and he thought he might wash his face. Kit kept his eye on his shoes, cautious of the slick cobbles. He wouldn't have looked up at all if a hurrying figure hadn't drawn back a startled step and gasped.

"M—Marley?"

God's blood. Kit looked into the eyes of a narrow little man with a narrow little face. He was well dressed and well wrapped against the rain, and he skittered back three steps and bared his teeth like a trapped rat as Kit advanced, reaching across his body for the rapier.

"Nicholas Skeres," Kit muttered between the draggled locks of his hair. He tasted lime and blood and soot, and spit them out upon the road. "Thou murdering bastard. I'll see thee hang."

Skeres' eyes widened so the white showed in a ring. He gave a scream like a startled girl and shuffled backward, tripped on a stone, and sat down hard in the slops. "Kit—stay thy hand—"

"As thou didst stay Ingrim's?" Another step forward, the naked blade in Kit's hand pointed at Skeres' left eye, only a few short steps distant. *The damage is done. You're recognized. You may as well get the pleasure of his blood—* Passersby were halting, drawing back, staring and muttering.

" 'Tis Master Marley's ghost." A woman's shocked voice: one he knew not, but he'd been well enough known. "The murdered playmaker—"

From some window open to the rain, a drift of music followed. Kit turned his head to regard the semicircle ranged on his blind side. A half-dozen men and women huddled in the rain, frozen with fear or fascination. He ran a cold eye over them and they drew back. He was all over whitewash and blood, and he knew what they must see: a tattered figure smeared with the lime of the grave, the blood of his fatal wound rolling from the socket of his missing eye, leveling a naked blade at a sobbing killer.

It was too much for a player's imagination. And a few reports of a dramatic revenant wouldn't risk the sort of intelligent questions that a dead man returning from the grave to slaughter his own murderer might. Skeres claiming a visit from Kit's ghost could be drunken fancy.

Or—*Hell*—a ghost, for all that.

Kit had been careless and greedy, and he wouldn't have Will or Francis or a true innocent like Burghley's changeling cousin Bull caught in the net of that carelessness.

Kit smiled through the blood and tilted his head to look his prey in the eye.

"You'll die screaming, Nick Skeres," he whispered. The man flinched down into the gutter, a fresh reek of urine hanging on the rain-wet air, and Kit whirled on the ball of his foot. Silent in his nail-less boots, carrying his naked blade, he ran into the storm and made himself gone.

Act II, scene vi

Pedro: I shall see thee ere I die, look pale with love.
Benedick: With anger, with sickness, or with hunger, my Lord, not
with love: prove that ever I loose more blood with love then I will get
again with drinking, pick out mine eyes with a Ballad-maker's pen, and
hang me up at the door of a brothel house for the sign of blind Cupid.

—WILLIAM SHAKESPEARE, *Much Ado About Nothing*

"Thou didst send for me, and I am here." Annie lay on his bed, her shoes lined side by side beneath it, her hair unpinned and spread like a river on his pillow, spilling over the hand and arm she propped her head upon. "I stink with travel, Will. Wouldst call up water?"

Will, fussing with the lamp, smiled. Her terseness had the welcome sound of home. "I'm glad thou didst come."

He stepped out the door and down the stairs, found the landlord's ten-year-old boy, Jack, dozing in the common room. "Warm water for my wife." Will dropped half a silver penny on Jack's lap. "And see if there's any of the pig left—"

He's only a little older than Hamnet. Jack vanished into the kitchen so fast he blurred. Will clumped back up the stairs, dizzy with the effects of a long day's work in the heat. "Water is imminent. And thy supper, too, if thou likst. How are Hamnet and the girls?"

"Growing. Susanna's tall as a willow. They're with thy sister Joan. Come home, Will."

He left the door unlatched and plumped down on the boards beside the bed in the flickering lamplight, the window thrown open despite the stench and sound of the streets. "Thou knowst I can't." He reached up without looking, caught her skirts, and tugged until her legs slid over the edge of the bed and her feet dropped into his lap. "I'm good at this, Annie. And—" The door swung open at John's tap. Will moved Anne's legs aside and rose to relieve the boy of his bucket and the cold pork and bread.

Will latched the door and set the food on the table, shoulders aching as he hefted the bucket. Anne peeled her stocking down, her leg raised in the air, her skirts in disarray and a wanton gleam in her eye. "Wash my feet for me, Will." Her bare foot ran up his calf, tickling the back of his knee.

"Annie." He set the bucket down and sat on the bed beside her, a careful six inches away. "Dost want thy supper?"

" 'Tis not supper I'm hungry for." She curled against his back, pressing her soft bosom against his shoulder, her hair across his shoulder like a veil. She smelled of dust and travel, of sweat and great distances, and of sachet lavender.

"I won't risk thy life for another babe, Annie."

" 'Tis not a babe I crave, sweet William. I'm too old to catch."

"Oh, Annie." He turned and put his hands through her hair, and closed her eyes with a kiss. "Not so old as that, I warrant. They say a love match never comes out well, but after all I went to winning thee, Wife, would I risk thee? Another birth like the twins would finish thee, and thou wert younger then—"

"It wasn't so bad."

"There was blood through the ticking, Anne."

"There's someone else." Flatly, a dead inflection that squeezed his heart like a fist.

"A player's dalliances. No one who matters—"

"A husband's prerogative, in the absence of his wife." She tugged her skirts out from under his leg and squatted beside the bucket, unlacing her bodice and pushing aside her smock as if the bitterness in her voice were the tones of idle conversation. He watched her wash her arms and neck, the shadows under the well-nursed softness of her breasts. The lamplight streaked her hair with an unfair quantity of gray. "I'm well provided for. Where does the money come from, Will?"

"I'm in favor at the court."

"And living over a tavern."

He looked around the Spartan room, seeing it through her eyes. "I'm not here often," he said at last. "I should see to better lodging."

"Thou canst write plays in Stratford. Thou canst see thy children grow. I'll content myself with stable-hands—"

He turned to her, startled, and saw her rock back on her heels and smile.

"If a husband may seek comfort elsewhere, Husband—"

"Mouse. Thou wouldst not."

She sighed and stood, her hands linked palm to palm before her thighs. "If thou'lt not risk me, should I risk myself? I die of idleness, Will."

"Three children and a cottage are not enough housewifery for thee?"

She kilted her skirts up, standing first on one leg and then the other to wash the grime from her feet. Will watched her toes flex, the arch of each foot grip the floor. "I'll clean my hair tomorrow," she decided, and stepped around the bucket, leaving footprints like jewels on the boards. Her hands on her hips again, challenging, and the curve of her clever neck—

—Not so different than she'd been when they'd conspired to marry over family objections, all those years ago. He coughed into his hand.

"If thou wilt not tumble me," she said as she came to him, "wilt at least come to thy bed and comfort me with thine arms?"

He blew out the lamp and did as she asked, and pretended not to hear her weep. Until the small hours, when the noise from the street below grew slighter and she moved against him, mumbling into the dark. "I want a business, Will. If thou hast playmaking, then give me something other than—stitchery and child-chasing—to fill the hours."

"What wouldst thou?"

He felt her smile against his shoulder, and knew he was lost. "My lord husband. I could make thee a wealthy man—" A long pause, and shimmering wryness. "I want to buy land."

Which she could do only in his name and person. "With the income I send?"

"And mine own portion."

Her held breath stilled against his cheek, he considered. "Annie —" he said, and still heard no hiss of breath through her lips. "Send me what needst my mark," he said. "Mean old biddy."

"Stripling," she answered, and kissed his cheek above the beard, and he was sorry that was all.

Act II, scene vii

Can kingly Lions fawn on creeping Ants?

—CHRISTOPHER MARLOWE, *Edward II*

"Sweet Kit." Murchaud shook his head, black curls uncoiling across the silver-shot gray silk taffeta of his doublet. He reclined beside the fire, an octavo volume propped on his knee.

Kit looked up from the papers spread on his worktable and smiled through the candlelight, wary at Murchaud's tone.

"You must not weary yourself on the affairs of mortals, my love. It will bring sorrow."

Kit blotted his quill and laid it across the pen rest. Methodically, he sanded black words, setting the letter aside unfolded when he stood. "A command, Your Highness?"

Murchaud set his book aside and stretched on the divan, gesturing Kit closer, but Kit stood his ground.

"Nay, my lord."

"Kit."

"*Nay*, my lord." He scraped a bootheel across the flags and frowned, turning to look into the flames of the cross-bricked hearth. "Where has Morgan been?"

"What mean you?"

"I mean," Kit said, watching ash crumble at the edges of a cave among the embers that glowed cherry red as a dragon's eye, "she has not summoned me in—" *How long has it been?* He shrugged, running his tongue across the cleft in his upper lip and then frowning as he nibbled his mustache. "—some time."

Kit heard the Elf-knight stand, his almost-silent footsteps as he closed the distance on Kit's blind side. "She has a cottage where she flees the court. It lies behind yonder beech wood. I will see that she knows of your sorrow. There's worse to come."

"What mean you?"

The hesitation was long enough for Kit's gut to clench. "I'm leaving in five days. The Mebd sends me on diplomacy."

"Where?"

"I cannot say. But it will be hard for you; Morgan must keep her distance now, and you must seem alone while I am gone. It must seem she has tired of you. You've played this game before. She said she warned you."

Kit looked up. "That I might be needed for skills beyond poetry. Am I naught but a Queen's toy, Murchaud?"

The Elf-knight smiled. "Is that so terrible a thing to be? You courted Papists for your former Mistress. There are factions in Faerie that are not so fond of your new one, or the Queen. You'll be attractive to them."

"The ugliness of the intelligencer's lot," Kit said. "Win a man's trust. Become his friend. Whisper words of love in his ear as you slip in the knife. Catholicism is as excellent a *religion* as any, I suppose, so I have no reason to prefer Protestants to Catholics. Nor this Fae to that Fae, Murchaud."

"No," Murchaud answered, a gentle hand on his elbow. "But thou didst serve a Queen those Papists would have seen murdered, didst not?"

Kit turned back to the fire. "I did."

Murchaud bent close amid a scent of new-mown grass. "And now you serve another, whose enemies are also manifold. Shall you serve her less well?"

That other service, for all its blackness, I chose.

Kit sighed and nodded, and Murchaud draped an arm around his shoulders. The Prince's tone grew intimate. "You mourn your other life? You miss smoky, brutal London and its pox-riddled stews, its painted Ganymedes, and its starving pickpockets, soon to be hanged?"

"Should I not?"

"Ah, Kit." Warmth, yes, and pity. "You'll outlive it. Outlive all your loves and hates. 'Tis easier to lose it now, all of a piece, than by shreds and tatters."

". . . outlive it?" He turned and looked, despite himself, and caught Murchaud's expression as the Elf-knight reached to steady him. "Outlive the mortal world?"

"Faerie does not move as the iron world, and you'll not age here. How long did you think you had lingered here?" Earnest eyes, and dark brows drawn together.

"Hast been a year and more in England—two, three summers here—" Kit swallowed. His voice trailed off at the smile in Murchaud's eyes. "How long?"

"We mark by the tithe," Murchaud answered. "The teind we pay to Hell for their protection. Every sevenyear we draw lots, or a criminal may be chosen to go, or a changeling stolen—or, rarely, someone will volunteer. Which last pays the debt not for seven years, but for seven times seven—" He shook his head. "Tribute to our overlords."

Kit shivered. Murchaud hadn't answered the question. Kit tried to think back, to count summers and winters, flowerings and fallings. He looked down at his right hand, turned it to examine the tendons strung across the back, the calluses ridging his palm. *How long?*

He had no answer. "When's the tithe, then?"

"Hallow's eve. Always." Murchaud shook his head.

"Hallows eve here or in the mortal world?"

"Time here is an illusion," Murchaud answered. "In the mortal world: Hallow's eve, fifteen ninety-eight."

"Four years hence."

"Not so very long. Do not pine so for your lost life, Sir Kit. Set it aside, and do what you can to make yourself a stronger place in this court."

"You suggest I could be sent, if the Mebd does not value me? Although your mother claimed my service? Kit Marley in Hell—it has a certain symmetry."

"The Mebd values you," Murchaud says. "But she trusts her sister, my mother, not at all. Wert wise to make as many friends in court here as thou couldst, and let thine old friends glide past. The river of time will bear them to their end more quickly than you imagine."

"I—" Kit swallowed. "Soon enough, then, I shall be beyond that. Had I no loyalty, what would I be worth to *you?*"

"So be it," Murchaud said. "Bloody thyself on the bars of thy cage, but know thou canst not straddle the flood between that world and this forever."

"I did not choose this world."

"No. This world chose you. Live in it, or it will cut you deep, my love. You cannot go home again."

"Have I leave to help my friends?"

"I will not forbid it," Murchaud answered. "But by the love you bear me, pay more mind to courting your Queen."

Kit nodded, watching the flames. *He didn't tell me how long I've been here. How much time could I have lost?*

The answer brought cold, sinking in his belly. *In a Faerie Court, Marley? You could lose your whole life in a night—*

He frowned, and didn't think of the letter to Walsingham on his desk, with its icy, alien words about Edward de Vere. "As you wish." He turned his back on the fire and walked to the cupboard, taking his time in selecting his clothes.

"Where are you going?"

Kit looked up, fingers stilling on the ruched sleeve of a padded doublet. He turned over his shoulder, enough to see Murchaud clearly. "I must dress if I am to dine with the Queen."

"Sit at the low table," Murchaud told him. "We shall pretend at a falling out. I cannot come to you tonight. Or any night until I return from my travel."

"How long—?" But then the Elf-knight kissed him, long hands cradling Kit's face as if he cupped a rose in his palms, and Kit forgot to pursue the question, after. If *after* had any meaning here, at all.

Morgan's rooms, on the third level of the palace, opened onto the gallery over the glass-roofed Great Hall. Murchaud's were a level lower, in a side hall near the Mebd's chambers. But Kit's chamber was in the east wing, and to come to the main level he descended a spiral stair rather than the Great Stair, as he had on his first night. From there, he passed through a corridor to the atrium in all its tapestried magnificence.

He drew up before towering ebony doors. Knights in armor, as unmoving as suits on stands, guarded the portal on either side. He ignored them for a moment and studied the dark, coffered carving: intricate spirals and knotworks, fancifully interleaved. *And what is it you've been seeking these past seasons? A melancholy existence in exile? How . . . romantic.*

Murchaud had threaded the stem of a pansy through the pearl-sewn embroidery on Kit's doublet; its golden-eyed, plum-colored face nodded against the mallard's-head green of the velvet—the color Murchaud had insisted he wear. *No knight should do battle without a favor from his lover. Green and violet are the Mebd's colors,* he had said. *If ever you learned to court it in the mortal realm, use that now, and know you walk a line even finer than mine own.*

Kit licked his lips into a smile for the bravado of it and stepped forward. The doors swung open smoothly, and he entered the great, galleried hall with its thousand torches burning with a golden, unholy light. The room was silent but for the faint, plucked twang of an un-tuned string: the bard Cairbre straightened over his lute and looked up at the swing of the door. He was alone in the Great Hall.

Kit was early.

So much for bravado. He laughed at himself and walked between the parallel trestles stretching the length of the hall. No fires burned at the hearths, and the high table sat on its dais swathed in silk that picked up the damasked colors of the marble tiles under Kit's boots. "Good even, Master Harper."

"And to you, Sir Christofer." The bard made as if to stand, reaching out to set his instrument aside, and Kit gestured him back onto his stool. "Come out of your self-exile after all?"

"There's only so long a man can take to his bed."

Cairbre's eyes flickered to his breast—*the blossom?*—and the bard frowned. "As you say. Will you grace us with a poem tonight?"

It wasn't a question Kit knew how to answer. He folded his right arm over his left and shrugged, silent until Cairbre took pity and tilted his chin to indicate the little stage, its assortment of harpsichord, gitar, lute, and archaic-looking instruments that Kit barely recognized. "Do you play?"

"Viola a little, though I am sadly out of practice."

"Every gentleman should know an instrument." Cairbre did stand then, his patch-worked cloak of multicolored tatters falling about him as he bent to pull a cased instrument from a cloth-draped stand. The bells on his epaulets rang sweetly as he laid it on the stool. "I have a viola here—" He chuckled, and indicated Kit's boutonniere with a flick of his fingers. "To match the one at your breast."

Kit laughed. "I'd only embarrass myself—"

"Nonsense." Cairbre's calloused thumbs stroked the clasps on the leather case, expertly flicking them open. "After the masque you gave us for Beltane—"

Masques. Silly things. "What's that to do with music?"

Cairbre shrugged broad shoulders, tucking a strand of hair behind an ear pointed like a leaf. His merry eyes fixed on Kit's face, and he smiled through a tidy black beard. "What has anything to do with music? We fools and poets must hang together— ah. Master Puck! Speak of the Devil."

Kit turned. Robin Goodfellow ducked under the high table and hopped down from the dais, twirling a bauble in time to the bobbing of his ears. "Devils for dinner? Not tonight, but mayhap on another. Do you like yours roasted, or baked?"

"My devils, or my soul?"

"Why, Sit Kit," the Puck said. "Do you have a soul? I'd think you half fey already, and as soul-less as any of us."

"Soulless?" Kit glanced over his shoulder at Cairbre, who opened the case and slowly folded back the layers of velvet and silk swaddling the viola.

"Soulless, aye," he answered, unconcerned. "As all Fae are. 'Tis the source of our power: Heaven has no hold over us, and Hell only the power we grant it. Our immortality is of the flesh. While your sort"—a dismissive gesture—"bloody yourselves over who has the right to interpret the will of *that* one, and worry at his will choosing those who govern you." A curt gesture of his chin upward; Fae, he couldn't say the Name.

If Heaven has no hold on you, why do you fear God's name? Instead, Kit said: "And who governs you?"

"Those that can. Go ahead and pick it up, Sir Christofer." Cairbre stepped away from the case, swinging his tattered cloak over his arm.

Kit stroked the cherry-dark neck. "I'm really not—" But his fingers slipped around the wood and lifted the beautiful instrument from its crimson bed. The varnish glowed in the torchlight, a rich auburn a master would have despaired of capturing in oils. "I've never *touched* something like that," he breathed, as if it were alive in his hands and might spread wings and spiral up into the vast galleried chamber, lost.

"It should be in tune."

Kit looked from Cairbre to Robin—whose ears waggled in amusement—and raised an eyebrow, but he took the rosined bow when Cairbre held it out, inhaling the dusty-sweet pine scent until he fought a sneeze. He closed his eye, settled the viola, raised the bow—

—and fluffed the third note. "I warned you."

"Lessons," Cairbre decided, and took the bow away. "Come. You'll give us a poem tonight, won't you?"

"Yes," Kit answered. "I'll give you a poem."

He expected they'd wait for Murchaud's departure, whoever *they* might be, but perhaps not too much longer. But that first night, as he sat sharing a trencher with Robin Goodfellow below the cloth of estate, he was bemused by the strangeness that filled him. In another setting he might have called the feeling *fey*: *back to what I was, when I was little more than a boy and full of myself and my secrets.*

Puck sat at Kit's right, on his blind side, and saw he ate, though his appetite forsook him in Murchaud's absence. Halfway through the meal, Kit realized the little elf had deserted his own place at the high table to stay with him.

Kit imagined he looked strange as a swan among magpies beside the lesser Fae. The Daoine Sidhe—the Tuatha de Danaan as they were called—claimed descent of the Old Gods of hill and dale, of moor and copse and ocean. A Church scholar might have said the blood in their veins was that of demons, not deities. Kit had long past given up his illusions that God kept his house in a church. Their sea-changing eyes and leaf-tipped ears marked them as something other than human, and their wincing aversion to the Name of the Divine might be evidence. But then, what god would abide the Name of his supplanter?

But they did, in broad, look *human*.

The elder, stranger Fae did not. Though they sometimes dined at the Mebd's table, served delicacies by brownies and sprites, and though many of them served in her palace, they were not Tuatha de Danaan, not Daoine Sidhe. And they were as strange now as ever they had been on Kit's first lonely walk into the throne room that lurked behind the second closed pair of doors.

Across the table rested a lovely maid-in-waiting whose forked tongue brushed the scent from each morsel she tasted before she lifted it to her mouth. On his left, a creature more wizened than even Robin crouched on the edge of the table and ate between his knees. Kit stifled a chuckle, thinking what his own mother would have said about boots on the table, and turned to murmur something in Robin's ear. A polite hiss from the scaly young lady across the table interrupted.

"Sir Christofer?"

Thread-fine snakes writhed like windblown curls about her temples. Her eyes were as flat and reflective as steel, the pupils horizontal bars. "Mistress—"

"Amaranth." It might have been a smile. Her lips were red and full, a cupid's bow disturbing behind the glitter of scales like powdered gold rubbed on her skin. Her hand darted with a swiftness that should not have surprised him, brushing the flower on his doublet before he could jerk back. "Does it not shame you to wear the love-in-idleness?"

There is more here than I understand. Remembering Cairbre's comment, and how Morgan and Murchaud had both adorned him with the blossoms. "Love-in-idleness?"

"Heartsease," she said, while Puck pretended not to hear. "The pansy or viola."

He pulled his bread apart in tidbits, setting the balance of it beside the trencher while he buttered a morsel, covering his confusion with concentration on the knife. It seemed dry as paste; he would never have choked it down without wine. "It pleases my lady, Mistress Amaranth."

The lamia's hair hissed again. He thought it was a chuckle. "Then she is cruel, is she? I am not surprised at that."

"Not so cruel as that."

"Cruel enough," she said, gesturing for a footman to lay a bloody slice of roast upon her plate.

"Kind as any woman," he answered. Amaranth's cold eyes widened; the Puck snorted. Kit toasted Amaranth, wondering what moved him to defend Morgan for all her late absence from the hall, and his bed. But his gaze traveled past the serpent, up to the dais and to Murchaud sitting near Cairbre, at what would have been the Mebd's right hand if the Mebd were there.

Even across that distance, the look Murchaud returned pressed Kit back as physically as a thumb in the notch of his collarbone. He reached for his wine, feeling as if he choked. *And now I truly am alone. Until he returns. Or until Morgan claims me. In deep deception, and in the hands of the enemy.*

He held the Elf-knight's withering glance until it seemed the whole room must have noticed. Until conversation flagged around him and Amaranth herself turned to follow the course of his one-eyed stare, then leaned aside as if she would not break the strung tension.

Murchaud looked down first, turning to laugh nastily at some comment whispered by the Mebd's advisor, stag-horned old Peaseblossom. Kit watched a moment longer, then dropped his eye to his dinner and haggled off a bit of roast as if he could bear to put it in his mouth.

"What's love-in-idleness?" Kit murmured, bringing his lips close to Puck's twitching ear.

"What you wear on your bosom," the Puck answered dryly. "That thing on your sleeve is your heart."

When Kit stood to give his poem—on Cairbre's signal—he chose something that spoke of the pastoral delights of summertime and never a chance of sorrow. But when he returned to his rooms after dinner, he worried an iron nail loose from his old riding boots, and slipped it into the sleeve pocket of his doublet, and felt just a little better for it.

Sweet Romeo:

    I apologize for the vagaries of my correspondence. My new masters it seems do not approve entirely that I maintain my friendships from service taken before but in this cause I am defiant. That I am your true friend do not doubt. I thank you for the word of little Mary & her nestling, that they are well.

    I will watch over you as my ability permits, & your letters (& those of FW) relating the situation in London fall most welcomely into my grateful hands. There is some change in my circumstances, not serious of yet but prone to developments, in which case you might say I am at mine old works again, & there are revelations that may suspend correspondence.

    These circumstances include the following: that I have been unfair in my judgement of TW, & rather those charges should have been levied at that abominable bastard in the peascod doublet he no doubt imagines conceals his paunch, you will know of whom I refer. Also, it is with sorrow that I must relate that he who I have considered your greatest ally (again you will know) is gravely ill. I have not managed a visit, or more than a word & a note, but I believe that the poison administered these four years since is at work again, & I do not think my dear friend will last through the winter in the lack of Doctor Lopez's care. This places you in graver danger than I can express. It is imperative that Peascod-doublet not learn we know of his duplicity.

    Her Majesty, as you know though it were sedition to speak it, grows in melancholy with the passing of each old friend & each treasured counselor. I cannot imagine that to lose mine old master will lie easy on her, for all their difficulties after the death of Mary Queen of Scots, & you must know it will make her more open to Essex & his machinations: the patron "they" have sought for you, Southampton, is useful as a link to Essex. There are rumors — but I am sure the conclusion lies within your powers.

    FW's illness means also we must find another path of correspondence. Will you have a looking glass placed in your chambers? Steelbacked is best for these purposes though flawed at reflecting, & less dear than silver.

    I pine without your company.

~~Should you speak to the younger Walsingham~~ Enclosed please find some verse I thought amusing.

I remain your true lover & truer friend—

—Mercutio

Post script: Amusing to put the speech on Queen Mab in the poor lad's mouth, then have him stabbed under his friend's arm. I wish Tricky Tom Watson were alive to see: he so would laugh. It reminds me of the time Will Bradley would have had my head if Tom hadn't got his blade between us, as I am sure you intended it to. Poor William should have known better than to start a quarrel with a poet; we travel, like starveling dogs, in packs. It saddens me to think now that all three of us who fought that night are dead.

Your loyalty warms me in a colder world than my words or yours could express, but you must have caution in these things, for all it flatters me to be remembered.

Dearest Mercutio,

London continues much of the same. Recusants and moneylenders pilloried in the north square, RB after me to pen more plays though I have given him four this year already. And I have spoken with FW, who is yes gravely ill and failing. He says he also had word from you that his cousin is genuine, and the peer you dub Peascod-doublet more truly the villain. I should tell you that TW spoke with me concerning you and I and the craft of playmending some time back. I gave him nothing then. In the light of new intelligence, is it your estimation that he may be trusted?

I asked RB to consider that slanders leveled against your name may source themselves in EDV. He thinks rather they come from Gloriana, though why she might wish your name blackened I know not.

MP and her son are well indeed, and under my care.

A story is making the rounds at the Mermaid that a half-dozen sober Londoners witnessed the blood-soaked ghost of Kit Marley on a Cheapside street in the rain this summer, prophesying doom on those who murdered him. The better versions of the story have lightning dancing around the ghost's shoulders like a cloak, a naked sword in its hand, and a whining Robert Poley cringing at its feet.

Of course, no one believes it. Where would you find six sober Londoners all at once?

There are a few stories the sober Londoners tell of EDV as well. I asked RB of the Spanish choirboy he's rumored to have imported, and RB assured me it was basest slander. The choirboy was Italian. Horatio something.

I suppose that's one way to stick it to the Papists.

Your true —
Romeo.

Act II, scene viii

Orlando: My fair Rosalind, I come within an hour of my promise.
Rosalind: Break an hour's promise in love! He that will divide a min-
ute into a thousand parts, and break but a part of the thousandth part
of a minute in the affairs of love, it may be said of him that Cupid
hath clapped him o'the shoulder, but I'll warrant him heart-whole.

—WILLIAM SHAKESPEARE, *As You Like It*

W ill stepped down from a hired coach weary, bruised to the bone, sorely afflicted with chilblains, and nibbled by fleas. He'd fallen uneasily half asleep with his fingers protruding from under a carriage robe clutched to his chin. He worked them now, trying to bring sensation to cold-chapped skin.

The coachman liberated his luggage and slid it down beside the wheels; the ground was too frozen for the trunk to be damaged by mud. The tired bay snorted. Will skirted the horse nervously, and caught one end handle on the trunk to drag it toward the cottage with its close-thatched roof. He closed his eyes, smelling kindled fire and baking bread, and stopped himself a half gesture before he rapped on his own front door.

Instead he breathed deep, then pulled the latch-cord and shoul-

They floundered through a snowdrift and into a deserted pasturage, Will half a step behind the boy. "Run, bear cub! The hounds are on you!"

Hamnet turned at bay against a hurdle, and Will drew up. "I'm Sackerson," the boy growled. "The strongest bear in Britain! I'll eat up any hound that comes after me!"

Will laughed and crouched down, hands spread, watching his boy coil to leap at him. That Hamnet would trust Will to catch him cracked his grin to show his teeth in more than mockery of a hunting dog's snarl.

"Hounds are smarter than bears—" He gasped as *something* took him, as if the snowy grass under his feet were yanked like a carpet, and he found himself flat on his back with Hamnet crouched over him, small fists clenched on the neck of his jerkin, roaring triumphantly. "Lad—" Will coughed. "Off!"

Hamnet jumped back, and suddenly Edmund's hands were on him, the Yule log abandoned in the lane, a worried brother brushing snow from his collar and hair, pulling him to his feet. "What happened?"

"Fell," Will said, and shoved his right hand into the slit in his jerkin and the pocket beneath so Edmund wouldn't see it shake. He wouldn't say more in front of Hamnet, but Edmund's lips pursed and he kept a hand on Will's elbow until they were back in the lane, and did the lion's share of the drawing.

Another half-hour's labor brought them through the festive streets of Stratford to the front door of Will's childhood home. Edmund pushed the door open to the parlor where the great bed stood, halloing unnecessarily as the whole family—Joan; her husband, Will; Gilbert; Richard—and guests turned with applause. The rich smell of brawn roasting and bread baking, of mince pie and fruit pie and plum porridge, was almost as sustaining as food itself. There would be no cold pottage in the Shakespeare house tonight. In the hall, where the hearth roared in readiness for their burden, some of the guests were playing at snapdragon, picking raisins from a bowl of flaming brandy. Will saw one man dressed in almost Puritan severity quench scorched fingers in his mouth.

Will dropped the traces and kicked snow from his boots against the threshold before stepping over onto rushes scattering the blue

dered the green-painted portal open, letting his trunk bump over the threshold. "Annie?"

She straightened and turned to him, aproned and dressed in good gray woolen, leather shoes on her stockinged feet against the winter chill of the rush-strewn floor, her befloured hands spread wide. "Will."

She stepped closer. Will kicked the door shut and bumped it with his heel to make certain of the latch. Leaving his trunk half blocking the threshold, he met her halfway between the door and the table and caught her wrists, holding her whitened hands back when he kissed her mouth. She giggled like a girl. He wiped flour off his cheek when he stepped away.

"I've a rental house for you to look at—"

"Annie, let a man get his boots off," he protested, and she laughed again. "I'm famous, wife. *Romeo and Juliet*. Dost care?"

"I'll read your plays," she said stolidly, turning to wash her hands, "when they bring you home again."

He came and poured the water for her so she would not beflour the ewer, and watched her hands tumble over each other like courting birds. "The bread smells wonderful."

"Wonderful enough to wake the children, do you suppose?" She glanced at him sideways, drying her hands on her apron.

"Still slugabed?" He smiled, looking up at the loft. "Did you tell them I was coming?"

"I—" She stopped. "I didn't want to disappoint them."

"Ah." The sour taste was no more than a night spent in the Davenant's Inn before resuming his coach seat to finish this journey. He nudged his trunk out of the doorway, pushing up a thin ridge of rush stems. Annie's eyes were on him, kinder than he had any right to. "Do you think I can get Hamnet down here over my shoulder before he wakes, the way I used to?"

"He's bigger than you remember—Will! Be careful. . . ."

But he was already halfway up the ladder, and turned to press a silencing finger to his lips. "At least let me try."

Annie laced her fingers behind her backside, half turned her head, and smiled and sighed as if they were a single gesture. But she held her tongue, and Will resumed his climb.

Soft morning sunlight from a casement under the eave filled the loft, the air cold enough that Will's breath steamed in coils. Will cat-footed to bedsteads ranged side by side along the left-hand wall; the wider held a pair of sweetly snoring lumps and the narrower only one. He paused, a few steps away from the children, and breathed their rich, sleeping scent. It made him lightheaded, as if he were breathing in the pale gold winter sunshine, filled up until he in-flated, buoyed, floating forward to unearth his son from quilts and comforters and the featherbed covering the rustling straw-filled tick.

Hamnet slept with his thumb in his mouth, knees drawn up, hips tucked forward, body turned fully at the waist so that his opposite shoulder was in contact with the featherbed. Golden eyelashes flut-tered against the boy's rosy cheeks as Will moved to block the square of sunlight dappling his face, dust motes flitting between them like atomies.

Will crouched, dislodging Hamnet's thumb gently, and with both hands picked up his sleeping son. He flopped the boy's slack warm arms around his neck and cradled him close. He squatted on the edge of the girls' bed, then, and leaned Hamnet's still-towheaded curls against his shoulder as he tugged the coverlet down.

Susanna lay with her arms widespread as if embracing the morn-ing, Judith's brown head resting on the soft part of her shoulder. The younger girl coiled around a pillow possessively, her braid snaking across her sister's breast.

Susanna's eyes flicked open when the light brushed her face, but Judith cuddled closer to her pillow and mumbled. And then Susanna's hazel eyes went wide, and as Will saw her draw breath to shriek in delight he put his finger to his lips. She choked on it, clapped her hand over her mouth, and giggled.

Will pointed to the ladder and to Judith, and Susanna nodded and reached to shake her sister awake.

He actually got Hamnet halfway down—to Anne's stifled laughter—before the boy squirmed awake and blinked sleepily through the tangled blond curls. And then Hamnet *did* squeal, and cling, while the girls laughed over the edge of the loft.

———

Will propped his feet on the bench before the fire while Susanna showed Judith how to sew the braids of ivy into swags to hang over the windows and the door, and Hamnet stole fallen leaves with which to tease Anne's calico cat. The cat, fat with winter mousing, purred and flattened her whiskers smugly, but she couldn't be bothered to extend a claw after the leaves.

Will, watching, covered his mouth and smiled into his sleeve. Still weary with the brutal coach ride, he must have dozed before the fire, because a knock on the door startled him awake. "That will be your brother Edmund," Anne said, crossing in a sweep of skirts. "He's come to take Hamnet to fetch the Yule log—"

"Uncle Edmund!" The boy bounced up even as Will dropped his feet on the floor. His youngest brother—a mere twice seven years—shook snow off his cloak and hefted an axe. "Ready to go out and slog through the snow with the men, puppy— Will!"

"Ted." Will stood, a broad grin stretching his cheeks. "You've grown."

"You're home." Edmund looked him up and down. He was al-ready almost Will's height, and his shoulders half filled the doorway. "Well, get your boots on, then."

Hamnet bounced on his toes. Will looked at Annie. Annie didn't quite nod—that would have been too much like permission—but she smiled. "Bring more ivy if you find it, or bay," she said. "Christmas eve supper shall be at your father's house; the girls and I will meet you. I promised to help cook."

The sun turned the western horizon to flame-colored taffeta while the three of them—Hamnet, Edmund, and Will—leaned into the traces and sledged an enormous log through ankle-deep snow. Or, in fair-ness, Will and Edmund sledged. Hamnet ran rings around them, the winter sunlight glimmering on his hair—now a hare, now a hound, now—"Uncle Edmund, look!"—a lumbering bear.

Edmund looked, and laughed, and Will looked at Edmund and understood, with a moment of bitterness he didn't deserve, who was raising his son. Will covered the hurt with a player's smile, and caught Edmund's eye before he ducked under the traces to chase his bear-cub down the lane, growling like a hound.

limestone floor. He and Edmund dragged the log in with Hamnet's interference. Then Will left it to his brother's labor, turning away from the precipitous stair on the left and into the hall, with its walls hung in holly and painted cloth. He could hear Hamnet and Edmund untying the Yule log, and he realized suddenly that they'd forgotten the ivy—or bay—and then his father's arms were around him, John Shakespeare stumping forward on a bentwood cane and wrapping his oldest son in palsied arms, leaning as much as embracing, clinging to his boy gone to London and mouthing words about Will come home in velvet and silk taffeta like a fine gentleman. His father's words were slurred, one running into the other, and Will knew from the stern, proud look on his mother Mary's face that he was not to remark on it.

The cousins close and distant huddled in a room hot with their bodies and the leaping flames of the hearth, among them men and women Will had never seen.

"Bring it in, bring it in," John Shakespeare said. "The feast is upon us."

Mary waited for her husband to step back before she came forward and looked up at Will. Her eyes were blue: she had the aristocratic cheekbones and the high brow she'd willed to all her children, the living and the dead. Will saw her noticing the snow and the earth staining his cloak and the knees of his breeches, but she met his eyes and held out a tankard of mulled cider, and only smiled. "Welcome home, Will."

"Mother," he said, and took the wine, searching the crowd for Annie and Susanna. Judith would be with the younger children. "God bless you."

Her kiss was roses and homecoming, and he let it drive the memory of balance lost and a lurch into a snowdrift away.

"How is Father?" An undertone, mumbled around his cider.

"Not much worse," she said, and shrugged. "And you?"

"My plays have been performed before the Queen," he answered, as he had imagined himself answering, and accepted her gasp and smile and delighted outcry as his due.

Annie found him before he finished the cider, and drew him through a low timbered archway into the crowded hall by a warm arm around his waist. "The brawn is almost ready," she said.

He breathed deep: cloves and crackling and the rich aroma of roasting pork. "Annie," he said. "Something happened today—"

"Not to Hamnet?" She crouched by the fire in the big bricked hearth, tucking her skirts in close as she ladled dripping over the roast. She wore neither bumroll nor farthingale, but a broad country skirt under her apron, and Will bit his tongue at the way those skirts draped between her haunches. Three children, and still—

"I fell," he said. "I think—"

"Fell?" She set the battered copper ladle aside and stood, turned, frowning. She took his wrists and drew his hands forward, glowering down at them—broad knuckles, long fingers, the last digit of the middle finger on the right one calloused on the inner edge and warped sideways from the pressure of the quill. The right one—

—trembled. "Oh, Will."

"Years yet," he said. "I swear I'll come home to you—"

"Broken and old so I can nurse thee through thy dotage? What good will you be to me then?" Her voice low, the bitterness hidden under the commonplace tone of wife to husband. "Pray it pass Hamnet by—"

"Annie, hush you. I—"

"There's a priest here tonight," she said suddenly, interrupting. "For Christ's birth. After the neighbors leave, there will be a midnight Mass."

A priest. She meant *a Catholic priest.*

A Catholic Mass.

A hanging affair.

Will swallowed dryness. "Annie, you must not tell me such things—"

"—Will—" *You were raised to it.* He knew.

He met her pale eyes and shook his head, tasting salt and sour like a reminder. "Anne. Wife. I'm a Queen's Man now. Do you know what that is?"

She shook her head. *No.* He drew a stool out from the table and sat, gesturing her to the bench. "Hast ever seen a Tyburn hanging, Annie?"

She blanched. "No." Not seen, perhaps. But heard.

"It is as well." *If I have my will,* he thought, *you never shall see one. Especially mine.* "I'll take Judith and Hamnet home after supper," he said. "You and Susanna may stay."

She did not argue.

Act II, scene ix

Fourscore is but a girl's age, love is sweet:—
My veins are withered, and my sinews dry,
Why do I think of love now I should die?

—CHRISTOPHER MARLOWE, *Dido, Queen of Carthage*

In the ten days or fortnight it took for Kit to sort out the social order of the low tables, he learned many things that had escaped his notice when he sat by Murchaud's side. The talk was freer, although his—Kit's—presence was greeted with sidelong glances at first. But when Murchaud left court, and Morgan was not seen, and Kit traded his green and violet and silver for the black velvet he truthfully preferred, the conversation flowed more free. Especially as he was seen in the company of the Mebd's Bard and her Puck, or sitting alone.

He couldn't bear the silence of his rooms, and spent long hours walking in the beech wood or along the strand, practicing music poorly with Cairbre or reading in the library. Kit had Latin, Greek, fair French, and slight German, yet he found them inadequate to the books and scrolls and stories there. The lamia Amaranth found him puzzling over books in strange languages, and with her dapple-scaled tail coiled between chair legs and occasionally, unsettlingly, brushing his calf, she set about to teach him the backward writings of Hebrews (which informed Kit of the names of three of the five symbols Baines and his friends had burned into his flesh: *mem*, *he*, and *lamel*) and Mohammadans, and the brush-sketched characters of far Cathay. Although her smile was cool and she would not answer questions about herself, Kit thought she courted him.

He permitted it, expecting her purpose to be revealed hesitantly, but before too long. Wrong again: her silence and amusement remained, counterpointed by her flickering tongue.

And so he continued, restless and—although often in company— alone. His thoughts were clearer now that he had a goal, but the passive means of accomplishing it—and his lack of success as bait— flustered him. More unsettling, it wasn't any easier to keep track of the days when he was focused on it. He went so far as to carve notches in a candle, and stopped when he began to realize that the number of notches *changed*.

As his head cleared further, though, the craving in his belly grew. He had to talk to Morgan. Jilted lover or no.

Of course, a jilted lover might be expected to wish to speak to her. If not too often. And I am tired of being treated as a pet.

He frowned, thinking that he would not trust himself with matters of import, as mooncalf as he had been.

Hell, I can ask her about love-in-idleness, too. And why Amaranth said she was cruel.

Kit dressed—as Will would have it—like a cobbler's son: a shirt of cambric, a leather jerkin, and brown wool breeches. He slipped the iron bootnail from the pocket of the doublet he had been wearing and was about to drop it into a lacquer box on the stand beside his bed when he hesitated. He could almost fancy the sound of a cobbler's hammer, familiar from childhood, and smiled for a moment at the memory of his father with a mouth full of tacks just like this one. It might have been the scent of leather, or the way the light caught on the worn surface of the nail, but he suddenly couldn't bear to set it aside. He slipped it into his purse and let it clink against coins he'd had no occasion to spend. *Here is the palace, and the court. But there is no Faerie city. No tradesman, no farmlands, no ports for ships trading the wide and wandering sea . . .*

How strange. And then Kit smiled, because there was a lyric in it.

dered the green-painted portal open, letting his trunk bump over the
threshold. "Annie?"

She straightened and turned to him, aproned and dressed in good
gray woolen, leather shoes on her stockinged feet against the winter chill
of the rush-strewn floor, her befloured hands spread wide. "Will."

She stepped closer. Will kicked the door shut and bumped it with
his heel to make certain of the latch. Leaving his trunk half blocking
the threshold, he met her halfway between the door and the table and
caught her wrists, holding her whitened hands back when he kissed
her mouth. She giggled like a girl. He wiped flour off his cheek when
he stepped away.

"I've a rental house for you to look at—"

"Annie, let a man get his boots off," he protested, and she laughed
again. "I'm famous, wife. *Romeo and Juliet*. Dost care?"

"I'll read your plays," she said stolidly, turning to wash her hands,
"when they bring you home again."

He came and poured the water for her so she would not beflour
the ewer, and watched her hands tumble over each other like courting
birds. "The bread smells wonderful."

"Wonderful enough to wake the children, do you suppose?" She
glanced at him sideways, drying her hands on her apron.

"Still slugabed?" He smiled, looking up at the loft. "Did you tell
them I was coming?"

"I—" She stopped. "I didn't want to disappoint them."

"Ah." The sour taste was no more than a night spent in the Davenant's Inn before resuming his coach seat to finish this journey. He
nudged his trunk out of the doorway, pushing up a thin ridge of rush
stems. Annie's eyes were on him, kinder than he had any right to. "Do
you think I can get Hamnet down here over my shoulder before he
wakes, the way I used to?"

"He's bigger than you remember—Will! Be careful. . . ."

But he was already halfway up the ladder, and turned to press a
silencing finger to his lips. "At least let me try."

Annie laced her fingers behind her backside, half turned her head,
and smiled and sighed as if they were a single gesture. But she held her
tongue, and Will resumed his climb.

Soft morning sunlight from a casement under the eave filled the loft, the air cold enough that Will's breath steamed in coils. Will cat-footed to bedsteads ranged side by side along the left-hand wall; the wider held a pair of sweetly snoring lumps and the narrower only one. He paused, a few steps away from the children, and breathed their rich, sleeping scent. It made him lightheaded, as if he were breathing in the pale gold winter sunshine, filled up until he in-flated, buoyed, floating forward to unearth his son from quilts and comforters and the featherbed covering the rustling straw-filled tick.

Hamnet slept with his thumb in his mouth, knees drawn up, hips tucked forward, body turned fully at the waist so that his opposite shoulder was in contact with the featherbed. Golden eyelashes flut-tered against the boy's rosy cheeks as Will moved to block the square of sunlight dappling his face, dust motes flitting between them like atomies.

Will crouched, dislodging Hamnet's thumb gently, and with both hands picked up his sleeping son. He flopped the boy's slack warm arms around his neck and cradled him close. He squatted on the edge of the girls' bed, then, and leaned Hamnet's still-towheaded curls against his shoulder as he tugged the coverlet down.

Susanna lay with her arms widespread as if embracing the morn-ing, Judith's brown head resting on the soft part of her shoulder. The younger girl coiled around a pillow possessively, her braid snaking across her sister's breast.

Susanna's eyes flicked open when the light brushed her face, but Judith cuddled closer to her pillow and mumbled. And then Susanna's hazel eyes went wide, and as Will saw her draw breath to shriek in delight he put his finger to his lips. She choked on it, clapped her hand over her mouth, and giggled.

Will pointed to the ladder and to Judith, and Susanna nodded and reached to shake her sister awake.

He actually got Hamnet halfway down—to Anne's stifled laughter—before the boy squirmed awake and blinked sleepily through the tangled blond curls. And then Hamnet *did* squeal, and cling, while the girls laughed over the edge of the loft.

Will propped his feet on the bench before the fire while Susanna showed Judith how to sew the braids of ivy into swags to hang over the windows and the door, and Hamnet stole fallen leaves with which to tease Anne's calico cat. The cat, fat with winter mousing, purred and flattened her whiskers smugly, but she couldn't be bothered to extend a claw after the leaves.

Will, watching, covered his mouth and smiled into his sleeve. Still weary with the brutal coach ride, he must have dozed before the fire, because a knock on the door startled him awake. "That will be your brother Edmund," Anne said, crossing in a sweep of skirts. "He's come to take Hamnet to fetch the Yule log—"

"Uncle Edmund!" The boy bounced up even as Will dropped his feet on the floor. His youngest brother—a mere twice seven years— shook snow off his cloak and hefted an axe. "Ready to go out and slog through the snow with the men, puppy— Will!"

"Ted." Will stood, a broad grin stretching his cheeks. "You've grown."

"You're home." Edmund looked him up and down. He was already almost Will's height, and his shoulders half filled the doorway. "Well, get your boots on, then."

Hamnet bounced on his toes. Will looked at Annie. Annie didn't quite nod—that would have been too much like permission— but she smiled. "Bring more ivy if you find it, or bay," she said. "Christmas eve supper shall be at your father's house; the girls and I will meet you. I promised to help cook."

The sun turned the western horizon to flame-colored taffeta while the three of them—Hamnet, Edmund, and Will—leaned into the traces and sledged an enormous log through ankle-deep snow. Or, in fairness, Will and Edmund sledged. Hamnet ran rings around them, the winter sunlight glimmering on his hair—now a hare, now a hound, now—"Uncle Edmund, look!"—a lumbering bear.

Edmund looked, and laughed, and Will looked at Edmund and understood, with a moment of bitterness he didn't deserve, who was raising his son. Will covered the hurt with a player's smile, and caught Edmund's eye before he ducked under the traces to chase his bear-cub down the lane, growling like a hound.

They floundered through a snowdrift and into a deserted pastur-age, Will half a step behind the boy. "Run, bear cub! The hounds are on you!"

Hamnet turned at bay against a hurdle, and Will drew up. "I'm Sackerson," the boy growled. "The strongest bear in Britain! I'll eat up any hound that comes after me!"

Will laughed and crouched down, hands spread, watching his boy coil to leap at him. That Hamnet would trust Will to catch him cracked his grin to show his teeth in more than mockery of a hunting dog's snarl.

"Hounds are smarter than bears—" He gasped as *something* took him, as if the snowy grass under his feet were yanked like a carpet, and he found himself flat on his back with Hamnet crouched over him, small fists clenched on the neck of his jerkin, roaring triumphantly. "Lad—" Will coughed. "Off!"

Hamnet jumped back, and suddenly Edmund's hands were on him, the Yule log abandoned in the lane, a worried brother brushing snow from his collar and hair, pulling him to his feet. "What happened?"

"Fell," Will said, and shoved his right hand into the slit in his jerkin and the pocket beneath so Edmund wouldn't see it shake. He wouldn't say more in front of Hamnet, but Edmund's lips pursed and he kept a hand on Will's elbow until they were back in the lane, and did the lion's share of the drawing.

Another half-hour's labor brought them through the festive streets of Stratford to the front door of Will's childhood home. Edmund pushed the door open to the parlor where the great bed stood, hal-loing unnecessarily as the whole family—Joan; her husband, Will; Gilbert; Richard—and guests turned with applause. The rich smell of brawn roasting and bread baking, of mince pie and fruit pie and plum porridge, was almost as sustaining as food itself. There would be no cold pottage in the Shakespeare house tonight. In the hall, where the hearth roared in readiness for their burden, some of the guests were playing at snapdragon, picking raisins from a bowl of flaming brandy. Will saw one man dressed in almost Puritan severity quench scorched fingers in his mouth.

Will dropped the traces and kicked snow from his boots against the threshold before stepping over onto rushes scattering the blue limestone floor. He and Edmund dragged the log in with Hamnet's interference. Then Will left it to his brother's labor, turning away from the precipitous stair on the left and into the hall, with its walls hung in holly and painted cloth. He could hear Hamnet and Edmund untying the Yule log, and he realized suddenly that they'd forgotten the ivy — or bay — and then his father's arms were around him, John Shakespeare stumping forward on a bentwood cane and wrapping his oldest son in palsied arms, leaning as much as embracing, clinging to his boy gone to London and mouthing words about Will come home in velvet and silk taffeta like a fine gentleman. His father's words were slurred, one running into the other, and Will knew from the stern, proud look on his mother Mary's face that he was not to remark on it.

The cousins close and distant huddled in a room hot with their bodies and the leaping flames of the hearth, among them men and women Will had never seen.

"Bring it in, bring it in," John Shakespeare said. "The feast is upon us."

Mary waited for her husband to step back before she came forward and looked up at Will. Her eyes were blue: she had the aristocratic cheekbones and the high brow she'd willed to all her children, the living and the dead. Will saw her noticing the snow and the earth staining his cloak and the knees of his breeches, but she met his eyes and held out a tankard of mulled cider, and only smiled. "Welcome home, Will."

"Mother," he said, and took the wine, searching the crowd for Annie and Susanna. Judith would be with the younger children. "God bless you."

Her kiss was roses and homecoming, and he let it drive the memory of balance lost and a lurch into a snowdrift away.

"How is Father?" An undertone, mumbled around his cider.

"Not much worse," she said, and shrugged. "And you?"

"My plays have been performed before the Queen," he answered, as he had imagined himself answering, and accepted her gasp and smile and delighted outcry as his due.

Annie found him before he finished the cider, and drew him through a low timbered archway into the crowded hall by a warm arm around his waist. "The brawn is almost ready," she said.

He breathed deep: cloves and crackling and the rich aroma of roasting pork. "Annie," he said. "Something happened today—"

"Not to Hamnet?" She crouched by the fire in the big bricked hearth, tucking her skirts in close as she ladled dripping over the roast. She wore neither bumroll nor farthingale, but a broad country skirt under her apron, and Will bit his tongue at the way those skirts draped between her haunches. Three children, and still—

"I fell," he said. "I think—"

"Fell?" She set the battered copper ladle aside and stood, turned, frowning. She took his wrists and drew his hands forward, glowering down at them—broad knuckles, long fingers, the last digit of the middle finger on the right one calloused on the inner edge and warped sideways from the pressure of the quill. The right one—

—trembled. "Oh, Will."

"Years yet," he said. "I swear I'll come home to you—"

"Broken and old so I can nurse thee through thy dotage? What good will you be to me then?" Her voice low, the bitterness hidden under the commonplace tone of wife to husband. "Pray it pass Hamnet by—"

"Annie, hush you. I—"

"There's a priest here tonight," she said suddenly, interrupting. "For Christ's birth. After the neighbors leave, there will be a midnight Mass."

A priest. She meant *a Catholic priest.*

A Catholic Mass.

A hanging affair.

Will swallowed dryness. "Annie, you must not tell me such things—"

"—Will—" *You were raised to it.* He knew.

He met her pale eyes and shook his head, tasting salt and sour like a reminder. "Anne. Wife. I'm a Queen's Man now. Do you know what that is?"

She shook her head. *No.* He drew a stool out from the table and sat, gesturing her to the bench. "Hast ever seen a Tyburn hanging, Annie?"

She blanched. "No." Not seen, perhaps. But heard.

"It is as well." *If I have my will,* he thought, *you never shall see one. Especially mine.* "I'll take Judith and Hamnet home after supper," he said. "You and Susanna may stay."

She did not argue.

Act II, scene ix

Fourscore is but a girl's age, love is sweet:—
My veins are withered, and my sinews dry,
Why do I think of love now I should die?

—CHRISTOPHER MARLOWE, *Dido, Queen of Carthage*

I n the ten days or fortnight it took for Kit to sort out the social order
of the low tables, he learned many things that had escaped his notice when he sat by Murchaud's side. The talk was freer, although
his—Kit's—presence was greeted with sidelong glances at first. But
when Murchaud left court, and Morgan was not seen, and Kit traded
his green and violet and silver for the black velvet he truthfully preferred, the conversation flowed more free. Especially as he was seen in
the company of the Mebd's Bard and her Puck, or sitting alone.

He couldn't bear the silence of his rooms, and spent long hours
walking in the beech wood or along the strand, practicing music
poorly with Cairbre or reading in the library. Kit had Latin, Greek,
fair French, and slight German, yet he found them inadequate to the
books and scrolls and stories there. The lamia Amaranth found him
puzzling over books in strange languages, and with her dapple-scaled
tail coiled between chair legs and occasionally, unsettlingly, brushing
his calf, she set about to teach him the backward writings of Hebrews

(which informed Kit of the names of three of the five symbols Baines and his friends had burned into his flesh: *mem*, *he*, and *lamel*) and Mohammadans, and the brush-sketched characters of far Cathay. Although her smile was cool and she would not answer questions about herself, Kit thought she courted him.

He permitted it, expecting her purpose to be revealed hesitantly, but before too long. Wrong again: her silence and amusement remained, counterpointed by her flickering tongue.

And so he continued, restless and—although often in company—alone. His thoughts were clearer now that he had a goal, but the passive means of accomplishing it—and his lack of success as bait—flustered him. More unsettling, it wasn't any easier to keep track of the days when he was focused on it. He went so far as to carve notches in a candle, and stopped when he began to realize that the number of notches *changed*.

As his head cleared further, though, the craving in his belly grew. He had to talk to Morgan. Jilted lover or no.

Of course, a jilted lover might be expected to wish to speak to her. If not too often. And I am tired of being treated as a pet.

He frowned, thinking that he would not trust himself with matters of import, as mooncalf as he had been.

Hell, I can ask her about love-in-idleness, too. And why Amaranth said she was cruel.

Kit dressed—as Will would have it—like a cobbler's son: a shirt of cambric, a leather jerkin, and brown wool breeches. He slipped the iron bootnail from the pocket of the doublet he had been wearing and was about to drop it into a lacquer box on the stand beside his bed when he hesitated. He could almost fancy the sound of a cobbler's hammer, familiar from childhood, and smiled for a moment at the memory of his father with a mouth full of tacks just like this one. It might have been the scent of leather, or the way the light caught on the worn surface of the nail, but he suddenly couldn't bear to set it aside. He slipped it into his purse and let it clink against coins he'd had no occasion to spend. *Here is the palace, and the court. But there is no Faerie city. No tradesman, no farmlands, no ports for ships trading the wide and wandering sea . . .*

How strange. And then Kit smiled, because there was a lyric in it.

He stomped into his boots, and left his cloak and his sword behind. Should anyone ask, he was only going for a ramble.

How far to Morgan's cottage, he could not estimate. Murchaud had said through the beech wood, but Kit's explorations had not found a farther edge. They *had* taught him that the wood changed from day to day; on one the brook might bend beside an enormous gray boulder like a menhir, caked with moss and lichen; on another it would run straight and tossing over rocks through the spraddled roots of a rogue oak, rough-barked and errant among the smooth-boled beeches, vast enough to build an Ark. Then again, there might be no brook at all, and the wood might sweep up the flanks of rolling hills, spacious and silent and lit like a green cathedral.

Kit followed a graveled trail through the palace's sprawling gardens. It became a sort of bridle path at the verge of the wood. He paused there for a moment to settle the leather bottle of water on his hip and get his bearings. Then—*Morgan's house*, he thought, and set his foot upon the path.

Today it was late summer under the trees, the day bright and serene, shade and a light breeze welcome in the morning's heat. He regretted the jerkin, but knew he'd want it if the sun set while he was in the wood. He didn't object to sleeping rough and hungry for a night, but he wasn't overfond of shivering in a pile of leaves until morning.

The trail tended east, gladdening Kit's heart, and it passed over the brook—there was a brook today, brown water dappled by sunshine—on a well-maintained footbridge. Kit was wise enough to step off the trail and leave prints down the muddy bank, crouching on gravel to cup water to his mouth. He drank deep to spare what he carried, smiling at the hop and splash of infant frogs the same bronze as the silt.

"Hurm," croaked the troll under the bridge as Kit hopped to the first of four rocks on the way to the far bank. "Harm."

"Good morning, Master Troll." Kit's hand would have dropped to his swordhilt if he had been wearing one.

"Good morning, Sir Poet."

"You know me."

"I know your eyepatch," the troll answered. "I know your errand."

Its eyes blinked like cloud-filtered moons from the gloom under

the bridge's arch. Kit saw a knobbed and swollen nose, slimy skin
reflecting the yellow glow of those eyes, and the splayed fingers of
one weird hand balancing the thing's crouch. He couldn't make out
enough of its body to get an idea of its size. The space under the bridge
was darker than it ought to be and there was no silhouette cast against
the light on the other side, so he saw only splinters of warty hide, the
hump of a shoulder illuminated in the thin bands of sunlight that fell
between planks.

"Mine errand?"

"Always on the Queen's business, aye."

"One Queen or another." Kit didn't like his footing on the stone,
which rocked under his boots. He stepped into the stream, calf-deep,
a cold gout of water soaking his leg to the thigh. "How may I assist
you, Master Troll?"

From the sound, Kit would say that the troll sucked snaggled teeth
as it thought that over. "Well. 'Tis a troll bridge, in'it? So logic says
you have to pay the troll—"

"I went around."

"That you did, that you did." The troll coughed, an unpleasant
fishy sound. "But you drank my water, and you scared my frogs—"

Kit sighed. He was in no mood to haggle, and losing light. "A piece
of silver?"

"And what does a troll need with silver, Sir Poet?"

"What does a poet need with a bridge?"

"Useful things, bridges—" The troll brightened. "You can pay me
with a song."

"A song. Mine own?"

"What use is a poet, else?"

"Do you intend to *keep* it, if I give it you?"

"Keep and pass along," the troll answered, lowering its glowing
eyes and curving its hand as if it studied the cracked yellow pegs of its
fingernails. "As anyone might a song. If anyone would listen to a troll
sing. But if you mean, will I take it from you—no, that's a price worth
more than a fording. And everything in Faerie has a price."

"I'm learning that." Kit turned in the water to put his blind side to
the bank, which was only marginally less discomforting than facing it
to the troll. He might not hear the rustle of leaves over the splash of

the brook, if anyone snuck close. "A love song, or a lament? Or something warlike, I know a few of those."

The troll sighed, and Kit saw his shadowed outline settle on its haunches. "Harm, hurm. A love song," he said in a dreaming voice. "There's little enough of love under bridges."

"But plenty of frogs." Kit winced as the words left his mouth. *Too clever by half, Master Marley. Or Sir Christofer. Whoever you are today.*

"Ah, yes," the troll answered. "A surfeit of frogs. Froggy frogs, froggy frogs." He followed it up with a froggy-sounding laugh; Kit glimpsed something like the white swell of a pouched throat. "Sing me a song, toad and prince."

"I know the song for you." Kit drew a breath and steadied it, and didn't sing so much as chant— *"Come live with me and be my love—"*

It was a simple song on the surface, an uncomplicated pastoral, but political on the bottom of it. Who was, after all, the famous shepherd who sheared his flock so close as to dine off golden plates?

Reciting it made Kit feel he was getting away with heresy.

The troll listened in silence, his hands with their old-man's knuckles and old-man's claws twined one about the other, and he chirruped once or twice in amphibian emotion. A few moments followed with only the wind in the trees and the water over the rocks, and then the troll said, "A right sunlit song." A sound like ripping cloth followed.

Kit stepped back, feeling his way over slick stones. "You're welcome."

"No fear, no fear," croaked the troll. He thrust a hand out from under the bridge, something brightly dripping knotted in the gnarl of it. "For your cloak. For the song."

Kit hesitated, but the troll stayed motionless, although its yellowgreen mottles pinked in the sun. "For my cloak?"

"Can't be a bard without a cloak," the troll said, and shook the bit of cloth. "Take it. Take it for your song."

Kit picked his way forward, following a sand bar scattered with stones. He stopped as far back as he could, and made an arch of his body to reach toward the troll. His hands closed on wet brocade, and the troll jerked its scalded hand out of the sun. "Hurm, harm. On your way then, bardling. I'll see you again ere your cloak is complete. And I say that knowing: trolls have the curse of prophecy."

It withdrew under its bridge. Kit scrambled to the far bank, turned back, and bowed in wet boots once he attained its height. "Rest ye merry, Master Troll."

There was no answer, but he fancied he heard a muted chant taken up in a croaking voice before he was quite out of sight of the bridge. *Come live with me and be my love, hurm, And we will all the pleasures prove, harm, That valleys, groves, hills, and fields, hurm —*

Three or ten hours later, he was forced to admit he was lost. Or, if not lost — for he had never left the bridle trail, or what-you-may-call-it, and thought he glimpsed the spires of the palace once or twice, when the trees grew thin at the top of a rise — at the very least he was sorely misplaced. He sat on a mossy trunk and drank water and inhaled the clean musty scent of the forest. The troll's scrap he spread on his knee to finish drying, and he considered it as he considered his options. With the water wrung out, the brocade was as satiny red as rose petals, woven of some fiber Kit couldn't identify. He rested his chin on his hand and scratched idly under his eyepatch, watching the light.

What filtered through the widely spaced pewter boles of the beech trees was growing golden, although the breeze was still balmy. He didn't think he'd find Morgan's cabin before sunset, and if he slept here, he'd have the fallen trunk and the hollow under it to break the wind. A hungry night, but —

crunch

— Kit's head came up, and otherwise he froze motionless against the trunk. *A footfall, perhaps something as simple as a wild pig or a stag.* Another crunch, and then a third. *Hooves*, he decided, the sound too crisp for a booted foot. He held his breath, hoping to see a stag or a hind and not wishing to disconcert a boar, if that was what minced toward him through last year's leaves.

Well. Not a stag, exactly, but the stag-headed adventurer whose poise and casual grip on his sword had so arrested Kit's attention on his very first night in Faerie. He dressed richly, an animal's smooth throat rising from the collar of his doublet, some Gyptian god made English.

The stag drew up, a brief rustle accompanying his cessation of motion. His finely etched head went back as if he considered flight, warm sunlight gilding the velvet of new antlers. "Sir Christofer," he said, and just as Kit was about to swing to his feet and remark on the unlikelihood of such an encounter, the stag pawed the earth and snorted. "I've been seeking you."

"Seeking — me?"

"Aye, Sir Christofer. Who else would be in the forest at this hour, save bogeys and creeping things?"

"I" — Kit peeled the damp scrap of brocade from his breeches and tucked it into a sleeve — "am embarrassed to say."

The stag tossed his horns. "And I am Geoffrey. A pleasure to make your more formal acquaintance."

"Geoffrey." Kit stood and stretched his shoulders. "Seeking me to what end?"

"Conversation. Were you bound for Queen Morgan's cottage?"

"Yes."

"And you found the way obscured. Unsurprising." Geoffrey strode along the bridle path, and Kit fell into step beside him, crunching through leaves in the half-light. "There's a glamourie on it: you cannot find the way unless you know the way."

"Ah."

"Fret not," Geoffrey continued, tilting his antlers. "I will show you."

"Thank you. To what do I owe this kindness?"

"My desire for a moment to talk."

Long practice kept Kit from checking his step. *At last.* "Surely a conversation could be had at less price —"

" 'Tis no price at all." Strange and stranger, to see a man's words fall from the lips of a hart. "A token of friendship."

"Friendship?"

"Oh, aye. Follow me —"

The stag left the path, leapt down a bank and pushed through a stand of laurel, Kit — on his heels — only stumbling once among the litter and sticks.

"Never step off the path," Geoffrey said. "Never look back" — he glanced over his shoulder at Kit, long neck twisting like a ribbon — "and never trust the guardian." A toss of his head back, westerly, toward the palace and the troll's bridge. "Unless you want to accomplish something. In which case you must risk, and intrigue, and sneak."

"And betray?"

"Betrayals are a tricky thing in Faerie. You don't wear Morgan's mark of shame any longer. Does that mean you're free?"

"The heartsease?" Half consciously, Kit brushed the breast of his jerkin with his left hand, feeling cool, supple leather. "Why should I be ashamed of it?"

Geoffrey stopped so suddenly that Kit almost slid into him. "Because of what it signifies."

"Curse it to Hell and beyond!" Kit stepped back stubbornly, folding his arms. "*Somebody* is going to tell me 'what it signifies,' or there is going to be blood."

"Blood." Geoffrey said the word tastingly. "Of course. Mortal man. We're all fools—"

"Fools?"

"Hast been so long since a true mortal walked among us. 'Tis changelings and half-Fae, and—well. It makes me wonder what the Mebd saw in advance of us, to steal a mortal away. Your obvious talents aside, no offense intended, etcetera."

Kit, amused: "Of course."

"And why Morgan would so lightly set you aside." He gestured Kit to follow with one expansive hoof. The beeches thinned, and yellow strands of grass began to thread between the leaves and roots.

"Why would a mortal man be important to the Fae?"

"We can't fight a war without one," Geoffrey answered, holding a branch aside. "A geas as old as the Fae. As for the heartsease. Its other name is love-in-idleness, did you know?"

"I've heard." The branch was whippy and fine: Kit almost lost his grip on it after Geoffrey handed it across. "Roses for passion and lilies for love—and for death. Amaranth"—he smiled—"is undying love, eternity. And crocus is gladness, and pansy is thoughts—but I do not think I'm so made mock of for a badge of *thinking*. So what, for the love of Hell, does a pansy signify?"

"Bondage," Geoffrey answered without turning. "There's your mistress' house, poet. We will talk again."

Kit turned to look through the gloom and the red twilight at a rose-twined cottage beyond a garden and a fieldstone wall. He turned back, to bid the stag thanks or—something, but Geoffrey had vanished in a silence as utter as that of the dark wood behind him.

"Edakrusen o christos," Kit muttered, because there was no Fae close enough to hear him. He placed one hand between the curling edges of lichen and vaulted the wall, rough stone gritting his palm and the turf denting under his feet. A white gravel trail led him between beds of roses, red and white, and under an arch of blossoms damasked both. The beds below the roses were planted with mint, melissa, verbena, rosemary, lavender, and what seemed a thousand other sweet and savory herbs. The scent filled Kit's head, almost dizzying, and he absently ran his hand across the bulge in his purse.

The cottage was as earthed under with brambles as any in a fairy tale, and Kit smiled appreciation of the image. It didn't look like the abode of a queen: the doorposts were skinned trunks, the door itself painted vermilion in a half-dozen coats that peeled as shaggy as the lichens. Lamplight gleamed through one small window, not yet shuttered against the night, and Kit's breath ached in his breast as a shadow moved behind it.

I can feel her, he realized. Like a hand twisted in his collar, drawing him forward, and although his strides stayed as crisp as if he knew what he intended, he shivered. He glanced over his shoulder, wondering if the stag watched after, but the wood was dark and silent. *Bondage.*

His shoulder ached in a memory, blow of a silver dagger hard across its ridge, and he tasted an also-remembered trickle of lukewarm mint, and for a moment he wished he had, after all, brought his sword. *Oh,* he thought. *Bondage. Yes, I see. More than her knight, her servant, her lover. More. Or less.*

Her slave.

"Hello the house!" Until the door swung open. "Good even, my lady—"

"Kit," she said, gray-green eyes dark as moss in the twilight. Her hair lay unbound upon her shoulders, tumbling to her waist, its darkness shot with silver threads like a moonlit river. She wore only a low-cut smock with blackwork around the neckline and petticoat-bodies over it; a working woman's home garb, her skirts kilted up to show a length of calf and a bare, clean foot, high-arched and more calloused than a lady's foot ought be.

She tilted her head, and he looked down, studying her feet. His hand tightened on the nail in his purse; it parted the cloth and pricked his hand, but he didn't let go.

"What brings you to my door, Sir Kit?" An arch smile, and her hand on his collar—her physical hand, twisting the cloth and bringing him inside. He moved as led, helpless under her touch, and thought of a stud horse rendered passive by the twist of a twitch on his lip.

Kit opened his mouth, would have spoken—accused her—but the taste of bloody iron choked him. A vividly tactile memory of powerlessness: the savage wrench of his dislocated shoulder, gory drool slicking his chin and choking his throat with the effort of screaming—and breathing—through a mouth full of barbed metal, thinking *If I could talk, I could explain my way out of this*—

There hadn't been any talking. Not for a long time.

And it was still better than what Essex's faction did to poor Thomas Kyd. What greater cruelty to a playmaker than shatter his hand?

Stop his tongue, show him his dignity and his sovereignty and his voice as easily rent from him as a girl's—Lavinia in Titus: *raped, dismembered, silenced. She could have been a poet too, for all the benefit it got her.*

Kit bit down on his tongue, knotted his fist on that nail, the pain shocking, before the memory went further.

—ah, but I lived. And there *was* satisfaction in that. "What have you—" *Like talking through a mouth full of blood. God help me. God have mercy* . . . "What have you *done* to me?"

"Claimed you," she said, and shut and latched the door, taking her time, giving him a moment to notice the airy interior of her cottage, the mud-chinked walls hung with tapestries and baubles and herbs. Roses grew through the gaps under the eaves to tangle across the loft where a high window gave them light: a perfumed, nodding mass of flowers. Her loom dominated the single room, her wide uncanopied bed against the far wall, a massive iron cauldron crouched upon the hearth.

"Iron," he said, and let his bloody hand fall to his side, spattering a few drops on the rush-strewn slates rammed into the earthen floor.

"Aye," she said. "I'm afraid a little steel won't protect you from Morgan le Fey. And I did no more to you than any lady might. I left you your freedom of speech and deed, which is more than the Mebd would have granted."

She took up his bleeding hand and studied it; he hadn't the strength to drag it away, and sagged against the wall beside the door, the stentorian echo of his own breath filling his ears. "Freedom of deed? When I come to your bidding like a mannerly stud to the breeding paddock—"

"Have I interfered in your comings and goings?" She raised his fingers to her mouth and kissed the blood away. He turned his head as if he could burrow into the rough wool of the tapestry behind him. Her mouth claimed his fingertips.

He moaned.

She let his hand fall, then, and whispered, "Have I forbidden you London, for all 'tis foolery that takes you there? Have I forbidden you to amuse yourself as you wish, or made you pace at my heels like a cur? Do I grant you dignity? Arrogance and errantry, and how like a *man* not to understand what he's given, and when his mistress is permissive, and how much more pleasant his station than it could be. At least a dog understands kindness."

He pressed his back against the wall, stomach-sick, eyes burning. Even when she stepped back, it was not distance enough. "A cur, is it? Shall I bark at your door, madam? What *dignity* includes a slave's collar and chains, a mark of shame?"

She turned away and moved toward her loom. He couldn't watch her: it was a sort of agony to be in her presence, and searing pride alone kept him from prostrating himself before her. His fingers stung, still dripping blood. The coolness of her voice cut through his fury. "I see the first approach has come, then. Who brought the flower to your attention?"

The wall was hard behind the tapestry. He blinked and straightened away from it. "Geoffrey the Stag. Wait—no. Puck and Cairbre, and the lamia Amaranth."

"Excellent." A rustle as she moved. He wished the taste of blood in his mouth were real; he wanted to spit. "Look at me."

He looked. She stood as proud as a lioness, her long neck a predatory arch under her hair. He could have wept with his need to bury his face in it, but he thought she would have smiled to see his tears.

"You're mine," she said, coming closer. "Don't fight me, Kit: I've outlived kings and outwitted princes, and bent the noblest of knights to my will. In the end, they all did as I bid, or they died: I was a goddess before I became as you see me now. Although"—her fingers cool on his throat—"even Lancelot never fought me as you do."

"Lancelot?" A froggy croak, clogged as the troll's.

"You're worth three of him," she answered with a storied smile. "Except on the battlefield. Where he *was* unstoppable. But that's the sort of swordsman I need least in this new world."

"Why me?"

"Because the Mebd wanted you, and I could get you for her. And get you *from* her."

He tried to speak, coughed instead. She stepped back, blessedly, and he battled the words until they came. "Geoffrey said the Faerie host cannot fight without a mortal man."

" 'Tis true. We have no reality apart from thy folk. And thy folk have no magic apart from us."

"And that's what you need me for?"

"Yes. That and the pleasure of your company." A wink turned his stomach and tightened his groin. "You're angry with me. You think what I've done to you is a sort of rape."

"Isn't it?"

"Rather," she answered. "But, then, so little of a woman's lot is what she wills, I cannot see it as much different from a husband's treatment of a wife."

"That is not a responsibility I will bear, strictly by merit of my sex." The spikes that had worn at his tongue and palate had been barely knobs, really. They had wanted him able to talk, afterward: the sort of bridle used for unruly wives, and not the sort reserved for heretics and blasphemers. *Which had been meant to be a humiliation, too.*

"No, I don't think you can be blamed for how men treat their wives and daughters. But." A pause as she laid a hand on his shoulder. "You might consider how much greater a dignity I grant you than *my* lord granted me. You, my sweet Christofer, have always your lady's leave to speak your mind. How many women have so much privilege?"

"You'll assess me the acts of a man a thousand years dust?"

"If I bear Eve's sins, you may as well have Lot's. No matter. You'll do as I bid, though I'd rather you do it willing."

"Willing—" Cold terror, suddenly. Worse because he knew that when she touched him, if he whimpered it would not be with disgust, or fear, as long as her hands were on him.

Her movements were like a dance: nearer, further. An increase and a decrease of pressure. Laughing behind the deadly earnest of her gaze. "If you fight me, Kit, I'll break you. I've seen your scars. I have some idea of what it would take."

His gut ached at the memory of her touch, the vagueness and blind lust with which she had afflicted his thoughts.

He fought his voice level. "And if I offer you my service—willing—in your coming battle, does that earn me your favor enough to beg the answer to a question?"

A shake of her skirts unkilted them; her petticoat fell to brush the floor. She sighed. "You may always question me. I consider it a fair payment for your inability to refuse. And I prefer a spirited mount to a brokenhearted nag."

"What if I wish—" He couldn't bring himself to say it.

She knew. "The sovereignty of thy person? 'Tis more than a wife gets, but I have the bond I need of thee." She winked. "Although I might miss a well-warmed bed now and again. I can drag that magic off thee."

She snapped her fingers. He felt as if something—a snapping branch, cracking ice—*broke* to make the sound.

"Lady." He relaxed as much as he dared, feeling suddenly—light. He straightened away from the wall. "Tell me of Bard's cloaks."

"Bard's cloaks? The cloaks of bards? What of them?"

"Is there virtue in them?"

"Aye, yes," she said. "The magic of goodwill, a protection woven of the pleasure they have given those they give pleasure to. Has someone offered to start you one?"

"A troll," he said, and shrugged when she glowered at him. "One more question an it please you?"

"Aye?" She shook her skirts again, unhappy with how they had settled, ducking her black head so the rivers of her hair washed over her.

Kit watched her move, and breathed a sigh to see only a lovely, dark woman, somewhat older than himself. "Who do we intend to do battle with?"

She looked up and smiled. "Elizabeth's enemies are mine own. Although we fight them differently. The Prometheus Club."

"Oh, bloody Hell. Morgan, you should have just *said* so."

Act II, scene x

Would they make peace? terrible hell make war
Upon their spotted souls for this offence!

—WILLIAM SHAKESPEARE, *The Life and Death of Richard II*

7th June anno Domini fifteen hundred & ninety five
Winding Lane
London

My beloved friend—

In the fervent hope & intention that this small note may pass to thee directly I will speak plain, for I feel what I must impart is of too much moment to conceal under circumlocutions. We shall have to trust the privy ink in which these lines are written, between the stanzas of my latest manuscript. If I am too forward in thine estimation, then shalt thou burn this missive when thou hast read.

I shall be as brief as I may: news in London is bad, & will unease thee. The Queen's physician is finally dead, hanged at Tyburn last week—I was in attendance for thy FW, who miraculously still holds fast to life & breath although I know not how. A terrible thing, & I believe—& FW & Lord Burghley with me—that it has much taken the heart from Her Majesty, for she was ever fond of Dr Lopez. In his last words, he swore his allegiance to HRM & to Christ, & died as thou mightst imagine, in exceeding pain. I will not say more; it is too close a memory for me of my mother's cousins, who were hanged & drawn on suspicion of treason some years past.

Thy letters tell me Poley watcheth me, & indeed I watch Poley, through the auspices of Poet Watson's sister who is as good a woman as thou hast indicated & in much improved circumstance now, along with Robin her boy. Fret not, gentle Christofer: I am as cautious as ever thou couldst wish. But she—although Robert her husband will not see her, Robert's friends will sometime pass her such nuggets & scrapings as they may—says also that he & Dick Baines have been said to be much pleased by this torture & execution & they have made many midnight comings & goings. More, they receive succor in their treasonous efforts from overseas, a Spaniard she thinks & I think as well keeps them supplied with coin. I have had this information to FW, but Oxford speaks well of Poley to the Queen, & so no action is taken. I suspect almost that Oxford has some secret hold on Her Majesty, for she is overkind to one who has not her best interests in heart. With what thou hast taught me I see how he doctors the plays that are meant to make Her Majesty strong, & his hand weakens every good line I put down, although I correct much of it more subtly than he knows. & still she loves him better than any but Burghley—

—Burghley, who is growing ill & aged, & his son takes more & more his place at the Queen's right hand. Raleigh is out of favor again, & Essex has become openly hostile. He grows bold & conceals not his disdain for the Queen & the woman who loved him. It is his hand no doubt behind the conspiracy to convict & murder—for I cannot call it a lawful execution—Lopez, & his success & the Queen's despair at it have made him drunk with power. & I have learned beyond a doubt that Poley is Essex's man. Mary says Poley bragged in a tavern that he got money from Southampton. Which means Essex. Which means—

—I do not need to draw the obvious conclusions for thee, when Southampton still in the guise of my patron & friend has asked for a play, a trifling thing. Thou wilt be unsurprised to learn that the topic of this play is Richard the second, & there is no way I can refuse without making it evident that I know more than I should. & that way lies a scuffle in a dark alley & a knife in the eye. More & more I feel I *tread—forgive the casual blasphemy—like our Lord Jesus Christ on tossing waves that might hurl me at my heavenly Father's least whim to the snapping jaws of the deep.*

More, & worse. I told thee of gold from Spain: with that gold comes its bearer, a Spaniard or a Portuguese, not so dark as Lopez—hair almost auburn in the sun, as if he had some English, French, or Dutch blood. Perhaps a Jew as well? I did not hear his name, but he attended the execution with Baines, & was almost as tall, with a knife-blade nose & very thin lips behind a close-trimmed beard. Most strange of all, he wore rings on every finger, and from what I glimpsed of them I should say they were wrought of twisted iron. He is, I mean, Promethean.

Mary has discovered his name: Xalbador de Parma, and heard as well in an unguarded moment one of Poley's associates, a recusant named Catesby who I know, for he spends time at the Mermaid, call him "Fray."

& still worse—& more interesting—concealed in the crowd & my hood at the hanging, I made shift to follow those men back into the city. There is famine in London, Kit, & in the countryside as well. I saw the foreigner speak with Baines; he went into a tavern, & Baines like an errand-boy went off to do his bidding. What his bidding was I can guess, for there were vagabonds & chiefly apprentices rioting in London by noontide over the price of food, cheese & ale smeared on the streets, two suspected Jews & a Moor & some goodwives & tradesmen who might have looked too prosperous dragged through the street, pummeled or killed for the error of being abroad.

Rumor has it culprits have been taken & are sure to be hanged at the Tower. Lads of 14, & I have no doubt that Baines who instigated shall not hang with them. I shall not attend. Lopez's torture was all I could stomach, & I feel no need to watch the ravens feast.

The riots mean the closing of the playhouses, & the Privy Council—influenced by the Puritans who thou thinkst & I think influenced by the Enemy—have ordered them torn down, although it has not happened yet. In some disgust, I contemplate spending the summer with Annie in Stratford, away from the stink & the plague that stalks London again. The drought is no better there, though, & the cattle sick with murrain. Bad omens, & the auguries poor as the Queen approaches her three score & three.

It is almost as if the hand of God himself is bent against us, but I know it must only be such changes & expectations in the minds of men as thee & me, ourselves, do wreak with our plain poesy. At least Lord Hunsdon is well, & he — & the Lord Chamberlain's Men, we his players, remain in good odor with Gloriana. So I can shield her a little, & perhaps set a word or two against Essex's murmurings & seditions, for plays go on at court even as the playhouses are shuttered.

FW informs me that our next act must be to forge evidence against Baines and Poley, if we cannot come by it honestly — and says to comfort me that there is no honor in it, but that we do it for the Queen.

I know through FW what Essex does not: for all her refusal to name an heir, the Queen favors James of Scotland & she does court him with secret letters, privily instructing him in her arts of governance. Of course this cannot be made public, as Her Majesty's position grows precarious & her wiles are not — ah, thou hast me penning sedition again — what they once were.

I fear some attack from our enemies. Something for which this abominable mess with poor Lopez is only the overture.

Lest I trouble thee unrelievedly, let me say in closing that I am well, & writing strongly, as thou mayst see, & Anne has written to inform me that she will be buying me the biggest house in Warwickshire before I know I am a gentleman.

yr Wm

Post script: I will set this by the mirror with a candle, as thou hast instructed, & write again when I have spoken with FW or Burghley.

Post post script: please forgive the awkwardness of my hand. I hope that thou canst unriddle it, as I am prone of late to monk's cramp, whose painful acquaintance I am sure thou, as a poet, hast made.

The tremors still subsided when Will put his fingers to a task. Such as flipping a silver shilling older than Annie. Mayhap as old as John Shakespeare: turning it in his fingers, over and over again, Will could just see the shadow of a hawk-nosed face when the light fell against it right. The shadow of Henry the Eighth, father of Elizabeth, founder of the English Protestant Church.

And author of all my troubles, Will thought, laying the coin on the table beside the inkwell. He spread his pages across the desk and recut a quill, nicking his finger on the knife when his right hand trembled. He thrust the knife into the tabletop and his left middle finger between his lips. "Damn it to Hell—"

"Now there's a scene from Faustus," an amused voice said from the corner. "Writing our plays in blood now, are we? That should be some sorcery."

Will pulled his bloody finger from his mouth and raised his eyes to the mirror. Kit lounged beside the fireplace, one elbow on the mantel, his left hand steering the hilt of a rapier. "You could have announced yourself."

"I was waiting for you to set down the knife," Kit said dryly. He straightened and came forward, producing a kerchief from his sleeve. "So you wouldn't cut yourself. Let me see."

Will held out his left hand, picking up his pen with the right one to conceal its tremors. " 'Tis just a scratch."

"Not so deep as a well, nor so wide as a church door? But deep enough, Will. Ah, you've missed the tendons and the bone. Good. It shouldn't bleed longer than half an hour. Morgan would say to wash it with soap—"

"Lye soap?"

"Aye, and it might be wise. She saved my face from taint that way. Is there water in the ewer?"

"Some." Bemused, Will suffered himself to be led to his bedroom and fussed over. He gasped when Kit scrubbed the wound, then pressed the edges of the cut tight and bound his first and middle fingers together with the kerchief to hold them closed and sop the oozing blood. "Who is Morgan?"

Deftly, Kit tightened the bulky bandage. He gave Will's hand a squeeze and let it go. "My mistress in Faerie. A sorceress. That will bleed less if you hold it up."

"*Morgan?*"

"Yes." The sidelong glance. Kit's face was pale, and Will thought if he touched his friend's cheek it would be cool. "*That* Morgana. Will, about your letter—"

The bandage pressed the pain back to a dull, warning throb. Will gestured widely with his bloodied hand, and went in search of a rag. "I've wine—hock. Can you stay a little?"

"I'd meant to. Are you expecting company?" The stress on that word brought Will to alertness.

He led Kit back into the sitting room. "*Company?* Burbage, you mean? Or Mary Poley—?"

"If they come, I can step through the looking glass. Give me that rag. I'll mop the blood. You pour the hock. Tell me what Mary says of Fray Xalbador de Parma."

That stress again, and Will puzzled it as he poured left-handed, despite his bandages. He got the harsh Rhennish white strained into the cups without spilling it and found bread and an end of cheese, which he set on the table beside the upright knife. "I've sugar for the wine—"

"I've gotten out of the habit," Kit answered, tasting. "And this is sweet enough without assistance."

"You know the name of the Spaniard."

"We were acquainted. He pretends to many things—but I had asked about Mary." Kit twisted the knife free of the boards and cut cheese dyed with carrot juice, broke bread, handed the first bit to Will. "More on the Spaniard when the wine is drunk."

"Everything she told me was in the letter. She'll come again when she can." The bread was hard to swallow. Will dipped it in his wine to soften it, much to Kit's amusement.

"I see. And little Robin?"

"Sleeping better."

Kit rubbed bread between his fingertips. He rolled the crumbs against the tabletop.

Will picked the shilling off the boards and turned it in his right hand. "Art jealous?" *Or is it that I'm jealous, and I pass it on to thee?*

"Jealous?" Kit looked up. He pushed the crust of bread away, and cupped both hands loosely around his wine, leaning back on his stool as if the scent of London—the reek of the gutters twining the perfume from the gardens—pleased him.

"Of Mary—"

"Why should I be jealous?"

"Robin's your son, isn't he?"

Kit's eye went wide, his face seeming to elongate as eyebrows rose and his jaw sank. "What gave you that idea?"

" 'Tis as good a reason as any for Poley to hate you. Beyond the political motives, which seem inadequate. Adequate for murder. Inadequate for *loathing*. I won't think less of you. . . ."

"Nor should you," Kit answered, reaching for his cup. "Given the somewhat hasty circumstances of your own marriage."

Will laughed, knowing he'd touched a nerve to draw that response. "Touché. Is he yours?"

"Why does it matter? I would not impugn the lady's honor. A man can have care for a dead friend's sister—"

"It matters," Will said, "because a man can also have a care for the children of a dead friend."

Kit balanced the knife across the palm of his hand. "Damn, Will. I don't know."

"What does that mean, you don't know?"

Kit reversed the knife in his hand like a juggler; Will jumped as he drove the blade neatly into the same gouge Will had left earlier, and a full inch deeper. "By Christ's sore buggered arse, Will. It means the possibility does exist. I shouldn't think I'd need to draw you a plan. Given *yours* come in litters."

The glare as Kit shoved himself to his feet left Will speechless and stung. He stood more slowly, holding out his bandaged hand, the right one tightened on the coin. "Kit—" Will swallowed, a task that was growing uncomfortable. "I apologize."

"Damn you." But the edge dropped from Kit's tone, and he settled onto his stool again, resting his forehead on the back of his hand. "Thy pardon, Will. I am overwrought."

Will nodded, and sat as well, reaching out right-handed to grab Kit's wrist, hoping his hand would not shake. "The boy will want apprenticing soon. Had you a desire to see him in some trade or another?"

"God." Kit's voice was shaky. He clapped his left hand over Will's right and squeezed. "Anything but a player, a moneylender, or an intelligencer."

"Not to follow in his father's footsteps, then?"

"Whatever those footsteps be."

The silence grew taut between them. Will drew his hand back and dropped it into his lap. "Right. Cobblery it is."

When he finished laughing, Kit emptied his cup and pushed it aside. "Xalbador de Parma. Fray Xalbador de Parma."

"A Promethean. I had discerned that."

"More than that." His voice seemed to dry in his throat. Will pushed his own barely touched cup of hock across the table, and Kit took it with a grateful nod. "A Mage, they call him, plural Magi. As if he had anything in common with great spirits such as Dee or Bruno. Fray Xalbador is also an Inquisitor, one of their infiltrators in the Catholic church."

Will wished suddenly he had not given his wine away, remembering Kit's voice on another occasion, in the dark kitchen of Francis Langley's house. *Still, an Inquisitor. I'm tempted to count it some species of honor.* "Oh."

"It bodes not well." Kit shoved the cup back at Will with still some wine in it. "You must see to it that Francis gives Thomas Walsingham the name. Or better, see to it yourself. I'm sure your status is enough, these days, that he would grant you an interview if you sent him a note."

"You sense a move against the Queen?"

"I can see no reason otherwise de Parma would be in England. You'll want to pour wine, if you've finished that."

"More wine?" But Will stood, and collected Kit's cup as well, and again filtered the dregs through cheesecloth to produce something potable. "Here."

"Sit," and Will sat.

"What is it?"

"The reason Elizabeth protects Oxford. And what will make your task all the harder, though Essex has o'erplayed his hand."

Will studied Kit's face, its deadly earnest placidity except for a sort of valley worn between the eyes. "I listen."

"You know Edward de Vere was raised as William Cecil, Baron Burghley's ward after the sixteenth Earl of Oxford died. At the Queen's request."

"I do."

"This does not leave this room."

"I understand."

Kit drank off his wine at a draft, and plucked the dagger from the tabletop to clean his nails. "Oxford is Elizabeth's bastard son."

Act II, scene xi

Mortimer: Madam, whither walks your majesty so fast?
Isabella: Unto the forest, gentle Mortimer,
To live in grief and baleful discontent;
For now my lord the King regards me not,
But dotes upon the love of Gaveston.
He claps his cheeks and hangs about his neck,
Smiles in his face, and whispers in his ears;
And, when I come, he frowns, as who should say,
"go whither thou wilt, seeing I have Gaveston."

—CHRISTOPHER MARLOWE, *Edward II*

Kit tugged his hood higher. "Latch the door after I leave."

Will folded his arms. "I fail to see what errand could be of so much import that you must risk yourself in the street."

"Some things," Kit said, "a man must simply do. I'll return by dawn. I swear it."

"I'll be at the Mermaid if you want me, then," Will said, shaking his head in stagy frustration.

Kit walked through London with a feeling in his breast like freedom, his left hand easy on the hilt of a silver rapier forged as hard and resilient as steel. Carts clattered in the twilight, whorish girls and boys called from doorways, and men and women hustled home from market or out to taverns for their dinners. A commonplace scene, London in the sunset, and one at odds with the determination that coiled in Kit. He kept his eyes downcast and let his hair fall in front of his face, concealing as best he could his eyepatch. *A sunny day for staging a vengeance tragedy, Marley.*

'Tis not vengeance, he told himself. *'Tis preclusion.*

Two hours' walking and half the Faerie gold in his purse bought him the location of Richard Baines' home: a house rather than a lodging, on Addle Street. He'd done well for himself.

Kit skulked through an alley almost too narrow for his shoulders to pass without scraping the wall on either side. The house had a little garden: he hoisted himself to peer over the wall, but every window was darkened. *Damn. At the Sergeant, do you suppose?* A bell tolled nine of the clock, and he let himself drop on the outside of the wall.

Wherever Baines is, Fray Xalbador will not be far behind.

Kit stroked the hilt of his sword again, thinking perhaps he should try his hand at finding Oxford, instead. *A dead man may accomplish many things a live one might balk at.* But he wanted Baines' blood, that was the truth, and wanted the false Inquisitor's more.

He could scale the wall and lie in wait, since it seemed not even a servant was at home. Or he could go in search, aimlessly pacing. His feet decided for him. He walked through the much-thinned crowds, amused at how little apprehension he felt at strolling London's streets in the darkness. *Dead men lay their burdens down.* But it was a lie, and he knew it.

With an intelligencer's assessment of risk and reward, Kit knew that Fray Xalbador was worth Kit's own lifeblood to put an end to. More than worth. *Might as well trade Faerie gold for a good English sovereign.* But as much as Kit would have liked to hunt Robert Poley to his death at the Groaning Sergeant, Kit knew his life wasn't worth Poley's. His secret wasn't even worth Poley's life.

Surprised at a familiar voice, Kit stopped, looked up, stepped away from the square of light cast by an open door. A slow baritone, with something of the luff and fill of thoughtful sails behind it.

"Chapman," he murmured. And indeed, his wandering footsteps — no doubt primed by Will's words on where to find him — had led him into Cheapside and onto Bread Street. As he looked up he saw George Chapman's portly girth silhouetted against the open door of the Mermaid.

Laughter followed Chapman's unheard bon mot. Kit drew into the shadows, hoping Chapman didn't think him a cutpurse or lurcher lying in wait. He need not have feared: Chapman never saw him, but set out whistling down the street, swinging a stout stick and holding a half-shuttered lantern.

Kit glanced longingly at the sharp-cut panel of lamplight on the cobbles, and swore. He could hear Will's laughter now, too, and some-one else — Tom Nashe? — a voice cut clean by the closing door. He turned on his heel and followed Chapman. *At least I can see him safe home. Arrant fool, walking through London alone after curfew.*

But Chapman moved east, and Kit followed at a little more distance, now curious more than worried as his old friend let that stick tap lightly on the cut stone kerb. Dark houses loomed: a crack of stars were visible only directly overhead, and only a few lights gleamed through the slits in shutters, stars of a different sort. The rats grew bolder after dark, and twice Kit heard the squealing of their private wars.

Chapman was walking to Westminster Palace, a goodly night's jaunt. The lantern was a godsend: its light both steered Kit and blinded Chapman, so Kit need fear neither recognition nor the loss of his quarry in the dark. He fell back a little as they passed Blackfri-ars: there were carriages in the streets, parties of walkers, and groups of armed men to keep the Queen's peace. King's Street was quieter, once they passed through the gates, and there was little traffic beyond Charing Cross.

Kit turned once at a footstep behind him, wary of a sense of being watched, but he saw only a few figures. Another lantern-decked car-riage rattled over the cobbles, forcing one pedestrian against the wall. *Probably just Morgan watching me through her damned Glass.* Matched bays drew the coach — a two-in-hand — and the gelding on the near side had one white sock on a hind foot, which flashed in the lanternlight along with the footman's livery.

Oh, that's just too much of a coincidence. Kit stepped up his pace, eyes trained forward. But of course it wasn't a coincidence at all. He had been following Chapman. And Chapman had been enroute from supper and conversation with his friends and fellow playmakers to meet his patron.

His patron, who had been Kit's patron as well. And friend. And more. Thomas Walsingham.

The June night was warm, the air humid enough that it felt as if Kit walked through veils of silk that clung and slipped. He followed the slowing carriage as he had followed Morgan, one footstep and then another. But this was thoughtful rather than blind obedience. *The meaning comes in the silences. Momentum comes from the instant before the foot leaves the ground.*

The white-footed gelding stamped as his mate jostled him, tugging the rein as the coachman drew them in. Kit heard the creak of leather, the rattle of iron-shod rims on stone. Someone hallooed Chapman; a lantern flickered.

Kit laid one hand on the wall and watched from the shadows, as if turned to stone. *Or salt*, he thought, as the coach door opened. *I could wish that. A pillar of salt, to melt in the endless London rain and flow down the Thames to the ocean. Like a river of tears—*

Oh, stop it, Marley. That's not even an original image. And still he could have wept at the contrast between what he felt, now, suddenly, that had been so long stepped upon—and the desperate, thoughtless, compliant passion that had marked his loves in Faerie. *Loves? How couldst even thou have mistaken* that *for* love, *Kit Marley?*

More to be ashamed, for he knew what love was.

It was the thing that held him now, a breathless kind of clarity that kept him in the shadows, waiting for one last glimpse of the man whose life and home he had shared before—

The footman moved to assist a tall, ginger-haired woman in a flat-fronted French gown down the iron step. Kit's breath lay like pooled lead in his chest as she lifted her skirts and set her pattened feet upon the cobbles with a clack. *Audrey Walsingham.* She stepped away, gliding toward Chapman, who leaned on his cudgel as if it were a cane and swept a thoroughly creditable bow.

The carriage door stayed open, the footman at attention. Kit heard Chapman's murmur, Mistress Walsingham's tinkling laugh as he steadied her toward the palace. *Leave,* Kit thought, and came a half step closer to the carriage lights.

Long legs in silk hose, a well-turned calf strong from time spent on horseback. The hair was dark by lamplight as *he* grasped the rail and stood, settling his doublet with a shrug of muscled shoulders, but Kit knew it would gleam with copper highlights in the sun. The footman stood aside as Thomas Walsingham descended, swinging the door shut with a casual gesture that brought Kit's heart into his throat. He stepped forward again, and halted his motion in midair. *What art thou imagining thou mightst do here, Marley? Apologize for thinking Tom conspired with thy killers? Explain that Frazier and Poley lied, and thou thyself never practiced against the Queen? Throw thyself at his feet and kiss the stones between his shoes? Beg him to take thee home to Chislehurst and swive until thou bleedst, stay from Faerie and die in his arms like a selkie kept from the sea, while the lovely Audrey cossets and possets thee?*

It had a certain appeal, like Dido leaping into the flames, like Cleopatra up to her elbows in a basket writhing with asps. Kit set his foot in the print he had lifted it from, and stayed in the shadows, his right hand closing on the collar of his doublet as to tug it open and cool his throat.

Such a small motion to so betray him.

Tom must have caught the gesture from the corner of his eye. He turned like a splendid stallion, nostrils flaring, six inches of steel flashing in the carriage light as his right hand gripped and half drew his sword. "Who goes?"

A low voice, not loud enough to turn the heads of Chapman and Audrey, but enough to bring the footman around to flank his master. Kit smiled in recognition of the caution. *Yes, Tom. Get the lady in the gates along with her escort. You stay and handle the trouble, and she none the wiser. Besides, the palace is close enough to rouse to a cry of murder in the street. But that could be embarrassing if it were a false alarm, couldn't it?*

He glanced over his shoulder as Tom and his man came a few steps closer. The coachman kept a tight rein on the stamping bays, but he turned to look, and Kit knew there was a loaded pistol in a box behind his seat. The way was deserted on either side, except for the figure who had dodged the carriage—some distance away and hurrying forward with running footsteps—and Chapman and Audrey, who would be out of casual earshot by now. A cross street lay a few steps away: Kit could turn, fly, and be gone before Tom glimpsed his face—

An excellent plan.

"What is thy name, villain?"

If I had ever been able to walk from that voice.

"Not a villain." Kit took two short steps forward, to the edge of the lanternlight, and tugged his hood back with his thumbs. The gesture revealed his sword, and showed his hands well away from it, and Tom's grip on his own hilt slackened.

And then Walsingham's jaw dropped, and the knuckles grew white again.

"Rather a gentleman, Tom."

By his expression, the footman didn't know Kit. *One small mercy.* Tom's jaw worked, but no sound emerged.

Kit couldn't spare a glance for the figure now running toward them. "Tom, you must know. Frazier lied to you. I never did what he said—"

"How do you know what he said?"

Kit jerked his chin at the candlelit windows of the palace. Tom's face grew so pale Kit could see by lanternlight. And Will Shakespeare drew up ten feet away, wobbling with the force of his stop, his arms widespread for balance as if he had suddenly realized he was about to run between two armed men. "Master Walsingham," he said softly.

Tom shot him a level, almost mocking look. Kit knew it, and breathed a little easier. "The playmaker Shakespeare. I take it you knew about this?"

Will nodded. Tom took his hand off his sword and turned to the footman. "Jenkins, see that Master Chapman and my wife understand that I will be delayed. Perhaps as much as an hour."

"Sir." Audible relief filled the man's voice as he took himself away from matters he did not understand and vanished in pursuit of his mistress.

"Now," Tom said. "Into the carriage, for lack of a tavern. Pity, for I am very much in need of a drink, but I can't stand talking in the street with a player and a dead man."

Kit tried not to notice how Tom's eyes lingered on his face. He turned his head to hide the scarred side, but could not stop a shiver when Tom took his elbow and almost lifted him into the coach. Will slipped on the step, but Tom steadied him too, and Will shrugged and smiled his apology.

Kit flinched at the misstep. He prodded the ache in his chest, and knew. Murchaud was right. *I can't stay here.*

They took their seats and Tom rapped on the coach roof. Wheels rattled on the cobblestones, the carriage swaying on its straps. "Where are we going?" Will asked.

"There and back again," Tom answered. "Twice, if we need more time."

Kit laughed. "You haven't changed."

"You have. Ingrim told me the Queen ordered your death. Through Burghley. Poley showed him a writ, and had him burn it."

"Would Ingrim know a forgery?" Kit rubbed his eyepatch.

Tom shrugged, leaning forward to speak over the creak and clatter of the coach. "He should. There's testimony, too—"

"Do you believe it?"

"When Her Majesty more or less forbade anyone to examine your death, and pardoned your killers, what else could I do? Tell me you're no agent of Spain, or the Romans. Or James of Scotland. Tell me where you've been. The Continent? It has been kind to thee. Thou hast not aged a day. Tell me thou art loyal, in thine own voice, Kit, and I'll believe it."

"I was loyal to the Queen, and the Queen gave me my life," he answered. "And then she returned to me mine oath. And now I am—" *A free man.* "—beholden to another. But faithful in my dealings with England, I vow."

Tom glanced at Will, who had withdrawn into a corner. He watched without speaking, making himself small. "And how does Master Shakespeare come into the ciphering?"

"I followed Kit," he said, folding his arms over each other as if he were cold. Kit felt him shiver, where their shoulders brushed. "He trailed Chapman from the Mermaid." A searing glance told Kit that he would have some explaining to do for his carelessness. "I had stepped outside to catch George and remind him of somewhat, and—"

Tom smiled, and Kit knew he was deciding to let his actual question go unanswered. Kit cleared his throat. "Tom, I can trust you?"

"As a brother," he said, and squeezed Kit's leg above the knee. Kit watched his face, and saw no flicker of deception.

"Very well," Kit said. "This will take longer than a coach ride. How much has Sir Francis told you?"

In the half-light of the swinging lanterns, Tom's face grew grim. "Not enough, apparently."

Kit nodded. "He's dying, Tom. For certain. And Burghley too." He lowered his voice. "And Her Majesty grows tired."

"Her Majesty has reason."

"They are old," Kit said, knowing that the words carried every trace of treason that his enemies could have wished. The coach's jolting seemed ready to drive his spine through his skull, but he kept on, though Tom sat back as if to increase the distance between them. "There's a reason your Ingrim put a knife in mine eye. Duped by Skeres and Poley, or conspiring with them, there's time enough for that later. There's a reason Oxford and Essex move against the Queen. The old Queen must have an heir."

Will's elbow banged against the side of the coach. "They *are* old. And we are young. Comparatively speaking."

"Fellows!" Tom's shock was evident.

"Listen."

And somehow, Tom did.

Kit drew a breath, but Will cut him short, surprising Kit with the depth of his understanding. "When Burghley and Sir Francis are gone, their successors can be thee and me, Master Walsingham. And Robert Cecil, and Thomas Carey's son George. Or they can be our enemies. Men like Poley and his masters."

"Baines. And the Spaniard."

"What of the Queen? And the—" Tom stopped himself before he said the unfavored word, *succession*.

Kit shrugged. "In any case, you must step into Sir Francis' shoes. And quickly."

Tom turned his face into the light. It illuminated his silhouette, limning lips and nose and brow in gold. "He's barely now begun to warm to me again, Kit. We did not speak o'ermuch after your—"

—*murder*.

"Mend it soon," Will said. "Or not at all."

"That bad?"

"We must sire our own conspiracy."

Kit could see Tom tasting the word. *Conspiracy*. He realized with shock that threads of silver wound Tom's hair. "Kit, and what of thee?"

Kit closed his eyes on pain, knowing the answer. Knowing what it had to be, as soon as Will had effortlessly picked up the thread of his thought, and explained it. Known from the way Will had tailed him so deftly that Kit — *Kit* — had barely even known he was watched, and how Tom had put Audrey and Chapman out of harm's way without taking time to think. *I am dead in this world. Everything I could do, they can do better.*

Sweet Christ, I love these men. Better to remember them young and fierce —

Than like Sir Francis.

"Tom, your man Frazier *was* duped?"

Tom's lips twitched. He nodded once, his eyes focused on Kit's scar.

"I am commanded elsewhere," Kit said. *You'll outlive it. Outlive all your loves and hates, and when your mortal span is past —* "Thou wilt not see me again. Nor shalt thou, Will, I warrant. But I leave my Queen in capable hands."

"Kit —"

Two voices as one, and the tone of them warmed him even as he shook his head. "I am commanded elsewhere," he repeated. "And so tonight I shall give you everything I know."

Kit laid the palm of his right hand on Will's mirror and pressed forward against a sensation as if jellied mercury flowed to admit him. He glanced over his shoulder at Will and at Tom Walsingham standing beside him, fixing the two men's faces in his memory. They had kissed and clipped him as brothers, and that embrace was a sort of hollowness resting on his skin. *Dead men must trust the living to get on with their business, I suppose.*

"I'll write," Will said.

"I don't think I shall reply." Kit looked away before Will's expression could change. "Tom, give my love to your wife." He pushed through the mirror. He emerged in the corridor between the curtains that flanked the Darkling Glass, tendrils of crystal loathe to resign their grips.

No sooner had his boot touched the tiles than he bowed his head, startled, and dropped a knee, his silver scabbard-tip clinking and skipping. The Mebd stood over him: he had almost stepped into her arms. A scent of roses and lilacs like a breeze from a June garden surrounded him; he lifted the embroidered hem of her robe to his lips, heavy cloth draping his fingers. "Your Majesty."

"Sweet Sir Kit." He heard the smile in her voice and clenched his teeth in anticipation of a hammerblow of emotion. Her hand touched his shoulder and he almost fell forward, realizing as he put a hasty hand to the floor that he had been braced against a raw spasm of desire.

It never came.

"Mayst rise."

He did as she bid, keeping his eyes on the woven net of wheat-gold braids that lay across her shoulders, pearls knotted at the interstices. She tilted his chin up with flowerlike fingers, forcing him to meet her eyes. "Needst not fear our games this night, Sir Poet." She released him and stepped back, her fingers curling in summoning as she walked on. "We've been most wicked to thee, my husband, my sister, and me."

"I've known wickeder."

The pressure of violet eyes in her passionless oval face was almost enough to force him against the wall. "Thou dost wonder at thy place in our court."

"I do."

She smiled, and reached into her sleeve. "When our royal sister Elizabeth dies, things will change."

"Your Highness?" He stepped back as she drew out a long fluid scarf of transparent silk and twined it between her fingers. It shifted color in the light, shimmers of violet, green, and gold chasing its surface.

"And there will be a war. If not that day, soon after."

"I am a poet, Your Highness. Not a soldier."

She smiled at him, and reaching out, wound the scarf around his throat three times, letting the silk brush his face, softer than petals. "For thy cloak," she said. "Give me a song."

"What sort of a song?"

"An old song."

She started forward again, and he paced her, reciting the oldest song he knew —

". . . Young oxen newly yoked are beaten more,
Than oxen which have drawn the plow before.
And rough jades' mouths with stubborn bits are torn,
But managed horses' heads are lightly borne,
Unwilling lovers, love doth more torment,
Then such as in their bondage feel content.
Lo! I confess, I am thy captive I,
And hold my conquered hands for thee to tie —"

"No," the Mebd whispered, interrupting him with a hand on his wrist and seeming for a moment a woman given to softness rather than a cold and mocking Queen. "Not that. An English song, for thou art an Englishman."

"Thomas the Rhymer?" he suggested waggishly, wondering if she would let him press the advantage. *A gamble, but they that never gamble have no wit.*

"Perhaps not that either. It's no mere seven years thou wilt serve." But she smiled, an honest smile, and tilted her head so her braids moved in disarray over her neck.

"I know it." He nibbled his mustache. "I've made my farewells, Your Highness. I'm ready to set it behind me."

"Thou shalt find it easier. And Morgan has released thee from what bondage she held thee in —"

He blushed. "It influenced my decision."

"Of course."

"Free, and myself," he said. "But never free to leave."

"No." Her sorrow was not for him. "Never that."

They walked on in silence. She led him through tall, many-paned glass doors and into a garden that smelled as she did of lilacs and roses.

"Mortals can be enchanted," she said, gravel rustling beneath her slippers and turning under the brush of her train, "but they cannot truly be bound the way the Fae can be bound—by their names, by iron. Every knot in my hair is a life I possess, Sir Kit, a Faerie entangled to my will forevermore. I could not bind thee so. Nor canst thou be released by the gift of a suit of clothes, or a new pair of shoes. So thy folk require more careful handling. 'Tis better to let them grieve at their own rate, and leave at their own rate, too." She smiled, and recited a scrap of song of her own. "*Ellum do grieve, Oak he do hate, Willow do walk if yew travels late.* Dost know that one?"

"No—"

"Ah, well. Thou wilt learn it, no doubt. Do you toss like an elm, or break like an oak, Sir Kit?" She stopped and bent to smell a rose.

"This war that you expect, Your Highness—"

"Aye?"

"—how will it be fought?"

Oh, her smile *was* lovely. Even through vision unclouded by fey magic and glamourie. "With song, Sir Poet. With song."

Act II, scene xii

Jessica: I am sorry thou wilt leave my father so:
Our house is hell, and thou, a merry devil.

—WILLIAM SHAKESPEARE, *The Merchant of Venice*

Will stood against the painted cloth covering the wall of Sir Francis Walsingham's bedroom, flanked by Richard Burbage's fair hair on one side and Thomas Walsingham's tall frame on the other. They leaned shoulder to shoulder, unspeaking, feet and lower backs aching, listening to the halting rhythm of a dying man's breath, watching his daughter bathe his brow with cool water and fret his spindled hands. Lopez was dead, and even if another could have been trusted to keep the secret of his identity, Sir Francis would not have accepted the ministrations of strange physicians.

Tom Walsingham shifted, his shoulder brushing Will's doublet. Will met his glance, but neither spoke, and they turned away again after a moment of consideration. Tom's guarded eyes reminded Will of the expression in the mirror.

They kept their vigil though the clock struck midnight and its hands began their long dark sweep through the downhill hours of the night. Sir Francis whined low on one intaken breath; his next expiration held a damaged clatter that Will knew better than he liked.

"Not long now," Burbage murmured, and Tom shook his head *no* but it wasn't a denial.

Thus began the seventh of September, 1595: the sixty-third anniversary of Queen Elizabeth's birth.

One oil lamp guttered. The other had burned out by the time the bell struck three of the clock, leaving a thin white coil of smoke ascending from the wick. Will stepped away from the wall, across the rush matting. He didn't understand how Sir Francis' daughter Frances bore it; the stench of putrefaction rising from the dying man's very pores and on his breath was enough to raise Will's gorge from across the room.

There was oil in a cupboard. Wordlessly, with exquisite care, he filled the extinguished lamp and trimmed the wick, relighting it before snuffing the second and repeating the process. He set the light left-handed on the stand beside the bed, acknowledging Frances' grateful glance with a smile. "We should send a messenger to Lord Burghley," he said to Burbage and Tom as he returned to his post by the wall. "And a messenger to the Queen. He will not last the—"

"The Queen will not come." A wheeze, a broken gasp followed by Frances' command to *lie back*.

Will turned in place and looked back to the bed with its coverlet drawn high and its curtains closed on two sides to keep the draft away. "Sir Francis."

The old man was up on one elbow, waving his nursemaid irritably aside, pain furrowing his face. His voice fragmented. "Master Shakespeare. Master Burbage—ah. Tom. Waste no—time on the Queen. She wouldn't—come. Unless she forgave me."

"Cousin, lie down," said Tom, crossing the rush mat heedlessly.

Frances moved out of his path in a graceful sweep of skirts and leaned against the window ledge to throw open the shutters, breathing gratefully of the rank Southwark night. Over the reek of the bear gardens, Will imagined he smelled fruiting lemons and apples ripening to the frost that would leave them sweet enough to be plucked. He brushed comforting fingers across Frances' arm and moved forward. Burbage hung back beside her, his nostrils flaring in a drinker's roseate nose.

Tom crouched beside the bed, heedless of the reek, and Will stood over his shoulder. "Cousin," Tom said.

Sir Francis coughed. Will flinched: the sound had torn flesh in it. Tom reached out and gripped Sir Francis' hand.

"Cousin," Sir Francis wheezed. "There's papers. Under a false bottom in my clothespress. Thou wilt need them."

"What are they?"

"There are men who will work for the love of their Prince. And there are those who must be cajoled, brutalized, or bribed."

"Your men," Thomas said, understanding.

"Filthy linen," Sir Francis answered. "Yes. 'Tis yours."

"Sir Francis—Her Majesty would not come to your deathbed?" Will felt the vibration of his own voice, but did not at first understand that he had spoken.

It took him longer to recognize the wet, desperate sound that escaped Sir Francis' throat as laughter; it was like the sounds a man might make being broken on the rack. "Serve your Prince," Sir Francis choked, waving Will closer. Breathing shallowly, Will bent forward, extending a hand. Francis Walsingham's yellowed nails dented the flesh of his wrist as the spymaster fell back against the bed. "Do not expect thanks of her. Not if you serve her well."

Will flinched. Blood and something thick and yellow crusted the corners of Sir Francis' mouth. A thin trickle of watery red dripped from his nose, as if the effort of holding his head up had burst a vessel somewhere, one with barely any blood left in it. "Sir Francis."

For all its feebleness, Sir Francis' voice brushed Will's aside as casually as a hand lifting a curtain. "You were young. When the Queen's Men I built for Gloriana toured Stratford, and they took you on." Will thought the sound of the dying man's laugh would make him vomit. "Dick—"

Burbage shuffled forward as if through mud. Sir Francis didn't release Will's wrist, and Will stayed bent over the crouching Tom, wondering if Sir Francis could feel the tremor starting now in his biceps, shivering down his arm to his hand.

"Sir Francis."

"Didst know what we had here, Dick?"

Wordlessly, Burbage shook his head.

"Ah." Walsingham slipped lower in the bed. "Now we do."

Tom dabbed his cousin's upper lip, rubbing thin blood into his beard. Sir Francis' hand slid from Will's wrist and lay slack and open on the coverlet, as if waiting to receive.

"Let me be, Tom." Sir Francis closed his eyes. "Let me be."

Tom stood easily and backed up, looking up as he took a second step away from the bed. And then kept moving, stumbling, his left arm catching Will across the chest and bearing him away as Will too raised his eyes.

A warm wind scented with tobacco smoke blew the bedcurtains back. They rippled heavily, the lamps guttering in their chimneys. The sound that fell from Will's parted lips was almost a *quack*.

The angel's wings, white and strong as a swan's, filled the room from floor to ceiling, even folded tight. Tom's shove turned into a clutch; Will looked up at a serene, unsmiling alabaster face, blue eyes dark as the ocean stern under a mannered wheat-gold mane.

Those candent wings rose not from robes, but a black silk-velvet doublet gleaming with ruby buttons, slashed in flame-colored taffeta and showing a gentleman's cobweb lawn collar at the neck: nothing so lordlike unwieldy as a ruff. The rapier at his hip wore a matching ruby in its pommel—pigeon's-blood, and big as a pigeon's egg. The angel's neck was long and fine, his elegant chin unshadowed by beard. His curls hung in oiled array behind his shoulders, one snagged disobedient on his collar. His lips were palest pink as dog rose, matching the blush in his cheeks. A heavy chain of office lay across his shoulders, a golden circlet crossed his noble brow, but his head was crowned in twining, writhing shadows like silhouettes tormented by flames, and so Will realized he wasn't *exactly* an angel.

:Be not afraid: the Devil said in the voice of a harpsichord, and reached down to stroke Sir Francis' matted iron-color curls. Then he raised those indigo eyes. They examined Tom's face for a moment, then flicked to the side and studied Will more carefully. :Master Shakespeare the playmaker:

Will nodded. Tom gripped his arm tightly enough to leave a perfect handprint through the cloth of Will's padded murrey doublet. "I am."

"Will?" Burbage stepped forward. From the corner of his eye,

Will glimpsed Frances a half step behind him. Both stared at him —
and Tom — as if they had grown donkey's heads. "Who are you talking
to?"

The Prince of Darkness took no notice of the player, except to wait
with elegant, amused politeness until Burbage had finished speaking.
:I have enjoyed your *Titus Andronicus*. And your *A Midsummer Night's
Dream*:

"I haven't written a play by that name. Your—" *Highness? Grace?
That can't be right. Get thee behind me, Satan—*

*—God help me, if you hear me. Who would have thought the Devil so
polite?*

:You shall. As good a play as Master Marley's *Faustus*, which I saw
in Exeter. I understand I gave poor Master Alleyn quite a fright: He
smiled, showing even white teeth. :No matter. We will meet again:

Tom's death grip, impossibly, tightened. Will clamped his lips
shut on a squeak. Burbage froze, hands outstretched as if he con-
fronted a madman; Will wondered what Burbage saw. The Devil
looked down at Sir Francis' breathless corpse and dipped his hands
into the dead man softly as if tickling trout from a stream. He raised
his eyes to the ceiling, with an expression of pure concentration, and
a moment later he smiled. :Master Shakespeare. Master Walsingham. Good day—:

A bit of a bow as he withdrew something small and fragile, gleaming like opal, from Sir Francis' breast. The Devil caught Will's eye one
last time, winked, and turned away.

Frances washed her father's body with sponges and warm water, the
valet and the gardener assisting. White linen lay at her feet, neatly
folded, for the winding sheets. Will sat forward on a bench in the corner, his elbows on his knees, and rested his face in his hands. "Richard.
Thou sawst nothing?"

Burbage sighed, back on his heels. He held in his hands the cup
that Will had refused to take. "I saw you talk at nothing and then
nearly faint into frothing fit upon the floor, Will. I'm taking you to a
doctor on the morrow — Simon Forman, if he'll see us — and you'll not
be playing for Gloriana today."

Will shook his head. Sir Francis dead, on Her Majesty's critical birthday. Will felt the power —*stirring*— in London's bones as he had not since that long-ago Twelfth Night. "I'm in that play. I must be in that play, Richard. Can't *you* feel it?"

He must be there, to bring his strength to bear directly on the enemy. No intermediaries this time. His urgency must have informed his voice. Burbage gave him a curious glance, and nodded slowly. "It's like *that?*"

"It is."

"What play?" Tom asked in what could have been innocent curiosity, but Will rather thought was shock.

"*Richard III.*"

"Wilt thou be seeing visions on the stage before Her Majesty?"

"Tom —" Will turned to Walsingham.

Tom scratched behind his ear, dark hair sliding across his high forehead. "I saw it. Him. As well. The Devil was in this room, Richard. And he spoke to Will and I, passing polite, and pinched my cousin's soul out between his fingers like a ring."

Will and Burbage exchanged a long stare. Will nodded. Burbage swallowed once, his Adam's apple bobbing under his pointed blond beard. "He —*spoke* to thee?"

"He said he'd seen *Faustus* in Exeter. God have mercy."

"We need a priest," Burbage said, but Will shook his head, glancing to Tom for permission.

Tom nodded.

"Richard, what would we tell him? We were at the deathbed of the Queen's spymaster, buried these five years, and Lucifer Morningstar showed up to drag him like Faustus to Hell?"

"Ah."

Tom turned Sir Francis' signet between his fingers. "I wonder why Will and I saw him, and you and Cousin Frances did not." Silence followed, heavy with the thin scent of morning, broken as a cock's crow was answered by rivals.

"We can discuss it later." Will heaved himself to his feet. "I wish householders would leave the chickens in the countryside. They're overloud when a man sleeps of a morning."

Burbage laughed, then looked at Sir Francis' corpse, abashed. "But what would you do for eggs?"

"There's swans on the Thames," Will answered. "They're tolerably silent."

"They're also," Burbage reminded, "the Queen's."

"Then let *her* charge tuppence an egg."

Will managed scarce three dream-torn hours before the nones bell dragged him from under his prickly woolen blanket. He pissed, washed, and dressed for court with a fussy, practiced care that would have amused his wife.

Tightening the points on loose breeches, Will resolved to gain weight if he had to subsist on possets and cream. His hand trembled with exhaustion; he glared at it until the tremors subsided enough to get his sleeve buttoned, then poured ale and broke bread for his breakfast. The bread caught in his throat; he crumbled it into the ale and choked the mess down, grimacing. His shoulders ached. He swore under his breath and left by the garden gate, in a vile enough mood that he wanted a walk to calm himself before he had to face company.

Winding Lane bustled. Will stepped around a woman whose dark orange skirts swayed over a farthingale, his left shoulder almost brushing the dark wood frontage of shops and houses under the overhang. Pale scars from that summer's violent hailstorms marked the facade; they might take years to fade.

He at last turned westward on Leadenhall Street, following it out Aldgate and then south outside of the city wall so he would not have to walk within sight of the Tower gallows and its somber-feathered attendants. The Queen was not at Westminster, but rather at her favorite palace in Greenwich. Will sought the barge that would carry the Lord Chamberlain's Men and their carts of props and costumes down the Thames; it was docked above the city, as convenient to the Theatre some two miles north as possible without hauling carts through London.

Burbage was aboard, eyes red-rimmed, hair damp. He eyed Will critically, a corner of his expressive mouth twitching upward, as Will came up the gangway. Will smiled at how Burbage found his frame between the pilings and the upturned poles at the front of the cart: a master player's unconscious authority of whatever stage he trod.

"Slept?" Burbage asked.

"We'll sleep in the grave," Will answered.

Burbage coughed. "So long as we don't die tonight."

"On the stage?"

"Or after it."

"The company is aboard?"

"But Kemp is late."

"Kemp is drunk, you mean —"

"Kemp is late," William Kemp called from the dockside. "Some of us hold our liquor better than others, sweet William. Now, Burbage drunk, I'd believe it. And you not drinking; 'tis put about that you're unfriendly. Step aside and let your betters in the boat."

"Not so much unfriendly as unhumored for it." Will moved three steps toward the heavy-necked Suffolk who dozed at the center of the barge. These were the horses he grew up with, placid liver mares with flaxen manes braided over the brands at their crests.

Kemp danced up the gangplank backward, his sack thrown carelessly over his shoulder, looking at any moment as if he might fall. He never did, of course, and Will laughed. "I will write a clown as hero one of these plays, Will."

"I will you to it, Will." Kemp grinned and folded himself onto a pile of well-stuffed woolbags. Wherries and skiffs flitted across the sunlit surface of the Thames behind him. "Wake me in Greenwich."

The barge slipped with the current between green muddy banks scattered with half-timbered or brick or stone houses that swam into view and subsided behind. The tide was with them, but Will's belly rumbled for dinner before Greenwich Palace's riverside face appeared, pink-red and white, leaden roofs gleaming obscurely. Towers and chimneys stood bravely against a blue September sky and the rich green of the trees. The horror of the night before could have been but another pageant; devils and men dying in their own rot had no place in the same world as *this* concrete dignity.

The players' barge passed through the water gate just as the Queen's might, and Burbage clapped Will on the arm and grinned. Will pushed a hand through his hair and walked forward past the dozing mare, holding a rail, to watch as the barge bobbed up to the stair that ran down the bank to the landing.

"Lovely," Kemp said over Will's shoulder. "How do we get the mare and the cart up *that*?"

With difficulty, it proved, but they had made the river passage with hours to spare before the performance, and Will helped haul trunks with a light heart. His hands didn't shake and his balance didn't fail, although he was aware of Burbage's supervision. *In case I should glimpse a Devil, doubtlesss.*

Will punched his thigh with a fist, stilling a shiver. *We're here to play a play.*

Servants showed them within, through tapestried halls whose floors were covered like any housewife's with a scatter of herbed rushes. The presence chamber was large, Queen Elizabeth's chair already in place and identifiable by its weight of gilt and crimson cushions. Burbage, son of a carpenter, got down on one knee among the rushes and poked his head under the stage as soon as their escort withdrew. "Will, a light—"

Will looked up, and Kemp did too, but Kemp was the first one to go in search of a candle and spark. Will simply mounted the stair and tested the boards with his weight, so that Burbage pulled back cursing and brushing sawdust out of his blond-red hair. "Seems sturdy," Will said, hiding a hesitation in his right leg that wanted to become a limp.

Burbage opened his mouth to curse and sneezed instead, his eyes screwing into slits. Edward—well bearded now and beyond playing girls—hauled rolls of painted cloth, stifling a laugh.

"As sturdy as thee, thou beggar." Burbage levered himself up against the stage. " 'Twill serve. If thou dost not stomp like a carthorse. What's the hour?"

"Two of the clock."

"Her Majesty will enter after six." Burbage brushed fragments of rush from his knee. "So let us make haste."

The sets were less even than what they used on the bare boards of the Theatre, but the rig to hold the painted backdrop took three cursing players to erect. Will stayed back, knowing he hadn't the remaining strength to be more than an annoyance. Instead he sorted through trunks and laid out costumes and changes in the order they would be needed, taking advantage of a trestle that had been provided for the players' convenience and concealed behind a red-and-green tapestry.

By the time servants came with lamps to augment the failing light from the windows, the whole improbable structure was cobbled together and stood up to Edward swinging on the crossbeam to test its strength. The players tidied themselves and dressed and hastily ate, beer and bread and a bit of cold meat. *We'll have an appetite for our suppers*, Will thought, pinning gold lace with his fingers while Will Sly basted it.

They were just finishing when the Lord Chamberlain arrived, his starched ruff standing high under a gray fringe of beard. Lord Hunsdon wore a black doublet fretted with golden stitchery, a sapphire glinting almost black on the little finger of his broad left hand. He drew up a few steps short of Burbage, who hopped quickly down from the stage and bowed. Will thrust the mended costume at Sly and moved to flank Burbage, bowing also.

"Master Burbage, Master Shakespeare. Is all in order?"

"My lord." Burbage glanced at Will, who nodded. "All is well."

"Expect Her Majesty within the hour. The court will be admitted first: the players may stand at the back of the reception line. Where are your liveries?"

"Ready, my lord."

Lord Hunsdon nodded. His eye caught Will's. "Master Shakespeare."

"Yes, my lord?"

"I must speak with you a moment." His gesture made it plain he meant for Will to follow him, so Will fell in behind. Hunsdon lowered his voice as they walked to the center of the presence chamber, far from the tapestried walls. He paused beside a heap of jewel-toned cushions intended to provide comfort to the Queen's ladies-in-waiting as they sat upon the floor. "Tell me what you saw last night, William."

Will looked up, surprised. "My lord, how did you hear?"

Hunsdon just smiled.

"I believe I saw the Prince of Darkness. My lord."

"Well, I cannot say Sir Francis lived in a good expectation of God's eternal grace, but that is unsettling. And a bad omen on top of ill auguries, and Dee's horoscope for the coming year—" Hunsdon rubbed his chin one-handed, hard enough that Will heard the wiry rasp of threads of beard against his skin. "This is the Queen's nine-times-seventh birth day, and Dr. Dee's charts indicate that it will be an auspicious night to bring forces to bear against her such as we have not yet encountered."

"Worse than the plague?"

No answer but a level look, and Will swallowed and glanced up at the beamed ceiling, far overhead.

"Yes. What think you of Tom Walsingham?" A level look from the Lord Chamberlain.

Kit trusted him. But that wasn't what Hunsdon asked. Will closed his eyes, feeling in a pocket for the slick outline of his now-habitual shilling. He turned it in his fingers, staring down in thought. "Mine impression of him is—very fair, my lord. Quick to act. Protective of those around him."

"Could he serve his Queen?"

"As well as any man, I warrant, although I'm not sure he has his cousin's . . ."

Hunsdon, inimitably plainspoken, smiled. "Ruthlessness?"

"Yes."

"That can be achieved. You may find yourself opposed tonight."

"My lord, how does one oppose a play?"

Hunsdon's elaborate doublet, covered by a gown, rose and fell over the narrow old-man's shoulders it padded. He knotted his fingers to control their palsied trembling; Will looked away. "On a day when devils arise from Hell to pull down our allies, anything is possible." He stepped away, turned back, the pointed tip of his beard quivering. "Long live the Queen."

"Long live the Queen," Will replied.

16 August 1596

~~*My dear compatriot & frie*~~

~~*Dear Christofer*~~

Old friend—

I write not knowing if I will have the courage to send this, or, if I attempt its dispatch, if or when it may reach thee. Forgive the abomination of my much distorted secretary's hand: I scribble this missive in the belly of Tom Walsingham's coach, where I have begged a ride for as thou knowst I am no assured horseman & I have need of very much haste: we were touring in Kent near Tom's house when the news came, for the new Lord Chamberlain has closed London's playhouses—I race ahead. I race ahead.

I may burn it, the letter I mean: I have no secret inks & no privacy in which to use them, although I suppose I could thrust my quill into an onion & squeeze the milk thereof.

But that will come later. First I must acquaint thee with a year & two months that have passed since last we spoke. Thou hast been true to thy word in keeping from me, & I have not wished to trouble thee with my letters. Forgive me for writing now: I am very much in need of the comfort of thy presence in this hour; ~~I am distrau~~

Sir Francis is dead. I do not know if thou wilt have heard, he passed this Sep. previous, attended by devils as befits the sorcery he oversaw. God forgives not crimes in good cause.

The devil is fair; if thou shouldst encounter him be not o'erawed by his beauty, as I was. The morn of that night Lord Hunsdon's Men — no, we were still at that date the Lord Chamberlain's Men — & myself did betake us to Greenwich, where we performed Richard III *before the Queen & her court to much approval. It was her anniversary of her birth, & my master commended me to have extra care in the performance, that forces "might oppose us."*

Kit, they did. It is Essex & his troupe, and I think them allied to Baines & yr Inquisitor.

The Queen might have died that night or fallen ill: it was a terrible thing, a black miasma that seemed to overtake the performance, made us stumble lines & the prompter lose his place. I could feel it, as if I waded the current when the Thames drops with the tide & thou canst walk the breadth standing upright, the water not even cresting thy knee, much to the dismay of the watermen.

But I contrived to trip on a board that was really not so loose after all & drop a bladder of pig's blood over Essex & some book he was reading in his lap, where he sat beside the stage. Her Majesty, thankfully, was unstained.

With that action came an easing of the—tide—& brief interruption of the play although Her Majesty being much amused insisted we continue to completion. Much to Essex's dismay. The ensuing acts proceeded smoothly, & all could recall their lines as necessary. That little action has earned me Oxford's enmity: I believe he has decided with Sir Francis' death — of which he seemed unaccountably early advised, for I know neither Tom Walsingham, Burghley, Burbage, nor the Lord Chamberlain informed him — that he may well end his pretense of alliance with us & show his true colors in courting Essex.

Fortunately with Lord Hunsdon's protection I shall be safe.

Our little magic worked, Essex's counterspell — so I believe it — being thwarted, & our gracious Queen was in very good spirits after & consented even to dance with rude players & commend her ladies likewise, for as I am sure thou knowest she is a great dancer esp. of galliards.

Forgive thee me if I ramble overmuch. I find the core of this tale wiggles from my quill like a fish in weir; penned, but seeking escape.

In November of last year, a book was published which caused great furor, but it seemed the Queen's will & a playmender's small magics still held all things concise. That book was called A Conference about the next Succession to the Crown of England, *& dedicated to Essex, which I am sure thou wilt see as the bold move on the part of his supporters it was. While I am not o'ermerry at the thought of James VI as our next King, there are those in mine acquaintance who think it no bad thing, & the Queen herself seems to have made him the best of a bad lot — Oh, I shall have to burn this letter, my friend — & surely he would be better than that popinjay Essex, whose sole recommendation is that Gloriana once thought him handsome.*

The fuss that followed was something to behold. My distant cousins Robert Catesby and Francis Tresham were jailed in London with many Catholics and suspected Essex sympathizers; I did make shift to see them fed & clothed during their stay at the Queen's hostelry, although it was not so long as some.

Still our grip held steady, & I felt it safe to return to Annie & my children for Lent when the playhouses were closed; I had seen to Robin and Francis' comfort, & all in London quiet. & I thank the Lord my God for the grace that I did that thing —

Oh, Kit. London is terrible. I cannot know what has changed, or how what we have done was broken, but I feel the power gone out of our mighty lines & I feel Oxford must have poets to oppose us. Spenser is returned to London: Lord Hunsdon has informed me that Edmund is

one of ours & always has been (I wonder at the secrets kept & the acts
of one hand kept hidden from the other, but who can truly trust whom in
a game where crowns are hostage?), but I fear he is not well; although
he struggles to complete his Faerie Queen I cannot feel but that we will
soon lose his light. There is famine in the streets: it is all I can do to
provide for Annie, as so many starve that there are carts come to collect
the bodies as in a plague year. Babes swim not in their mother's blood,
but rather starve & sicken for there is no milk at the breast—

—no, I will write no more of it.

On Easter Sunday, Burghley saw men taken into service through
the timely expedient of impressing those able-bodied who attended
Easter service for communion, as is of course required by law. England's stronghold at Calais is fallen to the Spanish: I see thy Fray
Xalbador's hand in this event. Drake's ship has returned: Drake has
not, & it has very much taken the heart out of our Queen that her
other Sir Francis is dead. Essex won some favor, the knave, taking a
fleet to Cadiz by leave of thine old patron the Lord Admiral, where they
sacked that Spanish city.

There is a new playmaker in London, a University man & the son
of a bricklayer or some would have it the posthumous son of a priest.
I have enclosed some of his pages: he fancies himself a comedian. His
name is Jonson, & I have some thought of bringing him into the fold
if I can prove he is not Essex's man. Not easy to do, as I myself have
served Southampton—a man's patron does not show his heart. Chapman is too pompous to trust.

Also there is a man Spencer, Gabriel is his Christian name, who is
not related to Edmund the poet & who seems to wish to attach himself
to Lord Hunsdon's Men. I have spoken to Richard of it. There are players & there are players, & I suspect this one is both.

Thou wilt laugh to learn that I am under interdict—with Francis
Langley! owner of the Swan—by a Southwark justice of the peace one
William Gardner who says we have threatened him bodily. I have not
done so, but thou mayst be assured I will see to it does he trouble us
further. These are petty lawsuits, & I—thou seest my hand is fairer
now, & I write this by candlelight in the Davenant's Inn where I rest
my night before resuming my pell-mell flight on the morrow—but I
believe this Gardner is one of the whoresons in Poley's employ. Of course

if Oxford no longer believes the players under control—such petty ha-
rassments can only continue. & since the death of Henry Carey & his
son George's accession to his place as Lord Hunsdon we are less secure.
The new Lord Chamberlain, Cobham, is of Puritan sympathies, &
he would the playhouses closed, torn down, & I think the players &
playmenders hung, drawn, & quartered. Or at least whipped through
the town. I wonder at how much of our famine is his doing—

—he must be Theirs.

It is down to Burghley now, & the Queen still loves him, but he is
ill, Kit, & in his dotage he grows enamored of oppressing the Catholics
rather than defending his Gloriana. I am desperate. Soon it shall be
only Tom, Lord Hunsdon, Robert Cecil, & myself. We are not the men
our forerunners were. . . .

No. I will not send thee this letter. I will write it for mine ease of
spirit & I will burn it, for I will not tempt thee with troubles to return
to a world that thou hast sanely left.

We starve & we bleed & we die.

& yet the only grief in my heart that is too deep for speaking,
the thing that I must write now & never send to thee. The reason I
am again in thy Tom's coach rattling over unsanded roads & Roman
ditches, & yet there is no haste that can carry me home in time—

I cannot write these words.

Kit, I am going home to Stratford because my son is dead. Dead
seven days now of this writing. Dead & in the ground before I knew of it.

Kit, what have I done?

Act II, scene xiii

She wore no gloves, for neither sun nor wind
Would burn or parch her hands, but to her mind,
Or warm or cool them: for they took delight
To play upon those hands, they were so white.

—CHRISTOPHER MARLOWE, *Hero and Leander*

Kit and Amaranth strolled together through the airy corridors of
the Mebd's palace, her coils dragging behind like the train of a
queen. He walked with a flute in his hands, practicing the fingerings,
keeping the lamia on his left side where he could see her hair writhing.
"You should make a start on your cloak," she said. "I would help you
sew the patches." He wondered how she spoke so clearly, when her
forked tongue flickered with every breath.

Magic and more magic. "Cairbre says I must stitch them myself. 'Tis
part of the protection."

"Then I will teach you to sew." Lightly scaled fingers demonstrated
a minnowlike dart.

Kit frowned, not looking up. "I am," he said with asperity, "a cobbler's son. I can handle a needle very well indeed."

"So I've heard rumored." She laughed when he shook his head.
"Tell me of this protection. I haven't heard the tale."

"The Queen's Bard wants me for an apprentice, I think. A true one, and not a hanger-on. It seems to involve rather a lot of memorizing antique ballads—"

"They were great memorizers of all things, the Druids."

"They would have gotten along well with my Latin tutor. I wonder if the Druids also believed in the recollective power of birchings." He slid the flute into its case on his hip opposite the rapier, and stretched his fingers one against the other. "I am restless, Lady Amaranth."

"You have seemed less anguished of late, Sir Poet."

"I have." *I am busy playing the student again, and making poems to please the Mebd. Morgan leaves me alone, more or less. Is pleasant when I report to her, and gives me no hint to what use she puts mine information, or if it is of use at all. Will not answer my questions about Murchaud, and neither will the Queen. And there is no news from England—*

—Leave it, Christofer. England is done with thee, and thee with she.

How is it that writing for royals is not so rewarding as the bloody rush of the common stage?

"I should be writing," he said, aware as he spoke that Amaranth's last few comments had fallen into silence unanswered, and he could not recall them.

"Ah," she said. Something in her cool, melodious voice caught him; he turned to study her eyes. "Such a lovely man," she said, stroking his cheek. Her fingers felt like cool leather, the scales catching his rough-shaven cheek. "Pity about your scars."

"There's nothing to be done for it," he said. "Many a man's survived worse than half a blinding, and to more sorrow."

"What would you do for your sight returned?" she asked, as if idly.

"Can you do such a thing?"

She shook her head. "There might be those that could. It's in the songs: *If I had known, Tam Lin, that for a lady you would leave, I would have taken your eyes and put in dew from a tree.*"

"I do not know that song. Cairbre has not taught it me."

"We do not sing it here." She smiled, a curve of bloodless lips. His footsteps padded beside the rustle of her belly sliding on stone. "It has not been written yet. And what would you write, if you were writing?"

"A play. Something of Greek descent, perhaps. Has ever a play-maker had such a cast as here, that could play satyrs and centaurs convincing?"

"A tragedy?"

" 'Tis what I'm good for. Tragedy and black farce." He ran the fin-gertips of his right hand along the wall, feeling slight dimples between the cool stones. "You know much of my history, Lady Amaranth. And I know little of yours."

"I have no history." As they turned the corner, the way opened wide. Cushioned benches lined the windows on the west wall; on the east were glass doors made of a thousand diamond-shaped panes as small as Kit's palm. Beyond them, sunlight lay on autumn gardens, begging comparisons to Elysium. "Shall we wander? I know why you are overset, Sir Christofer."

"I never said I was unhappy." But he held the door for her, wait-ing until the last slender inches of her massive tail whipped past, and stepped out onto the balcony behind.

Amaranth rose like a charmed cobra, the power of her lower body lifting her human torso fifteen feet into the air. She draped her coils over the thick stone banister and stretched down it, scorning the steps Kit descended. He enjoyed watching her move; she didn't slither side to side, like a garden snake. Rather, her scaled belly pulsed in ripples like waves rebounding in a fountain, pushing her forward, leaving not so much as a depression in the gravel path to mark where she had gone.

"Neither did you say you were not," she replied, stretching her arms to the sun. The snakes of her hair yawned wider than cats and twisted sleepily in the warmth of a St.-Martin's-summer day, tiny fangs glittering white.

"Clever Amaranth."

"Snakes *are* a symbol of wisdom." She turned to him, winked one of her expressionless eyes.

"If you're so wise, then what is it troubles my well-known, imper-turbable calm?"

Her laughter was a hiss. "The Prince-consort, of course."

"I have not seen him . . ." Kit paused. *Time in Faerie—ah.* "I cannot say how long it's been. Years."

"Then you have not been informed. Curious." Without inflection, as she sank her face into the enormous, late-blooming starburst of a peony.

Kit turned so fast that he tripped, his throat closing in fear. Some detached, intelligencer's fragment of his mind observed his sudden panic wryly. *So. It was not all enchantment, was it, Sir Christofer?* "Been informed of *what?*"

She cupped the blossom in her hand as she rose like a pillar to face him, so its crimson petals shredded and scattered through her fingers. "He has returned."

"I— No. No, I had not known. When, Lady Amaranth?"

"Two days gone. He's been closeted with his mother, and then his wife. But I would have thought—"

Kit rubbed his eyepatch. "So would I," he said, cold between his shoulders. "I would have thought, as well."

He hadn't a key, but locks as ancient and massive as the one on Murchaud's chamber door were a formality, a politeness more than a measure of security. He almost could have flipped the pins from the tumblers with his finger; a shorn quill and the shank of a heavy brooch sufficed. Kit sprang the lock and glanced over his shoulder to see if anyone had noted his unorthodox entry. It seemed unlikely. He slipped inside and let the latch click tight behind.

Twilight filled the bedchamber. Such decadence, in Faerie; even servants slept in their own beds. The first time in his life that Kit had had a bed and a room to himself was at Chislehurst, and that was a function of Tom Walsingham's great house understaffed and underoccupied. Kit walked to the window and threw the panes open, leaning out over the broad carpeted ledge on his elbows and breathing deep of the sweet air of Faerie. The sun had slid under the horizon, and mackerel clouds banded a violet sky. Dying rays stained the misty tops silver as mirrors: their bellies gleamed pewter-dark.

A tiny knot had snagged in the carpet. Kit worried it with a thumbnail, as if he could press it back into place among the red- and black- and mustard-colored wool. The evening smelled of rain, but only change-of-weather clouds hung across the sky. Kit at last closed his eye and leaned his forehead on the back of his fingers, thinking about what Amaranth had said. A remembered taste of blood came with the thought of a glittering blade, poised just above his eye—

He pressed the heel of his hand against his eyepatch. *How long can you play invulnerable, Kit?*

He drew one last breath and turned from the window. First, Murchaud's correspondence. And then—

And then whatever follows.

Night was long fallen when the turn of a key in the lock woke Kit—propped upright against a bedpost with his naked blade across his knees—from a doze. He opened his eye on darkness and rose to his feet, groping his way by the edge of the mattress. No servant had arrived to kindle a fire; perhaps the locked door had been barrier enough.

Murchaud entered alone, bearing a flickering lamp. Kit recognized the turn of his head and prayed himself invisible against the bedcurtains as Murchaud pulled the key and locked the door behind him. The flutter in his throat was excitement and apprehension, nothing more. The memory of Tom and Audrey—companionship, conversation, *family*—unoccluded by sorcery or betrayal, still burned brighter than Murchaud's presence. Kit swallowed against the feeling that he betrayed them, somehow.

You'll never see them again. This is Faerie. There is no love here. Use what you have.

Murchaud set the lamp on a stool and unbuttoned his doublet at the collar, turning toward a wardrobe cupboard against the interior wall. Kit moved across the carpets soundlessly and—as Murchaud hung his doublet on a peg—set the tip of his rapier between Murchaud's shoulder blades, just a half inch to the left of his spine. Kit remembered the spring of ribs, the curve of muscle under his hand, and pressed forward until the point of the blade slid through snow-white silk and a stain the size of a shilling started up.

"If I blotted a pen," Kit said softly, "why should I not write my displeasure on your skin?"

"No reason," Murchaud answered, lifting both hands into sight. "As welcomes go, this is more dramatic than most. Might I unhood the lantern, or do you plan to kill me in the dark?"

"Only if you wish to die tonight." Kit stepped back, sword whispering into its sheath in a snake-tongue flicker.

"What sort of a death are we discussing?" Murchaud's long fingers darkened the lantern for a moment and then were silhouetted; Kit looked down to avoid sudden brightness.

He ran his tongue along the back of his teeth before he answered. "Thou couldst have told me."

"Told thee which?" Murchaud came toward him, as if to pull him into an embrace.

Kit turned aside, feeling unfaithful still, and not to Murchaud. He went to the window and flung the sash open, leaning out into the night. A cold moon gilded the lawns and gardens below, tossing thoughtfully on the ocean. He did not turn back when he spoke. "Hell, Murchaud?"

"What dost thou mean?" The voice close behind him, Murchaud's footsteps soft as a breeze. A hand on his shoulder, fingers brushing his throat. Kit smiled, and didn't shiver.

"Thou hast been—what—five years in Hell? I know thou didst write to thy mother and thy Queen. Yet not to me—"

"I thought—" Murchaud halted. "My mother worked a particularly vile sorcery on thee."

Kit snorted and shook the hand from his shoulder. "Thou claimst to be a *friend* to me? Thy pardon, *dear heart*, if I mock the claim—"

" 'Tis true."

" 'Tis words." Kit moved away. He leaned against the wall between tapestries and crossed his arms, watching Murchaud spread his hands in conciliation, all the night and the nighttime sea behind him. "Just words."

"How didst thou know?"

"Know that it was only words?"

"Know I was in Hell."

"A man has ways," Kit answered. And he was assured that he had set Murchaud's memorized papers back in order so neatly that no one would know they had been riffled. "Thou didst travel to negotiate the tithe. The seven-year's teind."

"We will need Hell's protection as much as ever we have when Gloriana passes."

"What of thy Queen?"

"What of her?" Murchaud let his hands fall to his knees. "Marriages are what they are, and politics are what they are. Surely"—and the note of pain in his voice was masterful: so little, so bright, and so manfully repressed that Kit could almost believe it—"all that love thou didst show me was not merely black magic and bindings?"

Almost believe it. "All that love?" Kit smiled, and reached down with his left hand to slip his scabbard from his belt and lean the sword against the wall. He came to Murchaud, and ran his fingers through the other man's jet-black curls, lips so near to lips that Kit could taste Murchaud's breath, with a trace of wine on it, and a scent like roses. "All the love I have given thee in subjugation is but shadows of the love thou shalt have."

We keep nothing, who serve. And he pressed Murchaud's head back against the window frame and kissed him as if Kit's mouth were a branding iron and Murchaud the property it marked.

Kit did not ask himself to whom his service went. And it was he who rose from the warmth of the bed in the darkest hour of morning, retrieved his sword, and dressed. And turned the key in the lock. And left.

There were mirrors in Faerie, after a fashion: glass, water in a bowl, wine in the bell of a glass. Morgan had not precisely been truthful in saying there were *none*. What was true was that they did not *reflect*. The Darkling Glass drew all reflections to itself: into its embrace, and into its power. All reflections—save those in a blade.

A silver dagger polished to mirror brightness gleamed on the marble mantel over his fire, which lay as cold and unkindled as the one in Murchaud's chamber. Kit stripped to his shirt and washed in cold water from the ewer beside the bed. He rinsed his mouth and spat, combed his hair, and went to throw the window wide so the autumn nighttime could fill his chamber.

Which is when the light dancing in the polished blade of that dagger caught his eye. A light he hadn't seen in—

—How long?

He left the window open and walked toward the dagger, which glittered as if reflecting the light of a single candleflame. "Will," Kit whispered. "How long has it been?"

He lifted his hand toward the thick bundle of papers that lay beside the blade, visible in shadowy outline. A letter, he knew, with his name written on it in Will's fast-scrawled secretary's hand. Set on the mantel before a mirror, with a candle lit beside it. News of Robin, perhaps. Mary, Chapman, Sir Francis, Tom.

England. The Queen.

The papers were insubstantial, glimmering like shadows: a reflection cast on air by the light in the dagger's bright blade. If Kit's hand touched them, they would appear in his grip, firm and crumpled.

He reached out and willfully tipped the dagger over. The light in the blade died as if snuffed. The bundle of papers flickered like a blown candle and vanished.

Kit bit down until he tasted blood, and took himself to bed.

Act II, scene xiv

Gloucester: O, madam, my old heart is crack'd, it's crack'd!

—WILLIAM SHAKESPEARE, *King Lear*

The house was dark when Tom Walsingham's carriage rattled to a stop on the summer-baked road. Will put his foot on the iron step, clinging to the door for support as lathered horses stamped. "There's an inn not far, John—"

The coachman tipped his cap. "I know it, Master Shakespeare. I'll see to the horses and—"

"I shall find you tomorrow. I am grateful." Will would have tipped the coachman—another man's servant, after all—but John clucked to his horses, gentling them into the twilight as if he hadn't seen Will's outreached hand. It was a measure of the trust of the horses that the coachman never reached for the whip, and they went willing though their hides heaved like bellows.

Their clatter receding, Will turned toward the thatched and half-timbered cottage as swaying exhausted as if he had run from Kent on his own two legs. The door was latched, painted wood tight against timbers set in stucco that gleamed a soft pink-gray, stained with ochre earths.

Anne had let the flowers by the doorstep die.

Will tugged twice to free the latch, although he knew before the door opened that his house was empty: no smoke rose from the chimney, and he could smell cold ash. Twilight streamed down from the loft. Annie had left the windows under the eaves unshuttered. He fumbled his habitual shilling as he stepped inside, the glass-smooth coin ringing on the door stone.

He crouched to retrieve it, feeling among the rushes strewing the floor, and suddenly found he had not the strength to stand. Cold silver between his fingers, he crouched on the threshold in the open doorway and buried his face in his hands.

It was Edmund who found him. Will had curled forward, his knees drawn up against his forehead and his back pressed to the timber. He heard the footsteps up the walk and looked up, blinking in the twilight, scrubbing a hand across his face although his eyes stayed dry.

"Will. You should have written you were coming."

"I got here faster than a letter would have," Will said, and covered his mouth as he coughed. "From Kent. We only stopped to rest the horses. Where is Annie?"

"With Mother. Are you . . . ?" Edmund's voice trailed off.

Will pushed himself to one knee and stood. "No, I'm not well. How did you know to find me?"

Edmund took Will's elbow as Will hid his shaking hand in his sleeve, the shilling folded tight inside his palm. "Bill the landlord had it from your driver. He sent his boy. Come." Both men pretended it was exhaustion alone that left Will leaning on his brother's strong young arm. "Let's go home."

He dreaded Anne. Feared anything she might be—speaking, unspeaking. Eyes black with weeping. Eyes cold with consideration. *Was there anything I could have done? If I had been here, surely t'were something I could have done.*

She sat by the fire when he came into his parents' house, her dress overdyed drab in black that would fade as one might expect mourning to fade: eventually. One expected to lose babies. Or young children to the flush of their illnesses, the measles and the scarlet fevers and the great and small pox. Will's parents had lost three girls before Will, one of them—the first Joan of two—at nearly Hamnet's age. Children of schooling age, however, an only and an eldest son . . .

Will didn't notice if Edmund came through the door with him. His father might already be abed; Susanna and Judith were nowhere in sight. Will's mother left her darning in a pile on the board and came around it, past Annie, who looked up, but no more than that. Mary Shakespeare squeezed her own child's shoulders and leaned her forehead briefly on his neck. She kissed the corner of his mouth. "Oh, Will—"

Her voice broke and he clutched her tight for a moment, then set her back the length of his arms. "Thank you."

She nodded and ducked away, knuckling her eye, a hasty clatter on the stairs telling her passage.

Will went to his wife.

Annie's hands were white on her skirts. She crouched on a three-legged stool as if warming herself before the fire, but Will knew her chill would take more melting than that. He knelt down before her. The stool wobbled under her when he took her hands, the one leg shorter than the other that his father hadn't mended in fifteen years gone past. He opened his mouth; she closed it with a look.

"You came," she said. She leaned forward, her unbound fair hair falling around him, tangled with her lack of care.

"Would you doubt it?" Her look was answer enough. "Annie, what happened?"

She lifted her shoulders and shrugged. The hasty dye at her collar had rubbed off onto the linen of her smock. Her palms were calloused enough to rasp his skin, no lady's white soft hands. "Fffuh—" she started, and her throat must have closed on the words.

Will heard the front door latched; no one spoke. A stealthy creak that was Edmund climbing the stairs to bed. Saving candles, Will wondered, or too weary still with grief to face a long evening in company? He held his peace and held Annie's hands, and she neither flinched nor closed her eyes.

"Fell," she said again, more clearly, leaning back on her stool until only his grip held her upright, their arms taut between them like a rigging. "Fell from an oak. Dashed his brains upon a stone."

"Annie—"

"Hush," she said more clearly, and shook her head. "If you had been here—"

Each word might have cost her blood. Will clutched her hands in terror. She continued on a second breath.

"—nothing would have changed."

"Annie, my love," he said as the tears silenced her, finally. "Come upstairs." He pushed a tangle off her cheek. "I'll brush your hair."

"Will, come home." She stood when he tugged her upright, leaning heavily on his arm.

"I am home. . . ."

"Or let us come to London—"

"Plague," he said.

She stopped, one foot raised, and pivoted toward the hearth, drawing him. "We should bank the fire. Everyone's abed."

Will crouched on the sun-warm hearthstone. The poker had a curved point on the back like the beak on a halberd; he raked coals together with the edge and knocked ash over them, and the last bit of a log that had fallen out of the fire. He stayed there, hiding his right hand between his knees, fingers steadied by the twisted iron handle. Warmth bathed his face, his fingers, warmed his breeches until he felt the weave of the cloth.

Annie reached down and pulled his right hand into the light. "Worse?"

"No better," he answered, drawing the poker back so it scraped a white line through ash and across the stone.

Annie flinched. "You're thin."

"Eating's—" He pressed a hand to his throat. "Hard. And there's famine in London."

She swallowed and leaned closer. "Stratford as well. I wish thou wouldst have a care for thyself."

"I am taking care of myself, Annie."

"Shall I warm you a posset before we go up?"

"I subsist on the things," he said. "I wish only thy company. Let us to bed, wife." He hung the poker on the rack, muting the clatter with his hand, and thrust himself to his feet. She swayed as he slid an arm around her waist and drew her against his side.

Upstairs, he petted her until she slept—she rarely cried, his Annie.

Even when he thought she better might. And held her until a sliver of moonlight fell through the shutters, revealing the dark hollows bruised like thumbprints under her eyes, and she rolled away to bury her face against the wall.

Will rose in his shirt and smallclothes and crossed the floor. Breathless warmth surrounded him as he threw the shutters back and leaned out over the garden, imagining the colors of the late-summer blooms whose nodding faces reflected the flood of moonlight — thistle, daisies, and poppies. The Dutch bulbs would be over, but the too-ripe scent of late honeysuckle lay on the air like the scent of rot, and Will drew his head back inside.

Someone — Edmund? — had carried his bags up the stairs. Must have retrieved them from John the carriageman at the inn. Will lifted the smaller case and dug in it for paper and pen, finding first the sealed and bundled pages of his uncollected letter to Kit. He pushed them aside to uncover his inkhorn, silencing the rustle of papers as best he could, and left the case standing open when he went to the window.

The moonlight was bright enough. He wouldn't need a candle.

Will laid his sheets on the ledge and worked the plug out of the inkhorn before sliding the nib inside. He let the excess ink ooze back into the palm-sized container, propped it against the edge of the window, and hesitated, the quill almost brushing the creamy sheet. *A Midsummer Night's Dream*, he thought, remembering the impossible blue of Lucifer's eye.

I'd dream myself home safe in bed, and Hamnet clattering down the ladder to shake Annie and me awake —

The ink dried while he watched the moon-silvered garden. He dipped again and set it to the page in better haste, and wrote:

Ill met by Moone-light, proud Tytania . . .

Will drowsed, half waking, and mumbled as Anne smoothed his hair back to let the sunlight rouse him. The morning was unkind to the weary lines around her eyes. "The household is awake." The clatter of pots confirmed it. "How was your sleep?"

"Broken." He sat upright to knuckle the crusts from his eyes. He swung his legs over the edge of the bed. "Show me the grave today, Annie?"

She hesitated, reaching for her kirtle. "Of course. We—"

"What?"

"Thy father had a mass performed."

"Christ, Annie, I don't care what religion my boy is dead in." It came out sharper than intended, but she didn't flinch.

Her brows rose, as if she were about to deliver a tongue-lashing, and her mouth opened and shut. She covered her eyes. "Will, I'm sorry. It was hard, that thou wert gone."

"Would that I had not been. Would that none of this were necessary at all." *Would that I were still in Kent with Lord Hunsdon's Men. Would that I could have taken— Stop it, Will.* "I'm home now, Annie."

"For how long?" She turned her back on him as she wriggled into her petticoat-bodies.

Annie waited long enough to be certain he wouldn't answer, and turned over her shoulder. "That traveling priest is here more than you are, Will. If he were Anglican, I'd say I should have married him."

"Traveling priests and cottage intrigues—" he said, lacing his points with hands that almost didn't tremble. He heard her indrawn breath and rolled over it, refusing to look her in the eye. "I would not fight with you, Annie."

Her shoulders went back and she whirled on him, whispering so her words would not carry. "Well, and what if I would fight with *you*, Master William Shakespeare? Or shall I put that *want* on the shelf with all mine other *wants*, and will you talk to me of duty?"

She leaned forward, hands on her hips, her hair still unbraided and tangled over her shoulders. The little room seemed even closer as she stamped one bare foot among the rushes and then threw up her hands in exasperation at his silence. He felt as if he might choke on all the things he could not say to her.

"Annie, my love—"

"Go back to London," she said, and turned away to open the door. "If your plays are more to you than your children. Go."

"It's not—" he began. But the door swung softly shut behind her, and Will let his mouth do the same. "Damn," he said, and narrowly avoided punching the wall.

———

A sunny afternoon followed Will from the graveside. Fleeing its relentless cheer, he pushed open the door of Burbage's Tavern and nodded to the landlord in the cooler, airy common room. "Good day, Bill."

"Will." He hesitated, a rag in his hand, and cleared his throat. Three or four other men sat about the lower level of the tavern, the silence hanging between them redolent of an interrupted conversation. "I'm sorry—"

"We're all sorry," Will said into the heavy quiet. He nodded up the smooth-worn wooden stairs. "Have you anyone at work in the gallery today?"

"Not until suppertime. Sit down over here." A gesture at one of the long trestles, flanked on both sides by sturdy benches. "I'll see you get some dinner, for all the bread's gone cold by now."

"They fed me at home," Will lied, taking a seat in a sunbeam, which caught flashes of silver from the coin that he fussed. He couldn't face choking down bread and cheese before these pitying men. "Ale would go kindly." Served warm, and in a leather cup.

"Ale it will be. Is there news from London, Will?"

Will shrugged. "There's starvation in the streets, want and privation, consumption and plague. The usual, only worse. Preserve us from cities."

Footsteps from the more occupied corner of the tavern, and a voice unexpected enough to knock the shilling from his fingertips to clatter on the trestle board. "Oh, Master Shakespeare. Surely if London were so unhealthy as all that, none of us city rats would ever return, given a view of the country and a breath of fresh air."

Will held the mouthful of ale until it could trickle past the tightness in his throat. He laced his fingers under the table and let the silver spiral, jingling, to a stop. "Master Poley," he said, and didn't look up. "What brings you to Stratford?" Expecting the easy charm, the intelligencer's lie. Surely Poley wouldn't try to start an argument here, surrounded by Will's childhood friends and his family's neighbors.

"I came to look in on your family," Poley said, swinging a leg over the bench opposite Will. "I'm a father myself. It seemed the least I could do, considering the care you've taken of Mary. And little Robin, too."

Will did raise his eyes then, and dropped his voice. "Am I intended to understand this as a threat?"

"Understand it as you wish." Poley's trustworthy smile turned Will's stomach. The intelligencer held up a pair of silver tuppence to catch the landlord's eye, and traded them a moment later for a cup of wine. "Have you considered how much your family must miss you? How much the worst it would be if anything should befall you in London, so far from home? Cities are dangerous—"

"And *your* family? Do you consider the future of your son?"

Poley just smiled, and it struck Will like a kick in the gut. *I am not like this man. I am not like this man.*

But how, then, do we differ?

Will unlaced his fingers, lifted his tankard with his left hand, and only touched the ale to his lips. He wiped his beard to cover the smile. "My wife may curse me to my face," Will said. "And I can't deny she's a reason to. But neither my Annie nor your Mary will cross the street not to catch mine eye."

"My Mary?" Poley turned his cup between the flats of his hands, scraping the board. "I haven't a virgin thought in my head. Many a cheerful one, but not of Mary. Take her—"

" 'Tis not so."

"Pity for thee, Will. She's a wildcat."

"I'll not be thee'd by thee, either. *Master* Poley."

"Ah." The shilling lay shining between them. Poley picked it up, balanced it on edge. "An old one."

"A toy. Too debased to spend."

"It rings fine."

"It's shaved to half its size," Will said, as Poley made it jingle against the table again, the note of silver bell-clean.

"But the loyalty it buys is a whole loyalty, no?"

"Your point, man?"

A scrape as Poley pushed the rough bench back, quaffed his wine and stood. He extracted a short knife from his belt and pared his fingernails over the table. Will edged his cup away. "Mine only point is this." A flick nimble as a cutpurse's razor. Poley wore hammered rings on both thumbs, rings that glittered the dark hard radiance of steel. "You made an enemy in Essex."

"My clumsiness is renowned."

"A wonder you can stay on a stage at all—but no matter. Think hard, Master Shakespeare."

"Think on what, Master Poley?"

"Think whether your family might be better served by your return to Stratford. Or by your choosing a master longer for the world than Lord Burghley. Or Lord Hunsdon. Or Tom Walsingham."

"Tom's young."

"Aye," Poley said, and sheathed his dagger again. "Nearly of an age with you and Kit Marley, as I recall."

Will neither stood nor looked up as Poley moved toward the door; nor did he finish his ale. He sat for some time in silence, and then he picked that poor shaved shilling up with his fingertips and rolled it twice across their backs—as Tarleton had shown him, almost a decade before—and made it vanish into his sleeve. "Well," he said under his breath, "that was *interesting*. Bill—"

The last louder, so the landlord looked up. "Will?"

"Is John the carriageman still in residence?"

"Not in at the moment, but he did say he'd be staying as long as you did—"

"Send me a tally," Will said. He stood. "Let him know I'll be a week or so here, and then back to Kent. If he needs to attend his master I'll find other transportation."

"I shall. For home already? It's barely noon."

"For home," Will said, and went.

Act II, scene xv

Rome if thou take delight in impious war,
First conquer all the earth, then turn thy force
Against thy self: as yet thou wants not foes.

—M. ANNAEUS LUCANUS, *Pharsalia, First Book*
(translated Christopher Marlowe)

It begins in a confessional at nightfall.

The subtle bitterness of myrrh, the richness of frankincense, the sweat of the penitent lingering in age-calmed wood. Kit bows his head, leans close to the grille. Above the frankincense, the perfumed soap of the Spanish priest on the other side. With the cloying scent came cloying fear, knotting his belly like hunger, although he is successful. Accepted.

Soon, he will be going home.

Christ, not this one.

Not this —

Kit heard his own voice, Latin, the words of ritual. He fixes his eyes before him. 'Tis a good ritual. Comforting. "Bless me, Father, for I have sinned."

"Indeed, my child, you have. But fear not. Your penitence will be adequate before Heaven." English, and a voice he knows.

Blurs, a jumble of unclarity, of time slowed beyond time. The door of the confessional slides open, Kit blinking in the light as he moves to stand. Each heartbeat distinct as enormous hands close on his wrists, implacable as iron manacles, haul him up; he tries to kick—

—Kit: slender, not tall, barely bearded, without yet a grown man's shoulders. He might break nine stone after a hearty supper. Richard Baines simply lifts him off his feet like an ill-tempered child, like a spitting virago, veins bulging in Baines' muscle-ribboned forearms as the black robes fall back. Baines *bounces* him, once, and nausea fills Kit's throat as his shoulder rips inside like twisted cloth snagging on thorns.

"There's our cat, Fray Xalbador. Oh, don't like that much, do you, puss? Got your claws now—"

Baines shakes Kit; white flashes occlude Kit's vision. Hands fumble his belt as the Spaniard claims his dagger.

"Where shall we have him, Fray?"

The priest's accented voice. "The basement, I think. 'Tis pity my tools are not here—"

Baines answers, "Mine are."

Baines' iron rings pinch Kit's flesh. The skin at his wrist breaks; blood trickles. He fights, but the other Kit, who watched him, already knowing—*that* Kit curled tight and hugged himself in resignation. *Wake up. Wake up. Wake up.*

"I'll see him settled—wildcat!"—another bounce, with a kind of a twist to it, and this time Kit screams as his shoulder pops with a sound like a drawn cork—"well, that should make him easier to manage."

"Broken?"

"Just slipped, I think. Fetch the others, Fray Xalbador."

This Kit chokes on pain, keening the agony as Baines twists his dislocated arm behind his back to make him march— *This* Kit thinks— *Others. This is the core. These are the names Sir Francis needs. All I have to do is talk my way out of this. All I have to do is live through this.*

That Kit wept for his own innocence.

He blinked, and *this* Kit closes his eyes in pain and opens his eyes in pain, in a room prepared with a half-dozen torches, two braziers, and a fireplace for warmth.

Dark, clean, the floor of rammed earth and the walls of mortared

stone. Long tables against the walls, and Kit sees—chalk, a small heap
of candles, twine, and some things he can't identify as Baines shoves
him to his knees and twists his left arm behind him. He opens his mouth
to argue, and Baines bends the arm higher. Not much, an inch.

Kit wheezes with pain and locks his tongue behind his teeth. And
then there are men in the room, and he can't beg if he wants to, because spiked iron fills his mouth.

He *did* know the names of four of the other five. Easton, Carter,
Saunders, Silver. The last one is a slender-hipped, broad-shouldered
blond, barely a man in years, whom Kit would have eyed with some
appreciation under other circumstances. Catesby, Fray Xalbador calls
him, and Baines calls him Robin.

*Easton, Carter, Saunders, Silver. Catesby. Richard Baines. Xalbador de
Parma. Easton, Carter, Saunders, Silver—*

I can remember that.

In the dream, the rough iron of the bridle already wears at
his cheeks and nose. In the dream, the ruin of his right eye weeps
blood and matter down his face. In the dream he kneels quietly at
Baines' feet, domesticated. *And rough jades' mouths with stubborn bits
are torn . . .*

History had been different, but dreams were what they were. *Puke
with that thing in your mouth, Kit, and you'll die of it.*

Kit strains to overhear the quiet discussion without attracting
Baines' attention. The Spaniard seems to be instructing the others
with careful hand gestures. Kit presses at the gag in his mouth experi-
mentally with his tongue, moans as fresh blood flows. Baines catches
the iron straps around Kit's skull in a free hand and gives it a little
shake, playfully rattling the scold's bridle, bruising Kit's cheeks and
tearing at his mouth. Baines reaches through the bars and smoothes
Kit's hair, leans down and whispers—"Holla, ye pampered Jades of
Asia, / What, can ye draw but twenty miles a day?"

Catesby, the splendid blond, turns from the rest and crosses to
Baines, looking down at Kit with something like dismay. "He's a bit
unprepossessing."

Baines laughs, petting. "He's a poet. One of their sorcerer-
playmakers, a darling of Walsingham's. Already known around Cambridge for his filthy translations of Ovid, and London for a bloody

travesty of a pagan play. Aren't you, puss?" Another little shake, a caress, and more blood.

This Kit nods, biding his time, a chip of tooth working into his gum.

"Good puss. Pick of the litter."

"It's distasteful—"

" 'Twill break their black arts." Baines jerks his head at Fray Xalbador. "Between me and he, you've two priests who say it. Desperate times."

Catesby smiles bitterly, as *that* Kit thought *but you weren't there. It was only the five of them.* Panic. *I would remember if it had been six. I would* remember.

This is not how it happened. Catesby *had* been at Rheims, arriving just as Kit took his leave forever. Kit remembered the worn sword, the good clothes, the expansive grin. But Catesby had not, could not have been in that close basement room.

He still speaks. "It doesn't sit well. But, to the glory of God and the Holy Mother Church."

"To the glory of God," Baines answers. Kit doesn't think Catesby feels the lie in the big man's words, but Kit does. Feels it in the way his hand tightens on Kit's tattered arm.

Does Will know how much I left from that I told him?

"Which will it be, the pentangle or the circle of Solomon?"

Oh, God.

No.

Marley, I conjure thee, awake.

The braziers smoke as they make him ready, twisted rodstock heating in each one. It's copies of the poker with which he'd threatened Will, not the irons de Parma actually used, and *I fought. I fought and they had to drag me* he goes docile and willing to Baines' command.

It would be easier if they would bend him over the table, like Edward, so he can't see their faces. But they want him on his back.

That Kit remembered how he had turned his head, cursing, pulling against the agony of Baines' hands, and sunk his teeth in the base of the big man's thumb. *This* Kit tries, but the weight of his head presses the bands of the bridle forward, drags the barbs on the bit across the soft ridges on the roof of his mouth in a mockery of a lover's kiss.

Still, *that* Kit remembered the taste of Baines' blood with bitter triumph, and Baines' mockery as he inserted the bit. *Now, puss, if thou'rt going to bite we'll have to muzzle thee sooner instead of later.*

A fair idea, the Spaniard had answered, *to stop his pagan poetry in his mouth.*

It's why I had it with my mage-tools. That and in case we laid hands on a fay after all. Disorientation, time out of joint. Baines, laughing at the wound on his hand as the Inquisitor fetched the bridle. *Jesu Christi, she even fights like a wench.*

They come one by one into the circle and de Parma seals them one by one within. They take turns, every expression etched on Kit like the scars on his breast, his belly, his thigh. Catesby dispassionate, Silver mocking, Easton with closed eyes and a bitten lip—

—except in the dream, it's Edward de Vere who rapes him, and sweet Tom Walsingham, and over them falls the shadow of vast, bright wings. He feels the power they filter through him, the cool edgy blade of a magery so different from his own visceral poetry that he has no name for it. As different as blood-tempered, cross-hilted steel is to a crown wrought of raw reddish gold and fistfuls of the gaudy jewels of Asia.

And through it all, Richard Baines, hands as sure as irons pressing him to the table, a soft voice in his ear encouraging him, making a mockery of comfort, calling him *kitten* and *puss* as it bids him be brave, good puss, it will all be over soon.

And he cannot even scream.

God, enough.

God didn't seem to be listening. Again.

Consummatum est—

When they release him he rolls to the floor and lies there, drools blood as fast as it fills his mouth, mumbles through the agony, amazed his tongue will shape words at all. His knees curve to his belly. His chin curves to his chest. The bloody earth of the floor clings to his bloody flank.

"You're for the Queen's destruction," he rasps.

The priest nods, unafraid of him. Unsurprising: Kit couldn't stand if the roof were on fire. "We are."

"Let me help."

"You hate her so much? I'm not inclined to trust you right now, poet. But you've earned a quick garroting; I'm not an unreasonable man."

"Was not—" He spits again, smearing at his bloody mouth with a bloodier hand. "Was not Job tested in his faith?"

The priest watches, unimpressed. Kit rolls prone, whimpering as his left arm touches the floor. He shoves himself upright with his right, drags forward, more on his belly than his knees. He slumps down on the chill earth and kisses the man's boot with his broken mouth.

"I—beg you. Let me help."

It isn't enough, and he knows it. He closes his eyes. Both of them.

"If we have a chance to complete the wreaking in London," Baines says, over the sound of the well-pump he works to wash his hands, "it would help to use the same vessel. Even more if he were willing, of course. Although mayhap our little catamite liked it, considering his tastes. Did you like it, puss?" He crouches beside Kit almost congenially, and tousles the poet's blood-matted hair with clean, wet fingers. A look passes between Baines and de Parma that Kit does not understand, does not wish to understand.

De Parma turns away. "Then let him live."

This Kit covers his face with the hand he can move, curling like an inchworm at the touch, and *that* Kit finally managed to wake, whimpering, clinging to a pillow wet with sweat and red with the blood from his bitten tongue.

"God in Hell," he said under his breath, checking guiltily through the darkness to be sure Murchaud still slept. Kit rolled against the Prince-consort and buried his face in Murchaud's hair until his gorge settled and his heartbeat slowed.

A nightmare. *Nothing but Queen Mab running her chariot over your neck.* He'd *lived.* And three weeks later he had stood in front of Sir Francis Walsingham, his arm still useless in a sling, and reported that the Queen's enemies were resorting to sorcery and had fully infiltrated Essex's service. And that he, Kit, had engineered a connection to one of them and the guise of a double agent.

He'd worked shoulder to shoulder with Baines, ostensibly as a turncoat on the Walsinghams—like Baines himself—until 1592, in

Flushing, where he had somehow slipped and given away the game and Baines had nearly gotten him hanged for counterfeiting.

The only thing that had kept him sane those five years was the knowledge that one day he would look Richard Baines in the eye as a hangman slipped a noose around his neck. And the determination that nothing—*nothing*—that had happened at Rheims would *change* Kit Marley.

And what a fabulous lie that was, sweet Christofer. Because he had walked away from his chance at Baines in London, so terrified of the man he couldn't have looked him in the eye if it meant his salvation.

Murchaud smelled of clean sweat and violets. Kit lay against him in the darkness and tried without success to chase the reek of frankincense from his lungs.

Act II, scene xvi

O absence! what a torment would'st thou prove . . .

—WILLIAM SHAKESPEARE, Sonnet 39

October, 1597

I should have burned this letter.

I should write no more.

I know now I'm writing not to thee, but to myself. Still I imagine I might see thee again. But I am a poet, & poets are liars, as Ben Jonson —you would have hated Ben, sweet Kit —reminded me over supper at the Mermaid yesterday.

Still, I've managed to hold my peace a year. Perhaps I am learning independence after all. That was what sent thee back to Faerie so hastily, wasn't it, my friend? The worry that Tom & I wouldn't stand alone —

Thou wert probably right.

There is the usual news, fair & foul. Mary & Robin are well — Robin tall as a weed, & Mary we've found work as a seamstress with the Lord Chamberlain's Men. We're the Lord Chamberlain's Men again, George Carey Lord Hunsdon has taken his father's old place in the wake of Cobham's death —God rest his eternal soul, merrily, & in a place where entertainments are shown daily, much may it chafe him.

Oh, Kit, the litany of the dead grows long.

The gossip might as well grow on trees. Gabriel Spencer, who I mentioned when I wrote you last, killed a man in a duel before Christmas. And he and Ben Jonson were arrested in July—Ben says Spencer's a secret Catholic, not that that means overmuch, but it doesn't ease my suspicions that he's Promethean. James Burbage died in February; Richard & his brother Cuthbert head the company now. We had to tour last summer, & next summer again likely. There's lease trouble with the Theatre: we shall have to relocate & though they have purchased the indoor theatre at Blackfriars (the one that was used by Chapman's boy company, from whence so many of our apprentices on the common stage did come) a lawsuit by the neighbors there keeps us from using it.

I suspect Baines. Or Oxford, more likely. Not that there's a blade's width between them.

Annie bought me only the second-biggest house in Stratford, after all: she's moved the whole family therein. My father was awarded arms in London last fall. Life seems to go on most merrily, & yet I find nothing in it to put my teeth in. Perhaps because I have lost one or two.

Ned Alleyn has left playing, for good he says, & truly he has everything a man could want from it. I think he finds the modern masques & satires as wearying as I do, & misses thy pen & thy wit, sweet Christofer. Truly, he & thee were a match. Half the new satires have no play behind them but a series of jibes.

Or perhaps I am old & out of fashion. Although my plays do very well. I include my Midsummer Night's Dream*—a foul copy, forgive me—on the thought it might amuse thy mistress a little. Thou shalt judge if it is fit for her eyes.*

Thou wilt however be amused to know Ned's still wearing that cross—and since mine encounter with the Devil claiming he appeared at Faustus *(I had heard the story but never credited it) September last, I'm inclined to wear one of mine own.*

The other news is not so cheerful. Thou wilt however laugh—I can see thee laughing—to know that Her Majesty clouted Essex alongside the head recently when Essex turned his back on her. She created your old patron, the Lord Admiral, Earl of Nottingham after Cadiz, & Essex was outraged that he, the Queen's favorite, should be passed over—Burghley says he nearly drew his sword on the Queen, & the

Lord Admiral now Nottingham pinned him to the floor before he could clear the scabbard, thus saving Essex's life.

Pity.

My Richard II *has been pirated, & I recognize the draft of the manuscript I circulated through mine old patron Southampton & his friends. I shall not make that mistake again.*

Sleeping, waking, heart beating or cold in earth, 'tis all the same. I've no taste for anything of late but putting words on paper. Kemp claims I must have taken a pox, I have so little will for sport. Mary's a relief. The plays go well. I write better when I'm unhappy. There's comfort in that of a sort.

I fear I am growing old. Four & a half years ago I was young, Kit. The age most men are when they marry. My career ahead of me, London bright, Gloriana strong. Thou wert alive, & we were rivals and chambermates. The poetry we were going to write, each of us outdoing the other!

Now I am famous & a gentleman with a fine house. ~~What good~~

Edmund my brother is with us in London now: he said he could not bear to stay in Stratford ~~after they~~*. He's a hired man with another company—not with the Chamberlain's, he said he wished to make his own way & I cannot grudge it—& courting the girls. Good news there at least.*

Well. I'll leave this on the mantel tonight, again, and again you will not take it—

Nay, enough. More later, perhaps. As the spirit moves me.

The place on the Mermaid's weathered door where a hand might rest to make it open was refined smooth and fair, the wood so oiled with the grease of men's palms that it retained a fine polish although its sea-blue paint was worn into the grain. Will found the spot and pushed, holding it wide to let little Mary slip through before him.

A few ragged voices greeted them, rising from an enclave of players in the corner by the fire, half under the gallery. The October afternoon was gone chilly as the sun slipped behind a layer of overcast unlikely to bring desperately needed rain.

Mary headed for the publican as Burbage waved Will to a cluster of benches maintained by the other Wills—Sly and Kemp—along with the amiable, red-goateed playmender John Fletcher, whose unbuttoned red doublet made him look like a fashion-conscious demon, and Kit's old collaborator Thomas Nashe with his ridiculous curls. Will limped close enough to speak in a normal tone. "Wills. Jack, Tom, Richard." They embraced and kissed him before he sat, which eased Will's sore heart. He hadn't the spleen to be angry when they treated him like Italian glass; it was, he knew, a measure of their love. "A spare crowd tonight. Tom, you're neither in the country nor in jail."

It had been a play called *The Isle of Dogs* that had seen Nashe flee London before he could be locked away on suspicion of sedition; Will glanced around the Mermaid for its second author, Ben Jonson. These satirists sailed very close to the wind. Admirable — but the wind changed frequently.

"Not jailed, and drinking to it."

"Chapman claims he's close to ending his revisions on Master Marley's *Hero*, and he'll be along when 'tis finished." Fletcher's eyes sparkled above his freckled cheeks, a comment on the likeliness of that.

Nashe snorted into his wine. "Kit's four years dead. I think he would have had the poem finished in a month at most —"

"Chapman has to be sure he's eradicated all the bawdy bits. It takes a while to find them all, it being Kit's work —" Will replied, dropping into a chair as laughter rose around him. He waited for the pause, and filled it to an approving roar. " — and for George, longer than most. Where's the bricklayer, Tom?"

Nashe tapped a pipe out on the edge of the table and twisted a knife in its clay bowl. "Ben? Still jailed —"

"No one stood his bail?"

Burbage, stretching until his shoulders cracked. "Henslowe loaned him four pound to eat on."

"Four pound? At what rate?" Will raised an eyebrow.

Fletcher laughed. "Better than borrowing from Poley."

"Aye, at least with Henslowe you'll see the money and not a pile of lute strings you're supposed to sell to recoup."

Mary came to the table balancing two mugs of thick ale, and Nashe let whatever else he might have been about to say about Robert Poley's moneylending practices die in his throat. Mary perched on

Burbage's knee and kept one mug for herself, sliding the other neatly to Will. He cupped it, too cheerfully tired to think of fighting to swallow. The mug was cool from the cellar. "I'll stand Ben's bail. How bad can it be?"

"Fifteen pound." Nashe drained his wine.

"Significant. I'll go tomorrow. I want him to owe me a favor —"

"You'll have him teach you satire?" Will Sly was sly enough, on the rare occasions when he troubled himself to add to the conversation.

Will snorted. "Something like that. Richard, especially for you — I come with fair news to tide us through a cold winter."

Burbage's head came up. "The playhouses."

"Yes, my merry men —"

"Hah!" That from Burbage, who slammed his fist on the trestle and kissed Mary hard enough to spill her ale.

Every man in the room looked or jumped, but Will followed the motion of one fellow in the corner, who started to his feet as if expecting a brawl, feeling for his swordhilt; Will's cousin, the Earl of Essex's friend, the golden-haired recusant Robert Catesby. Will blinked: he knew both of the men at Catesby's table. One was Gabriel Spencer, who had also been jailed for *Isle of Dogs* as one of the principal players, and whom Will would have expected to be sitting with the players: he raised his mug to Will as Will turned. The second, in a plain brown jerkin, was the Catholic recusant Francis Tresham. *Interesting. If Sir Francis Walsingham was alive —*

There was not a chance that Will would inform Burghley and Robert Cecil of the same. There was comfortably Protestant and conforming in the name of the Queen, and then there were the Cecils and their mad-dog desire to see every Catholic whipped from England, and every priest hung.

Burbage clapped Will on the shoulder, drawing his attention to the table. "Oh, yes, bail Ben for that. I'll stand half the fee. I'll buy that Bankside property —"

"Buy?"

"No more landlords." Burbage spat into the rushes.

Kemp muttered assent. "What about the timbers?"

Burbage shrugged. " 'Tis small carpentry, but great labor. We'll pull the Theatre down."

"And cart it over the Bridge?"

"Float. Or—wait for the ice to set and skid it over."

"Won't your landlord have something to say on that?" Nashe asked, hunched over peppery warmed wine. He was lucky to be free of the Marshalsea. Kit and Tom Watson had spent time in Newgate themselves, an experience Will envied not.

"We'll do it at Christmas," Burbage said. "Betimes, I know an inn-yard or two would be glad of us—"

The Mermaid's blue door rattled a little on its hinges when it opened. Will turned to see who had come in, and understand why Burbage's voice had stopped so abruptly that it still seemed to hang in the air around them.

Sir Thomas Walsingham stood for a moment framed against the door, resplendent in a ruff starched pale yellow to compliment the canary slashes on his doublet of sanguine figured satin. A touch of gold at the buttons, the hilt of his sword, the clasp that held his cloak askew, and the pin in his hat. He'd come from court, quite obviously, and quite obviously in a hurry; his horse's sweat stained the knees of his breeches and the insides of his hose, and his clothes were quite unsuited to riding.

"Master Shakespeare," he said from the door. "If you would be so kind—"

Will stood, pushing his still-brimming tankard at Mary, and followed Walsingham out into the hubbub of the autumn afternoon. "You look like you've had a hard ride, Sir Thomas."

"A fast one, in any case. And have I stopped being Tom in private through some offense, or—"

"A public thoroughfare is hardly private."

Tom dismissed it with a tip of his well-gloved hand. "Robert Cecil sent me. After a fashion."

"On what case?"

"Have you any progress on the Inquisitor?"

"God's blood, man—" Will looked up as Tom's eyebrows rose. "I forget myself, Sir Thomas."

"I like that in a friend. You were about to say you had been on tour."

"Aye."

"But the playhouses are opening."

"Aye. Oh!"

"Yes. And Cecil wants his results half yesterday." Oh, that Walsingham smile. As if Tom looked right through you, and weighed what he saw, and was amused. A softer voice, almost too quiet to be heard over the street: "Any word of Kit?"

"No. You?"

"No." Tom swallowed. "He always was marvelously good at making a threat stick. Will, bring Poley's head at least to Cecil if you can, preferably Baines or de Parma. His father's health is failing, I think, and—"

Will sighed, following Tom's smooth stride over the cobbles almost without a limp. "And 'tis down to me and you, and Dick. I'd thought of recruiting Ben Jonson. If anything happens to me, you'll need a poet. Things are not good, Sir Thomas."

"Nay, not good at all. No one can remember such a drought. Jonson's rumored a recusant, isn't he?"

"And he seems to spend most of his time in jail." Will shrugged. "But he has talent."

"Cecil won't hear of it."

"Then Cecil won't hear of it."

Tom coughed, and smiled. "He wants you at Westminster tonight. Privily."

"You're a most discreet messenger. In your court suit."

"A more usual one follows. I thought you deserved warning."

"By Sir Thomas Walsingham."

"William Shakespeare, Gentleman. How does it feel?"

"Like ashes rubbed between my hands," Will said bitterly. "I've never written better in my life."

The way forked. The two men glanced at one another, and turned back in the direction they had come, annoying a goodwife with a basket full of greens. "Is there more?" Will asked.

Tom shook his head, and they continued in silence to the Mermaid's door. "I'd offer you my horse, but it would be a little obvious."

"I don't ride," Will answered. "I'll just slip inside and await the messenger."

"And do try to look surprised—" Tom stopped and laughed at the expression on Will's face. "Very well, Master Player, I shan't teach you tricks that were old when you were a new dog too. Have a care tonight. He's a very devil, Robert Cecil."

"I think," Will said, "it goes with the name."

Act II, scene xvii

Like untun'd golden strings all women are,
Which long time lie untouched, will harshly jar.
Vessels of Brass oft handled, brightly shine —

—CHRISTOPHER MARLOWE, *Hero and Leander*

Kit leaned back on Murchaud's shoulder, his right side to the wall and his rapier twisted aside so he could rest his heels on the padded bench while they watched the dancers. The prince's warmth soaked the knot between Kit's shoulders, and the warmed wine at least began to ease the pain in his neck. And contributed to the headache he still carried, since waking from another evil dream in the black hours of the morning.

"A pavane," he said amusedly. "It will be country dances next —"

"Country dances. You like them for kissing the ladies in passing," Murchaud said, elbowing Kit in the ribs.

"Better in passing than in matrimony," Kit answered, turning his head to watch Morgan whirl across the floor, her wild hair spinning around her, her ivory silk skirts swaying heavily as she moved. "We're failing utterly to look disaffected with one another, love."

"We'll quarrel after the dancing." Murchaud draped his right arm over Kit's shoulder and around his chest. "I'm expected in my lady's chamber's tonight, and perhaps tomorrow as well. Besides, a stormy love affair is so much more intriguing to a gossip or conspirator than a quiet one, or a simple parting of the ways. You might after all be disaffected enough to turn, and yet still close enough to exert influence."

Kit shivered, nodded. *I'll just sit up tonight,* he thought. *I've that masque on Orpheus to turn to a proper play, anyway.* "Renewed interest?" Relief, that the tone in his voice was amused pique and not the terror of waking alone that knotted his gut. *Six days' nightmares,* he thought. *Perhaps on the seventh day my demons will let me rest.*

"Renewed interest in getting an heir," Murchaud said.

"I'd presumed thee childless by inclination," Kit admitted, and Murchaud laughed.

"The Fae are not known for our overwhelming fertility, save when we breed with mortals. And even then—" Murchaud shifted against Kit's shoulder. "The Mebd's one daughter, Findabair, is dead these thousand years. I barely knew her: she married a mortal king a short time before I was born, and died barren. There has not been another."

"And the Mebd is suddenly keen to get an heir?"

"War is brewing," Murchaud answered. "I'm her heir, as it stands: there is no spare."

"Ah," Kit said, as the music shifted. "There's my country dancing. Come pick a fight when you're ready to go to bed."

"Kiss enough pretty women to make it look convincing."

Oh. Never fear on that account, my dear.

The wine was cool, and sharp enough to cut the exhaustion cloying Kit's throat. He'd probably had too much of it, and the hall was nearly empty, false silver creeping across the blackness of the high windows. But he couldn't face the trek from his lonely seat at the end of the high table upstairs to his bed and his nightmares yet.

Kit leaned on the back of his fingers and contemplated lifting the tall glass goblet again. It seemed like a lot of effort for very little reward, and he raised his gaze to the last few dancers on the floor below. He saw Geoffrey and Cairbre, whom Morgan was relieving at the music stand. He knew the names of the others by now, but did not *know* most of them beyond a casual conversation. *I should remedy that tonight.*

It took a moment to grope out the edge of the table and grasp it. Oiled silk and linen slipped under his hands; he took a firmer grip and hoisted himself to his feet, the floor lurching. He leaned on the table edge heavily, reached for his cup, and overset it. He righted the glass in the midst of spilled wine and looked up again, glancing around the room for someone to talk to. *Geoffrey*, he thought. *Perhaps the stag will be a little more forthcoming tonight. Given the obvious disrepair of my love affair with the Prince.* But the stag was nowhere to be seen, and, in fact, Kit found himself quite alone.

He didn't recall hearing the music stop, but the hall echoed in its emptiness, and he realized that everything was tidied except for his own place at the table and that single glass of wine. He imagined the castle's corps of brownies and elves sweeping the place clean in a matter of instants, and rubbed his face with his hand. *Well, passing out drunk at the high table will certainly convince them your heart is in disarray. Hast no dignity at all?*

At least it wasn't face-down in a puddle of vomit.

To bed, he decided, and set about working out how best to clamber down the low steps from the dais without breaking a limb. There was no railing, and misperceived heights were enough of a problem sober and fresh.

"Sir Christofer—"

Kit closed his eye. "Robin." Drunk enough that gratitude soaked his voice effusively. "Your assistance, good Puck?"

"Ah." A jingle as the Puck took his arm. "No one bothered to inform you that the wine was fortified, I take it?"

Kit giggled. "Is that what it was? I thought I was merely a shame— a shame*ful* drunk."

"You have your reasons." The little creature steadied him; Kit clung to his hand. "I'll see you to bed."

The spiral stair wasn't as bad as Kit had anticipated, for all his head reeled. Robin's long fingers were cool and soothing, and there was a railing to cleave to. Left on his own, he thought, he probably would have had to crawl.

"Oh," he said, surprised to recognize his own door. "Here we are."

"Yes, Kit. Come inside—" Robin turned the knob and chivvied him into the bedroom, kindling a light from the lamp at the top of the stairs. "Can you get your boots off on your own?"

"Not." Kit swallowed. His throat burned, which was bad: it meant he was sobering. "Not going to bed."

"Suit yourself," Robin said. "How's the stomach?"

"I am unlikely to—dis*grace* myself. Further."

"Good. You knew he was married, Kit."

"Not that," Kit said, then cursed himself for honesty. "Nightmares," he explained, as Robin led him to a chair. "Do you dream, Robin?"

"These nightmares," the Puck said, jumping up on the arm and turning to face him. "Are they new?"

Kit shook his head. He reached out and gently caught Puck's wrist, turning it to see the way the spidery fingers joined each other in a palm no bigger than a shilling coin. "Amazing," he said. "New? No. But worse of late. And dif—dif*fer*ent."

The Puck's bells rustled. He twined his other long hand around Kit's wrist: a gesture of comfort. "They'll get worse before they get better. Are you stitching your cloak yet?"

Kit shook his head, regretted it when the room kept wobbling after. "Should I be?"

"Tomorrow. The sooner the better. You'll have to claim this, or it will claim you."

"What is it?"

Great brown goat eyes examined Kit, their horizontal pupils swelling in interest. "A bardic gift," Robin said plainly. "The gift of prophecy. If a gift you can call it—"

"Cassandra," Kit said thickly. "Wonderful. Serve forth Apollo: I'll fuck him. Cairbre didn't warn me . . ."

"Cairbre doesn't have it." Robin laid his hand in his lap, and curled cross-legged on the arm of the chair. " 'Tis rare, even among bards. Taliesin had it, if you know that name."

"Nay—"

"Merlin?" The Puck smiled at Kit's expression.

"The slip of a clerk's pen nearly—metamorphosed—this Marley into a Merlin in younger years," Kit said, remembering amusement at the name misrendered on his scholarship papers. And his sisters' good-natured cruelty over the mistake. *Merlin's going to university, Father—*

"A turn of prophecy, then. Make your cloak, Sir Kit. You're close on becoming a bard: you'll need it."

"So hang thee me in thy rags of honor," Kit said after a considering pause. "In the tatters of Autumn's fair fastness clothe me in patches of moss-shag'd boulders that all who attest shall know thy banner, thy brand, thy choice, thy mark in this vastness for all the world, thy witness: my shoulders—bah. It needs internal rhyme. And banner/honor, that's not so good."

"Pretty," Robin commented. "What is it?"

"Slightly less than the back half of a very bad sonnet. The Italian form. The scansion limps outrageously and it doesn't close properly; I was never very good at them. But that—Oxford could do better. I am most foully drunk, Master Goodfellow."

Puck laughed, and turned on the arm of the chair so he could lean back on Kit's shoulder, as Kit had leaned on Murchaud. Kit shifted to make the creature more comfortable; his rapier hilt jabbed floating ribs, and he lifted his chin to clear the Puck's half-floppy ear from his field of view. They settled into companionable silence while the room grew brighter.

"There are many sorts of bindings," Puck said. "I myself am knotted in the Mebd's hair, and have no choice but to serve her loyally inasmuch as she commands me. I feel your grief, Kit."

"There are bindings and bindings," Kit said, as the sun peeked the horizon and Kit's wine-soaked dizziness receded like the tide before morning.

"Have you heard from your playmaker in England?"

"No—" Kit sighed. "I thought it best to make a clean break, after all."

"His son has died."

Kit blinked. He arched his neck and angled his head to get a look at the Puck, who snuggled closer on Kit's blind side. The words hung in the air, unaltered. "I beg your pardon?"

"His son. A year past now, of a fall from an oak—"

Kit heard a Queen's voice, a smiling rhyme. *Ellum do grieve; Oak he do hate; Willow do walk if yew travels late—*

"Hamnet," Kit said. "Dead."

"Aye."

"Oh, God." Numbly, remembering an undelivered letter—*a year past, though I am no judge of time in Faerie*. And then hugged the Fae close as Robin flinched, covering his ears with his spidery hands. "I beg your pardon, Master Robin Goodfellow."

" 'Tis nothing." Robin hopped up, his moist eyes dark. "I must to mine own tasks, Sir Kit. I hope you find your surcease."

"Perhaps," Kit said, a little soberer and sadder. He grasped the arms of his chair and pulled himself to his feet to walk Robin to the door. They exchanged a handclasp, and Kit closed and latched the door behind the Fae.

He turned and leaned his back against it, eyeing the smooth-tugged counterpane of his broad, empty bed. A few rays of sunlight lay across it, but the bedcurtains would see to those—

His son.

Oh, Will.

Decisively, he turned again, steady enough if he did not bend or stand, and pulled his door open. Mouse-soft footsteps carried him up the stairs and through the gallery, to a door he had not tapped in quite some little while. His knock wavered more than he liked; he was about to turn and walk away, almost with a sense of relief, when it swung open and Morgan stood framed against the morning, blinking, in a white nightshirt and a nightgown of apricot silk, barefoot, no nightcap and her hair a wilderness of brambles on her shoulders.

"Madam—" Kit said, shifting from one foot to the other.

She stood aside, and let him enter.

Act II, scene xviii

Now let it work. Mischief, thou art afoot,
Take thou what course thou wilt!

—WILLIAM SHAKESPEARE, *Julius Caesar*

The chamber was large enough for a royal audience, bare but for fresh rush matting on the floor and the figured richness of the red gilt leather walls. Will wouldn't have wanted to sit, and it satisfied him to have the excuse to pace, tumbling his shilling through ink-stained fingers. "Will I, nil I," he muttered, staring up at the dark beams vaulting the underside of the roof, and grinned. That wasn't half bad—

"Master Shakespeare."

Will stopped and turned, hopping a little when his right foot dragged on the rush mat and tripped him. He blushed, and stammered a greeting. "Sir Robert."

Cecil smiled, sharp brown goatee bristling over his carefully pressed ruff and increasing his startling resemblance to his father. His robes fell in rich, simple black folds to his knees, his shoes and stockings as black behind them. His beautiful hands were ringless, the thumb of the left one hooked as if by habit behind the broad maroon ribbon from which depended his only jewelry, a finely detailed golden lion's head, mouth yawning to show its pointed teeth. He came to the center of the room, limping slightly, and Will went to meet him, slipping the shilling into his sleeve and stilling the trembling in his hand as best he could, but limping as well.

Cecil noticed. A frown at suspected mockery became a raised eyebrow of interest. "Art injured, Master Poet?"

"No, sir. A weakness in the leg is all."

"It doesn't impede thee on the stage?"

"The stage is smooth," Will said. He didn't ask after Cecil's limp: rumor had the man born with a twisted spine, and Will could see that one shoulder rode higher than the other. "You wished to instruct me, Sir Robert."

"Instruct? It had been mine intent rather to seek answers of thee." Cecil's voice lowered as the two men came together, almost shoulder to shoulder, far from any wall. Will understood Cecil's choice of the room, now. "How proceeds thine investigation of Master Richard Baines?"

"Surely you have men better equipped for such than I?"

Cecil's mouth twisted, and he lifted his chin. "I have few men who have worked neither with—nor for—Baines nor Poley."

"Ah," Will said. "I see. Why has Her Majesty not had him hanged, Sir Robert?"

Cecil stopped his pacing and looked Will square in the eye. "The letter of the law must be upheld," he said, "and Her Majesty persists in seeing our struggles with these vipers in her own bosom, as it were, as the sort of squabbles among snotty boys upon which she has built her power, her reign, and her control. She has ever maintained and strengthened her power through the skillful manipulation of factions, and perhaps . . ." Cecil's voice trailed off, as if he examined all the ways he could say what he needed to say, and came up wanting. "She is Gloriana," he said at last. "She has not failed us yet."

"Ah," Will said, when the silence began to drag. "I can prove nothing on Poley, Sir Robert. Less on Baines. They are as scrupulous as anyone could wish. Or unwish, in this case."

Cecil straightened, and Will heard the click of his bones as he pulled his shoulders back. "Then invent something," he said. "As soon as thou mayst, but not too hasty; it must hold up on inspection. I will be waiting."

———

Ben Jonson's shoulders almost filled the doorway he ducked through. Young, barely bearded, scarecrow-thin despite his height and frame, he looked more like the soldier and bricklayer he had been than the playmaker he'd become, with a face like a mutton-chop. He straightened, tugging the grayed collar of his shirt and wrinkling his broad, broken nose at the steady drizzle. He shifted a bundle on his shoulder. "Will," he said. "I can imagine kinder sights, but not many."

Will fell in beside him, boots slipping on filthy cobbles in the rain, not willing to answer his unspoken questions just yet. "If thou couldst only circumspect thy pen—" he said, and then shook his head. "Then thou wouldst bear some other name than Ben." And grinned, as Ben clouted him on the shoulder.

"And let the first thing I hear as a free man be rhyming doggerel? O terrible Shakespeare." He scratched with broad hands at hair gone shaggy, and cursed. "I'm crawling. May I prevail—"

"Of course, Master Jonson," Will said. "Is there a barber thou preferest?"

"At the sign of the black boar's as good as any. You could do with a barbering yourself. Unless you mean to make up for the hairs falling on top by growing them at the bottom."

"It's the damned satires," Will answered. "And the humors comedies. I go, I clutch my hairs in horror, and they unravel from the top and hang a fringe about my neck. I'll have to find some goodwife to knit them up for me again, like a stocking cap." The rainswept street was empty; Will contemplated ducking into a church or cookshop, but it didn't seem half worth it.

"Will, why did you stand my bail?"

"I'm collecting favors owed."

Ben hesitated. "Some playmending you'd as soon elude?"

"No," Will said. "Come, Ben. We'll see thee barbered, deloused, and fed. Then we've an appointment with the crown."

"Her Majesty?" Ben tripped on a cobblestone and caught himself, checking his stride so he didn't outpace Will.

"Well," Will said. "Her Majesty's servant. But so are we all, in the end."

"I'm no Queen's Man."

"You will be." Will grinned. "I hear thou wentst Catholic in prison. That's useful, if thou'rt loyal."

"I heard a sermon or two," Ben admitted. "But a conversion is news to me."

"See, it's familiar news."

"Will," Ben said, in the gentle tone he could take between tirades, "what's the enmity between you and Robert Poley?"

"Who told thee about Poley?"

Ben's eyes were cleverer than they had any right to be under a glowering Cyclopean brow. "Richard Ede," he said, lowering his voice further. "A keeper at the Marshalsea. Not a bad man, I think. They put Poley in with me, Will."

"Poley's no prisoner—"

"Aye, an informant. There to prove sedition or treason on me. Ede warned me. What are you playing at, Will?"

"A sudden question. And an unnerving one, following on the heels of Poley."

"He was curious about you. Very much so." Ben's concern turned to a pleased sort of mockery as he began walking again. "Which I might have attributed to your undeserved fame, you ill-educated lout, but then with Ede's warning—"

"What toldst thou him of me?" Even over the sound of the rain, Will knew by the way his voice shivered at the end that he'd misread the line.

Ben almost reached out to lay a filthy hand on Will's shoulder, but caught himself and withdrew it. "I should be grateful for the rain," he said, wiping streaked dirt from his face on a grayed linen sleeve. "I told him naught, Will. Well—"

"What?"

"I had to tell him something, or he'd assume I had something to hide."

"So?"

Ben's eyes flickered sideways, and his heavy jowls twitched with humor. "I told him the 'William the Conqueror' story."

"Christ on the cross," Will swore. "And I was hoping that one would die a deserved death—"

"If you'd seen the disconsolate look on Burbage's face when he wandered into the Mermaid alone, you'd think it worth it."

"There are greater challenges than to outcharm Richard," Will said. "And the citizen in question a comely lass. But 'tis not the gentlemanly thing to spread tales."

Ben choked. "Not gentlemanly at all," he agreed. "And yet some *spread* them anyway—ah, here we are."

Will opted for the barbering after all, and saw Ben decently clothed and fed at a tavern by the time the rain began to taper. Ben ate with the appetite Will associated with stevedores, while Will picked through a mincemeat pastry, choking down what he could. Finally, Ben wiped his mouth on his new, clean kerchief and sat back with a sigh. "Unwell, William?"

"In pain," Will answered, rinsing his mouth on the dregs of the wine. "I shall be fine in a bit." He tucked his hand into his pocket and stood. "Art content?"

"Aye." Ben pushed his bench back. "Whence?"

"Upstairs," Will said, turning away. "He's waiting for us."

"He?"

Will nodded. "Sir Thomas Walsingham." He turned his head and glanced over his shoulder. The well-worn shilling was between his fingers. On an impulse, he drew it forth and tumbled it through the air on a high, lamplit arc.

Ben was quicker than he looked. Blunt fingers plucked the shilling at the apex of its climb; he frowned. "What's that?"

A grand gesture, Will thought, and smiled. "Come on, Queen's Man. Thou hast a craft to learn."

"Do I have an option?" But Jonson fell into step beside him, although Will took his elbow to lead him up the stairs.

"Not if you expect to write plays like that and live."

Eleven months and two weeks later, Tom Walsingham leaned against the shutters in Ben's lodging, which were closed against an unseasonable late-September chill, and tossed a gray kidskin pouch idly in his hand. Something jingled within it.

By Tom's smile, Will had a pretty clear idea what. He rose from his perch on a three-legged stood beside the hearth and crossed to where Ben crumpled his tallness over a trestle, papers unrolled and weighted at the corners with an inkhorn, a candlestick, and a pot of sand. Will leaned over his shoulder.

"What's Tom brought us, then?"

Ben's thick finger tapped the middle of the paper, shifting it under the weights. It was a plan of a house and garden, well drawn in black lines, with a steady hand Will envied. Ben raised his eyes to Tom, who was still fighting that inscrutable smile. "Richard Baines' house and garden," Ben guessed. "How did you come by these?"

"Bribery," Tom said succinctly. "Catch." He tossed his bundle through the air; Will fumbled it, and it landed on the map with a clunking sound entirely unlike the fairy jingle of silver or the sharp clean sound of gold.

Will struggled with the knot, the fingers of his right hand momentarily failing to answer, and got it untangled. He upended the pouch and dragged it, whistling as it spawned a river of coin. "There must be a hundred pound here."

"Hundred fifty," Tom said. "Or a few pounds worth of pewter," he said, that grin returning. "It seemed appropriate, somehow, given Baines has used the trick himself. I thought it best to attend to Cecil's—pardon, Sir Robert's demands regarding the inestimable Master Baines while he was still occupied with the affairs of his late father."

"How do you intend to pass it to them?"

"Plant, not pass." Tom drew his dagger and picked at a cuticle with the point, not quite as idly as Will thought he meant to make it look.

"Interesting," Will said. "I don't see you clambering in windows—"

"The clambering is Ben's part."

"Sir Thomas—" Ben looked up from arranging the debased nobles and sovereigns in tidy rows across the face of the map.

"You're youngest, Ben. And"—a circular gesture of the knife—"strongest."

Ben sighed, his brow wrinkling like that of a bull-baiting dog. "Aye. And once the coins are placed, Sir Thomas, how do we make sure Baines spends them rather than dispensing with them?"

"The property will be searched." Tom sheathed his knife and picked up a silvery coin, turning it in the light. "Leave that to me. These are better than some I've seen —"

Will wasn't sure what drew his attention to the window; a shadow across the shutters or the faintest of sounds. "Ben," he said in Jonson's ear, "is there a stair out your window?"

"A drainpipe," Ben answered in an undertone, following his gaze. "Over the kitchen garden. Sir Thomas, you were followed —"

"—but far from the best. I'm minded of a time in France —" Tom continued, never missing a beat as he drew his sword and moved to the window in silent footsteps.

Ben came around the board, catching his sword from the back of the chair it hung on and easing it from the soft leather sheath. He caught Tom's eye, and Tom nodded as Will hastily scooped the jingling counters of a hanging offense back into their bag.

Ben hurled the shutters open and Tom lunged, reaching, cursing softly and jerking back a moment later. "Missed him," he said, over a rustling crash and then the sound of running footsteps. "Ben, go after —"

Jonson didn't hesitate. He dropped his rapier inside the window and planted one hand on the sill, vaulting over with a grace that belied his height. Will winced at the thump from ten feet below, but Ben sounded unhurt as he called up *"Blade!"* He must have stepped aside as Tom snatched the sword up and dropped it, point-first so it would stick in the earth. " 'Tis Gabriel Spencer —"

Tom was already moving for the door. Will grabbed his sleeve as he went by. Tom couldn't: too much chance of being spotted and recognized, even in that nondescript, unfashionably blue doublet that was too broad across the shoulders. "No."

A moment's startled regard, and then— "Will?" Tom's voice was suddenly his cousin's, his eyes as full of cold necessity as Sir Francis' had ever been. "Make sure Ben understands —"

Oh, Christ on the Cross. Will nodded and stuffed the coins inside his doublet, hitching his stubborn right leg as he stumbled for the stairs. He wasn't about to catapult out a window like a man eight years younger, but Will was surprised how fast his halting gait, assisted by a grip on the banister, brought him into the courtyard.

Ben must have caught up with Gabriel Spencer by the innyard gate. He had the smaller man lifted off the ground by the collar, Spencer's hand—and a dagger—pinned high against the timbers. *I'm about to order a man to kill.*

Will swallowed, as best he could, conscious of the clunk of the coins inside his shirt. *Tyburn hanging,* he thought, and then he thought about Kit in a hearth-warmed kitchen, trying so hard and so falsely to smile. "Ben," Will said. "Let him down."

Ben turned over his shoulder, startled. Will nodded, and picked up the blade that Ben must have dropped when he manhandled Spencer against the wall.

Will held the rapier toward Ben, hilt-first, careful of the edge. Ben dropped Spencer—more tossed him to his feet—and stepped back far enough to grasp it, keeping a questioning sideways attention on Will. "He heard everything," Will said in an undertone, hearing a different voice in the place of Spencer's sudden, comprehending pleading. *This is what a Queen's Man is. This is what a Queen's Man does.*

Why, so it is.

Ben stared for a moment, aghast. And then a soldier's composure settled over the rough features, and he stepped to block Spencer's rabbity bolt for the gate. "Draw, Gabe," he said tiredly, as his blade came up and he turned to extend the line of his arm.

Spencer glanced from Will to Ben, and back. He slipped his main gauche into the proper hand, and reached across his belt to his rapier hilt. "This is murder, Ben. It's a hanging."

"Right of clergy," Ben said, piggy eyes narrowing under the cave of his brow. "I read Latin. It's a branding. Counterfeiting is a hanging. Draw your blade, and you've got a chance—"

He didn't, of course: quick as Spencer was, Ben was half again his size, half again his reach, and almost as fast, with a soldier's nerve. The blades rang silver on silver, with a purity of tone the debased coins burning Will's chest couldn't hope to match. Spencer lunged and shouted—above, at the window, a cry of *murder!* went up—Ben parried, riposted, the passage too fast for Will's eye, trained only to stage combat, to follow. The big man moved in, Spencer's main gauche tearing his sleeve but not the arm beneath, and a moment later blood stained eight inches of steel at the tip of Ben's blade.

Shouting and running footsteps rang down the street. Will never saw how it happened.

Ben wiped the blade on his kerchief before he sheathed it, while the witnesses and then the watch crowded close around them. "You tell Tom he'd better stand my bail," Ben muttered, and Will nodded as Ben was led away.

Act II, scene xix

It lies not in our power to love, or hate,
For will in us is over-rul'd by fate.

—CHRISTOPHER MARLOWE, *Hero and Leander*

In absolute blackness, Kit paced in the cramped circle afforded him.
His right hand trailed on the damp stones of the wall. He had no
fear of tripping; his feet knew the path, and the dank earth was where
he slept when he grew too tired to walk. *Wasting energy,* he thought,
but he could not sit still. "The sink wherein the filth of all the castle
falls," he mumbled, but it wasn't, quite. More an old, almost-dry well,
lidded in iron as much to keep light out as the prisoner in, for the sides
were twenty foot and steeply angled.

He had paced forever.

He would be pacing forevermore.

A strange sort of irritation, first an itching and then a raw, hot
pain, grew in patches on his torso and his thighs. To pass the time
he told himself stories. Bits of verse—Nashe's plays, half memorized,
Kyd's *Tragedy*, Will's *Titus*. The Greeks and the Romans and his newest acquisition, the Celts.

And none of them could drive the mocking voice of Richard Baines
out of his mind. *Good puss. Wait there, I'll be back for thee when I can.*

Damn you, Baines, don't leave me alone down here —

Oh, thou wilt not be alone. There's rats and frogs. And they tell me Edward's ghost still screams. He'll be company for thee; thou hast so much in common. Dost remember the irons, puss? Thou canst look forward to their acquaintance again.

Kit closed both eyes. It made no difference: he walked, and turned, and walked, and turned. "Christ, Richard. For the love of God, what made you such a monster?"

"Froggy frogs," someone answered. Kit startled, felt about him. He kicked something that rolled and rattled in darkness, a heavy iron jangle, but nothing that felt like flesh.

"Master Troll?"

"Froggy frogs. Froggy frogs. Froggy frogs —" faint as an echo up a drain pipe.

Kit felt after whatever had rolled. Maybe a tool, something that could be used to dig, or pry, or climb. He found it after some scrabbling and sat down against the wall to explore it with his fingers. Round, a sort of ball of iron straps. . . . It smelled of rust, the cold savor of iron. He felt inside it, and yelped when something pricked his thumb.

Oh.

Of course he would have left this here for me to think on.

Carefully, almost reverently, Kit laid the scold's bridle aside and scrubbed his hands on his breeches as if he had inadvertently grabbed two fistfuls of meat writhing with worms. His breast burned, his belly, his thighs. In five discrete patches, now, one for each brand, an agony as fresh as the day they had been seared into his skin. *How did I get here?*

He didn't know.

"*Hurm.* And *harm.*"

"Master Troll? Is there a way out of this pit? This oubliette?" *A forgetter,* some helpful portion of his mind supplied. *Where you put someone to forget them.*

But Baines said he'd be back.

Listen carefully, Kit. Can you hear Edward screaming?

"There must be a way out of this."

:Ah, Sir Christofer: A voice like brushed silk. :There is always a way. Come with me, my love. I am the way:

There was light, suddenly. Light cast from over his shoulder, and as he found himself standing he turned to it, turned into it. The scent of pipe tobacco surrounded him, a comforting memory of Sir Walter Raleigh's chill parlor and many late nights. He walked through it, heard voices hanging on a glittering arpeggio, felt air stirred by a suggestion of wings.

God.

He walked past, and through. Found himself elsewhere, in a tower room, high in the air: an autumn or early winter evening and the unmistakable reek of the Thames, the cry of ravens in the graying light. Harsh wood scraped Kit's knuckles; something writhed ineffectually against his grip. He looked down, at the skinny, stripped man of middle years he pinned against the rough table, in an all-too-familiar pose.

God.

God, hear me now —

The man was familiar too: his black hair, high forehead, terrified gray-blue eyes. As familiar as the lazy oval scarred by a set of good young teeth at the base of Kit's left thumb, the saddler's muscle ridging his forearms under thick golden hair. The pain from his brands was a symphony now, bright as holy words written in his flesh. *Will. What is —*

Oh, God.

That's Will.

I'm Baines.

A flurry of wings, and the cries of falcons, or perhaps of women in unimaginable grief or unspeakable pleasure. The light shattered like a hurled looking glass —

Kit awakened in the evening dimness behind Morgan's bedcurtains, his head pillowed on her nightgown-covered thigh, and groaned with the simple agony of opening his eye. "Where is he?"

Her voice, lazy and collected and very much awake. "Where is who, Sir Kit?"

He raised his head, wincing, and looked up her body at the woman lowering her book to regard him. "Whosoever it was that beat me in my sleep."

"All your own doing, I fear." She laid the cloth-bound volume aside and reached down lazily to smooth his rumpled hair. "You're a sorry drunk, Kit. Do try to avoid it in future."

"I don't recall," he answered. Vaguely, a memory of walking ever-so-carefully through her door, the click of the latch, her hands unbuttoning his pearl-embroidered doublet and unbuckling his sword. A brief check informed him that he was half dressed, at least, and Morgan seemed clothed and composed. "What befell?"

"You fell into mine arms," she said, quite gently, "and wailed like a pup pulled from his mother's teat. And when I thought you'd cried a whole world's tears, you cried a few more in your sleep, and tossed and turned. But slept the morning through and then the afternoon, and whimpered whenever I rose or left your side. Still dreaming?"

Her fingers were gentle. He laid his head down on her thigh again, and sighed in the simple comfort of her touch. *I could have liked her, if things had been different, for all she is wild and cold.* "Aye," he said, and then sat upright, the spinning room competing for his attention with remembered horror. *Baines. And Will. Prophetic dreams.*

She let her hand fall from his arm. "What of?"

"How did you know of my dreams?"

"Sweet, Murchaud isn't so sound a sleeper as that. They are somewhat—spectacular." She smiled. He blinked, considering.

"Morgan, thank you." It fell from his lips unheralded, and he paused a moment to examine the sentiment behind it. *Thank you for— saving my life? Letting me awaken with some shred of my dignity intact, after last night's display? Just—being there?* He didn't know. He stood and collected his clothes from the back of her chair, and struggled into them while she laughed.

"People will talk."

"Let them," he answered, and licked his palm to push his hair back from his face. Impulsively, he bent and kissed her on the cheek.

She covered the place with her hand, her expression unreadable. "Such haste—"

"I've an obligation," he said, stamping his boots down, still quite dishevelled. "Anon?"

"Anon," she answered, and did not rise to see him to the door. But he could hear her laughter chasing him as he fled back to his own room, and—

Someone had been there before him. A single candle burned on the mantel, and propped up beside it was a tall silver blade. Something shimmered before them, half real. A bundle of papers of mismatched size and color, ragged at the edges, so thick it was rolled and tied with a grosgrain ribbon instead of folded and sealed. Kit hesitated in the doorway, his sleeves unbuttoned, head aching and stomach sour, his rich court doublet hanging open over last night's crumpled shirt. *Do you ever feel at the mercy of conspirators, Sir Christofer?*

Why, no. Never in my life. " 'Sblood," he cursed, and kicked the door shut with his heel before he crossed the room. He snatched the letter from the mantel, and brought it across the room to the window and the last light of sunset to read. Sorting the pages rapidly, he recognized sheets of plays and poetry, Will's hand and someone else's, shoving them all aside until he found the thick ten pages of letter.

"Oh, Will."

Head pounding but no longer spinning, Kit sat on the edge of the bed to read Will's shaky, hasty secretary's hand. When he finished, he set the pages aside and stared for a moment out the window, watching the pale phosphorescence of the twilit sea, hoping it would calm the cold terror in his chest. As if entranced, he stood, buttoned his sleeves and laced his points, buttoned the doublet, adjusted the hang of his sword, and settled a dagger on the right side of his belt. As an afterthought, he slipped a dirk into his boot, and then as he reached for the door he glanced down and laughed at himself, going to war in court silks and pearls.

Act II, scene xx

Good things of day begin to droop and drowse;
While night's black agents to their preys do rouse.

—WILLIAM SHAKESPEARE, *Macbeth*

September, 1598

Thou wouldst have hated Ben Jonson, Kit.

& as I write that line, & read it over, it strikes me; I write as if to a dead man truly, & now I wonder if I have in some madness invented thy survival.

Ben is brilliant. I mocked him for writing in humors, & he presented a comedy—Every Man, 'tis called—that I cannot overly fault. To prove me wrong as much as himself right. Brilliant, & of much use to Tom & I.

Tom asks after you. He's been knighted. Audrey is pregnant again. Mary's son Robin is apprenticed a chandler.

Her Majesty has survived another anniversary of her birth, by the grace of God, & Richard has procured a property in Southwark not far from the beargarden & the Rose, where he will raise our new playhouse, which we have decided will be called the Globe. If we can free our materials from the odious Master Allen, our old landlord, we'll have it up by Spring. & no near neighbors to answer to, by God, for all we'll have to

build it on timbers over a sewer ditch. Like an ark—when God sends
His rains to cleanse the unfaithful, we vile players can clamber into our
sinful playhouse & raft to safety on the swollen Thames.

So we will have only the Lord Mayor to contend with.

The flag is already painted, & the motto chosen. "Totus mundus
agit histrionem" which thou wilt be able to translate as well as ever I
could.

Ben, whom I did mention previous, has found himself new trouble.
His temper might o'ershadow even thine: I oft imagine if thou wert still
with us, thee & he would likely have come to blows. You would have
loathed him with a passion I'm sorry I shall not witness.

Let me set the stage: Master Jonson is near sixteen stone of man,
trained as a soldier & he wears a sword daily. His wits are quicker on
paper than in a tavern, for all he is an excellent poet, & he's as quick
to take offense as any man. Thus it is not too much questioned that he
killed the rattish Gabriel Spencer in a duel. It wasn't a duel, but out
of unpleasant necessity, for Spencer became too well acquainted with
our plans, & our Ben only avoided the Tyburn tree through claiming
benefit of clergy—for he reads Latin—& forfeiting his chattels. Also
he was branded on the hand, & cannot write until it heals.

I've sent him to Stratford to stay with Annie for a week or two,
which is not so unwise as it seems: better than to keep him in the city;
lest another quarrel be provoked, or he insist even now in taking part in
the merriment Tom and I have planned.

The foolishness of this is that it forces advancement of mine own
plans. Lord Burghley too has left us; the Queen's guiding Spirit died,
they say, in Her Majesty's arms last month, after even her cosseting
could not save him. The mood is somber.

His son, Sir Robert, has become secretary of state.

Which leads me to my current problems. I've been charged by that
selfsame Robert Cecil with the eradication of Master Poley & Mas-
ter Baines. & the additional complication that Ben writes to say he's
seen thine old acquaintance Nick Skeres in Stratford. I have a sense of
things moving under the surface, Kit, & I wish I could gaff them & lift
them into the light.

Still, Tom & Ben & I have hit upon a plan for dealing with
Baines & Poley. All it needs is a little expedition to plant some false

coin—kindly provided by Sir Robert—in their chambers, & a search.
Thou wilt appreciate the irony of this.

 Ben was to make the entrance, but his circumstances now forbid
it. If I could be assured that this letter would reach thee, I should beg
thine assistance, for thy habit of walking through walls would be most
salutary in this cause.

 I've thought long on this, & in addition to my ms. of the Dream,
I've included a fair copy an act or two of Ben's. & some poems.

 Which will discuss later, as I do not believe I would have the courage
to include them if I thought thou wouldst ever collect this thy letter.

 Be glad thou canst not see what poor George has wrought on thy
Leander. *To be fair, 'tisn't bad.*

 But it is not Kit.

"A fool and more than a fool," Will cursed himself under his breath, stepping into the stirrup Tom Walsingham made of his hands. He bent his head close to Tom's ear. "Why am I shinnying in the window?"

"Could you pick me up?"

There was that. He put a hand on Tom's shoulder and gripped his dagger in his teeth, steadying himself against the wall. Tom's strength surprised him—*He's three years older than I am, damn it.* Tom's shoulders moved under Will's soft-soled shoes, his hands bracing Will's thighs, and Will was glad of the growing darkness in the garden, as his face heated at a sudden image of Tom, and Kit—

Will spat the dagger into his hand and slipped its narrow blade between the shutters. On the second try, he caught the bar. On the third try, he lifted it successfully, and held his breath as it clunked rather than clattered to the window ledge between the shutters and the glass. The sash shifted easily, and the space was sufficient for a skinny man to slip through. What lights still burned in the house were under the gables, and Will and Tom had been lurking in an upstairs room of an inn down the street long enough to see Baines set off, alone, a little before dusk. Curfew was nine o'clock, if he bothered to come home before it; they should have an hour at least, and Will expected the sojourn into the house to take less than five minutes.

He looked down, and spoke softly. "Tom, as soon as I'm inside, you leave."

"Will—"

"No. If . . . If. You've Ben. You keep working."

He felt Tom's rebellion, knew he had no right or precedence with which to command the other man. And then felt Tom's resignation at the logic of it. *This is what a Queen's Man does.* "All right, Will. Hurry— I'll meet you at the Mermaid."

False coins shifted against his breast in their soft leather bag. Tom got a hand on each ankle and lifted as Will pulled, and a moment later Will was inside the window and standing in absolute blackness. *And how did you intend to find a place to hide a sack full of counterfeit coins in pitch blackness, Master Shakespeare?*

Purity of spirit, sir.

He crouched, realizing he was silhouetted against the window, and then thought to swing the shutters and the glass closed so a draft wouldn't bring some servant looking for the source. He traced the baseboard with hesitant fingers, following it into the corner of the room. *This was supposed to be a bedroom—ah. And so it is.*

His fingers found the featherbed, straw ticking, the twine binding the edge. He bit through a knot with his teeth and tugged edges open, heartbeat pulsing in his throat as he shoved the bag arm-deep in rustling straw and tugged the mattress' edges together, knotting the cord as best he could in the dark.

And very nearly wet himself when the door swung open, and a darkly clad figure held a single flickering candle high in his left hand. "You must be Shakespeare," he said, and set the candle on a table by the door. The brass and wood fittings of a pistol gleamed in his other hand; Will recognized the black-red color of his hair, the thin, aristocratic line of his nose.

"Fray Xalbador de Parma. I am delighted to make your acquaintance, sir." Amazed at how steady his voice stayed, although his eyes betrayed him with a flicker at the window. Will started to stand.

De Parma cleared his throat and gestured slightly with the pistol. Will sat back against the bed.

De Parma crossed the room, staying enough away that Will wouldn't risk a grab for the snaphaunce flintlock in his hand. *That's right, Tom. Just head on home. I'll be along shortly.*

Oh. Rather a bad miscalculation, this.

A miscalculation compounded as another figure stepped into the room: slender, blond, with a mischievous twist to his lips. "Fray Xalbador," Robert Poley said, slouching on his left shoulder against the door frame. "I thought I'd heard a mouse scratching up here."

"Poley—"

The blond man clucked and shook his head. "After all that fuss killing Spencer," he said, "you should have known we'd be expecting your visit."

"Yes," Will answered. "I should have known."

Barabas: Your extreme right does me exceeding wrong.
—CHRISTOPHER MARLOWE, *The Jew of Malta*

Kit pressed fingertips to the cold, black glass and hesitated, his right hand going to the hilt of his sword. The other Prometheans were warded from the gaze of the glass. But Will was not, and so Kit saw Poley turn, saw clearly the half-inch bore of the weapon pointed unwaveringly at Will's midsection. Saw, as if he floated overhead like a one-eyed angel, Tom's occasional guilty glances over his shoulder as—against his better judgment—he followed Will's instructions and paused by the warmth of the well-lit tavern. Until he cursed, stopped, and turned to retrace his steps.

Just what I need. Bad enough to have to rescue one of them.

"Tom, don't."

Kit didn't expect Tom to hear him. Most of Kit's attention remained on Will, anyway, and the two images layered each other like an oil painting held up against the back of a stained-glass saint. Until Tom stopped, and glanced over his shoulder, as if he'd imagined he'd heard someone call his name.

Kit cleared his throat, forgetful in his fear. "Tom, love."

Wide eyes, a whisper barely shaped. "Kit?"

"I'll take care of him," he said, and then let the scrying end before he said anything else, turning his attention entirely to Will. Will, who had drawn his knees up and kept his back to the bed as if it could afford him some protection. Poley moved about the bedroom, lighting candles, and Kit nibbled his lip at Robert's expression. *If only I had been a half step quicker—*

Or a half a year. No time for recriminations, sir.

The pistol was his worst worry. It wouldn't take more than a glancing shot to shatter bone, tear flesh, crush limbs—assuming the thing didn't misfire. *Oh, I wish I had Morgan's magic now. But—if I step into the room behind de Parma, Poley only has a dagger. I just have to make enough noise that the Inquisitor will turn instead of making sure of Will.*

Good Will. Stay there on the floor, roll under the bed when the fighting starts—

Thank God Baines is nowhere in sight.

Kit drew his rapier and his main gauche, pulled a single shallow breath through his nose to still the trembling in his hands, and stepped through the Darkling Glass.

O conspiracy,
Shamst thou to show thy dang'rous brow by night,
When evils are most free?
—WILLIAM SHAKESPEARE, *Julius Caesar*

Will could never quite describe what he saw: whether the shuttered window seemed to fall open on a starry night, or whether the shadows of the flickering candles twisted together in some glimmering reminder of the span of black wings. But he gasped, and when he did, Poley turned to follow the line of his vision. De Parma brought the pistol up and danced a half step back, angling his left foot with perfect balance, a sidestep that would have brought him around, his back to the wall beside the shuttered window—

—if several narrow, blooded inches of Kit Marley's main gauche hadn't emerged from his chest as he moved, his own momentum carrying the blade through his body and dragging it out of Kit's hand. De Parma completed his turn before he realized he was dead, the pistol still rising, finger tightening on the trigger as he staggered back against the wall beside the window. The scrape and then the roar of the flintlock was so enormous that Will imagined for an instant that he hadn't actually *heard* anything, just tasted all the brimstone of Hell in a concussion as if God Himself had boxed Will's ears.

De Parma fell against the wall, the narrow blade leaping a few more inches from his chest, and slid down like a pile of discarded clothing.

Kit was already sidestepping to face Poley. "Will," he shouted, loud enough for Will to hear it through ears that would never stop ringing. *"Run!"*

Will forced himself to his feet, de Parma's blood already soaking through his shoes. It shone on the floorboards, *glossy*, and Will tore his eyes away with a grunt. Kit extended like a dancer, infinitely more graceful than Ben, the totality of his body and his will focused, it seemed, on the firelit silver of his swordpoint.

Running wasn't possible. Will staggered toward the door.

"Marley. God. You're *dead*, you son of a whore."

"Oh," Kit said cheerfully. "God has very little to do with it, and my mother's virtuous to a fault, I fear. What shall it be, Master Poley? Thy heart?"

But a bulky shadow filled the doorway, and Will skidded to a stop fast enough that he went to one knee in the rushes and the blood.

"How about an eye, and into thy brain, dying instantly? Too good for thee, but time is short and we must make—"

"Kit."

"—do."

"Good evening, puss," said Richard Baines, as Kit turned to face him. "I should have known my kitten would never be so uncouth as to die without bidding me one last farewell."

I am Envy. I cannot read and therefore wish all books burned.
—CHRISTOPHER MARLOWE, *Faustus*

The tip of the blade *shimmered*, so close, so close. Kit settled himself for the lunge, the perfect motion of body and sword and strength that would carry his blade into Poley's left eye and carry with it a perfect, a *holy* revenge. And then Will's panicked squeak, and the voice—God. The silken, caressing voice of Richard Baines.

Bile and blood cloyed Kit's tongue. He stepped back from Poley, unable to turn his blind side on Baines for the second it would take to make sure. "Dick," he said, and extended the rapier over Will's shoulder. He let the tip sway on a gentle arc between Poley and Baines, a motion including both of them. Kit feigned deafness to the shiver in his own voice, swallowed a mouthful of saliva and put his back to the window as he croaked, "Will, come back here, please."

Will didn't stand, just skittered backward in a crouch that looked like it hurt him. De Parma's blood reddened the palms of his hands, the knees of his hose. Across the line of Kit's rapier, Baines smiled and came a half step closer, a half step beyond the reach of Kit's lunge. "Thou hast aged not a day. And the eyepatch suits thee. Did it hurt very much?"

"No," Kit answered. "No. It didn't hurt. Much."

Baines nodded. "Not compared to some things, aye? Sweet puss. There's nowhere to run, thou knowest. Back to the wall, and I can wait here all night, and thou hast nowhere to go."

"There's a knife in my boot, Will." Kit felt fingers fumble it as much as he felt anything but the ice snarling his limbs.

"Kit," Will hissed, grasping the window ledge to stand a little behind him, where he could not foul Kit's arm, "he's unarmed. Kill him—"

And it was true. Baines stood just inside the doorway, limned by candlelight, those big hands hanging open at his sides. Kit could imagine he saw the outline of his own teeth, sunk in the heel of the left one. He shuddered, and brought his gaze back up to Baines' eyes. Better the eyes than those gentle, terrible hands. *He never needed weapons before—*

Kit, shut up.

Poley had a dagger, no good for throwing or he would have thrown it. Kit barely spared him a glance. He caught the light winking off the blade in Will's hand as Will skinned it.

"What are we doing?"

Will spoke in an undertone that Kit matched with a murmur, aware of Baines watching his lips for a hint of what he said. "Get ready, William, my love. If this doesn't work, I'm sorry."

"Put down the little knife, puss, and I'll be gentle—" Baines stepped forward. Kit flinched, and Baines smiled.

"What are we doing, Kit?"

Kit never dropped his eyes. He felt with his left hand, slipped it around Will's waist, shifted his weight in a way he hoped Will would understand. Will switched the dagger to his left hand and gripped Kit's belt with his right. He moved with Kit, in unison, and Kit nodded. *No hesitation.* "Running away," Kit answered, and let his knees go as weak as they wanted to, dragging Will backward through the window and the glass.

Intra-act: Chorus

These things, with many other shall by good &
honest witness be approved to be his opinions and
Common Speeches, and that this Marlow doth not
only hold them himself, but almost into every
Company he Cometh he persuades men to Atheism
willing them not to be afeared of bugbears and
hobgoblins, and utterly scorning both god and his
ministers as I Richard Baines will Justify &
approve both by mine oath and the testimony
of many honest men, and almost all men with
whom he hath Conversed any time will
testify the same, and as I think all men in
Christianity ought to endeavor that the mouth of
so dangerous a member may be stopped.

—RICHARD BAINES, "A note Containing the opinion of one
Christopher Marly Concerning his Damnable Judgment of
Religion, and scorn of gods word," recorded May of 1593

Baines lunged, shouldering Marley's slender blade aside. A half
second too late; the edge of Marley's doublet brushed his fingers,
and Kit and the crippled playmaker hit the glass with—

—no sound of splintering. They vanished as if they'd tumbled into peat-blackened water. Baines caught himself hard against the windowsill before he could follow, headfirst through shattered glass and the shutters knocked wide, into the garden below. Something in his elbow popped, and he grunted as he pushed back. Fray Xalbador's blood slipped and stuck under the soles of his boots. "Damme." Quiet and wry, an edge of admiration in it Baines would not have permitted Marley to hear.

"Christofer Marley," Poley said, not releasing his dagger. "Jesus fucked Mary and Joseph. Nick wasn't drunk after all."

Baines pressed his palm against cool glass, tentatively. The sensation was mundane, diamond-shaped panes and strips of lead between. He strode across blood and stopped not far from Poley. "You sound like our pussycat, Robert. Such blasphemy—"

Poley looked up at him, blowing the hair out of his eyes. "I buried that man, Dick—"

"Aye, and he's come back from the grave?" Baines rolled his shirtsleeves up. "Put the damned dagger away, as it did you so much benefit last time. Are you sure you killed the right poet?"

Poley turned his head and spat. "I checked his brands before we buried him. But that was no ghost managed the friar so neatly. And— you saw the eyepatch: Ingrim struck him fairly and laid him down." The slender blond agent nudged de Parma's flaccid corpse with his toe. "We'll have to dispose of this."

"We'll wall him in the cellar," Baines answered, already calculating the losses and advantages of the Inquisitor's bloody death. "Damme, we're short a sorcerer."

"Aye. And moreover, it seems our Kit's exhumed himself with a touch of the glamourie." Poley raised a hand and rapped lightly on the window glass, tilting his head as if to assess the rattle of the sash against the frame. "The old bitch must have had him off overseas, or he's been laying low. Still. As long as he's living—"

Baines lifted his chin in comprehension. "We won't have to enchant another, when the time comes. How did he survive a stabbing *and* a burial, then?"

Poley wiped his blade, unnecessarily, on his breeches and slipped the dagger into its sheath. "Sorcery?"

"If he were a sorcerer, I would know it. A poet, yes, and a good one, but the real use of him was —" Baines saw Poley's eyes widen as he, Baines, hesitated. If the light were better, he imagined he would have seen Poley blanch.

"You think Mehiel had something to do with it."

"I think," Baines answered, considering, "we may find Master Marley difficult to keep dead, if that is indeed what happened to him. An unexpected incidental result." He shrugged. "But I mastered him once. Can do it again."

"He slipped your lead once," Poley reminded.

"Only because de Vere gave him too much rope."

"Come, Dick. Help me wrap the friar so he doesn't drip down the hall."

Baines crouched, dragging a woolen blanket from the bed. He lifted de Parma's body by the sticky dark auburn hair, and heaved in unison with Poley. The little man was strong for his size. "If our pussycat's returned to my safekeeping, I can promise you *that* won't happen again."

Act III, scene i

Orlando: Then in mine own person I die.
Rosalind: No, faith, die by attorney. The poor world is
almost six thousand years old, and in all this time
there was not any man died in his own person,
videlicit, in a love-cause. Troilus had his brains
dashed out with a Grecian club; yet he did what he
could to die before, and he is one of the patterns
of love. Leander, he would have lived many a fair
year, though Hero had turned nun, if it had not been
for a hot midsummer night; for, good youth, he went
but forth to wash him in the Hellespont and being
taken with the cramp was drowned and the foolish
chroniclers of that age found it was "Hero of Sestos."
But these are all lies: men have died from time to
time and worms have eaten them, but not for love.

—WILLIAM SHAKESPEARE, *As You Like It*

Kit grunted as Will fell atop him. The hard landing broke Will's
startled shout, for all Kit cushioned them both as best he could
without losing his grip either on Will or his rapier. Threads on Kit's
doublet snapped, pearls splashing, powdering between bodies and

stones. Will rolled, scrambling to his feet with the dagger at the ready, bad leg dragging. He turned, trying to cover Kit and still stay out of his way, and then hesitated, amazed. "Kit—"

Kit pushed himself to a crouch, wheezing. "Damme, but that was closer than I like them."

"Where are we?" *William, my love.* Will dismissed it with a half-formed judgment on Kit's habitual extravagance.

"Faerie." Kit dragged himself up the wall as if his ribs pained him. Will winced. "Drink nothing while thou here lingerest. Neither shalt thou dine, lest like Proserpine thou dost find thyself obligated to the underworld."

"Faerie." Will shook himself, a chill only half excitement crawling the length of his spine. "Why this course? With the Inquisitor dead, I don't see why you left Baines and Poley—"

Kit straightened, consternation a furrow across his forehead. "I should have had Poley," he admitted. "I couldn't see Baines well enough to know if he was armed, and I didn't dare risk keeping my back to him if he was. It was a mistake."

"Why did we come here instead of going after Baines, then?" *And why was he talking to you like that?* The bitter taste of something half understood, which he understood no better when Kit glanced at the floor and turned away.

"Come along, Will. We'll get you cleaned up a little, and I'll see if you can be presented to the Queen. Or I suppose I could send you back through the Glass now, safe and sound in your lodging—"

"I'm in Faerie, and all you can think of is sending me home?" Will struggled to keep up; still shedding pearls like snowflakes from his shoulders, Kit caught Will's blood-covered sleeve and helped. "Before I've seen the place?"

"You could lose your life in a night. Or be trapped here."

"I'll risk it." *Just this once. For an hour.* "Why did you pass your chance at Baines?"

"Because I wasn't sure I could kill him."

"He wasn't armed—"

"Christ wept!" Kit turned on Will with enough force that Will staggered a step. "I wasn't sure I could kill him, Will. Why are you after me? I came to help, didn't I?"

Perversity flared in Will. *Came to help. Aye. And where were you all the long last year, and the one before that, and the one before that —* "How did you know about Baines?"

"I read thy letter."

"You read my . . . oh. How did you —" *And this is the night he chooses to take it?* "Did you read any of the papers with it?"

"Ben's play?" Kit shook his head. "I read the letter only, and panicked. And a good thing: you would not have wished to make an intimate acquaintance of Master Richard Baines."

"I'm glad you have the poems." Will hoped his voice hid his desperation. They moved through narrow corridors; with a little amusement, he realized — despite rich hangings and the smooth golden stone underfoot — that Kit shepherded him through the castle on the servants' trails. Just as well — Will's blood-soaked shoes left brushmarks on the flags. The walls were almost translucent, glowing mellow amber. Will laid a hand on one, surprised to find it cool. "Do you suppose I could reclaim those? Ben has my other copy, and I don't expect him back from Stratford for a month."

"It may be a month gone by when you return home," Kit said, and Will couldn't miss the relief in his voice at *Baines* as a dropped subject. "But, aye, of course. May I keep the plays?"

"In addition to Ben's," Will answered. He ducked so Kit wouldn't see his blush. "There's two comedies of mine."

"Oh?"

"*A Midsummer Night's Dream.*" *Which Satan said he rather liked. Rather in advance.* "And *As You Like It*," Will said. "If thou couldst see the boys we have now, thou wouldst strangle me in my sleep for a chance to write for them."

Kit changed the subject again, leaving Will to wonder at his discomfort. "Here's my door. There's half a chance hot water awaits thee, if I know the castle's staff. I'm off to fetch Morgan. I won't be above half an hour."

"With blood all over thy breast?" Will asked gently.

Kit brushed at it with the backs of his fingers, scattering another pearl. "She's seen worse," he said. "Your poems are on the bed. Drink *nothing*, not even the water." He shut the door before Will could thank him, or make sense of the ragged darkness in Kit's expression.

Kit's chamber was big enough for a Prince, the floor covered in a stun-
ning extravagance of Araby carpets, the curtained bed broad enough
for five. *I wonder who he shares it with,* Will thought, and put the thought
away. Tapestries and painted cloths muffled the walls; their subject
was pastoral, and Will did not think Kit had chosen them.

The aftermath of combat made him dizzy. He washed, then sorted
his poems from the other papers and rolled them tight, finding a bit
of ribbon in his purse to tie them with. Will breathed easier once
those too-revealing sonnets were tucked inside his doublet; less easily
when the door opened and Kit led a woman of middle years and black
Roman beauty in. A woman clad in a man's white cambric shirt, riding
boots, and green breeches that were almost trunk hose, cut tight and
close to her hips and thighs. "My lady," Will said, making a somewhat
unsteady leg, noticing Kit's discomfiture as an adjunct to his own. *It's
a bit of a pleasure to see Marley flustered.*

She snorted like a mare and scanned him lengthwise, shaking her
head hard enough that the peridot clusters in her ears tangled in the
escaping tendrils of her hair. "The legendary William Shakespeare,"
she said, and turned to Kit. "A little unprepossessing, isn't he?" Her
smile softened the comment into a flirtation; Will didn't understand
why Kit blanched and leaned heavily on the edge of the clothespress.

"My lady," Will said, feigning hurt, "I am accounted the most
charming of playmakers —"

"Given thy competition, I do not wonder," she said. Her hips
moved marvelously under the tight dark brocade as she crossed the
carpet. Will kept his eyes on her face, the green-black eyes she never
lowered. "Wert injured?"

"No," he said.

She reached up and tilted his face side to side, clucking her tongue.
Despite himself, her fingers stroking his beard, the scent of her skin
like mint and citrus, he couldn't help but smile. "What is't?"

"You sound exactly like my wife."

"I hope that's a better compliment than if I said you sounded like
my husband."

" 'Tis the greatest compliment I can offer," Will said as she stepped
away. "Do I pass inspection, madam?"

"You seem unhurt. We'll talk of the other things later—" Before he could do more than startle, she moved toward the door. "You washed your hair, at least. I'll see you clothed; we'll present you to the Mebd tonight, after supper—"

Kit cleared his throat. Morgan turned to him and smiled, and Will's breath swelled his throat for a moment as he tried to decide if the smile was a lover's, or that of an indulgent guardian. "My boon, my Queen," he murmured.

Her chin lifted, and the smile grew amused. "Of course." A little show of feeling in her pockets, until Kit touched his collar—Will realized that the other poet had changed clothes, or his shirt and doublet at least, and washed the rusty red spatters from his hands. *He keeps clothes in her rooms. That answers one question. Or does it?* Morgan laughed and unpinned something winking gold from the cambric of her shirt, coming back to Will. "Have you a place for an earring, Master Shakespeare?"

He lifted his hair, showing the bit of silk that kept the hole from closing. Kit nodded when Will caught his eye, and so Will ducked his head and let her untie the cord and slip it from his ear. A little gasp as she tugged the hole open and slipped something into it: a substantial ring, warm from the heat of her bosom. "There," she said. "A favor from a lady. A favor that will permit thee, Master Shakespeare, to come and go from *this* land to *that* land as thou wilt, without years cut from thy life whilst thou in Faerie dwelleth."

Kit came forward beside her, rubbing at his eyepatch as an exhausted man might rub his eye. As Morgan stepped back, Will touched the earring, feeling heavy gold swing. "A rich gift, Your Highness."

"We have a special love of poets here," she said. "Don't we, Sir Christofer?" She turned to kiss Kit on the cheek. Will saw his friend pale, but Kit did not step away, and in fact smiled as if at a favor.

The door shut behind her, concealing the sway of her hips, and Will touched the earring again. "Do you trust this?"

"Her word is good. When you can get her to give it."

"An impressive woman."

"If thou knowst what's wise," Kit said, "that will be the last time thou thinkst so. Come, lay thee in my bed and rest. I'm too long slept, myself: I'll sit and read thy Jonson's plays while thou dost slumber, and wake thee when thy clothes arrive."

Who ever loved, that loved not at first sight?
—CHRISTOPHER MARLOWE, *Hero and Leander*

Once Will fell into exhausted slumber, Kit dragged the fireplace armchair to the window for better light, muttering amiable profanity as ornately worked legs snagged on the carpets. Taking up the remaining papers, he settled down to study. Jonson's play he set aside, for perusal when his concentration improved, while he spread the sheets of Will's comedy across his knees and held them up, unfolded one by one, to read. Five or ten leaves in, he stifled laughter against his sleeve and read faster. At the end of the third act, he turned the already-read pages over and laid them on the floor, sitting back in the chair to regard their slumbering author.

He gazed for long minutes, blinking thoughtfully, and at last picked up the remaining sheets to read: more slowly now, and with attention. "Ganymede, eh?" But it was no more than a murmur, the shape of a name on his lips.

He read the play twice over before he set it aside, and then he stood and paced the width of the room once or twice, stealing glances at Will now and again, shaking his head each time. Will showed no signs of stirring, sleeping the sleep of utter weariness, and Kit at last stopped pacing and returned to the window and Jonson's play. The wit was sharp, the rhyme fitting, if the tone a little dismissive of both players and audience—but Kit could not concentrate long enough to read a page complete. He laid them aside and picked up Will's play again, thumbing through it to read a line here and there. Again shook his head, and again laid the papers aside. At last, in frustration, he stood and fetched a bundle, thread, and a needle-book from the clothespress: a task to busy his hands enough, he hoped, to silence the breathless longing that had sprung painfully to life in his breast.

Who ever loved, that loved not at first sight?
—WILLIAM SHAKESPEARE, *As You Like It*

Will found himself turning and turning again, trying not to stare at one improbable being after another as Kit led him through the soaring hall. It took concentration not to crowd Kit for the transitory feeling of safety the brush of his shoulder gave. Will stole another look at his friend's ragged cloak, almost a motley, a panoply of richest fabric stitched with a tight and tidy hand. *Court garb in Faerie.*

Will looked longingly at the wine in his glass, but set it on the edge of the table.

"Go ahead and drink," Kit said. "You've a Queen's surety you may return home without fear. The Fae keep their word. And now, come and meet my lover."

"Another one? Haven't you enough problems?"

"Mix with the men of power and rise." Kit shrugged. "They teach that at Cambridge, too."

The banter, the sparkle. It was tinsel, Will thought, understanding. *There's a reason no one ever let you on a stage, Marley.* But as Kit led him forward, he followed on.

Act III, scene ii

Faustus: *Was not that Lucifer an Angel once?*
Mephostophilis: *Yes Faustus, and most dearly loved of God.*
Faustus: *How comes it then that he is Prince of Devils?*
Mephostophilis: *O by aspiring pride and insolence,*
For which God threw him from the face of heaven.

—CHRISTOPHER MARLOWE, *Faustus*

The rill of Cairbre's harpstrings shivered through the air as Murchaud brushed a courtier aside and came across the floor—currently otherwise occupied by clusters of conversationalists—to Will and Kit. Kit bowed, found it useless as Murchaud closed the distance between them and took Kit's doublet in both hands, lifting him to his toes to claim a possessing kiss. Kit's ragged new cloak, only a single layer of a few dozen patches yet, dragged at his collar as Murchaud bent him backward. He pressed one hand to the Elf-knight's breast, feeling the racing beat of his heart under velvet and silk.

Murchaud released him and stepped back, left Kit wiping his mouth on his hand, stinging with the suddenness of the release. Kit turned to Will, still tasting the kiss, watching the blood rise in Will's ghost-pale cheeks. "Your Highness, Master William Shakespeare," he said formally. "Will, Murchaud ap Launcelot, Prince of the Daoine Sidhe."

"Fitz," Murchaud corrected. "How did you know that?"

"Your mother hinted strongly," Kit said, his eye on Will, who shifted a flustered gaze from one to the other of them as if uncertain where to rest it. "Welcome to Faerie, Will. Things are a bit different here."

"Your Highness," Will said, bending a knee. Kit thought he looked striking in a saffron-colored doublet pinked in peach and gold, the padding enough to make him seem a little less painfully thin. If nothing else, those cheekbones and the startling blue eyes would have made up for a multitude of sins —

Kit.

Stop.

"Call me Murchaud," he answered, to Kit's surprised pleasure and then jealousy. "We needn't stand on ceremony. Come, let me introduce you to my wife —" He took Will's elbow and led him toward the dais, Kit trailing uncomfortably.

The Mebd was garbed in gold and white, the floor-length sleeves of her gown wrought with fantastical chains of green embroidery. The dress resembled an antique style called a bliaut, belted with golden chains encrusted with emeralds. She drifted down the steps with her arms spread wide, poised like a dove at the bottom of the dais, her train spread behind her glittering with crystal and silver thread.

"Kneel," Murchaud instructed Will as they came before her. Kit stepped forward and dropped a knee: uneasiness still troubled his stomach as Will sank correctly beside him and Murchaud bowed low.

The Mebd looked from one face to another, and smiled. "My lord husband. Sir Kit. And Master William Shakespeare. Has ever a court been so graced with jewels of verse as ours?"

"Your Majesty," Will answered, bowing his head. "You do me more credit than I deserve."

"Nay," she answered. "Sir Christofer, we see thou hast claimed thy rank as journeyman-bard. We are pleased." A hesitation, and Kit felt her smile like a brand. "Poets, rise. You will grace us tonight?" *You, not thou. Both of us. She means to make a little rivalry between us. Faerie —*

—and their games.

Will glanced sidelong at Kit, who nodded, barely. Will answered, "It shall be as you wish it, Your Majesty. We will be pleased to. If I may beg a boon . . . ?"

Kit nibbled the edge of his mustache, keeping his eyes on the floor. *Careful, Will.*

And, *Ganymede.* Jove's fancy-boy, his pretty cup-bearer, and by extension, the painted boys who worked in London's alleys. *Do I want to know if it means what I think it means, that Will named so his woman-dressed-as-lad?*

Kit's stomach knotted again.

"Ask what thou wilt, Master Poet."

"To stay in your court a little, that I may sing its praises the more extravagantly when I return to England."

She made a show of considering, but Kit—risking a glance—perfectly understood the small smile playing at her lips. "Thou mayst stay," she said. "A little. And"—before Kit could do more than nudge Will warningly with an elbow—"thou mayst leave when thou wisheth. For the rent of a song or seven, while thou art with us. Art agreed?"

"Aye, Your Majesty."

"It will be as we have said." She smiled, and graced Kit and then Will with a touch of her hand, and then took Murchaud's arm and permitted it to seem as if he led her away, although Kit could see the hesitance of the Prince's step.

"Are they all like her?" Will asked under his breath.

Kit shook his head. "She's the most—"

"Fey."

"Yes. Foolish to ask, but dost feel—ensorceled?"

Will turned a stare on him, and then stopped, lips thinning as he considered. "How would I know if I were?"

"An excellent question," Kit admitted. "Let me know if anyone pins a pansy to your bosom. Will you write to Burbage to see to your affairs?"

"I'll tell him I was called away, aye. We won't have a playhouse until after Christmas, as it is."

Tear down the Theatre, Kit thought, shaking his head at a bit of his world gone forever. Sharp as a stone in his shoe. *Murchaud did warn you—the world changes, and you will not.* "Ah, there's someone you should

meet. The lady Amaranth." Kit stole a sidelong glance at Will, whose
jaw was literally hanging open. "Striking, is she not?"

"Astoundingly. Is she venomous?"

"She assures me she is. I have never sought an opportunity to
discover it first hand."

"Methinks 'tis probably as well."

"Aye," Kit said, taking Will by the elbow. "I do agree. I've spoken
with Morgan. Thou wilt share my quarters, an it please thee. The
bed's big enough for four, and to be frank I find it strange having
so large a room to myself." *And it will present a barrier to keep thee from
Morgan's clutches. And perhaps buy me some peace as well.* The thought
of returning to Murchaud's bed made him sick. *Rosalind. Dressed as
Ganymede.*

Oh, Will.

Oh, God in Hell. "Amaranth," Kit said as they came up to her. "Meet
my friend William Shakespeare. Will, Lady Amaranth."

"Charmed," Will said, and to his credit bent over her cold, scaled
hand and brushed it with his lips.

Amaranth's snakes swelled, pleased, about her elfin face as she
mocked a smile. "Master Shakespeare," she hissed. "Your reputation
precedes you."

Will glanced at Kit. Kit shrugged. "We stay current," he said.
"What poem do you plan to recite?"

Will closed his eyes, as if considering. "Something you haven't
read, I think. Are you reciting Hero?"

"They've heard it," Kit said, lifting his shoulders in a shrug. The
ragged hem of his cloak swayed against his calves. "The Mebd hinted
she wanted me to play Bard, so I thought I would sing something not
of mine own composing."

"When do we—"

Kit pointed with his chin to the dais. "Go and tell Cairbre there
you're sent to claim the stage. He'll advise you when."

"Come with me?"

Kit smiled. "Aye, I will. Amaranth, will you accompany?"

She tilted her head in gracious refusal as she flicked herself into a
tidy tower of coils. "I must seek Master Goodfellow," she said. "Anon,
gentle Poets."

"Anon, my lady," Will said.

Kit bowed slightly, but did not speak as she glided away. "She likes thee."

"How knowst thou?"

Kit flinched as they turned toward the small stage. Cairbre had been joined by Morgan le Fey, who gathered her gown—*thank God she's decently dressed*—in both fists as she seated herself before the virginals. "I can tell."

"Your Morgan plays?" Will asked in his ear, a tender thrill in his voice that drew another shiver from Kit.

"Very well," Kit answered, and walked forward.

Kit leaned against the pillar between two silk-shrouded windows, arms folded over his breast, and unsuccessfully fought a smile. Will was correct: he didn't know this poem, and its simple style masked Will's eternal cleverness very well.

Half Kit's mind was elsewhere, hastily revising the words of a whimsically chosen song to remove references to "the Divine." But with his remaining attention, he watched Will put on a player's confidence and take the stage like a master, broad gestures and subtle expressions as he declaimed.

> *. . . Truth may seem, but cannot be;*
> *Beauty brag, but 'tis not she;*
> *Truth and beauty buried be.*
>
> *To this urn let those repair*
> *That are either true or fair;*
> *For these dead birds sigh a prayer.*

Applause, and Will soaked it in for a moment before doffing his borrowed hat and taking a long, savoring bow. Kit watched, his stomach still twisting. *No Ned, nor will he ever be, but the man has grown. Even if he is losing his hair. Congratulations, my love: an ovation in Faerie, such as most poets only dream.*

Will's smile, when he stood, cast his face in the architecture of delight. He turned to Kit, summoning him on an airy gesture. *Sweet*

Christ harrowing Hell, how am I supposed to sleep in a bed with that man all night after reading that play?

Kit mounted the steps, acknowledged to a ripple of applause, and leaned down and whispered in Cairbre's ear, enjoying the expression on the Bard's face when he said, "That Tudor song I taught you, Sir—"

"Bold," Cairbre said, and laced his fingers over the strings of his harp.

"This is not mine," Kit said, turning to the Fae, "but is said to have been written by a King himself not known for his faith to his ladies." He drew breath, and found Murchaud in the crowd as Cairbre and Morgan gave him the first plaintive notes.

Alas, my love, you do me wrong,
To cast me off discourteously.
For I have loved you well and long,
Delighting in your company.

Your vows you've broken, like my heart,
Oh, why did you so enrapture me?
Now I remain in a world apart
But my heart remains in captivity.

The Prince's eyes widened in shock at the boldness of the gesture. *And after that kiss, he shouldn't be surprised—* Kit looked away, to find the rest of his audience, aware that his voice hadn't the richness of Cairbre's deep baritone, but finding its notes with confidence. Kit sang a line for Amaranth, and one for Geoffrey, and discovered other eyes in the crowd as well. A sly glance at Morgan, giving her a phrase or two as she ran her fingers over the keys, and she smiled back as if enjoying his bravura.

Goodfellow's glance, there, and a tight little smile as the Puck tugged at his own short motley cape. Kit smiled back, and gave him a verse, for the only friendship Kit had known in Faerie. And then he turned his head and gave Will a verse, one of the changed ones, his throat tight enough that he prayed not to squeak like a mouse.

To Murchaud, the last verse, and to the Mebd's cruel, amused, approving smile and her whisper in her husband's ear — *See, love? Your pet has teeth* — and then he closed his eyes and back to the beginning again, for the final hanging, dying line.

> *Alas, my love, you do me wrong,*
> *To cast me off discourteously.*
> *For I have loved you well and long,*
> *Delighting in your company.*

Shock, not applause, and Kit let the old armored smile slide over his face like a visor at the paleness in Murchaud's cheeks and Kit's own unexpected success. *I've found a way to scandalize Faerie at last,* he thought, and took himself down from the stage.

Act III, scene iii

> **Mercutio:** *Without his roe, like a dried herring: O flesh,*
> *flesh, how art thou fishified! Now is he for the numbers*
> *that Petrarch flowed in: Laura to his lady was but a*
> *kitchen-wench; marry, she had a better love to*
> *be-rhyme her; Dido a dowdy; Cleopatra a gipsy;*
> *Helen and Hero hildings and harlots; Thisbe a gray*
> *eye or so, but not to the purpose.*
>
> —WILLIAM SHAKESPEARE, *Romeo and Juliet*

William knew something had happened, that Kit's rendition of "Greensleeves" had somehow been a challenge, the smack of a gauntlet against an unprepared face. Knew it more when the music that resumed after Kit left the small stage was wordless, and Morgan excused herself, smiling, and went to climb the dais beside the Queen and the Prince.

Who shortly thereafter removed themselves from the hall.

Will, rested from the afternoon's nap, mingled joyously with musicians and poets, with the Faerie players that Kit had recruited for his masques and plays, until at last Kit found him and tugged his sleeve toward the stair. "It looks desperate to be the last one at the party," Kit said. "Unless you were planning on leaving with the brunette—"

Will glanced back at her. She smiled coquettishly behind a fan of painted mauve silk, and he waved and turned away. "The fangs are a bit disconcerting."

"She's Leannan Sidhe. You'd never be the same." Kit lit a candle at the base of the spiral stair, and Will climbed in silence beside him.

"Leannan Sidhe?" He tried to mimic Kit's pronunciation.

Kit hesitated, his hand still warm on Will's arm as they made their way up the stairs. "Blood drinkers. A man can't be too careful, in Faerie."

Will watched Kit open the door. "Black Annie," he said. "Only men, not children."

"She's got a special affection for poets." Kit ushered Will inside, latched the door, and found cups and a bottle in the cupboard, upon which he left the candle. " 'Tis said her love gives inspiration."

"And have you availed yourself of this inspiration?" Will took the cup Kit offered him and held it under his nose. The scent made his eyes tear. "Brandywine?"

"Better. 'Tis called uisge. Be careful—" As Will sipped, and coughed, and Kit laughed at him. "No, dying young once was enough. But I wanted to talk to you about your play."

The fire of the liquor sliding down Will's throat did nothing to calm the tension in his shoulders. He told himself any ripples shivering across the tawny fluid in his cup were just the effects of his palsy, and set it down before he could spill it. "You disliked it."

"I could not adore it more," Kit said, refilling his cup. He leaned against the great carved post of the bed, curtains rumpling against his cloak. As if irritated, he unfastened the clasp and leaned forward enough to free himself of the tattered finery, tossing it to the bed. The single candle cast gentle shadows across his face; he drank and continued talking into Will's silence. "You've cast me again, haven't you? As you like your Rosalind. Your Ganymede."

Will laughed. "You caught me out. The first to notice it enough to warrant a mention."

"How could they miss? Ganymede, Leander, dead shepherds. A crack about 'a great reckoning in a little room' and another about incompetent historians? You should not take such risks."

"Not a risk if no one notices."

Kit laughed, staring down into his cup. "Kit in skirts—I should be offended, I suppose, but she's a delightful girl. Although to call her Ganymede were an ungentle jest—"

"Ungentle? I thought to reference your *Dido*. . . ."

"And not painted boys untrussing in doorways? I suppose that's all right—"

"I beg your pardon—" Will picked up his cup and gulped more liquor, liking the second swallow better. "I intended no offense." *Naive, Will.*

Kit dismissed it with a tilt of his hand. "She's a marvelous character. Any man with the wit to choose a resolute wench would die for such a maid." And then hastily, as if afeared—"Is that how thou seest me, Will?"

"How I—" *Damn. How does he always manage to weasel me into the honesty I don't want to give?* The liquor gave Will courage, and he wondered if Kit had intended it so. "Perhaps how I would see thee, if I could."

That beautiful, ruined face turned toward him, and Kit set down his cup on a relief-carved trunk and closed the distance a few hesitant steps. His forehead shone pale, candlelight burnishing a thin gloss of sweat. Will swallowed. Kit's careful, measured voice coiled his limbs like the tendrils of a fog, cat-amused. "And were I a woman, a maid, what wouldst will of me?"

Will grinned and stepped back, far enough that he could breathe again. The closer Kit came, the vaster grew the tightness in Will's throat. He tossed back what was in his glass; it seemed easier to swallow, and a pleasant looseness imbued his muscles. "Wouldst measure thy will 'gainst mine? I'd say a maid at thine age hadn't been striving for another state."

"I'd be inclined to agree. Dost wish more drink?"

"Wine, an thou hast it." His throat was dry; wine would comfort it.

"By all means, put me to use."

Kit busied himself at the sideboard; Will watched how his curls snagged and slid on the velvet across his shoulders. *He would have made a lovely girl.* "To use? Pouring and fetching?"

Kit checked as if Will had flicked his nose for overcuriosity. "Pity mine impertinence. 'Tis queer to see oneself given a woman's body.

And, in my situation, a rare pleasure to be remembered." Bitterness on that last word, and Will flinched from it as Kit returned his cup.

Will drank, and Kit drank too. The silence lasted until they'd drained the wine. Will set his cup on the window ledge with a soft click and twisted his heavy new earring in his ear before he spoke. The words that came were not the words he'd intended. "Kit, why would any man permit . . ." He swallowed, stuffed his traitor right hand into the pocket of the borrowed sunflower doublet. "Isn't it—agonizing?"

Kit cleared his throat, looking away, dispossessing himself of his cup as well. "Rather thou shouldst say, exquisite."

"I find it difficult to comprehend."

"I"—Kit paused, still looking down, face suddenly pale around a flush that marked consumptive circles on his cheeks, bright enough to show by candlelight—"could show thee."

Ah. Will's mouth that had been so dry was full of juice now. He swallowed it. "Thou—"

Kit was trembling. Like a leaf, like a girl, like a rose petal twisting in the breeze, about to be lifted from the stem. "Do not I possess mine own body, to pray God as I wish, to speak as I wish, to love with as I wish?"

Which was heresy again, and sedition, and half a dozen other things. To which Will had no answer. Kit smelled of sweet wine and herbs, and that fiery taint of uisge. Soft boots silent on red-and-gold carpet, in one endless moment, he came the few short steps to Will diffidently, like a man wooing a maid. Gaze on gaze, as if watching for the instant when Will might startle, he raised spread fingers and slid them up Will's cheeks, brushed his ears, combed his curls with them. Then took Will's face tenderly between his hands and, tugging him down, nibbled Will's lips until they parted. *William, my love—*

A kiss at first as hesitant as a maiden's, but then deepening as Will softened into it; and yet unlike kissing a maid, for all Kit's lush mouth and pouting lip, because that mouth and tongue were knowing. There was the aggression of it, the light control exerted by Kit's hands in his hair, the yielding lips fronting a seeking tongue, the brush of beard against beard, the hardness of a man's muscled body in his arms. Literally in his arms; Will blinked to realize he'd pulled Kit close, dust-colored curls between his fingers, leaning into the forbidden, erotic kiss that drained blood from a suddenly light head to warm and throb in his loins. A swarm of moths beat hungry wings toward the candle flaring in his breast—

—he jerked free.

A string of saliva stretched between their mouths, glistening. "Pity," Kit said, and broke it with a fingertip, stepping away. "More wine before we sleep?"

"No," Will said. "I think I've had too much already. Art ready, for sleep?"

"Aye," Kit answered, unbuttoning his doublet's collar. "To sleep."

Will lay in darkness, listening to Kit's slow breathing, hugging his nightshirt close to his sides. *How can he sleep like that, as if nothing transpired*—

Sleep is what you should be doing as well, he reminded himself, and closed his eyes resolutely on the faintly moonlit swells and valleys of the canopy overhead. Will nibbled his thumbnail, stopped quickly at the subtle reminder of the pressure of lips on lips. He turned on his side, careful not to shift the coverlet, and buried his face in a tightly clutched pillow as if the greater darkness could silence the voice in his heart. *What if I had shown him those poems?*

He knows. He must know. Or was he just—

—being Kit? He shocked all Faerie with that song of old Harry's. Did he want to shock me too?

Did I want him to know?

Kit never stirred. Will cursed him his complacency, the even rhythm of his breath, the relaxation in his shoulders under the whiteness of his nightshirt when Will turned to look at him in the moonlight. Wondered what would happen if he, Will, put out his right hand and took Kit by the shoulder and turned him to the center of the bed, and stole another kiss. *It would be more than a kiss now, and that, thou knowest.*

He sighed, and rolled back to his own side of the bed. *O let my books be then the eloquence, And dumb presagers of my speaking breast*—

And what if I told him that? Would he—

—kiss me like that again? What else would he do?

Would I want him to?

An unanswerable question, for all Will would have known the answer short hours before.

The night passed in discomfort, until the last grayness before the first gold of morning, when Kit's muttered whimpers and bedding-snarled struggles drew Will upright. "Kit?"

No answer, but a low, tangled moan. Kit's hand reached out, as if to grasp something, or ward it away, and Will impulsively caught his wrist with both hands. *"Kit."*

Who blinked, and drew the hand back, self-consciously, rubbing at his scar. Who looked strange in the half-light, divested of the eyepatch Will still hadn't quite accepted; Will wanted to reach out and touch that long white scar, the drooping eyelid, the bland, pallid orb underneath. He tucked his hands below the covers. "Dream," Kit said softly, turning aside as if Will's gaze discomfited him. "Damn me to Hell, Robert said they were supposed to get better after I made the cloak—"

"What sort of a dream?" Will drew back among the pillows, propped against the bedpost. "Nightmares?"

"Robert said they were prophecy, and indeed I had one of you in Baines' clutches. 'Twas what drove me to your rescue. But stitching that cloak was meant to bring their power under control. Prophetic dreams are all very handy, I'm sure, but if I cannot sleep at night, any night, I'll be of no use to anyone—"

"You slept a little," Will said.

"I had . . ." Kit stopped, his hands fretting the bedclothes. "Just drifted off a moment ago."

"Oh." Wariness, and then a cold sort of delight. *Not so cool as he pretends—*

Master Shakespeare. It will not behoove you to be cruel. "The cloak," Will said; anything to break the fraught, gray silence. "What if you spread it over the bed? There's herbs that keep dreams off if placed under your pillow. Perhaps it holds the same sort of virtue."

Kit lifted his chin and slid his legs out of the bed. He'd pulled the cloak off its foot the night before and folded it neatly over the back of the chair; now he shook it open and laid it over the coverlet. The fabrics dark and bright, rich and plain, were hypnotic; Will reached out and stroked a rose-colored trapezoid of brocade. "Why a patchwork?"

Kit smiled. "Morgan and Cairbre say it signifies all the hearts a bard has pleased with his music; it represents protection, for the good will of all those listeners and lovers interlinks to a garment that keeps ill magic and ill fate away like ill weather. A very old kind of sympathy."

"So not a fool's motley, then?"

"They both represent something sacrosanct." Kit clambered back into bed, making a show of pushing his pillow around, and lay down with his back to Will again. "A tatterdemalion sort of magic, but there you are."

"Which patch is from your Prince?"

"He hasn't given one." A hesitation. "The green-figured velvet embroidered with the unicorn, though. That was from Morgan, and oddly formal for a thing that's meant to be made of scraps and ragged leavings."

As if the Bard, in exchanging pleasure and truth with many, isn't entitled to a single whole life of his own. "Rest easy, Kit," Will said, because he could not think what else to say. "I'll wake you again, if need be."

Act III, scene iv

For such outrageous passions cloy my soul,
As with the wings of rancor and disdain,
Full often am I soaring up to heaven,
To plaint me to the gods against them both:

—CHRISTOPHER MARLOWE, *Edward II*

Kit awakened for the second time almost rested, and he wasn't entirely certain whether it was the mingled silken and harsh fabrics of the cloak bunched in his fists that made the difference, or Will's arm around his shoulders, bridging the careful four inches that separated their bodies. The rhythm of Will's breathing told him the other poet was not sleeping. "Was I dreaming again?"

"Complexly, I gather, from thy conversations." Will drew back as Kit turned to face him, and Kit frowned.

Aye, Marley. And your own damned fault it is. What wert thou thinking? More to the point, what wert thou thinking with?

"Conversations? What did I say?" Kit sat upright, reaching for his eyepatch. "At least I didn't wake up screaming this time; the cloak must have its uses."

Will blushed, and as Kit asked, he remembered—a flurry of wild white wings like Icarus—doves? Swans? *If it's swans, does it mean*

Elizabeth? There seems to be a symbolism running through these dreams of mine, rather than a literal thread. And there had been blood, and pentagrams.

"Thou didst call on Christ to save thee. Begged someone to finish something, or make it done. And then—"

"Consummatum est." Kit stood and pulled his nightshirt over his head, stumbling across the carpet to the wash-basin. He all but felt Will avert his eyes. "I remember now." *If I could only remember what it is that was done. . . .*

"Yes. Kit—"

Kit turned back, preserving some semblance of modesty with the nightshirt in his hand, amused at Will's reaction to his nudity. *Unkind, Christofer.*

I am what I am.

"What is that mark on thy side? Oh, there's another."

"Five," Kit answered, remembering how they had burned as if writ anew on his flesh, in the dream. "One on my breast. One to each side, just below the ribs on my belly. One gracing each thigh, like the points of a star." *The circle of Solomon or the pentangle? I imagine the circle would have required more men. And then, circles are for keeping something out; pentagrams for keeping something in.*

Stopping my voice in my throat, like the bridle. And when my Edward proved to them they had failed to break me, they killed me. God in heaven, I hope I never know what Oxford was thinking when we— Lacrima Christi. When we were together. How much did he know?

All of it?

"Not an accident, then."

"Rheims," Kit said, and waited. *Did you think I was kidding about the irons, Will?* When Will said nothing more, he turned away again and went to wash himself in the icy water before finding a clean shirt and leaving the basin to Will. " 'Tis nigh on afternoon. Not surprising; we scarcely slept till morning. Have you plans for the evening?"

"Will we be expected at dinner?"

"Dinner is cold shoulder. The court prefers to gather for supper, and for sport and entertainments after. Thou'rt still nine days' wonder enough that thou shouldst appear. I certainly will." Kit's clothing seemed to have expanded overnight, some brighter colors among the blacks and greens Morgan favored on him: clothes narrower in the shoulder and longer in the arm. "Your wardrobe has arrived."

"Does it involve a clean shirt?"

"Aye, a selection—" Kit stepped aside so Will could pick through the pile. "Wilt explore Faerie?"

"Is it safe?"

"No—" Kit said. "But I'm only writing a play on Orfeo gone to Faerie now, or perhaps 'tis Orpheus gone to Hell. I could accompany you."

"If it's not an inconvenience. Is there a difference, between Faerie and Hell?"

"When I've seen Hell, I'll tell thee—" A light knock interrupted. "A moment!" Kit caught his cloak up from the bed and hesitated. "Will, is this thine?"

Something gleamed in the middle of the coverlet, as if it had been slipped beneath Kit's cloak. A quill—he guessed it a swan's quill, by the strength and color—the tip cut to a nib but with the vanes of the feather unstripped.

"I think not," Will said, hunching to twist his hose smooth at the back of his knee. "A pen?"

"Indeed." Some unidentifiable thrill ran through Kit as he held it, a sensation like beating wings, and with it came undefinable sorrow and joy. He set it on the table near the bed but was unable to resist one last, soft touch. "I wonder how it found its way onto the coverlet. Who's there?" Tucking his shirt hastily into his untied breeches as a second round of knocking commenced, he hastened to the door and unlatched it.

Morgan stepped inside and regarded Kit with amusement. "So you rise to greet the nightingale, and not the lark?" And then, over his shoulder: "Good day, Master Shakespeare."

"Your Highness." Will came forward, fastening his buttons one-handed. "A fine reception last night. I thank you."

"There's dancing tonight," she offered, brushing past Kit to lay a hand on Will. "I wished to speak with thee. Kit, Cairbre wishes your attendance when you are decent—"

Kit swung his cloak up. "Will, wouldst care to accompany me?" *I am not leaving him alone with Morgan le Fey.*

"I—"

"I shall send him along when I've finished with him," she promised. "Don't worry. It shan't be long."

Kit looked from one to the other: Will had a certain bemused curiosity on his face, and Morgan's tone was one step shy of command. He sighed and finished dressing. "Very well." He bowed over Morgan's hand. "Treat kindly with my friend, my Queen." Knowing she would hear everything he put into the title, both promises and obligations.

"I shall be sure to," she answered, and there was nothing for it but to excuse himself and go.

Act III, scene v

For all that beauty that doth cover thee,
Is but the seemly raiment of my heart,
Which in thy breast doth live, as thine in me:
How can I then be elder than thou art?

—WILLIAM SHAKESPEARE, from Sonnet 22

"Now, Master Shakespeare," Morgan said, after the door drifted reluctantly closed behind Kit, "this illness thou'rt concealing so effectively. We're going to discuss it."

Will blinked and sat down on the edge of Kit's bed. "Not such effective concealment if you noticed it in the span of a few hours' acquaintance."

"I am she who notices such things," she said, dark eyes sparkling. She settled on the floor, her gown puddling around her, and drew her knees to her breast. "What afflicts thee, other than the tremors and the shortened stride?"

"Lack of balance," Will answered, amazed at how easily the words came. *Do not trust what the Faeries offer,* he reminded himself. "Easy exhaustion. My throat aches, as do my breast and back, and I have no appetite. Of late I notice the palsy in my left hand too—"

"The next stage of the illness," Morgan said, resting her chin on her crossed arms and her knees, "is likely a more shuffling step and a — nodding palsy, and a paralysis of the face. If it follows the course I've seen. Thou'rt no more likely to suffer dementia than any man, for what comfort it offers."

"Likely," Will answered. "My father is well aged and still in his right mind, though ill for years. I have my hopes."

"Thou shouldst." She rose, uncoiling, posed for a moment like a caryatid, and as she came toward him he saw her feet were bare upon the carpets. The loose gown caressed the heavy curve of her hips and breasts such that it left Will's throat aching more than his illness could excuse. "I've aught for thee: a tincture of hellebore and arnica, and powdered root of aconite."

"Monkshood?" Will thought of nodding blue flowers. "All poisons, Your Highness—"

"Aye," she said. He would have stood when she came before him, but her long-fingered hand on his shoulder pressed him down. "Herbs of great virtue are often dangerous." She smoothed her fingers under the line of his jaw, where his blood fluttered close to the skin, and felt of it for a moment, unhurried.

She smelled of something sharply bitter and over it a musky, resinous scent: warmed amber, he thought. The frustrations of the night flooded back at her touch, and he prayed she thought the shiver that ran through him was illness and not the raw, physical reaction that it was. *Always a weakness for older women.* He bit down on a chuckle. *Much older.*

She nodded and stepped away, her hand lingering for a moment. "I've brought a salve imbued with amber oil and camphor as well, to anoint the sore places. Some say it helps—" A facile shrug, and then she dug in her pockets for a tin box, a stoppered bottle no bigger than an inkhorn, and a casket of carven stone. "We can try poison nut if none of these avail. Thou needst be cautious of the dosage: there is no remedy for monkshood or arnica poisoning, and neither is a pleasant death."

Will held out his hands: they trembled less as she laid each gift in his cupped palms. "Thank you, Your Highness. You will show me how?"

She nodded and went to the fireside, leaning against the edge of the hearth, watching him with a sort of birdlike brightness. He stilled his face to hide the longing in it. "None of this is a cure, gentle Shakespeare."

"I understand." Curiously, he examined the bottle; it was carven from the tine of a stag's horn, and the stopper was finished with a knotty gray pearl. He laid it on the bed beside him, along with the other trinkets. "Your Highness—"

"Ask it, William. I have little time for reticence, as Sir Christofer will no doubt inform thee."

"Why am I permitted my freedom and vouchsafed your aid, and that of the Mebd, when my friend Kit is so obviously bound here against his will, and in durance?"

"A good question," she said, and went to find glasses on the sideboard. "Thou shouldst not too much drink ale or wine with those herbs—a little will not hurt, but be sparing. But I can offer thee a drink of lemons and ginger—"

"A good question that will go unanswered," he said with some amusement, smiling as she placed the cup in his hands. It steamed, and the metal warmed his palms: more casual witchcraft.

"Nay," she said. "I'll answer thee."

She sipped her own drink, and Will only held his for a moment and watched her face and the way her hair moved against her cheek, showing bands of silver among the black.

She said, "Because thou art of more use to Faerie in the mortal realm than thou art here, and Sir Christofer has that in him which we need, and can bargain with, and can use as a weapon. And thus we keep him here."

"Has that in him—his magic? His poetry?"

"No, though we have our ways of making profit on that."

"Does he know this?"

"He knows we have uses for him. He knows what some of them entail: his poetry, his plays. We use him as your own Gloriana did—and there is more to it, of course."

"And you have not told him—"

"Because," she said, pressing the back of her hand to her eye, "he is not ready to know. Thy Kit Marley is a deeply broken thing, gentle William, and I do not think he could bear the knowledge of what use he has been put to."

Will's hands tightened on the cup. He lifted it to his mouth and tasted the sweetness of honey, the sharpness of ginger, infused with a silvery aftertaste. Her candor left him nauseated: the ginger helped. "What use is that, Your Highness?"

"No," she said, after a considering stare. "I do not believe thou couldst keep it from him long, even an thou understood why it must be kept. Suffice it to say he is safer with us, and kept distracted with small tasks."

"He's not a man for small tasks, Your Highness."

This smile sparkled, parting her lips for a low, sugared laugh. "Perhaps not," she answered, setting her cup on the mantel and strolling toward the door. She opened it and paused within its frame, turning back for a parting smile. "But then, neither art thou, I consider."

Will paused in the doorway to the conservatory, blinking in the light as its occupants turned to face him, and then blinking again to bring the splendor of the enormous room into focus. Music surrounded him, an eldritch sort of a reel on two flutes and viola; he gazed about in wonder as he paused atop the broad, time-hollowed marble steps. Some vining plant—a type of fig, he realized, for the fruit that hung in purple-black profusion along its stem—ascended a trellis, contorted branches a latticework against the crystal of the ceiling. A wisteria's waterfall blossoms dangled among the fig's glossy leaves, and all about the glass-domed marble space were fountains and benches and statuary, a profusion of half-private niches and mossy grottoes.

A small group of people both nearly human and quite outlandish gathered by the splashing fountains: Kit and the bard Cairbre in their gaily colored patchworks, and beside them the snake-tailed Amaranth. There was a foppishly dressed gallant with a stag's head on his shoulders, shiny above the ears where he must have shed his antlers, and Robin Goodfellow perched on the head of a statue, reed flute raised to pursed lips and his ears waggling in time. Will *did* feel better for Morgan's herbwifery, he realized; the ache across his shoulders ebbed, and his hands shook less as he took the banister to descend, hushing his footsteps so as not to disturb the musicians. Kit caught his eye over the restless motion of the bow, offering a smile that brought with it a frisson that Will could almost convince himself was aversion. *Or should that word be "fascination," Will?*

He paused outside the circle until Kit, Cairbre, and the Puck lowered their instruments, then joined the polite applause. Kit, that smile still intact, handed his viola and the bow to Amaranth, who settled it under her chin amidst much inconvenienced hissing from her hair. "Well played," Will said.

Kit shrugged it off. He laid a hand on Will's shoulder and drew him gently aside, where the sound of the fountain and the flurry of music would cover their speech. "I've not much to do but practice and play the Prince's favorite. How went your—interview with my mistress?"

"She is most gracious," Will answered. "And most mysterious. I hope you have been careful what she has asked of you, Kit—"

"As careful as a man may be, where he owes his life—"

"Aye, there's the rub."

" 'Tis not the rub that concerns us so much as the result."

Will chuckled, dabbling his hands in the fountain. He leaned back, rested against the edge, remembering the paleness of Kit's scars. *The man's entitled to nightmares,* he thought. *He's also entitled to the truth of what Morgan said of him: as well she knows I won't be used against my friend.* "She hinted at things that troubled me, my friend. Sorcery and subtlety."

Kit snorted, turning to sit on the marble edge, shoulder to shoulder with Will and on his left. "Did she tell you it was she who ensorceled me, when first I came to Faerie?"

"No. And yet she released you?"

"After a fashion. Or I won my way free. I am still bound here, though."

Will raised his left hand to brush his earring. Kit nodded. "I envy you that, a bit. It seems I can be gone from Faerie three days, perhaps four, before my body begins to fail."

"An unkind sentence."

"I comfort myself that at least I left no family, save that in Canterbury."

What dost thou then think I am, Kit? And the Toms, and Mary and Robin, and Ned Alleyn? But he nodded, and bumped Kit's shoulder with his own. "She also hinted—and wisely said she would not say more, as I might run direct to thee with the tidings"—a deprecating laugh— "that thou wert bound, somehow, still. She suggested that there was a power in thee, something trapped and broken." He moved to see Kit's profile. Kit had put his blind side to Will, Will realized with a rush of affection.

"She has a gift for manipulation," Kit said. "But she does not understand, always, mortal men."

"I see."

"What did she say, exactly?"

Will drew a breath, watching Amaranth rise up on the tower of her tail, her scales catching the light that rippled from the fountains until it seemed she shone. "She said that I was free to go because of being more use in the mortal world than here, and that you 'have that in you which she needs, and might bargain with, and may find to be a weapon.' And that you were too deeply wounded to be told this secret, because it would damage you further to know."

"I see," Kit said. " 'Tis so satisfying to have the trust and good faith of one's patrons."

Will held back a laugh at Kit's dry, weary tone. "Wilt beard her on this?"

"Morgan le Fey? Might as easily draw the claws from a lion's paw as secrets from that one. She's fair as thorn in bloom, and twice as daggery. No. I'll pursue where I can." Kit folded his arms across his chest, the angle of his chin telling Will that he watched the Puck cavorting about the shoulders of Hercules. He sighed. "Sweet William. How did we ever get from there to here?"

Will shrugged. "Where? London? Where is *here*, then?"

"Sorcery, intrigue, intelligencing, Faerie."

"Poetry."

"Poetry is how we got here? Who would have thought poetry so dangerous?" Kit kicked one heel up, resting it against the base of the statue. "My father made shoes. Yours made gloves. There's a certain symmetry there, and to ending up here."

"The Cobbler's Boy, the Glover's Lad, and the Queen of Faerie. I hope this isn't an ending."

"I was hoping for *happily ever after in wealth and contentment*."

"It should be a ballad."

"If I know Cairbre, it will be." A facile comment, but Will thought there was more behind it. Kit hummed a familiar melody, and sang under the rise and fall of the flutes and the viola: *"All hail the mighty Queen of Heaven! Oh, no, True Thomas, that name does not belong to me."*

"Old songs?"

"Old songs, old poems. Old poets."

"Getting older."

Silence for a minute, as they listened to the melody of the instruments and the falling water. "I think I know, then, what's bound in me that they mean to use as a weapon."

"You do?"

"I can guess—" The arms unfolded. Kit leaned back, his hands flat on the edge of the fountain. Will imitated the gesture, cool marble smooth and damp under his hands.

"What then?"

"At a guess? Something to do with the spells we build with our poetry. It would go a deal toward explaining why thou hast been unable to break the drought, if they've . . . Baines"—and Will felt Kit's shiver—"said the bridle, the stopping of a poet's voice, was the symbol that drove the spell—"

Spell? Will turned again, and laid a hand on Kit's shoulder, watching him swallow and continue to stare straight ahead at the musicians. "Spell?"

"You're too easy to talk to, Will."

"As it may be. Spell. You said nothing—"

"What happened in Rheims," Kit said, "was some sort of black magic. Promethean magic. Baines called me a"—deadly levelness, the tone of a boy reciting Latin verbs—"vessel."

"Christ, Kit—"

Kit didn't turn, but a casual gesture dismissed Will's fury. "So logically, if that's what's bottled up in me, and how they did it . . ."

"Canst prove it?"

"Nay. 'Tis speculation of the rankest sort."

"What are we going to do about it?"

We. He felt Kit's relief at the word, the way the smaller man relaxed as he turned to give Will a fragment of a smile. "Damn, Will. We haven't an idea. But we'll be sure to let us know when we figure it out, won't we?"

Will squeezed and let his hand drop, turning back to the music, aware that the appraising eyes of Cairbre and the stag-headed Fae rested upon them. "We'll certainly do our best."

Act III, scene vi

That love is childish which consists in words.

—CHRISTOPHER MARLOWE, *Dido, Queen of Carthage*

K it watched Will turn away, admiring the resplendent and obviously uncomfortable figure he cut in trunk hose, a starched ruff,
a plumed hat, and a gold-and-aquamarine-wrought doublet of the
vivid blue called inciannomati. Blues were unfashionable in London; it
was the color of apprentice gowns and Elizabeth detested it, but here
in Faerie there were no such considerations. The color looked very
fine with Will's dark hair and startling eyes, the trunk hose showing a
sinewy leg. *Give Morgan that,* Kit thought. *She can dress a man —*

And then he laughed, remembering many an attempt to dress Will
up in years gone by. Will glanced over his shoulder as Kit pushed
away from the fountain and fell into step beside him. Together, they
wandered away from the little clutch of musicians and observers to
circumnavigate the conservatory. "What?"

"My William doesn't look like a Puritan today." Kit watched Will's
eyes to see if his friend flinched at the endearment, and was relieved
when it seemed to pass unremarked except by a flicker of smile.

"Can you call it a day, here? And would a Puritan be welcomed
in Faerie?"

"That's a ballad of a different sort," Kit said. "A bawdy one, or I miss my mark. Perhaps I should write it—"

"With a black cloth coat / and a starch'd white ruff / all strewn o'er the greensward—" Will sang to the tune of a common tavern song, and Kit laughed. "So, sweet Christofer, how shall we entertain ourselves until the dinner hour?"

"Hast eaten?"

"A pastry and a bit of small beer. It will do."

"I could introduce thee to the gardens."

"If they outshine the conservatory—" Will's stagy gesture took in the glittering dome overhead, the marble planters full—without regard to season—of nodding blossoms, the scent of the wisteria as heavy and sweet as treacle. "Shall I be called upon to sing for my supper again tonight?"

I should count on it, my friend. "The Fae," Kit said softly, as they came up on the rest of the group, "will pay handsomely to be made to feel. They are cold and strange, and I sometimes think . . ."

Will's curious gaze stroked his face.

Kit felt it as a palpable touch, and sighed. He stopped, and turned aside to toy with the cool, silken petals of a chimerical chrysanthemum. *Put it aside, Marley—* "I sometimes think they envy us our passions, and half the reason they steal us mortals away is to keep us hothoused like these blossoms. Nothing ever *dies* in Faerie. It just grows chill and dark."

"I could wish a little chillness in trade for a little life."

Kit glanced up at the bitterness in Will's tone, and almost reached to take Will's arm. The stiffness of the other man's posture, his averted eyes, gnawed at Kit with sorrowful teeth, and he let his hand sink back to his side. "Will, I'm sorry—"

"No," Will said. "You've nothing to be sorry for. There's nothing you can make better, Kit."

I could have been there, Kit thought. *You said it yourself.* But he waited, dumb, as Will wandered away to plunge his hands into the fountain again. A tug on Kit's sleeve startled him; he jumped and turned to his blind side. "Geoffrey!"

"Your pardon, Sir Poet. You seemed pensive."

"I am pensive, Geoff. Has the music lost its charm for you already?"

He tilted his head suggestively at Amaranth, Puck, and Cairbre, who were still in full swing.

The stag shrugged, which Kit found anatomically interesting, and looked down his long muzzle at the poet. "This Shakespeare is a friend of yours?"

"Aye," Kit said, "a good one —"

Geoffrey raised a placating hoof at the warning tone in Kit's voice. "I meant nothing by it. One tries to stay apprised of the poetical rivalries in court, of course, and it's been long since we had bards to choose between."

Kit laughed. "Friendship has never stopped us being rivals. The two are not exclusive. Is politics and poetry the main course tonight, then?"

Geoffrey's cloven forehoof moved like a scissors. He lifted the dark violet, golden-eyed blossom he'd snipped from the planter to his nostrils and sniffed. "Do you remember when we spoke of war, and bondage?"

"Love-in-idleness. I couldn't forget."

"Then you know 'tis always politics."

"Politics and poetry. Politics and love. Politics and fairy tales. This is the introduction to a seducement, Geoffrey."

"Am I so transparent?"

Kit let his voice go low, but kept the banter in his tone for the sake of eavesdroppers. "It's been a long time coming," he said. "What does it entail? The overthrow of the Queen?"

"Nothing so dire," the stag answered, just as soft. "Merely a little magic. Which you well began in song already, I wot."

"Why now? Why not last year, or the year before?"

The stag arched his head, observing the musicians and Will both through the advantage of his wide-spaced eyes. "You're reclaiming yourself at last. You show you are a man of loyalty, once that loyalty is won —"

"I wouldn't be so hasty as to think so. I've never been known for choosing sides based on anything other than expedience."

"Haven't you? You've been careful *not* to choose, here, Sir Christofer. It has not gone unnoticed that you share your gifts between factions, and permit none of them, quite, to claim you."

Kit caught himself chewing a thumbnail, made himself stop and tuck his hands inside crossed arms. "What can you offer me that Morgan can't, or, failing that, the Mebd?"

"Freedom," Geoffrey answered, the sunlight shining on the silvergray patches where his antlers would grow come the fall. His wet nose quivered softly. "If you like—"

Kit felt Puck's curious eyes on him when he reached out and eased the flower from Geoffrey's hoof. He crushed it in his hand—satiny moisture and a violet stain that vanished when he brushed the ruined remains on the raven's-wing velvet of his doublet. "We'll talk again," he said, and nodded once before he walked away.

Leaning against a marble satyr, Kit folded his arms and watched Cairbre and the towering Amaranth show Will the esoteric fingerings of a silver Faerie flute. He covered a momentary pang of jealousy with an idle smile. *Give him his glory: a poet in Faerie.*

Kit laughed silently. *If Orfeo stole his lover back from the Faerie king, what does that make of me, having done the reverse?* A moment before the fallacy sank in and his mouth twisted in bitter whimsy rather than humor. *That is to say, if I had any claim on him at all. Mayhap Annie can come steal him back from me, and keep the legend intact.*

He sighed and looked down at his hands. *Most men are married,* he reminded himself. *It is the custom of the age.*

And what of you, Sir Christofer?

Ah, the unanswerable questions.

He straightened and left Will there, slipping through the glass door to the garden. Gravel settled under his boots; the scent of roses overwhelmed the sticky, lingering perfume of the crushed blossom upon Kit's skin. Kit turned his face to the sky, reveling in the warming sunlight.

He recognized the step on the walk behind him and didn't turn to face who came. A warm breeze lifted Kit's hair; a warm hand followed it, stroking the nape of his neck. "Wanton." A whisper against his ear.

"Murchaud."

"Sweet Christofer. Your friend has charmed the court already."

Kit bit his tongue on his first reply and forced his manner to calm. "He's for the ladies, lover."

"Poor Kit, that he should disappoint thee so. And more fool he."
Murchaud knotted a hand in Kit's fine, full hair and turned his head
to kiss him on the mouth. Kit fairly burned with unexpected shame,
knowing the embrace plainly visible from within the conservatory.
Knowing Will would think Kit had abandoned him among strangers
to go out to his lover.

*A Prince's licentious favorite. Ganymede, indeed. Even if he were so given,
how could he ever believe thy love more than this travesty?*

Tom did—

Murchaud spoke against his ear. "You're thinking."

"Aye." Kit cast about for the plausible lie, hesitated. Drew back
enough to look Murchaud in the face when he spoke. "The Mebd—"

"Aye."

"What do you think I owe her, Murchaud?" He turned as he spoke
and strode slowly along the path, leading Murchaud among the roses
and their lesser brethren.

"Aside from your life?"

"She's got payment in service for that," Kit answered. "And surely
I owe your mother as much."

"Aye." Murchaud cocked his head to follow the flitting progress
of an exaltation of larks. His right hand rested possessively on Kit's
elbow.

"Everyone pushes me in one direction or another, Murchaud. As
if the whole world held its breath, waiting to see which way I'll bend.
And yet I feel I am not vouchsafed information enough to do so intelli-
gently." Kit kicked at the gravel. They came beside a path of cypresses.
Kit did not remember having gone this way before.

"And when you chose for England and her Queen, what details
were you vouchsafed then?"

Kit stifled a laugh at himself. "That was simply naive patriotism,
I'm afraid. And there was only one side that wanted me—"—*untrue,* he
realized as he said it. *Or I wouldn't have been able to enter Rheims at all.*

"Well, then, to be wanted so desperately now tells thee something."
Murchaud drifted away, plucking dusky blue berries from the ever-
greens hedging the walk and flicking them away with his thumbnail.

Kit caught their resinous scent and thought it erotic. "And what
am I taught, my love?"

"Thou art important to someone. Come, I wish to show something to thee."

Kit considered that as he followed the suddenly animated Prince across a wide green lawn toward a copse of thorn trees hung with berries red as blood. Curiosity galled him, but he wouldn't give Murchaud the satisfaction of seeing it manifest. *You'll know soon enough.* "The Mebd said once that when Queen Elizabeth passes there will be a rade. A procession." Murchaud's strides were long. Kit hastened to keep up, soft greensward dimpling under his boots.

"Aye, we'll go to honor your Gloriana."

"And your wife"—the faintest emphasis—"said also that there would be a war. A war of song."

"A war of spells. Not that they are much different, in Faerie or on Earth." Murchaud led Kit under the bowering thorn trees, lifting the branches aside. Red blood welled from the Prince's thumb; he licked it and laughed. Beyond the trees rose a simple pavilion of classical design, a miniature Parthenon of milk-white stone.

"How can she know what will happen when Elizabeth is dead?" *How can any of us know?* To contemplate her death alone was a marvel: Iron Bess had reigned—and ruled—longer than Kit had been alive.

"We can't," Murchaud answered, turning impatiently to Kit, who must have mounted the steps more slowly than the Elf-knight liked. "I can only guess. And it may not be hard on the heels of her death. I rather expect there will be a few years' subtlety and manipulation, first. Edging the pieces about the board."

"The midgame starts when Elizabeth dies. Why?"

"Because faith in Elizabeth herself is half the faith that holds England and the Protestants together," Murchaud said. "And that faith alone is enough to send enemy ships stormlost at sea, and bring forth men like Burghley and Walsingham and Shakespeare and Marley to serve."

"What's that?" Kit gestured to the long marble box, chest-high and seemingly hollow within, that dominated the center of the pavilion. The only other furniture was a pair of marble benches along the walls.

"England," Murchaud answered. "Come forward, Sir Christofer, and meet my family."

Curious, Kit walked up beside him, through the softly breezy shadows, until he stood beside Murchaud over the tall plinth, as long as a coffin. An apt comparison, because — *A plinth*, he realized. *Or a bier.*

Its high marble sides enclosed the form of a man on a platform some twelve inches below: what Kit would have taken for a waxwork had not the impossible profusion of copper-blond hair stirred in the passage of the sleeper's even breaths. Someone had combed those locks to softness, shining like hanks of silk in the filtered light, and Kit judged it would reach beyond the sleeper's knees if he stood, on a man as tall and as broad as Murchaud. A golden circlet crossed his splendid brow, and a scattering of freckles dusted the skin over the aristocratic bones of his face: last stars fading at dawn. By contrast with his hair, his beard was neatly barbered and as red as Kit's, but streaked with steel under the corners of the mouth. Powerful elegant fingers enfolding the hilt of the bronze Roman sword laid down the centerline of his chest gave Kit the first soft inkling of who this was. "How long has he lain here?"

"A thousand years." Breathless, and the weight of all those years was in the Prince's voice. Fingers very like the fingers of the sleeper twined Kit's own, and Murchaud drew Kit's hand out to brush Arthur's warm and pliant cheek.

"I always rather liked the tale," Kit said, just to break the hush, "that he had become a raven. And that is why ravens are sacrosanct, and why should they all ever leave the Tower, it is assured that England will fall. Pity it isn't true."

Murchaud smiled. "But it is true. As true as the story that he sleeps here in Faerie—"

"How can that be?" Kit, softly, wondering.

"All tales are true," Murchaud answered, squeezing Kit's hand before he let it fall. "Some are simply more true than others. Look here, unto thy lover, Sir Poet: here stands a man born nigh unto Roman times, son of a story not invented until seven hundred years later—"

Kit couldn't bear to break the silence. He stepped away from the bier, his eyes stinging, and turned away for a moment to watch the sunlight move through the branches of the thorn trees. *A thousand years.* When he re-collected himself, he asked, "What do all these factions want of me, Highness?"

Silk rustled; Kit thought Murchaud shrugged. "What do you suppose they wanted of *him?*"

"Conquest," Kit said promptly, and then a moment after—"Salvation."

"Love?"

"Do you suppose?"

"My father loved him," Murchaud said softly, and Kit turned to him in surprise. The Elf-knight hadn't moved: he stood, still, with bowed head over Arthur's bier.

"Your father betrayed him."

"Aye," Murchaud answered, glancing up with shining eyes. "That's what makes it a tragedy, my dear."

Act III, scene vii

Had my friend's Muse grown with this growing age,
A dearer birth then this his love had brought:
To march in ranks of better equipage:
But since he died and Poets better prove,
Theirs for their style I'll read, his for his love.

—WILLIAM SHAKESPEARE, Sonnet 32

K it lay on his back against the emerald coverlet, lamplight snarled in his light brown hair, and idly turned the swan-white quill between his fingers while Will watched from the chair by the window. The ornately carved back was winning the war against Will's spine; Will leaned forward, resting his elbows on his knees. "These lamps are very fine. They burn paraffin?"

"Spirits of some sort," Kit said. " 'Tis a lovely bright light, isn't it?"

"I might sit up a little," Will said, feeling dishonest. "If the light will bother you, I can retreat to the library."

"No need," Kit said, kicking his legs high to swing himself out of the bed. He dropped the pen onto a shelf as he stood, his fingers returning to stroke the stainless plume briefly before he turned away. "What a little mystery this is, isn't it?"

"What will you do with it?"

Kit shrugged, his eyebrows arching in cheerful mockery. " 'Tis too lovely to strip and stain with ink. Keep it as a token of affection, I suppose; I must have an unconfessed admirer."

"Perhaps she wants you to write a sonnet to her loveliness. Or"— Will grinned—"*on* her loveliness, for that matter."

"Ah, but sonnets are thy idiom, not mine—"

Will leaned back into the shadows, feeling the grin slide down his face. "Where have you read my sonnets, Kit?" He managed to hide a guilty look at his cloak and the brownie-cleaned boots that he had come to Faerie in. They were tucked into the corner beside the clothespress with his sonnets rolled up inside them. Surely Kit would be, if anything, too proud to sneak—

"*Romeo and Juliet*," Kit answered. "And nicely done it was. I wouldn't mind seeing those others you mentioned, though, when you think they're fit for the public eye."

Somehow, Will managed not to choke. "They may never be so."

"Really? Not as off-color as Tom's dildo poem, I trust—" Kit poured water to wash his hands and face and made a little ceremony of it.

"With a better meter, at least."

Kit turned to him surprised, reaching for linen to dry his hands, and Will laughed.

"No; I've a touch more decorum than Tom, though I've read the poem in question. I rather imagine *that* one will never see printer's ink. You don't mind my rustling papers and cursing by lamplight while you try to sleep?"

"Not at all." Kit shrugged. "You're not like to have much time for work here. You're a puzzle to them, a toy, and if you claim the library, this palace holds enough creatures who do not sleep to distract you with their demands. Besides, if you're here, you can wake me if I start to dream."

"Sensible," Will said. "May I have that lamp by the bedside as well?"

"Yes, and use my table." Kit brought the squat globe with its odd, tall chimney over to the broad walnut writing table, shoving layers of papers aside. Will picked up the lamp from the square table beside the window and joined him, angling the two so they gave enough light to write by. "That's not bad—"

"Better than candles."

"Aye. Sleep well, Kit."

Kit pursed his lips as he turned away. "Just don't wish me dream sweetly, I pray."

A few hours later, Will rolled the mismatched sheets of sonnetry into a tube again and fastened them with a ribbon. He weighed the poems in his hand: a few ounces of ink and paper and emotion and clever wordplay. Surely nothing to feel such pride and consternation over.

He'd lied to Kit when he said Jonson had a copy; a few he'd shown to friends, but not most of them. Certainly not to anyone who might recognize the subject.

Poley and Baines know Kit is alive now, he realized suddenly. *I have to draft a letter to Tom Walsingham.* Which he did, hastily, and sanded and sealed it, explaining the situation and that he, Will, would return by Christmas. *And may I meet my promise to a conspirator better than I meet my promises to my wife.*

Will stood, the poems in one hand, the letter in the other, and hesitated. *I don't know how to send it.*

He stole a glance at Marley, curled like a child under his spotted cloak, and stifled a yawn against the back of the hand that held the sonnets. He didn't feel like sleeping, and he propped the letter and the poems upon the mantel and stepped into his boots before he blew the lamps out. The latch clicked softly, well oiled, when he turned the handle, and he walked into the darkness of the hall.

The Mebd's palace changed in darkness and solitude. The airy corridors closed in, became low and medieval, and Will thought he saw things scuttle in the corners near the floor. He stopped his hand before he could cross himself, wondering where *that* ancient reflex had arisen from, and picked his way past the roiling shadows of infrequent torches, certain of restlessness, uncertain of his goal.

He found the spiral stair with ease and followed it down, noting landmarks so he would be able to find his way back when his wandering tired him. An unusual sense of well-being buoyed him; he wasn't sure if Morgan's medicines deserved the credit, or if it was simply the magic of Faerie.

Will paused in the atrium, in the mellow moonlight drifting through high windows and magical skylights, and nodded to the unmoving suits of armor flanking the relief-wrought doors. He wasn't *sure* they were inhabited, but in the very least they *felt* alive. *Felt alive, Master Shakespeare? Can you explain what precisely that means, for our academic interest?*

Well . . .

. . . no. But he nodded anyway, and continued past, down the winding side corridor that would bring him to the library. A library worthy of a Cambridge man's glee, in Will's admittedly under-experienced opinion. The light was better, candles that never seemed to drip or smoke ranged every few feet along the wall, and Will found the tall red cherry doors easily enough. They gleamed strangely in the candlelight as he pulled a taper from its sconce and fumbled for the crystal knob, pleased his hand didn't shake.

A dim strand of light crossed the floor as he eased the door; he slipped in and let it latch softly. "Good night?"

"Master Shakespeare." A pleased voice, a thrill of velvet that reminded him of the furry backs of fox moth caterpillars inching along a twig. Morgan le Fey looked up from reading, her light gilding one side of her face and casting the other into shadow. A folio whose illuminated leaves were shiny umber under the ink and gilt lay open before her; she held a thin glass rod in her right hand which she used, delicately, to turn the pages.

"Your Highness." He bowed, balancing his candle, careful to spatter no wax. The scent of paper and leather filled the library. "An unexpected pleasure."

"I haunt the place," she said, laying her wand aside. "Sleepless? Too ill? I have herbs for that, too—"

"Rather, I am too well to sleep, Your Highness," he answered. "And I thank you for it."

As he came forward, he saw that the light gleaming over her shoulder was neither lamp nor candle, but what seemed a swarm of green and golden atomies hovering in midair. He tucked his candle into a wall sconce, well away from the ancient tome, and seated himself across from her in acquiescence to her gesture.

She smiled. "I'm pleased to find I'm not the only one who seeks the dusty comfort of books when I am restless at night."

She did not behave in the manner he expected of Queens, and truth to be told he *was* restless; restless with a sort of longing that his own poetry and his sleepless exhaustion had reawakened in his breast. He ached with the need of it, instead of the pain that had haunted him so much of late. He licked his lips and looked down at her text. "What are you reading?"

She wrapped her fingertips in her sleeve and turned the book so he could see, but the thick hand-drawn letters defeated him. The illuminations told him it was an herbal, though, and he thought it one in verse. "It's beautiful."

"Not quite so old as I am." She smiled. Her near-black eyes caught sparks of light from her attendant atomies; they swirled about her hair like a tiara of jewels on invisible threads.

Unbidden, Will thought of a line of Kit's poetry — *O, thou art fairer than the evening air / Clad in the beauty of a thousand stars*. And then, unbidden, a response — *and dark within that light; not so much a star herself. There's a poem in that — no, not a star, not so much a sun . . .*

Her calm voice broke his reverie. "I could grow accustomed to being looked upon so, Master Shakespeare."

He blushed, and blinked. "My lady is lovely," he said, and blushed harder when she moved the priceless book aside and reached to take his hand.

Her fingers were rough at the tips with callus, the hands shapely and long and the tendons plain against her skin as she turned his over to study the palm. "Have you ever had your fortune told, Master Shakespeare?"

He bit his lip and shook his head. The dancing lights grew brighter, flitting like the fire-bugs that were supposed to inhabit the darkness of a New World country called Virginia. Her thumb traced the lines of his hand, and as she bent to study them her hair cascaded across his wrist. "The old women of the gipsy caravaneers practice an art handed down from ancient times, they say. They claim a man's destiny is written in his hand, a predetermined fate —"

"The Puritans agree," Will said with a smile that hurt the corners of his mouth. "And the Greeks."

"And the Prometheans," Morgan continued, without raising her eyes. "Their ideas are not so revolutionary as they believe. My history gives us prophecies of a different order: geas and fulfillment. You won't have heard of them—"

"No, madam." He watched, fascinated, as she stroked a deep crease beside the heel of his hand.

"This is called Apollo's. 'Tis said to indicate creativity and potential for greatness. Combined with the shape of your thumb, a fortune-teller would say that you are intuitive, passionate, intellectual. Quick of wit and great of talent—"

"A fortune-teller would say so?"

"Aye," she said, with a caressing touch that made him shiver. "I am not a fortune-teller, Master Shakespeare." Her gaze rose again, her eyes blacker than ever. His shiver redoubled. "I am a witch."

Strangely, his face tingled as if she stroked his cheek rather than his hand. He looked away, down, anywhere but into her laughing eyes. "Great of talent, you say."

A chuckle. "Aye. Great enough for most purposes. And here: this line belongs to Saturn. It shows a destiny, as well. . . ." Her voice trailed away.

He focused on amusement, on keeping his breaths even and slow when they wanted to flutter in his throat. "What destiny is that, Your Highness?"

"I cannot say," she answered. "But if I were a fortune-teller, I would say that you would find it within twenty years, and no longer."

"Anything could happen in two decades. That's a fair spread."

"Not so long as it now seems," she answered. "Here is the fold that dictates your romantic nature. See how it curves up, and extends long?" She bent closer. "Ah, and it is braided—"

"Braided?"

"Aye. You've not one great love in store, Master Shakespeare, but three."

He laughed. "Surely one great love is enough for any man—"

Her fingers moved again, and he thanked the opaque surface of the table between them for preserving his dignity. "And this is your life line—"

"And what does that tell you, Morgan le Fey?" The challenge in his own voice surprised him. Her fingers followed the tracery down and under his thumb, stroking the soft flesh at the inside of his wrist. He caught his breath in shock at the delicacy of that touch.

"You will live to go home again, William Shakespeare," she said.

"Do you say any of this will come true, Your Highness?"

" 'Tis the rankest charlatanry," she answered. Bending her head further, she placed a moth's-wing kiss in the center of his palm. He gasped again and almost pulled his hand away; she held the wrist and transferred her attentions there.

"Your Highness—"

"Hush," she said, glancing up at him through the pall of her hair. "Say nothing, Poet, save *yes* or *no*."

Will closed his eyes, aching. *Annie,* he thought hopelessly, and then almost laughed aloud at the next thing he thought: *That was in another country, and besides, the wench is dead. Oh, Kit, trust you to make a hellish sort of sense of this.* "Yes," he said, and waited endless instants while Morgan sent her pixy-lights to bar and watch the door.

Act III, scene viii

Rejoice, ye sons of wickedness; mourn, unoffending one, with hair in disorder over your pitiable neck.

—CHRISTOPHER MARLOWE, *On the Death of Sir Roger Manwood*
(translated from the Latin by Arthur F. Stocker)

Kit rolled over and lifted his head from the pillow as the bedroom door opened and Will slipped inside, half invisible in the starlit darkness. "You were gone a while," he said softly, smiling when Will startled and jumped.

"I went to the library after all."

Will's doublet was unbuttoned, his hair disheveled. Kit's smile broadened. "Didst find what thou sought?"

"Nay—" Will started, pulling off his clothes. And then he stopped and moved toward the cupboard, a paler shape in the darkness. "Well, perhaps. After a fashion. So many books, Kit!"

"Faerie has some joys." He turned away as Will struggled into a nightshirt. Plumage rustled as Will made himself a place in the featherbed, the perfume of a woman coming with him. *Just as well,* Kit sighed. *Perhaps he'll lie easier now that he's reclaimed that.* And then he caught the scent of rosemary and lemon balm on Will's hair, and turned, mouth half open, before he stopped himself. *I could wish he'd chosen differently—*

—or do you simply wish that you had chosen differently, Marley?

Will, half settled among the pillows, returned Kit's stare wide-eyed. That as much as anything told Kit how fey his expression must be. "Kit?"

"Will." *But what do you say? You haven't a claim on him—* "Thou hastn't anything to prove to me—"

"Perhaps I had something to prove to myself."

Ah. Of course. Kit opened his mouth again, to say whatever he had been about to say, and closed it before the words could escape. "Just be careful, Will."

Will laughed, softly, and tugged the covers. "What chance have I against the likes of *her*, sweet Christofer, an she decides she wants me?"

For which Kit had no answer. The thrill of delight in Will's voice told him more than the words, anyway. He lay back down, a serpent gnawing his bosom, and dreamed of sunlight and herb gardens and the beating wings of ravens and of swans.

He woke again before Will did and stretched in the morning sunlight, surprised by how rested he felt. He stood and performed his toilet, stealing a glance at Will before he dressed. The other poet had burrowed so deeply beneath the covers that all Kit glimpsed of him was one ink-stained hand.

Kit smiled fondly, for all he still felt seasick with jealousy, and went to collect his rapier from the stand beside the fireplace. *I'll have to get another main gauche,* he thought, although he wasn't sorry to have left the slender blade in de Parma's back. *I wonder what the coroner will make of a silver dagger, beyond the estimate of price?* He turned to check his hair in the mirror over the mantel, tilting his head in curiosity as he noticed the papers stacked there. The roll of poetry didn't surprise him. The letter addressed in Will's cramped hand to Thomas Walsingham *did*, and Kit's fingers almost brushed it before he tugged his hand back. *It's not as if he made any effort to hide it from me. I could always just ask.*

If I weren't so out of the habit. He settled the rapier on his hip one last time, turning for the door. *Which reminds me, I should write Tom myself and let him know I've queered the game with Baines and Poley.*

So early, the palace was still as quiet as Kit had ever seen it in daylight. He wandered downstairs, idling, and made his way into the hall to see what there might be to break his fast upon, if anything had yet been laid.

A few Fae clumped at trestles along each wall, sipping steaming mugs and carrying on quiet conversation. Kit was first surprised to see brownies among those present, but quickly nodded. The kitchen staff dines early everywhere.

He was less pleased to see Morgan le Fey rise from the sole occupied chair at the high table and beckon him, but he went. She looked composed this morning, lovely, robed in some fine, unrestrained black fabric that clung to her body when she gestured. Kit swallowed sharpness and moved forward, ascending the steps. "Your Highness," he said, and bowed.

"What, so formal, Kit?" She reached out and took his hands, drawing him to her side. She did not sit, and neither did he, aware that they made a lovely picture in their sable finery, framed against the crimson hangings at the back of the dais. Her hair was dressed, today, into a high elegant coil, a single strand of tiny pearls wound through its blackness. Her changeable eyes were poison green over the cheekbones of a goddess, and she suddenly took his breath away. "Art unhappy?"

"What have you done to my William, Madam?"

A raven-black eyebrow arched. "*Your* William, is it? And yet I heard you said to Murchaud that he was for the ladies, and in the manner of one who knows for himself the truth of his words—no matter," she said, shifting abruptly, turning away from the hall without releasing his hand. She led him between the draperies, to a passage he had suspected but never walked down. "Come, spend a little time with me."

"You are my mistress," he said, and fell into step.

"Am I?" Her voice was hushed; if he didn't look at her he could imagine they walked hand in hand like old friends, like brother and sister. When he turned to catch her words more clearly—as he half suspected she intended, with the soft risings and dips in her tone—a barbed spiral he recognized as lust and jealousy and covetousness and the bitter dregs of a hundred other mortal sins caught under his breastbone, and he drew each breath in pain.

Why should she have what I want so badly?

A bitter thought. An unkind thought. And unfair to Will, who was kindness personified—

"Are you my mistress? I come to your whistle."

"Still you have not forgiven me?" They came from the cloth-draped passageway into the throne room, and Morgan led him down from the dais with its chair of estate and the massive cloth-draped throne that Kit had never seen, nor seen the Mebd sit in.

"How can I forgive—" He caught the words in his teeth before they quite got away from him. She held his arm, leaning close enough that he could smell not only her own pungency of rosemary and rue, but the traces of another's scent on her hair and clothes. He breathed in through his mouth, and told himself it was against the pain in his bosom. "That is to say, Madam, whatever your sins, they must be out-weighed by your favors."

She laughed. "My favors weigh so heavily on thee? If 'tis jealousy that drives thee, Sir Christofer, then my favors can be thine for the asking. It was not I who ended our arrangement."

He coughed and tugged away. She kept walking while he stood, her gown trailing like the train of a jet-black peacock, and turned back only when her hand touched the door.

"I wish my friend safe," he said.

Her eyes glittered as she smiled and inclined her head. "You wish more than that."

"Aye—" A groan. He turned away. "As if something buried, once watered, has sprung into the sun and flowered on a day, and now will not be withered no matter how I scorn and strike it."

"I could give thee a spell to make him love thee—"

"He loves me well enough," Kit answered, hating his own honesty. "And that I should be content with."

Her skirts rustled across the tile as she drifted to him. Her hands encircled his waist, her chin resting on the padded shoulder of his doublet. "Could give thee a spell to do more."

Kit bit his lip as her breath stroked his ear. Her breasts pressed his back, her fingers demonstrating what he was sure she already knew. *She could*. The experience that proved it was as painful as the experience that proved it was not just her magic that aroused him, although free of the sorcery he could almost pretend it was the touch alone, nothing more than a whore's practiced hand. *She could give me Will —*

"Madam," he whispered. "What do you take your Marley for?"

She laughed in his ear; he turned in her arms and laid his own around her shoulders, holding her away as much as close. "Anything he'll offer me," she said. And then, more kindly: "No, thou wouldst not be my Christofer if thou wert so base as thy Morgan in such matters." She smiled and would have stepped back, but his arms restrained her.

She turned half a step; they moved as if dancing, her train winding their ankles, binding them together. She ran fingers up the breast of his doublet and touched his lip. He frowned, and she brushed the corner of his eye as if something gleamed there.

"Hard," she said. "Hard it is to love something, to need something, and to have it taken from thee. There are simples to ease that pain as well —"

"That pain," he said, "is sheerest poetry."

"He would not like it if you bedded me today —"

"I do not like that he bedded you last night."

"There was" — she smiled, her breath against his skin — "no bed."

"Ah." And indrawn breath. It cut.

"Come to my room, Christofer."

He shook his head, but he didn't step away. "I should go. Go to Murchaud — Morgan. I can smell him on your skin."

"I know," she said, brushing her lips across his lips. "I left it for you. Come upstairs —"

As if he had always known he would, he went.

Morgan curled against Kit's side, her sweat drying on his arm. She laid her head on his shoulder, the pearls half worked loose and falling across his throat. Blessedly, she held her peace until his pulse no longer rasped in his ears, and he opened his eye again and turned to look at her.

"Such passion, Kit." She knotted a fistful of the linen sheet in her hand and dried her face; offered him the same.

He rubbed the sweat from her body and untangled the pearls from her hair, laying the strand aside before pulling her down beside him again. "That was—different."

"Thou wert not ensorceled." *Silly man,* her pursed lips said, and he had to agree.

What do I here? "Is that all?"

"Enough." She drew the damp sheet over them, idly toying with his hair. "Tell me whence comes this sudden affection of thine for poets."

He brushed her bare leg with the side of his foot. A tremendous hollowness still haunted him, something as consuming as a flame, but for now he could set it aside—along with the images it taunted him with—and draw the silence of his heart over himself as Morgan drew the sheet. "Not sudden," he admitted. "I knew it—years ago."

"Oh?" A quiet sound of interest, after a long and companionable wait.

Damme, what an intelligencer she would have made— He sighed, and managed not to sound sullen. "Damn you, Corinna. Is't not enough to *have* us both? Must also step between?"

She turned against his neck, tasting his skin with her smile.

"There are reasons I stopped going to London."

"When knew you, then?"

Kit laughed. "He tripped climbing a stair and I almost swallowed my tongue in panic."

Her fingers coiled his hair and pressed unerringly against the sore places in his neck. "Speaking of falling. You should have come to me after you did."

His and Will's ignominious tumble through the Darkling Glass, of course. "How did you know I fell?"

"The bruises on your arse."

Their laughter drew the tension out of his shoulders almost as effectively as her fingers; he rolled on his stomach and let her lean over him, working the pain from his back. "The teind is soon," she said, stressing every other word as she leaned into him, an oddly artificial pattern of iambs. "The sacrifice will have to be chosen."

"Ow."

"When you tense, it hurts." Warmed oil drizzled onto his back; he didn't ask where it came from, as her hands never left his body.

"How is that done?"

"This?"

"The sacrifice chosen." He groaned as she ran strong thumbs from the top of his spine to the base, and did not stop there. "Gently, my Queen—"

"Poor Kit. Black and blue from here to here." Her fingers measured a span bigger than his palm. "Thou'rt lucky didst not break thy tail."

"Art certain 'tis unbroken?" And realized he'd *thee*'d her, and thought *and would it not be an irony to "you" her so engaged?*

"Evidence would suggest."

He gasped, burying his face against her herb-scented pillow, and she laughed. "Wilt urge me proceed gently here as well, Sir Poet? Will you write me poems on this?"

Her hair swept his shoulders; he shivered, jolted from his fantasy of whose touch he labored under. "When will we know who is chosen?"

"When they bring the horse before the one who will ride him to Hell. There. Is that nice, my darling?" A kiss between his shoulder blades; another brushing the downy, well-oiled hollow at the small of his back. "Are you thinking of your poet now?"

He couldn't bring himself to answer.

Act III, scene ix

The Queen's withdrawing room, revealed through an opening door, wasn't as grand as Will had expected; rather a quiet sunlit place appointed with rich paintings and more of the extravagant carpets, these in harvest-gold and winter-white, with touches of emerald and sapphire in the plumed weave. A small table stood in the center of it, a cushioned chair at either end, a service of silver-gilt and golden plates laid on linen as white as Morgan's sheets.

He smiled at the memory and executed a sweeping bow, resisting the urge to reach into his pocket and fumble the scrap of iron nail Kit had pressed upon him before the appointment. The Mebd stood before the window, her hair gleaming under her veil; she turned to acknowledge him. "Gentle William. You brighten our court. Pray rise."

"Your Highness is most gracious." They were seated, and attendants Will could not see poured wine and served them both. Nervousness robbed him of his appetite: his knife shivered on the richly decorated plate. The Queen herself ate delicately; he was surprised to

see that what she cut so tidily and placed in her mouth was wine and
capon, and not flower petals and dew.

"You hunger not, Master Shakespeare?"

"I am curious," he admitted with whatever charm he could muster.
And now I've met three Queens, he thought. And swallowed a broader grin
as he also thought, *and bedded one.*

"Curious?"

"Curious what Your Highness would have of me."

She smiled and laid her knife across the plate. "Perhaps you and
Sir Christofer would consent to honor us with a play."

"A collaboration? We've done it before, Your Highness. I'm sure
Kit would agree."

"We have faith in your ability to convince him," she said. Will
picked up his goblet as she contemplated her words. "We were favor-
ably impressed with your *Midsummer Night's Dream*. Although it sad-
dened us to see your Queen in the end humiliated and defeated by her
unsavory husband. It seems to us that she, Titania, had the right of it,
and that is not merely our sympathy for a sister Queen."

Will frowned, tasting the unfairness of his own life in the irony of
his words. "It is the experience of this poet, Your Highness, that just
women are often misruled by their husbands."

"And just peoples misruled by their Princes, by extension?"

Too late, he saw the trap. He nodded. "And yet such is the way of
the world: many a man abuses the trust of a woman who deserves better, and yet they and the world are so made that they must accept the
dominion of men. Many a Prince abuses the trust of his subjects, and
yet how few men are born to rule?"

She rolled her silver-handled knife between fingers white and soft
as cambric. "And yet thou dost serve a woman who is also a Prince. Is
she deserving of thy sacrifices?"

"Your Highness, aye."

"Why is that?"

"Because—" He shrugged. "Because she has made her own sacrifices, to keep her people safe."

"Ah." The Mebd closed eyes that had shifted from green to lavender and then to gray. When she blinked them open, they were the

color of thistles under gold lashes worthy of a Hero. "So the sacrifices a husband makes for his wife earn her loyalty."

"If he is worthy of her." He lowered his eyes, unable to support her inquiry, and dissected a morsel upon his plate, sopping the meat in sweet-spiced gravy. The flavor cloyed.

"And are you worthy of your wife, Master Shakespeare?"

"No," he answered, without looking up. "Madam, I am not."

"And yet she serves you as you serve your Prince."

"Aye."

"This is what we adore our poets for." He was surprised by the tenderness in her voice into glancing up again. "They lie with such honesty."

"Lie, Your Highness?"

"Aye." A smile on her lips like petals. "Sweet William is a flower. Didst know it?"

"Aye, Your Highness."

"Perhaps we shall have some sown."

Will nodded, dizzied. Emboldened, a little, by the frankness of her conversation, he asked a question. "Your Highness. Like Gloriana, you have no King—"

"I will be subject to no man," she answered. "Even a God."

"And yet from what Morgan tells me, Faerie is subject to Hell and its Lord."

"Women," she answered, extending her white-clad wrist to pour him wine with her own pale, delicate hands, "have long learned to simper in the presence of their conquerors. And not only women, Master Poet."

"No," he answered, tipping his goblet to her in salute before he drank. "Not women alone."

"We are glad," the Mebd said, "you have agreed to dine with us today. We trust you will never find yourself bound in an— *unpleasant*—subjugation."

"Your Highness."

"Yes." She smiled as she touched his sleeve. "I am."

Act III, scene x

Had I as many souls, as there be Stars,
I'd give them all for Mephostophilis.

—CHRISTOPHER MARLOWE, *Faustus*

K it unhooked his cloak and threw it over the high back of his
chair. He leaned on Murchaud's velveted sleeve and watched the
dancers eddy across the rose-and-green marble tiles, wondering if he
could afford another glass of wine. The way Will's head bent smiling
as he whispered in Morgan's ear was making him *want* one, badly, but
he suspected that it would be unwise to indulge.

"It looks as if thou mightst have room in thy bed tonight," Murchaud said conversationally, drawing his arm from under Kit's head
and dropping it around his shoulders.

Aye. I'll sleep alone tonight. And in the morning, Morgan will find me.
Sweet buggered Jesus, how have I come to this?

"If thou wouldst wish companionship—"

"Perhaps," Kit said, and poured water into his glass. He sat upright to drink it, as Murchaud played idly with the strands of his hair.
"Aye. Dice and wine, perhaps a pipe?"

"To begin with. Thou canst defeat me at tables again."

Kit chuckled. Murchaud's luck with dice was abysmal enough to be notorious. "For a start."

Murchaud reached past him for a tart and leaned forward to eat it over the table, scattering crumbs. "Hast spoken more with Geoffrey?"

"Words in passing." Kit drew up a knee and laced his fingers before it.

"Wilt give him thine answer?"

It wasn't really a question, Kit knew. "Shall I offer to betray you, then?"

"That would be kind." Murchaud leaned back beside him, crossing long legs, his right foot flipping in time with Cairbre's fiddling. The song wound down; the dancers paused. "We need to know the nature of the plotting."

"Ah. Yes." Kit stood and glanced over his shoulder at Murchaud, sweeping his gaudy cloak around his shoulders as he did. "Thy mother seems to have abandoned my poet," he said. "I'm off to comfort him. And yes."

"Yes?"

Kit turned away. "By all means, come and see me tonight."

The stairs were less trouble sober, although he cursed the lack of a railing under his breath. He skirted the applauding dancers on the side away from the musicians, not wishing to capture Cairbre's eye and be summoned to perform. Will must have seen him across the floor, because he met Kit halfway.

Kit ached to look at him, giddy with dancing, color high and eyes sparkling like the gold ring in his ear in the light of the thousands of candles and torches. *They love him because they cannot keep him,* he reminded himself, and forced himself to smile. "Will. Come have a drink with me."

"No dancing for you, Kit?"

"I don't pavane," Kit said dryly. "Neither do I galliard. Stuffy dances for stuffy dancers. Come, there's spiced ale by the fire." He led Will to the corner by the tables and filled cups with the steaming drink, redolent of cloves and sandalwood. They leaned between windows, shoulder to shoulder, and Kit buried his nose in his tankard, breathing deep.

"The Queen wants us collaborating," Will said, swirling his ale to cool it. "A play by Hallowmas, it seems."

"A play?" Kit turned to regard Will with his good eye. "Did she assign a topic?"

"Not even a suggestion. Please, overwhelm me with your brilliance."

"The Passion of Christ," Kit answered promptly, and was rewarded by a gurgle as Will clapped a hand over his face to keep his mouthful of ale from spraying across the dance floor.

Choking. "Seriously."

"Damme, Will. I don't know. Thou hast had longer to think it than I have. They won't care for English history."

"I left my *Holinshed* in London, in any case."

"Coincidentally, so did I. I wonder who has it now?"

"Tom," Will answered. "Unless he burned it. He was very angry with you for some time."

"Only fair. I was very angry with him."

Silence for a little. They drank, and Will took the cups to refill them. When he returned, he rolled his shoulders and kicked one heel against the stones. "Why the Passion?"

"Suitably medieval," Kit replied. "Like so much of our religion."

"Still no faith in God, my Christofer?"

"Faith, William?" Kit tasted the ale; this cup was stronger. "Died blaspheming, indeed. Do you suppose He eavesdrops on those who call His name in passion? *Oh, God! Oh, God!* Mayhap He finds it titillating—"

"Kit!"

Kit snorted into his cup. "Faith. I'faith, the Fae, who ought to know it, say God is in the pay of the Prometheans. I imagine He'd little want me in any case—" *No, and never did. No matter how badly I wanted him.*

A little like Will in that regard, come to think of it.

"I sometimes suspect," Will said softly, "that God finds all this wrangling over His name and His word and His son somewhat tiresome. But I am constrained to believe in Hell."

"Hell? Aye, hard not to when we're living in an argument on metaphysics." Kit kicked the wall with his heel for emphasis.

"Say that again once the Devil's complimented you to your face. But I am the Queen's man, and the Queen's church suits me as well as any, and I should not like, I think, to live in a world without God."

"An admirable solution," Kit said. "I flattered myself for a little that God did care for me, but I felt a small martyrdom in His name was enough, and He has never been one to settle for half a loaf. And I am maudlin, and talking too much."

"I do not think your martyrdom little."

"Sadly, it is not our opinion that matters." Kit had finished the ale, he realized, and felt light-headed. He set his cup on the window ledge and leaned against the wall, letting the cool breeze through the open panes stir his hair. He put a smile into his voice. "Your celebrity here is not little, either."

Will laughed, and leaned against Kit's shoulder. "I find the affection in which I am held—adequate."

"For most purposes?"

"The purposes that suit me. Are all poets admired in Faerie?"

"Only the good ones," Kit answered. "And yet I envy you your freedom to go home."

"If I knew a way to bargain for yours—"

"Poley would simply have me killed again."

"He might find it harder this time."

"Ah, Will. Everyone in London who loved me is gone. What had I to return to, even were it so?" Kit shook himself, annoyed at his own sorrow, and knowing as he said it—"Will, forgive me. Those words were untrue, and unfair."

"I understand," Will answered. "As for me, I am half ready to flee London overall. Our epics are not in fashion any longer, Kit. Shallow masques and shallower satires, performances good for nothing but jibing. More backstabbing and slyness than old Robin Greene ever dreamed of. Stuff and nonsense, plague and death. Stabbings in alleyways, and I'm as much to blame as any man, because my plays do not catch at conscience as they once did. My power is failing with the turning of the century."

"Failing?" Kit laid a hand on Will's shoulder and shook him, not hard but enough to slosh the ale in his cup. "Foolishness. The power is there as always; in every line thou dost write. It's merely"—Kit squeezed, and shrugged, and let his hand fall—"in abeyance. Because it depends, in some measure, on the strength of the crown."

"Another raven." Will set his cup aside and pushed away from the wall. "Waiting for Gloriana to die."

Kit plucked the figured silk taffeta of Will's sleeve between his fingers, drawing his hand back before the urge to stroke Will's arm overwhelmed him. Across the hall, he saw Morgan mounting the steps to take a seat at the virginals. "At least our feathers glisten. Look, Will. Smile, go dance attendance. Your lady takes the stage."

Will looked him over carefully, boots to eyepatch, a frown crinkling the corners of his eyes. Kit held his breath as the poet leaned so close that Kit almost thought his lips might brush Kit's cheek. But his hand fell heavily on Kit's shoulder, and his frown became a smile. "I'll see you."

Kit turned and took himself upstairs, to wait for Murchaud and the backgammon board.

Act III, scene xi

A woman's face with Nature's own hand painted
Hast thou, the master-mistress of my passion;
A woman's gentle heart, but not acquainted
With shifting change, as is false women's fashion;

—WILLIAM SHAKESPEARE, Sonnet 20

A tankard of Morgan's brew—bittersweet and redolent of gin-ger and lemons—cooled by Will's elbow. He dipped his pen in raven-black ink, so different from accustomed irongall, and watched it trickle, glossy, down the crystal belly of the well.

"Stop playing with your pen and write, Master Shakespeare." Kit curled like a goblin on the window ledge, wrapped in his parti-color cloak against the chill breeze through the sash. "Commit mine immortal words to paper—"

"Thine immortal words?" Will smiled. He touched pen to paper and let the ink describe the arcs and knots symbolizing Kit's *immortal words*. "I was just thinking, we haven't done this since Harry and Edward met their fates."

"We've improved," Kit answered. He turned his back to the window and kicked his heels against the wall. "I heard from Tom last night. Another letter."

"And?"

"All is as well as can be expected. I'll read it to thee later. When didst thou think to return to London?"

A little too casual, that question. Will laid the pen down and turned to regard Kit, silhouetted against an autumn light. "I've been here three, four weeks now? I thought I might stay another month, perhaps, and go home to Annie before Christmas."

Will thought of Morgan, and the way his hand was steadier on the pen than it had been in years. He'd stay as long as he could. He tried not to think that once he left, the chances of being invited to return were slim.

"I'm glad of the company. And then there's our *Chiron*."

"I couldn't leave that unfinished. Although it will never be performed in London. Difficult to find a centaur to play the lead." Kit's gaze unsettled Will. He looked down at the paper again. "I think it might prove a challenge even for Ned, if Henslowe still had him."

"He'd be fine as Achilles—"

"He'd be brilliant as Achilles." The pen wasn't flowing well; Will dried the nib and searched out his penknife to recut it. He couldn't quite forget the stiffness and hesitance in his muscles, but simply being *better* was such a blessing he couldn't bear to question it too closely.

"We should give Dian a stronger role. Mayhap an archery contest— Don't cut yourself, Will."

"Very funny." But he looked up and saw Kit's concern was genuine, and looked down again quickly. "Archery would give us a chance to bring Hercules in earlier, and show him at play with his arrows."

"Aye. Will—"

The tension in Kit's voice drew Will's head up. "We could still do Circe, instead."

"Nay," Kit answered. "There's a thing that happens here, every seven years. A tithe—"

"The teind. Morgan told me." No, no mistaking that flicker of Kit's lashes when Will said Morgan's name. Nor was there any mistaking the relief on Kit's face when Will continued. "She said I am a guest, and needn't worry; hospitality protects me."

"Then you'll stay; 'tis settled." Kit braided his fingers in his lap for a moment, stood abruptly and began to pace, almost walking into a three-legged stool that Will had absently left out of its place. "We'll be like Romeo and Mercutio: inseparable. What happens after the archery, Will?"

"Mayhap a philosophical argument. Chiron and Bacchus. We could trade off verses, give each a different voice."

"And I suppose I am meant to versify Bacchus?"

The sharpness of Kit's tone halted Will's bantering retort in his throat. "If you prefer the noble centaur, by all means — Kit, what ails thee?"

Will saw the other man pause before he answered, the moment of contemplation that told him Kit was framing some bit of wit or evasion. But then Kit looked him in the eye and frowned, and said straight out, "I'm jealous."

"Of Morgan?"

"Dost love her, Will?"

Will picked up his cold tisane and gulped it, almost choking. "Love is not a seemly word, where vows are broken."

Kit's lips thinned. "Grant I forgive thee for Annie's sake."

Will stood and crossed the room, crouched by the cold, dead fire. "Kit—yes. I love her."

"Then I *am* jealous. Of thee, not Morgan. And canst swear thou feelst nothing of the like?"

Will stopped. Thought. Closed his eyes. *I could lie.* Could he? "What I feel frightens me. I love thee—"

"Is my love for thee less than thine for me, that I would kiss thee? You've not held a rose unless pricked by a thorn, sweet William."

Will shot Kit a hard look; Kit's eye shone with his silent cat-laugh. Will spread his hands wide and swore, then: "Here."

He kicked the stool toward Kit, and tossed a roll of papers tied with ribbon at him. Kit more batted them out of the air than caught, but wound up holding the roll securely.

"What?"

"Read." He turned his back on Kit, and the stool, and the golden Faerie sunlight that poured over both. The light illuminated Kit's flyaway curls with the sort of halo usually registered in oils, dry-brushing the dark mulberry velvet of his doublet, making the crumpled sheaf of papers in his hands shine translucent.

Will slapped wine into a cup perhaps overquickly. "You may skip the first"—he counted on his fingers—"seventeen. Or so."

"Starting from *Shall I compare thee . . .?*" But then Kit's voice trailed off into the rustle of thick pages, and Will stared out the window over Kit's shoulder and drank his wine without tasting it, small sips past the tightness in his throat, until enough time went by for the sun to shift and warm the rug between his boots. He didn't dare look directly at the young man reading—surely Kit hadn't aged a day in six years—but the calm expression of concentration on his face dizzied Will more than rejection or horror would have.

Finally, Kit looked up. "There must be a hundred of these."

"One hundred and two. So far. Not counting those terrible ones I wrote for Oxford."

"One hundred and two." Kit cleared his throat, and read—

"So oft have I invoked thee for my Muse,
And found such fair assistance in my verse
As every alien pen hath got my use
And under thee their poesy disperse —

"—that says a dozen things, all different, half of them bawdy. These are wonderful, Will."

"They're yours," Will answered carelessly. He brought a second cup to Kit. "I have perhaps been cowardly."

"These—" Kit lay the papers on the floor and his cup on the windowsill, expression neutral as Will sank down on the floor nearby. Shades of red colored Kit's cheek in waves. "I am not accustomed to being the subject of poetry."

"Are we not as brothers? Like Romeo and Mercutio—"

Kit stood with a young man's nimbleness and knelt—in the same movement—on the floor before Will, who set his cup aside.

"I should not use a brother thus," he said, and knotted his right hand in Will's hair, meeting Will's gasp with a wet, swift kiss. A kiss that bore Will over, slowly, with perfect control, until he lay flat on the carpet, Kit straddling his hips. Kit's lips moved on his lips, his cheek, his eyelids: a little tickle of mustache, the lessened ache and stiffness in Will's muscles forgotten as he raised his hands to encircle Kit's waist. Kit leaned forward, slick mouth wanton on Will's ear and then his throat, until Will felt the flutter of Kit's heart, the bulge of his prick, and the pressure of his thighs. The velvet covering his body was warmer than the sunlight —

"What of thy Prince?" Soft, afraid to startle Kit away.

"He is in no position to bargain for fidelity," Kit answered, between kisses, deft fingers unfastening Will's buttons in a manner that presumed no argument. "And I would rather thee than he, my heart, on a thousand stormy afternoons. Ask me to choose, Will."

"I've no right," Will answered, and swallowed around pain.

"Fear not," Kit said, drawing back as if he saw the discomfort twist Will's face. "No harm will touch thee at my hand." He stroked Will's breast as if he could feel the rigidity in those muscles, locked so tight they trembled. Finishing the buttons, he began to unlace Will's points. "Love," and Will closed his eyes as Kit quoted his own words back to him — *"Then give me welcome, next my heaven the best / Ev'n to thy pure and most most loving breast."*

Kit was bent over him, Will saw when he opened his eyes again, and Kit's hands were nimble at their undressing. "This will require conversation, William."

With a little shiver, Will identified the emotion that pinned him to the floor: it was fear, a cold knot of terror that blended with the honeyed rush of longing to render him helpless. "I am not certain I am capable."

"Well" — Kit opened Will's doublet and slid one rough hand under his shirt, letting his warm palm rest under the arch of Will's ribs — "Will, you're too thin."

"Aye," he answered, at last able to laugh. "Too thin, undereducated, set above my station, and disinclined of writing the sort of masques and humors in fashion in London, for all Faerie loves me. Chapman or Jonson will be happy to tell you more of my failings—"

But there was a sort of magic in that unmoving hand. Its warmth spread through him and unlocked the chains that held him taut, unknotted the fear in his belly. Will let one hand slide down Kit's leg, thumb caressing the inside of his thigh.

"Undereducated?" Kit leaned forward to claim another kiss. "I *had* promised to improve your understanding of classics. Shall we start with some Latin, then, before we move on to the Greek?"

"Think you my Latin insufficient?" Will opened his mouth for the kiss.

Kit hadn't touched his wine. His mouth was flavored with traces of pipe tobacco and the fainter bitterness that was just Kit. He stroked Will's hair as if gentling the wild thing Will suddenly felt himself to be.

Kit stretched like a cat while Will unlaced his collar—and then stopped, as sunlight caught the shiny unevenness of old scars. Will pushed the edges of lawn apart and reached up to brush Kit's breast with his fingertips, outlining a shape that had the look of a sigil in some arcane alphabet.

"Christ, Kit."

"Ancient history," Kit said, and kissed Will's fingers. "Thou'rt trembling. Art certain . . . ?"

"Aye," Will said, and put his fingers through Kit's hair. "I hate to think of thee—"

"Peace, Will. There's less that's pretty, I'm afraid." Kit shrugged out of his shirt, biting his lip, refusing to meet Will's eyes while they made a fresh inventory of his scars. And then Will reached for him, and it was all right, after all.

Someone's foot scattered papers across the jewel-red wool rug, and mismatched scraps of parchment and foolscap crinkled and adhered to skin. Will laughed, and Kit bit his shoulder gently, sliding up to cover him. "Skinny *and* furry," he said. "I apologize for the state of the poetry."

"I needed to make a fair copy anyway."

"The words could hardly be fairer." A lingering kiss, fraught with intricacies.

Will ran a slow hand up Kit's spine, enjoying the abandoned expression that followed his touch. Fear filled his throat, but he said, "Thou offerèd to instruct me—"

" 'Tis not often I'm privileged to instruct *thee*."

"Other than blank verse and buggery?"

Kit choked, turning his face aside until he mastered the giggles that warmed Will's throat. "Buggery," he recited, lips twitching with the effort to maintain a bored pedant's tone. "So-called in reference to the purported practices of the Bougres, gnostics of France, who held the world so evil that procreation was a sin—"

"Kit," Will interrupted, "surely you are the most erudite of sodomites."

Kit wheezed laughter. "Been said."

"Art . . . willing?" he asked when Kit's shoulders stopped shaking.

"Willing and more than willing—"

Will caught his breath. "Work thy will on thy William, then."

Kit, regarding him seriously, touched the tip of his nose. "Still frightened?

"Not enough to matter," Will answered, and let Kit lead him to the bed.

Act III, scene xii

Mortimer: *Why should you love him whom the world hates so?*
Edward: *Because he loves me more than all the world.*

—CHRISTOPHER MARLOWE, *Edward II*

M uch later, they dressed and trussed and sorted the scattered sonnets in silence and the morning light. Kit was concerned to see Will moving with stiffness as he crawled beneath a bench to reach out papers. "Will . . . have I hurt you?" *Possibly we could have exercised more restraint*—but Kit's lips twitched as he went to help. *Carpe noctem,* after all.

Will sat back on his heels, holding a bit of foolscap in a hand that shook enough to flutter the edge of the paper. He laid his left hand over the right, as if to silence the trembling. " 'Tis just a palsy," Will said. "Such as my father suffers, and one of his brothers had. It comes with aches and clumsiness, worse when I'm tired." He smiled, then, and pushed himself to his feet. "And I am—very delightfully tired. And thank you for it."

"You're young to be trembling, Will. Thirty-four is not such a great age—" The words seemed to swell until they stopped Kit's throat, and he could neither swallow nor speak past them. His fingers tightened on the sheaf of poems in his hand as the meaning of the words came plainer. *Presume not on thy heart when mine is slain, / Thou gav'st me thine not to give back again.*

Will handed papers to Kit, which Kit took to the table they shared. *Shared. 'Tis a fancy, Marley. He leaves thee soon. To return to London and his wife, and even here, he is not thine alone.* Oh, but it was a pleasant fancy—

And thou wilt outlive him, too.

But not in name, an he's writing poetry like that.

"Will you lie to me?"

"Fear not. Morgan's helping me. And I've decades left," Will answered, and let his shoulders rise and fall in a shrug as he stood. "More, if like my father— Well, 'tis not a bad death. The trembling grows, and the body perishes in the end for want of breath. Sir Francis died far worse. And I might still, on the path I walk. If Oxford has his way."

Decades. "That time of year you may in me behold / When yellow leaves, or none, or few, do hang / Upon those boughs which shake against the cold—"

Your poems don't speak of decades, love. "If I have mine," Kit replied, and lifted a candlestick to weight the poems. "Gloriana will protect you. But come. This is not an hour for such thoughts."

"No," Will said thoughtfully. "It's an hour for breakfast, I think. And perhaps I owe Morgan a little groveling—"

"Does she expect your attendance *every* night?" Kit regretted the words as soon as they left his lips, and fetched Will's boots to cover his discomfort.

Will laughed, paying with a kiss as he took them from Kit's hand. "No. But I rather suggested I would meet her for supper."

And she no doubt thought to find me this morning. There *had* been a tapping at the door a little after sunrise, which had not awakened Will and which Kit, roused by dreams, had ignored as unworthy of the price of lifting his head from its throne on Will's shoulder. "Well, we can't hide here forever, living on love." Kit sighed and shrugged, his doublet settling onto his back like duty. "I suppose 'tis brave the day and regroup when the enemy gives up an advantage."

"I'll see you at dinner," Will said. "And then this afternoon, more centaurs."

Kit opened the door, turned back, and smiled. "And satyrs?"

"Christ," Will grumbled, following. "A little pity on an old man."

Kit laughed as he left, bracing himself for the knowing smiles that certainly would greet his and Will's simultaneous reappearance after eighteen hours of silence and a locked door. Things were different in Faerie, aye; for one thing, the gossip galloped three times faster.

He picked his way down the stairs, one hand on the railing, as Will went up, and tried not to frown. *Trouble thyself not with that thou canst not command. Thou lovest, and art loved. 'Twill serve.*

Breakfast had no more formality in the Mebd's palace than it had at Cambridge or in a shoemaker's house in Canterbury, but Kit had paid in two missed meals for the pleasure of an uninterrupted afternoon and evening, and he made haste to the hall in the hope that there would be bread and butter and small beer left. The tables had not been cleared for dinner, but there wasn't much left to choose between. He piled curds and jam on thick slices of wheat bread with gloriously messy abandon, balancing two in his left hand and the third atop his tankard until he found a place at a crumb-scattered trestle and fell to with a passion.

He was halfway through the second slice, leaning forward over the board to save his doublet the spatters, when a shadow fell across the table. He looked up, chewing, into Morgan's eyes and swallowed hastily. "Your Highness."

Her smile had a flinty glitter as she hiked up her skirt and stepped over the bench opposite. "Sir Christofer. I see you're in good appetite."

"I missed my supper. Will was looking for you just now."

"I shall seek him. I trust you had a productive evening—"

"Most." Oh, that smile. Deadly. She helped herself to his tankard, sipped, and frowned over the beer before pushing it back at him. Kit never dropped his gaze as he drank.

"One *can* send down to the kitchens for a tray, if one is indisposed."

"If one wishes the distraction. Poetry waits for no man."

Now she gave him a better smile. "And was it poetry?"

"Of the sheerest sort."

"I expect you shan't be calling upon me this morning, in that case. Now that thou hast had thine use of me—"

The wrong tack; Kit tore bread with his teeth and swallowed more beer, giddiness in his newfound power. "Consider all debts paid for the use you had of me."

"Touché. You won't take him from me, you know." A possessiveness he wondered if she'd ever shown over him flickered across her face.

The jealousy he'd thought well-sated flared, and he chased it down with beer. *Must she own everything she touches?*

The question was the answer. "Madam, he is a married man, with a home and children. I won't see him bound to you."

"No? How will you stop me? If I offered him surcease from pain and a place in Faerie at my side? At your side too, Kit. Help me. He'd half like to stay here. He wouldn't deny us both."

Will.

Here. Alive, not ill any longer.

"He'd have to become like me. A changeling."

"An Elf-knight, Sir Kit. Where's your blade, I wonder?"

"In my room. An *Elf-knight?*"

"And yet you wear your rapier wit." She shook her head. "What else did you think you were become? Help me, Kit. Help me save your true love's life—"

Oh. Oh. He thought of Will's hand shaking. Knew Morgan had been waiting, lying in wait, and this was the opportunity he'd given her. Closed his eye for an instant, and covered his mouth with a hand that smelled of sugar and blackberries. "And damn his soul?"

He watched her face, the thin line between her crow-black brows, the way her eyes went green in passion and the mounting morning light, and realized he'd misjudged and misunderstood her again. "Morgan." She startled at her name, and at the tenderness in it, which startled him as well. "Wouldst take his family from him, my Queen? Bind him as thou hast bound Marley, and Murchaud, and Lancelot, and Arthur? Should the list of names continue? Accolon, Guiomar, Mordred, Bertilak. How many great men hast thou destroyed?"

"How many have I made greater than they were? How many have I healed and defended? I am not merely that evil that thou wouldst name me, Christofer."

"Morgan," he said, understanding. He took her immaculate hand and cupped it in his own. "I know what thou art."

She blinked. The tone in his voice held her; the revelation unscrolled. "Thou art that which nourishes and destroys: the deadly mother, the lover who is death. Because that is what we have made thee, with our tales of thy wit and sorcery. Thou art too much for mortal men to bear."

She sighed and sat back, but did not draw her hand away. "Wouldst see him die?"

Kit stuffed another piece of bread into his mouth with his left hand, refusing the bait. "Morgan. You're a *story*."

"Aye, Master Marley. Poet, Queen's Man, cobbler's boy," she said. "I'm a story. And now, so art thou."

He sat back. He would have let her fingers slide out of his own, but she held him fast and looked him hard in the eye. "A story who'll live to see his mortal lover grow old and gray, totter and break. Canst bear it, Kit? Canst thou bear to see that light extinguished in a few short years?"

He shook his head. "No. I cannot bear it. But I rather imagine Will couldn't bear to bury his son, either. And Morgan, I *will* not see him owned. Mortal men are not meant to live in your world; we cannot bear *that* either."

Heads were turning around the hall at the intensity of the whispered conversation, the white-knuckled grip across the table. Kit breathed deep. "Morgan. 'Tis true what I say."

"Aye." And it was a curse when she said it, and her eyes were blacker than he had ever seen them. "I was a *goddess*, Kit."

"Madam," he said with dignity. "You still are."

Act III, scene xiii

Rosalind: Oh how full of briers is this working-day world.
Celia: They are but burrs, Cousin, thrown upon thee in holiday foolery,
if we walk not in the trodden paths our very petticoats will catch them.
Rosalind: I could shake them off my coat, these burrs are in my heart.

—WILLIAM SHAKESPEARE, *As You Like It*

Will's days seemed longer than the span of their hours, a lan-
guorous blur of lovemaking, companionship, and poetry that
expanded to include time for every eventuality and sunsets too. The
nights he spent with Kit or Morgan by turns, the days in rehearsal for
Chiron—planned for the Hallowmas entertainment—or with his lovers.

He hadn't felt anything like it since the first flush of his affair with
Annie. *It cannot last.*

No, only through the autumn, and when winter came to England Will must be homeward bound. Still the days were endless, the
weeks longer than months, the perfection of his happiness such that
he almost did not move himself to ask how time passed in the mortal
world. "Worry not," Kit assured him as they sat on rocks over the
ocean, watching sunset stain the white manes of the waves, listening
to their whickering. "Hallowmas will be Hallowmas, here as there,
and then—"

"We'll have the bloody slaughter of the noblest of centaurs under our belts, and I will bid thee adieu." Will pulled a stalk of salt grass and slipped the tender inwards from its overcoat to chew. He gave the dry brown husk to the air; the sea wind blew it back over his shoulder. "Kit, what will we do?"

Kit tugged his slowly growing cloak around his shoulders and bumped Will's shoulder with his own. "Ford it when we come to it," he said. "We should—"

"Aye. We should."

"It will only grow harder—"

The wind stirred Will's hair. The locks had outstripped the length they should have in the time he'd been in Faerie. "I can picture myself pining by my window for my Faerie lover, growing gray and sere. A legend will grow up—"

"*Will!*" Kit grabbed his wrist, and jerked it. Will turned, startled; Kit's expression was wild. "Don't joke about such things. Never joke about such things; you're on the edge of legend here, and names have power, and things *listen*."

His plain fear brought an answering tingle to Will's spine, to his fingertips. "Morgan wants me to stay." The chewed stem grew bitter. Will tossed it away.

"I want thee to stay," Kit said, still staring. "And Morgan wishes me to plead with thee as well. But I will not permit it."

Kit's pulse flickered in the hollow of his throat. Will wrenched his eyes away. "Art my sovereign, Marley?" Soft as the ocean's breath playing over them both.

"Aye." The fingers on Will's wrist tightened. "Aye, in this thing, I am. What would thy girls do, without thee?"

"What they do now, I expect. I've hardly been an exemplary father and husband." Will kissed Kit's brow, by way of example.

Kit released him to pluck a smooth, moon-white stone from a crevice in their sand-worn perch. He tossed it thrice before it slipped between his fingers, rattling on the rocks below. "Blast. Thou hast the chance to be better at both, at least." His gaze lifted to the darkening horizon.

Abruptly, Will understood. "Kit, forgive me—"

"There's nothing to forgive. I'd live to bury any wife or child I'd left behind; aye, and their grandchildren, too. If I'm fortunate enough that no one puts a knife in the other eye."

The wind freshened. The day's warmth soaked the stone they sat upon; Will pressed his back against it. "After *Chiron*," he said, dropping his arm around Kit's shoulders, "I suppose I shall go home."

"I suppose that's best," Kit said, and leaned closer as the light drained the sky, replaced by the slow unveiling of the stars. "Hast heard there's an astrologer in Denmark claims the stars are not settled in crystal vaults? That they float unsupported, and other stars — comets and *stella novae* — move through them?"

"I imagine the Pope hates him."

"Not as much as he hates Copernicus, I imagine."

"O, thou art fairer than the evening air / Clad in the beauty of a thousand stars —"

Kit laughed. "I should write you a poem. Something better than that."

"Better than *Faustus*?"

"Christ wept, I hope I've improved."

Will earthed himself under the warm edge of Kit's cloak, kissed him where his throat blended into his jaw, the sticky musk of the ocean rich on moist, salty skin. "Thou'rt all the poetry I need."

"Sweet liar —"

"Sweeter when you know it cannot last." Will's voice shivered with his whisper. Kit's answer was slow.

"Christ. Damn me to Hell. Yes, Will. 'Tis sweet."

The old moon rose in the new moon's arms. The rocks grew cool around them. Kit's cloak concealed a multitude of sins.

And over the water, something listened and understood.

Act III, scene xiv

And here upon my knees, striking the earth,
I ban their souls to everlasting pains
And extreme tortures of the fiery deep,
That thus have dealt with me in my distress.

—CHRISTOPHER MARLOWE, *The Jew of Malta*

Kit rubbed a corner of his eye in the dimming room and thought of candles. He stretched against the back of his chair, his spine crackling, and stood a moment before a hesitant knock rattled the door.

"Come!" He crossed to the fire to light a rush. The door swung open, revealing Murchaud leaning against its frame in a pose at once consciously arrogant and restlessly self-aware.

"Christofer." The prince flipped a stray curl behind his ear, an un-characteristically tentative gesture. "Art thou . . . ?"

"Alone? Aye." Kit touched his spill among the embers, then stood to apply the resultant flame to a lamp wick. "Come in."

Murchaud stepped onto the jewel-patterned carpet, cautious as a stag. Kit blew out the rushlight, adjusted the lamp, and fitted its chimney, carrying it to his table as a scent of char filled the room. It spilled golden light across his poems and paper, and Kit slid them aside until he found pipe and tobacco pouch among the clutter.

"Filthy habit," the Elf-knight said, latching the door. "I'd thought thee quit of it."

Kit turned to face Murchaud, tamping the pipe with his thumb. "I was." He didn't know how to explain that he woke from his dreams of late with the smell of tobacco and whiskey clinging to his skin, full of strange cravings nothing would assuage. He dipped a second spill down the chimney of the lamp and lit his pipe from it. Settling down on his stool again, he let the first breath of smoke drip down his chin.

Murchaud leaned against the locked door and crossed his arms. "I came to wish thee well tomorrow."

"The *Chiron*? Thank you. Will needs your luck more than I do; my part is finished. He'll be on the stage."

"*Will*" — Murchaud grimaced — "is with my mother tonight."

"In rehearsal first."

"I know. And so I came to thee. I expect thou planst to be with him after the play."

"So I had anticipated," Kit answered slowly, cupping the warm bowl of his pipe in his hand. The embers had gone out from inattention: he reached for a rush. "He returns to London on All Saints' Day."

Murchaud straightened away from the door. "And will your cruelty to me end when he is gone, my love?"

Kit froze with the pipe between his teeth, the relit spill pressed to the weed within it. The poet forgot to draw; the flame flickered out and he laid pipe and burnt rush on a shallow pottery tray. "Cruel? To thee? As if I had the power—"

"Thou goest to Morgan still, and dost hide it from thy mortal lover, who sports with her quite openly. And yet to me, who was more a friend to thee than ever my mother proved, thou wilt barely speak in passing."

Kit pushed his stool back and stood as the Elf-knight came to him. The room was growing chill; he thought absently of tending the fire. He lifted his chin to meet Murchaud's gaze directly. "What couldst thou wish of me?"

Murchaud's fingers slid under Kit's hair, caressing his neck. "Tell thou me, O Elf-knight with thy human lover—"

"I'm not—"

"—what does he give thee that I cannot?" Murchaud's breath was warm on Kit's skin.

Kit swallowed, and considered. "The Fae are very cold," he said at last, hopelessly.

"And mortals a flame we warm ourselves upon."

Kit turned his head to avoid the kiss, but did not pull away as Murchaud bowed his face against the poet's throat. "I'll be thine again after tomorrow."

"Oh," Murchaud said. "I rather think thou wilt not." There was grief in his words; so much pain that Kit shivered in reaction. "Why Morgan and not me?"

"I do not know."

"Liar." Murchaud breathed deep, as if fastening Kit's scent in his memory, and stepped away—unruffled, his pale eyes chill. "Is it vengeance upon thy poet, for not loving thee alone?"

Kit shivered and shook his head. The words came strung on knotted wire: each one tore his throat. "Kissing thee—does not hurt enough."

Murchaud chuckled, his hand on the door. "Half Fae already," he said, and left Kit alone in the lamplight, unkissed.

> *Do I envy those jacks that nimble leap*
> *To kiss the tender inward of thy hand,*
> *Whilst my poor lips, which should that harvest reap,*
> *At the wood's boldness by thee blushing stand!*
> —WILLIAM SHAKESPEARE, from Sonnet 128

Will poured golden wine into Morgan's glass and then his own. It filled the fire-warmed air with a scent of summer, grape arbors, and clipped grass. He cupped the glass in both hands, leaning against Morgan's chair, stretching his feet to the fire. "I'll miss thee." Without looking at her. "And thou me?"

She leaned forward, knees pressing his shoulders, and took her glass from out his hand. Her lips brushed the top of his head; she sat back. "One becomes accustomed to loss."

"That is not an answer, my Queen." The rug beneath him was soft, her fingers kind in his thinning hair. Fine ripples trembled as he raised the wine to his lips.

"I will miss you. If it is important to you to be missed."

"To be missed? To be loved—"

"You are loved." Something in her voice reminded him of when she had read his palm: an assurance like prophecy. "And shall be more loved still."

"By whom?"

"One can never tell, until it is too late to do anything about it." A light click told him she set her glass on a low table. Her fingers found his shoulders, sought deep into his tension. "Do you regret this, Master Poet?"

"Regret leaving? Or regret Faerie?"

"If we shadows have offended—"

He laughed, and then her touch made him sigh. "It is rather like a dream. A dream of peace and healing. Is it your medicines or is it Faerie that mends me so well?"

"Both," Morgan answered. "Time stands still for thee here. And my herbwifery lends some relief. But when thou goest back to the world, thou wilt begin to die again."

"You still wish me to stay—"

"Thou hast ten years. Perhaps as much as fifteen." She bent and kissed his forehead, tilting his face up with a hand under his chin. "Go to him," Morgan le Fey whispered. Her lips brushed the heavy earring. He shivered.

"Tomorrow night—"

"Tomorrow is too late," she said, and stood out of her chair. She stepped over Will lightly, her kilted skirts sweeping his shoulders. "Go now. Tell him to wear his boots and cloak tomorrow, and his sword."

Will pushed himself to his knees. "I had written something for you—"

She stood facing the fire with squared shoulders and softened hands. "A sonnet?"

"About your music—"

"I do not need your poetry. It belongs to the mortal world. I have a poet of mine own."

Silence. Will rose to his feet. The fire popped, scattering coals on the hearthstones; Morgan's precisely applied shoe ended their escape. "Morgan—"

"I have a poet of mine own," she repeated. "If you are wise, you'll go to him now; you have so little time left before I reclaim him."

The cruelty in her tone left him gasping. His lips shaped her name again, but that very breathlessness kept it mercifully silent. She stood before the fire and did not look at him. He turned and left her presence.

The door of the room he shared with Kit was unlatched. Will pushed it open gently and found Kit bent over papers on their table. *Kit's table,* Will thought as the poet looked up.

"Forgotten something?"

Will hoped he imagined the chill in Kit's voice. He latched the door, breathing deep the aromas of woodsmoke and cold tobacco. "Morgan's finished with me: she couldn't make me stay. You said that quill was too beautiful to use."

Kit glanced at the gorgeous alabaster feather in his hand. "I changed my mind. It writes well. You have a play tomorrow: come to bed."

"You're working." But Will unfastened his doublet as he argued, struggling only a little with the golden buttons.

"I can work in November." Kit dropped the quill into jet-black ink and stood. He came around the table. "Will, I'm frightened."

"Frightened?"

"I think—" He shook his head. "If you stayed in Faerie, love, you could live—"

"I want to see my son again," Will said quietly, knowing Kit would not argue the point. "That's not what scares you."

Kit tugged the doublet from Will's shoulder and took it to lay out to air. "Murchaud was here. And very fey."

"He is—"

"No. Will, I think he's going to the teind."

"What do you mean?" Will laid his hand against Kit's cheek. The skin was cold and damp. Kit let the doublet drop on the floor and Will pulled him close, feeling Kit's heart like a terrified sparrow trapped in the cage of his ribs.

"I mean," Kit said, "I think it was farewell. And he'll be gone, and you'll be gone—"

"I'll write," Will said. "You'll visit."

Kit turned around and looked at him, unapproachably distant from inches away. "You'll die."

"I'll care for you. Morgan said she would have you back—"

"I have no plans. To return to Morgan."

So they were lovers, then. Will laid his hand on Kit's cheek. *I wonder who ended it.* "I misspoke. *Take* you back."

"I've worn her collar enough for one lifetime." Kit shivered and drifted away, running his fingers inside the band of his ruff, disarraying the careful pleats. Abrupt gestures betraying annoyance, he untied it and tossed it on the chest. "Morgan is a fool."

The thing on Kit's face approximated a smile, Will decided, but it wasn't, really. "Shakespeare is a bigger one," he answered, and was glad Kit kissed him before he could compound that foolishness somehow.

Act III, scene xv

Hermia: Out, dog! out, cur! thou drivest me past the bounds
Of maiden's patience. Hast thou slain him, then?
Henceforth be never number'd among men!
O, once tell true, tell true, even for my sake!
Durst thou have look'd upon him being awake,
And hast thou kill'd him sleeping? O brave touch!
Could not a worm, an adder, do so much?
An adder did it; for with doubler tongue
Than thine, thou serpent, never adder stung.

—WILLIAM SHAKESPEARE, *A Midsummer Night's Dream*

Will's role was small—Asklepios—and he'd written it so intentionally. After his own sad death, struck down by Zeus' thun-
derbolt, the erstwhile physician scrubbed the paint from his face and
made his way into the audience, seeking companionship.

The revelers were masked and gowned as gorgeously as Will had
ever seen; they bowed or curtseyed graciously—or, pleasing him more,
failed to, rapt in the performance—as he walked among them, seeking
Kit or Morgan.

He found neither, but Puck's small, twisted form beckoned among
the window draperies, and Will went there. The sounds and scents

of Faerie surrounded him; he sighed, settling into the window seat. "Master Goodfellow, well met."

"Master Shakespeare, as well." Spry as a goblin, Puck swung up the draperies and clung to them lightly, at a height from which to hold comfortable converse with a seated man. "They approve of your work."

"They seem to," Will answered, over the hollow clatter of hooves as the centaur playing Chiron took the stage, remonstrating with the Gods over Asklepios' death. "Kit and I put some magic of our own into the ending. When Prometheus takes Chiron's immortality, to permit Chiron death—"

"I should think our enemies would find that more to their liking than our allies, Master Poet—"

Will grinned and tilted his head to look Robin in the soft, goatlike eye. "Ah, but Prometheus dooms himself in doing so."

"Dooms to eternal torment," Puck answered, nodding. "Clever. But surely outside the scope of the play?"

"There is—an epilogue."

Silence, and then Puck tittered: a high fey giggle like a child. "Speaking of eternal torment—"

"Aye?"

"What think you of the teind?"

Will swallowed hard and looked away from the Puck, running his eyes once more across the crowd. Neither Kit, nor Morgan, nor Murchaud could be seen. "Kit thinks it will be Murchaud," he said. "I imagine he is making his farewells."

"Think how glorious the pain will be. How deep, how lasting. There's poetry in that."

"Pain?" Will hauled his legs up onto the window seat and hugged his knees. "Glorious pain? If you think pain is glorious, perhaps you have never known it practically."

"When you live as the Fey live, any sensation is precious."

"I see—"

"Not yet." Puck smiled. "But you will."

"I've had enough of prophecy," Will said. He sighed and stretched and stood; Robin swung on the drape and hopped to Will's shoulder, no more than a featherweight, holding Will's ear with his long bony fingers.

"Then don't listen to it." A jingle of bells, the tangling and untangling of improbable limbs. Puck shifted on the bones of Will's shoulder and made himself as steady a place as any horseman well accustomed to the saddle. " 'Tis not Murchaud going to the teind tonight, Will Shakespeare. And a sacrifice gone willing to Hell buys not seven, but seven times seven years."

On the stage, Chiron was dying, beasts and mortals gathered close about. Will stopped and watched as the noble centaur went to his knees, a majestic fall. "How do you know? It is kept close secret—"

"Will," the Puck said softly, "I'm the Queen's Fool. I know *everything*. I am just not often privileged to speak on it."

"Then who will it be?"

Crowds have a way of moving, of breathing, of falling silent at once as if they were some giant dreaming animal. Will looked up as the animal sighed and stretched and turned in its sleep, as it rolled and broke open along his line of sight. A tingle ran up his skin; he felt the nail that Kit had given him grow hot in his sleeve. *Sorcery?* But the thought was lost as a drape blew back from the curtained shadows of a window embrasure like the one he had just left, one toward the back of the hall and away from the crowd gathered before the stage.

Will, slowly walking, froze so abruptly that Robin clutched at his head in a most undignified manner. "Oh, Hell," Will said, reaching out a hand blindly for balance.

For Will recognized the figures intertwined within its moon-touched shelter, caught a kiss that seemed sheerest delight—the smaller all in black except his ragged cloak, his fair hair gleaming; the taller in a gown of palest green, her black hair tumbling over her lover's hands like a living thing.

"Kit," Will said, crossing his hands over his belly as if to press his vitals back inside. "Ah. No."

On his shoulder, Puck slid down, flexible as a squirrel, and threw both arms around Will's neck. "Yes. I'm sorry."

"Sorry?" Will mouthed. He was staring; the curtain fell back, mercifully, and he managed to turn and look away. The chorus took the stage for the epilogue. He raised his eyes. "You have no cause for sorrow, Master Goodfellow—"

"Sorry I could not tell you sooner," Puck said, as Will closed his ears on the savage poetry of the thing that he and Kit had created together. The words left a taste like vinegar in his mouth; if the floor were berushed over the soft-sheened marble, he would have spit the grit and savor of bitterness out.

"It was hardly your place to tell a man his loves betrayed him—" Even as he said the words, Will tasted their hypocrisy. Puck slid down his shoulder. He wobbled, half realized he was sitting on a bench when Puck thrust wine into his hands. Will drank it greedily and put the goblet under the bench; his fingers itched to hurl it, hard, against the wall. "Oh, Robin. I've nothing to complain."

"You feel betrayed? Then why not sing it?"

"Because," Will said around the taste of ashes that the wine could not rinse from his tongue, " 'tis neither Kit nor Morgan who broke a bed-vow to a wedded wife, is it?"

"You know he went back to her bed almost as soon as she took you into it."

Dear God in Hell. But Will kept enough control of his tongue not to say it. *Then what did either one of them have to do with me for?*

Unless 'twas pity. Yes, pity. For poor, inept, sickly Will. How could a balding poet hope to content things out of legend—

But Robin was still talking. "—and that's not what I'm sorry for."

Hopelessness, and the void in his belly sharp-edged as a fresh-dug hole. His eyes burned. His knees would not support him when he tried to rise. Somewhere, Will thought he heard a bell pealing; Chiron— resurrected—bowed for the end of the play. And the cold voice Will recognized as his own aggrieved conscience: *Say you deserved it not. Say Annie's courage in the face of your misbehavior was nothing.* "Then what?"

Robin sucked his wide lips into his mouth so that every rosy trace of color vanished from them. "Will," he said. "Murchaud isn't the teind. Sir Christofer is."

Will blinked, demanding that his ears report some other phrase. "Kit," he repeated, stupidly.

Robin laid a twiggy hand on William's arm. "I don't think he can bear it—"

Somehow, Will found his feet. "I *know* he can't. Robin—"

Enormous brown eyes turned upward, seeking Will's expression. Will schooled it to impassivity.

"Master Shakespeare?"

All a player's urgency and power of command imbued his tone when he found his words again. "Robin, what must I do?"

Faustus: How comes it then that thou art out of hell?
Mephostophilis: Why this is hell: nor am I out of it.
Think'st thou that I that saw the face of God,
And tasted the eternal Joys of heaven
Am not tormented with ten thousand hells,
In being depriv'd of everlasting bliss?
—CHRISTOPHER MARLOWE, *Faustus*

There in the shadows of the embrasure, behind the bowering curtains, Morgan put her arms around Kit and kissed him lingeringly. Blood rose in his face, ran singing through his veins. A storm-prickling wind swirled around them, rustling his cloak, lifting his hair like a lover's fingers. He pressed his body to hers, drunk on the heady beauty of the words that flowed from the incomparable players at the far end of the hall.

A measured cadence of church bells pealed close enough to reverberate in his head; Morgan's lips firmed and yielded by turns. "A bone healed twisted must be broken again," she murmured without pulling back. "What I do I do out of necessity, and I hope you find the courage to forgive me, someday. You have your boots and sword, your cloak and your wits. And now a lady's kiss. It will suffice."

Murchaud, he thought, panicky. "Morgan—" He pushed her back a moment before she would have stepped away on her own. "Your own son?"

She shook her head. "It is done."

The bells were hoofbeats, he realized; the tolling of silver horseshoes on the flags. He turned and looked up, stepping past the curtain, out of the recessed gap before the window, and into the suddenly silent hall.

A milk-white mare, caparisoned all in silver and blue, bowed her snow-soft nose before Kit and blinked amber eyes through the froth of her mane.

"Oh," Kit said, as Morgan moved away from him. "Of course. It's not Murchaud; it's me." And laid his hand quite calmly on the pommel, fumbling for the stirrup with his left foot.

> *Him have I lost; thou hast both him and me:*
> *He pays the whole, and yet am I not free.*
> —WILLIAM SHAKESPEARE, from Sonnet 134

The white mare's hooves rang on the cobbles; she shifted restlessly as Kit swung into her saddle. Will limped up with dreamer's footsteps—*too slow, too slow*—and came forward as Kit settled himself, feeling under her pale mane for the reins.

She was white, stark white to the tip of her nose—not a pale gray at all, but some Faerie breed—and she gazed at Will with a knowing eye as he came up to her. Kit's dark suit outlined him like a pen slash on the paper-white of her hide, his jewel-colored cloak spreading over her rump. The Fae parted before him, opened like the Red Sea before Moses, and Will stumbled forward and grabbed Kit's boot at the ankle. "No."

Kit looked down; looked Will in the eye, the strap of his eyepatch stark against the pallor of his brow. That grimace must be meant to be a smile. "Gentle William," he said, transferring the reins to his right hand and laying the left on Will's shoulder for a moment. "I must. I have no choice."

"No," Will said, a second time. And *"No."* A third, and he reached up and yanked the reins from Kit's hand as Kit was shifting them again. *A sacrifice gone willing,* he thought, *a sacrifice gone willing to Hell buys not seven, but seven times seven years.*

"Dammit, Will." Kit knotted his right hand in the white mare's mane, reached down to pluck the reins back. Will shivered as the mare sidled and shied, jerking against his inexpert touch. Kit slid and bit back a curse, struggling to regain his stirrups. "It's my place."

Will tilted his head back to look Kit in the face. *He's immortal. I'm dying. Why should I not do this thing? Annie would be better off a widow, given the husband I have been.*

Although I wanted to see Hamnet again.

And didn't admit even to himself he thought, *And let it punish him for loving Morgan more than me*—

"I understand." Will laid his hand on Kit's knee and offered up the reins, straight over his head. Kit leaned out to reach them; just as he overbalanced, Will let them fall. Will's right hand darted to Kit's swordbelt. Will's left closed on the cuff of his boot. "I understand 'tis not your place at all."

The mare shied in earnest as Will leaned backward and yanked, Kit's face blank with sudden panic. Leather creaked in Will's hands, velvet soft against his knuckles. The white mare sidestepped, and Kit tumbled all elbows and flailing into Will's waiting arms.

Will rolled with it, prepared, a stage fall that nonetheless knocked the wind out of him—though he made sure Kit landed on the bottom. They fell face-to-face for a moment, and Will pressed breathless Kit hard against the harder floor. "Mine," Will said, and kissed Kit roughly, briefly on the mouth.

He pushed himself back with both hands on Kit's collar, a knee still on the smaller man's belly, shoving him down, looking up into Murchaud's eyes and the amused, changing eyes of his wife. Puck stood between them, tugging them forward by their sleeves. Kit reached with both hands to clutch Will's wrists, opening his mouth, unwilling to strike Will hard enough to hurt him. Will doubled his fists and lifted, and banged Kit once against the floor.

"Your Majesty," Will said, with what dignity he could muster over Kit's betrayed shout. "I claim the right to go as your teind to Hell."

The Mebd's lips pursed. She stepped away from Murchaud and from her Puck, while Kit raised his voice in a string of incoherent objections. She crouched before Will, her skirts a pool of green water tumbling around her, and silenced Kit with a brush of her fingers across his angry lips.

He must have longed to shout, to rage. Will felt Kit's voice fluttering in his throat. But her magic held him silent, and—seething—he fell impotently still under Will's hands. And then Kit's trembling started in earnest, both hands pressed against his mouth, and Will thought, *Oh, Jesus. Rheims.*

"William Shakespeare," she murmured. "Dost know what thou offerest?"

"Nay," he said, sick in the bottom of his belly and determined nonetheless. Kit surged against his grip, and Will kneeled down. "But I am willing. Only tell me, Your Majesty, that you will spare my love."

Kit was weeping. His hands dropped from his mouth and circled Will's wrists, jerking, chafing, but he fought no more. The Mebd smiled, and nodded, and closed her eyes; Will thought they shone more than they should have. Kit pulled Will's hand to his mouth and kissed the fingers, a pleading gesture, even his hot gasping breath coming silent through the potency of the Mebd's negligent spell. Will tugged his hand free, the image of those lips kissing Morgan hot behind his eyes.

"You do us honor," the Mebd said softly; Will did not miss that she addressed him as an equal in that moment, before she rose and swept away.

Kit slumped as Will pushed himself to his feet; Kit pressed his fist against his mouth and curled on his side, dragging his face down to his knees. *"Jesu,"* Kit gasped, and Faeries ducked away, wincing; one sprite covered her ears and dropped to the floor. A circle had grown around them. Will stood at its center, turning slowly, and none of the Fae would look down from his regard, and none would quite meet his eyes.

Except Puck, and the Prince.

Robin Goodfellow stepped forward, and Murchaud followed him a half step behind. Murchaud bit his lip and nodded to Will. His lips parted as if he would speak, and Will, trembling now, stepped back from Kit's huddled form. Murchaud knelt, gathering him close, and Will turned away.

Puck laid a hand on his wrist, fingers dry as kindling and as knobby as knotted rope. "Master Shakespeare." He drew Will's attention to the wild-eyed mare. "You need to go now."

Will bit his lip, trembling harder under the mare's amber regard. She prodded him with her nose; he fell back. "Robin." His voice broke; he pretended he didn't see Kit's shuddering flinch at the sound. "I am at a loss. I do not ride —"

"Fear not," Puck answered, taking his elbow. "Thy steed knows the way."

Act III, scene xvi

I am a Lord, for so my deeds shall prove,
And yet a shepherd by my Parentage . . .

—CHRISTOPHER MARLOWE, *Tamburlaine the Great, Part I*

Murchaud knotted his fingers in Kit's hair and dragged Kit's face against his shoulder, whispering something that might have been intended as comfort. Kit couldn't understand over the tolling of somber bells, the jingle of the white mare's harness—or, more precisely, he didn't care to try. He stayed frozen, curled so tight in pain that his chest and shoulders ached. *No.*

Whatever Murchaud said, it vanished in the vanishing hoofbeats, and when Kit raised his head, avoiding the prince's face, both Will and his white steed were gone. Murchaud clung to him, trying to draw him close. *No.* Kit pressed his knuckles against the floor and got one foot under himself, and tore free of Murchaud's embrace. He turned to survey the room; every Fae watching ducked his eyes and withdrew. "Where is Morgan?"

No one answered. Kit reached across the ache filling his belly and grasped the hilt of his sword. "Where is the Queen?" She'd silenced him, a finger to his lips and his voice had swelled in his throat and choked him. He tasted blood.

"Gone with Will," Puck said quietly, when no one else would meet Kit's gaze. "Two Queens to guide him —"

" — to Hell. Christ on the Cross!" Satisfaction heated the emptiness within him as every Fae in the room cringed as if he'd kicked them. "Damn every one of you," Kit said, enunciating, the sweat-ridges on his swordhilt cutting hot welts his palm. "Damn you each and every one to Hell." He looked at Murchaud as he spoke, and the taste of smoke and whiskey filled his mouth.

Murchaud only blinked without dropping his gaze. "No doubt," he said, "it will be as you prophesy."

The silence lingered until Kit turned. "I'm going after them." He dropped his hand from the blade and shrugged his cloak back from his shoulders, sustaining rage lost. "It's in the songs, after all."

"Oh, yes, Orfeo." Not Murchaud's voice but Cairbre's, mocking. "Go win thou thy love back from Hell. It should be just a little task for a journeyman."

Kit didn't even trouble himself to turn. He kept his eyes trained on Murchaud, and smiled. "Someone has to."

"I forbid thee to leave this place," Murchaud said slowly, power and the right of command imbuing his words. The geas struck Kit like a backhanded blow; he rocked with it, felt it break on the protection of his iron-nailed boots and his patchwork cloak. *Thank thee, Morgan. And how did she know?*

Kit lifted his chin, hooked his fingers through his belt to keep them off the rapier's hilt. "Try again?"

His throat ached with something — pride, anguish — as Murchaud stepped so carefully between him and the door. "If thou wilt walk through me," Murchaud said, "wilt need thy blade."

"Good my lords."

Kit looked down reluctantly. He owed Robin the favor of his attention even now. "Puck —"

"Your Highness," the Puck said, bowing, ignoring Kit with pricked ears and a stiffly erect spine. "Prince Murchaud, an it please you — Sir Christofer must do this thing."

"There's no covenant to protect him if he goes."

"No," Puck said, shuffling a half step away from Kit. "But we need

Shakespeare in the world more than we need Marley in Faerie. And
furthermore, you cannot gainsay him."

"Thou darest tell me what I can do, and cannot, fool?"

Robin waggled donkey's ears. Soft bells jingled, like the bells on
the white mare's harness. He realized that every other Fae had withdrawn; only Puck, Murchaud, and Cairbre remained.

Puck abased himself. "It is in all the songs."

"*Blast!*" Kit jumped at the outburst before he realized it was his
own. "Am I to make my destiny as dead singers direct?"

"Exactly."

Kit glanced over his shoulder at Cairbre, finally, and was surprised
to see the master bard grin. "The Puck's right, Your Highness. Kit has
to follow his love to Hell."

Kit leaned his forehead against the gelding's sweet-smelling sorrel
neck, coarse straw rustling about his ankles, and steeled himself to
swing into the saddle. "All hope abandon, ye who enter here."

"Nay. You can save him," Robin said from his perch on the stall's
half-door.

The sorrel snorted, shaking his head as if in annoyed agreement.
*Pray stop teasing me with the prospect of an outing, Master Marley, and lead
me from this stall,* Kit extemporized. He chuckled bitterly under his
breath, and then caught a glimpse of the gelding's expression. *Damme
if he isn't thinking just that.*

"I can't even save myself, Master Goodfellow."

"Who among us can?" The Puck slid down from the door and
came forward to tug the reins from Kit's hand. Kit gave them up, and
the little Fae led both horse and man out of the stable and into the
courtyard. Silver shoes and iron bootnails rang on the pale cobblestones. The courtyard was empty in the moonlight except for the two
of them and the gelding; Kit refused on his pride to crane his neck to
the windows to see if Murchaud might be peering out. "Bargain well,"
Puck said, and held the stirrup.

Grief and gratitude welled into Kit's eye. He blinked them back
and took the reins when Robin held them up. "I know not how to
thank you."

The Fae skipped away from the gelding's hooves. "Come home safe, Christofer Marley." He stepped into a shadow and was gone.

Kit tucked his cloak about him to keep it from flapping, turned his mount with his knees, and urged the sorrel toward the palace gate.

What do you tremble, are you all afraid?
Alas, I blame you not, for you are mortal,
And mortal eyes cannot endure the devil.
—WILLIAM SHAKESPEARE, *Richard III*

The road stretched broad and easy before Will and his docile, mannerly, ghost-colored mare. Her shoes chimed carillon on the smooth cobblestones. She arched her neck as if proud of her burden, for all he slumped on her back like a bag of fresh-killed game. The stirrups cut through the arches of his court slippers; he did not even attempt to ride over the beat of her stride, as the women—riding astride—did.

The Mebd rode on Will's left side and Morgan on his right; as they had passed under the archway of the palace gate, Morgan caught his sleeve. When he had turned to her, unwilling to meet her eyes, the Mebd had reined her ink-black gelding shoulder to shoulder with the milk-white mare and reached over Will's bowed head and hunched shoulders to press something onto his brow. A circlet, a band of resilient gold; he saw its reflection in Morgan's eyes.

"You knew," he said to the woman he had loved.

She nodded and swept a hand through the wire-curled tumult of her hair. "I chose," she said simply, turning away again. Her bay horse dipped a white-blazed face as if to crop the grass at the roadside; Morgan twitched the reins and the mare snorted, soft purls steaming from her nostrils. "I thought it would help him, in the end. We need your Christofer whole, sweet William."

"Do not—" The mare tossed her head as his hands tightened on the reins. He forced himself drape them loose against her neck. She settled into her easy pace again. *The horse knows her own way home.*

"Don't . . . what, my love?"

The Mebd rode close, within hearing of the softest murmur.

Shadows seemed to grasp around the edge of things. Clutching branches and rustling limbs. *Willow he walk, if yew travels late.* "Don't call me pet names," he said, hoping his voice sounded disinterested. "I saw—"

She smiled. White teeth winked in the corner of his eye. "Kit and me?"

"Aye." The heat of his furious blush. And what did it matter now, lust or love, fornication or sacrament? He was damned. The clawing shadows crowded closer to the road; Will, with ease, could imagine them pitchfork-wielding demons.

"Ah," she said. "Yes. Lovely boy. Very sweet in bed. Far too easy to manipulate. 'Twas one of the flaws I had hoped Lucifer could correct in him."

"As if Hell were a schoolboy caning."

"But Master Shakespeare"—honest startlement, her gray eyes wide in the moonlight—"it is."

Whatever he might have found to say in response was ended by the flicker of a lantern a few hundred yards ahead, emerging through gaudy, rustling October leaves. The low yellow flame rested at ground level, silhouetting a square, glass-sided frame, the interleaved cobbles of a crossroads, and the shining dark hooves of a massive steed. It limned the figure on the stallion's back from beneath—the soft black velvet of his doublet, the sovereign shine of his hair. The kind alabaster arch of his enormous wings cast their own pale glow, feather edges stained gold over silver by the candlelight.

For Kit, Will thought, as Lucifer Morningstar lifted his chin and regarded the approaching trio.

His wings fanned softly; he leaned back in his saddle in feigned surprise. :Why, 'tis not the soul I was bid expect. Good even, Master Shakespeare. How pleasant to make thine acquaintance again:

Morgan placed a warm hand on the small of Will's back. He rode forward as much to elude the touch as because that was where his white mare took him. From the corner of his eye, Will thought perhaps he saw Morgan's cheeks shining. *Ridiculous that Morgan le Fay should weep for me—*

And then he smiled. *As ridiculous as that she should moan for me.* He turned back over his shoulder. Distantly, he thought for a moment he heard the echo of galloping hooves. Morgan wept indeed: Will forced himself to meet her eyes and speak coolly. *Love her all you will, foolish heart. She'll have no more kindness from thee.*

"Tell Kit," he said, his voice cracking. "Tell Kit I bid him care for my Annie and my girls."

Whatever she might have said in return died on her lips, or under the peals of the white mare's hooves as she bore Will forward beneath the mighty wings of the Prince of Hell. Lucifer turned his horse and, leaving the lantern where it lay, led Will and his strange knowing mount into darkness and down.

:You have the look of a man who will be hard to buy, Master Shakespeare:

"Buy, and not break?"

:And yet you have an imagination. That is well. I invite you to contemplate that we will be together for eternity. Will you serve willing?:

"I came willing," Will answered.

:No one comes willing: Lucifer said. :They come because they have no other choice. Or because they will accept no other choice presented them. Or rarely, as thy lover Marley learned, because they have come to understand that Hell is all around them, and that they have never been out of it once:

Will blinked. The sway of the white mare under him was growing comfortable. He forgot himself enough to turn in the saddle and look up at Lucifer's face. The rebel angel smiled down slantwise. "This is Hell? I had expected —"

:Torment. Aye: Lucifer hesitated. Will realized that his black steed wore no reins. :What torment, Master Shakespeare, could I heap upon thee worse that that which thou hast chosen for thyself?:

"Your . . . Highness?"

:Really, Master Shakespeare. How dost thou think thou can serve *us*, poet, when thou canst not keep even thy troth to thy wife, or thy Ganymede, or thy mistress? All three at once thou hast betrayed —:

Stung, Will reined his mount further from the Devil's side. She protested when he tried to bring her too far, and afraid of being thrown, he desisted. "Kit lied —"

:Nay: Lucifer's sky-blue regard spurned him. :He told thee whatever truth thou wouldst hear. How *darest* thou press thy lovers, thy wife to meet a standard thou canst not uphold?:

Will raised his right hand to his mouth, feeling the moment of re-alization like a dagger in the breast. *This is what Annie felt,* he realized. *Felt and forgave. And as I cannot love less —*

—neither then can she.

"I have," he said, the reins tumbling from his fingers. The white mare sidled next to Lucifer's black stud, rubbing her shoulder against his, brushing Will's knee against the Devil's with a tingle Will would have preferred to deny. "I have made mine own Hell. I deserve it."

:Every creature does: the Devil answered, and they rode on in silence for one hour or a thousand, until they passed the low-arched gates of Hell.

Act III, scene xvii

My bloodless body waxeth chill and cold,
And with my blood my life slides through my wound,
My soul begins to take her flight to hell:
And summons all my senses to depart.

—CHRISTOPHER MARLOWE, *Tamburlaine the Great*

The red gelding ran hard. Kit bent low over his neck, mane stinging his face, and did battle with the impulse that would have had
him clutch the reins like a fool and kick the willing horse faster. The
gelding's hooves rattled on gravel and then thudded on packed earth;
the way grew narrow and dark. Kit hunched closer to his horse and
reined the gelding back, swearing, as the long angry claws of leafless
oak trees reached across to bar the path and scrape his face, yank at
his cloak and hair. *This should be the beech wood. I should smell the sea.*

Somewhere ahead, unwavering, growing more distant despite
their deliberation and Kit's weeping haste, he could hear the even pace
of hooves laid against stone like church bells. Trees closed across the
path. Kit bulled the sorrel through branches; the horse went snorting,
plunging, shivering with eagerness to be free of the trees and *run*.

Kit closed his eye against welling tears of frustration, could do
nothing for the ones that soaked his eyepatch. He pulled his cloak

around his sore bruised body against a chill; *Morgan's patch, and the troll's. One from the Mebd and one from Will. Cairbre, Geoffrey, Puck —*

The wood was dark as the bottom of a well. Even the sorrel shivered.

A good gelding, steady and swift. Kit patted his neck. "I wish I had thought to ask your name."

Low and distant, a croak. *Froggy frogs.*

"Master Troll?" *How odd, when I was just now thinking of him —*
Trust the horse.

The voice came from the left. If it was a voice, and not Kit's desperation and the wind.

He can't possibly do a worse job of it than I have. Kit swore one more time, for good measure, and let the gelding have his head. He stroked the sorrel's rough mane and looped the reins around the pommel, then leaned forward to speak into a swiveling ear. "Find him for me." *Please.*

The red horse snorted, both ears back briefly, then switched his tail and walked boldly forward through the thickest stand of oak. The road lay beyond, broad and shining in the starlight. Kit reached for the reins again, let them fall when the gelding tossed his head.

"If you know what you're doing —" He caught the mane in both hands. "Well, let us make haste."

The horse struck out at an easy canter, clatter of hooves on stone. Over it Kit heard that pealing, *tang tang tang*, measured as a pavanne. *I don't pavanne.* But he kept up now, never gaining, rising in the saddle to see farther ahead. A glimmer of golden light shone on the pavement: a candleflame.

A lantern.

A crossroads.

Bloody Hell. Where went they?

The sorrel never hesitated. Kit touched the horse with his boots; he sprang past the abandoned light as if it had caught his heels on fire. The way was darker here, tending downward. Relief and horror did battle in Kit, and for a moment he thought he caught the acrid scent of whiskey and char. The trees fell back from the roadside. Alone in the night, Kit heard something huge rustling through leaves. *Just the wind.*

Of course.

But there was no breeze on his neck. And now the road descended through nothing at all but blackness to either side.

By the time he saw the broad-pillared gate, his tears had dried, leaving the taste of salt on his tongue. The sorrel snorted and struck sparks from the roadway, refusing the passage. Kit nodded and checked to make sure the reins were knotted so they wouldn't foul the horse's legs. "Brave enough," Kit said, swinging down. He rubbed the sorrel's nose, turned him back up the road, and slipped his bit. "I could not ask more. Go, get home. There's a warm stable for thee."

The gelding looked over his shoulder dubiously. Kit raised his left hand over the animal's lathered flank, trying for menace; the sorrel shrugged and ambled back up the road as if to say, *I might have waited a bit. Just to see if you were coming back. But if you insist —*

Kit squared his shoulders, turned his back on the sorrel, and walked quickly toward the gate. Quickly, because if he let his feet drag he would never pass under that plain black archway, no higher than the overhead reach of his hands.

It was as well he'd left the horse behind; within the gate the road turned to a narrow stair, and Kit fumbled down in the chill, over dank, slick stones. He leaned on the wall, sweat freezing in sequins on his skin, and willed his heart to beat. Cold, searing cold, and he chuckled nastily in memory of a scene he'd written so many years before, Mephostophilis warming Faustus' frozen blood with a brazier so that it would run through a pen.

This place smelled of leaf mold, of earthworms, of fresh-turned earth. Behind Kit, a gray light like morning was growing; he noticed when he glanced over his shoulder to see if the archway was still in sight, and did not look back a second time. He feared if he did turn he would keep turning, and keep walking, and never force himself downward again.

He counted as he descended.

On the one hundred and thirteenth step he lost the sound of hoof-beats. On the three hundred and eleventh step he lost the light. There was no railing; he leaned on the wall and felt for the edge of the step with his toe. The rattle of the iron nails in his boots gave him hope.

My father's hand. In hope. And then, bitterly, *I saw the back side of it often enough.*

He lost count.

His left hand fell on something leathery in the darkness; Kit jumped backward, squeaking like a wench who's brushed up against a rat in the cellar. He would have fallen—*Jesu*—all the bottomless way, but something moist and strong wrapped his wrist and pulled him hard against the wall. He grunted, scrabbled, found his footing with a twisted ankle that would have been much worse without the bracing of his boots.

A cold exhalation pressed his ear. The smell of loam and leaf mold redoubled; Kit held his breath until his heart no longer felt fit to leap through his chest. The predatory grip on his wrist never eased.

Another exhalation. A slow voice, inflectionless, half rumble and half hiss. "Who passes, and on what errand?" The demon's maw gleamed red when it spoke: the only light in the world, silhouetting serrated teeth as if on coals.

Kit swallowed. *This is real. Now.* "Marley." The smallness of his own voice angered him. "I come to bargain with your master. Let me pass."

"My master?" Silence, that Kit somehow knew was laughter. He wondered if the thing saw his own face lit red when its mouth opened. "My master treats with none that can not pass by me."

Kit himself glimpsed nothing but the fangs. *It can see in the dark,* he realized. "Must I fight you, then?"

"You must pay the toll," the demon said, releasing his wrist quite negligently. "What will you pay it with?"

Kit crowded back against the far wall of the narrow stair. He laid a hand on the hilt of his blade, did not yet dare draw it. *Well, I won't offer you the pound of flesh nearest my heart, and that's for certain.* "That depends on the going rate." It was eerie speaking so, as if the blackness itself could hear him and answer.

" 'Tis easier to buy thy way *in* to Hell than out," the demon allowed. "Your remaining eye, perhaps? Your good right hand?"

Kit blinked, understanding. *Just like bargaining in the marketplace. I'll not be thee'd down to by demons, either—* "I'm surprised thou didst not commence with mine immortal soul."

"Ah," the demon said, casting a glare as it licked its maw with a lingering tongue. Light between its teeth like pipe smoke; Kit caught a swift impression of clawed leathery paws, of scaled masculine tits and paunch over hair-thatched legs. The demon was impressively, unpleasantly male. "No such delicacies for me. But a taste of sweet man flesh—" It shrugged. "Or of a sweet, tight arse—"

Kit pressed himself against the wall and pulled his sword into his hand, the scrape of metal on scabbard reassuring. "My flesh is not for dining on."

Scales rasped on stone; hair rubbed on hair. Kit forced himself to look where the thing's mouth and, he supposed, its eyes would be, and not strain at the darkness for another glimpse of its talons or its forked, knobby member. It chuckled through its nose, a dying-ember glow limning its nostrils.

Kit swallowed hard. "Or any other sport thou mightst desire to make upon it."

"Pity," the thing said, its voice very close, the coals in its belly glaring. Kit tasted its cold breath on his face. "That blade is Faerie silver, mortal man."

"Aye." Kit brandished it at nothing, felt the tip prick nothing and slide through. A heavy slick sound, and he knew the thing had sidestepped upward. Kit turned to cover it with the blade, boots clattering on the steps. He kept his blind eye to the wall, although it restricted his sword arm; he suspected the sword wouldn't help him much, all in all.

"The sword will do for payment." The demon opened its mouth wide, the glow revealing more than Kit desired to see.

"And when thou hast it?"

"Thou mayst pass freely."

"And return?"

That silence that was laughter; the tilt of the scaled, fanged head. Horns broad as a bull's caught the unholy light. "That," the thing said, "is my master's to decide."

Well enough, Kit said, and reversed the sword in his hand to offer it to the demon.

"Pass," the thing said, and struck its fist against the wall.

Pallid and silver, starlight spilled through the opening. *A doorway*, Kit realized, and started forward, curiously lighter without his rapier.

He half expected the demon to snatch him back by the scruff, but he passed through unmolested and the stone of the wall ground closed like a prison door. Kit found himself standing in the midst of a vast blank plain, his nailed boots his only security on the slick surface beneath him. He could no longer hear the gay peal of hoofbeats on stone, and an ashen glow like starshine filled the air from no identifiable source, omnidirectional, shadowless. Some distance ahead, he saw the rippling movement of water between smooth, low banks. *Styx?* he wondered. *Acheron? Cocytus or Lethe, perhaps; not Phlegethon. No sign of fire.*

A shadow moved across it; the outline of a ferryman, tall and stooped, bent to the pole. Kit felt for his purse; there was gold in it enough to pay the passage there and back, he hoped. Boots skidding on the glasslike landscape beneath his feet, he struck out cautiously for the water's edge.

Whatever river that is, I know I don't want to fall in.

Kit watched his feet at first, until he saw vaporous things moving beneath the landscape like drowning men clawing under clear, thick ice. He wrenched his eyes upward; the shadows flinched when he walked across them, and yet they pressed their vaporous hands, their hollow-socketed faces against the barrier. He almost thought he heard them pleading, screaming. They swarmed after him like trout swirling toward crumbs cast on water: arms outreached in supplication, faces averted in pain.

He slipped sideways, almost went down. Then placed his feet the way Will did when Will was tired and staggering; short steps, straight up and down like walking on icy cobbles. He fixed his eyes on the ferryman poling to meet him and found his lips shaping Latin words. "Pater noster qui es in cœlis, Sanctificetur nomen tuum. Adveniat regnum tuum. Fiat voluntas tua, sicut in cœlo, et in terra—" He bit his cheek until blood flowed, and couldn't silence the litany. *Panem nostrum quotidiamum da nobis hodie et dimitte nobis debita nostra, sicut et nos dimittimus debitoribus nostris. Et ne nos inducas in tentationem. Sed libera nos a malo. Oremus.*

"Christ on the cross."

Kit.

Ridiculous.

Thou'rt in Hell, boy. Here to trade thyself for the freedom of your lewd, your unclean, your bestial and unnatural love. What maketh an abomination like thee to think thou'lt get any good from an Our Father?

Kit walked, exertion warming his body, failing to numb his thoughts. The words were as unstoppable as the gray water rippling in the haunting light so far ahead. He heard both parts of the litany, prompt and response, as if two voices spoke within. He hadn't prayed so in— Hell, in eleven years and more.

Domine salvum fac servum tuum qui suam fiduciam in te collocat. Mitte eum Domine angelum de sanctuario tuo. Et potenter defende eum. Nihil prævaleat inimicus in eo Et filius iniquitatis non noceat ei. Esto ei Domini turris fortitudinis a facie inimici. Domine exaudi orationem nostram et clamor noster ad te veniat.

Oremus.

Oremus.

"Deliver us from evil," Kit scoffed aloud. "Useless, methinks, when I'm plain walking into it." And yet he stopped and looked about, there on the barren moor of Hell, the damned writhing under his feet. *What, Kit? Art waiting for an answer?*

"Oh, Sweet Christofer."

An infinitely welcome voice from over his shoulder, and he closed his eye a moment in joy and relief, unwilling to believe.

But the voice continued. "My love, you came."

"Will." He turned, and looked up into his lover's face. "I can't believe it. It worked."

Will's smile folded the corners of gray-blue eyes. He raised his arms, and Kit came into them, lifting his mouth for a kiss that was suddenly the only thing in all the world he wanted.

"Thou hast forgiven me," Kit said, when the kiss was ended and still his lover held him tight.

"Thou dost taste of ashes," Will said, stepping back. "Was the way very long? Thou shouldst drink—"

"Ashes to ashes," Kit answered, releasing Will only with reluctance. "Drink of that river? I think not." Kit turned to look upon it, putting Will on his blind side. Kit frowned with cracked lips, scrubbing sore, itching palms. "What river is it?"

"What does it matter? Thou must drink—"

"—nay—"

"—else thou canst not stay here with me."

Kit blinked. He tasted blood from his bitten cheek. *Deliver us from evil.* He rubbed his hand across his lips, startled when red blood streaked his glove.

No. Not from his cheek. From his lips, from his tongue.

He turned his hand over, gasped when he saw the burned-through palms of his gloves, the blistered flesh of his palms, the smoldering scorches on his doublet where it showed under the patchwork of his cloak. His cloak smoked too, but seemed unharmed, and the flesh beneath it was not burning. Kit raised his eyes; something red and supple as a lizard winked at him with a slitted yellow eye, gleaming in colors like fire.

"Salamander."

"Ifrit," it said with a mocking bow, flickering through shapes like a windblown torch—a red-haired woman, a stallion with a mane aflame, a dragon no bigger than a hummingbird. "I am the second guardian. I'll have your cloak before you pass."

Kit drew it close about his shoulders with his blistered hand. "This cloak that saved me from you?"

"Aye, well," the ifrit answered. "There's a price for everything. You'll also need to pay the ferryman."

Kit thought of edging past it. Sparks flashed from its eyes; it grew again into the image of Will Shakespeare, but flames flickered at its fingertips. He saw that the damned underfoot squirmed away from its footsteps, huddling behind Kit as if Kit could defend them.

"This cloak is valued of me," Kit said.

"That's why it buys you passage." The ifrit extended an imperious hand. " 'Tis that, or thy smoking heart. Thou goest before my master clad in thine own power only, and nothing borrowed may come."

"Ah," Kit said, and shrugged the heavy cloth off of his shoulders. He folded it over his arm, twice and then again, running his fingers over scraps of velvet and silk and brocade. *Thank you, Morgan. Thank you, Master Troll.* "I'll have it back when I return."

"Perhaps," the ifrit said, and plucked the cloak off Kit's arm. Both cloak and spirit vanished in a swirl of hot wind and shadows, and Kit swore under his breath.

Lighter still, he walked to the ferry. It seemed easier now; he closed the distance in the space of a few heartbeats, and stood waiting while the boat grounded on the glassy shore and the ropy, bare-chested figure at the pole beckoned.

Kit stepped over the gunnels and found a place near the prow, facing the pilot. "What is the fare, Master Ferryman?"

"The thing that you can least afford to lose," the figure answered, scrubbing a hand over his bald scalp before pushing off. His trews seemed gray in the dim, directionless light, and they were rolled almost to the knee and belted with a bit of ivory rope. His horny feet were bare.

No rope bound the ferry on its path too and fro—and yet the boat cut clear and straight across the rushing river, making a clean angle to the farther shore. "What river is this?" he asked, once the ferryman had settled into a rhythm.

"Lethe."

Kit licked blistered lips. "So the ifrit urged me drink."

"Drink, and forget all pain."

Kit leaned back against the bow. The bank they had left retreated rapidly. He turned to look over his shoulder; the far bank seemed no nearer. "All pain. All joy. No, thank you."

The ferryman poled in silence for a little. "You were eight years old in 1572."

"I turned nine—"

"At the end of it, aye. But in November? December?"

"I had measured eight summers. Aye. How do you know me so well, Master Ferryman?"

"It is my task to know. Do you remember what was special about that Christmas, Master Poet?"

Kit thought back. "The new star. Bright orange, it was. Visible by daylight—"

"Aye. A new star in the heavens. A change upon the face of what many said was ineluctable destiny. It tormented the learned astrologers greatly."

Kit swallowed frustration; even though he spoke, the man poled fast. Surely they must be nearing the far bank shortly. He turned, and was surprised by the distance still to cover. "What purpose these questions?"

"Idle conversation," the ferryman said, and fell silent.

Kit glanced over his shoulder again. "How wide is this river, Master Ferryman?"

"As wide as it needs to be." The steady rhythm of the pole continued, a little wake lifting in curls beside the bow. "You cannot land until you pay."

Kit pressed his blistered palms together. He needed the gloves off, and to bathe his hands; not in *this* water, but he started peeling off the ruined kidskin anyway. "The thing I can least afford to lose? My life? I cannot pay that—"

"There's something that has done you great service in your life, though you oft have denied it." The ferryman never looked up from the water.

"Not Will either—"

"You lost *that* yourself. Hell had naught to do with it."

Lost. Kit threw his gloves at his feet. Blood welled from his burns; he'd torn the skin. *Lost.* "Then what?"

The ferryman kicked the soles of Kit's boots, never skipping a beat with his pole. The river made sounds against the boat like a maiden's kisses. "Those will do for a symbol."

Because it is. It's symbols and the manipulation of symbols. Names and poetry. Even here. Kit's brows rose in comprehension; the band of his eyepatch cut his forehead. "Those are all I have from my father."

"No," the ferryman said. "You have also his love, which led him to let you become this thing he could not understand. Because you needed it so desperately, my boy."

Oh, Christ.

The ferryman shrugged. "One thing is the other."

Kit hesitated. "My father did not love me—"

"Didn't he? Doesn't he? In his own narrow, thoughtless, assuming tradesman's way? Hast never wished thou couldst love so, without the burden of thinking? Always *thinking?*"

Silence. And then, "Aye."

"Hast never wished to be free of his love, his demands?"

". . . aye." Kit's voice had gone small again. He didn't bother, this time, to correct it.

"Then take off his boots."

Kit lifted his foot across his knee and touched the leather. It smelled of saddle soap and bootblack. The old hide was supple and well-worn under his hand. His wrist had no strength suddenly; he hooked his fingers around the heel and wriggled his foot, and the boot would not shift.

Or perhaps, more precisely, Kit would not shift it.

He looked once more. The shore was no closer.

" 'Tis the same to me if we never arrive. I pole eternally."

Will.

Kit closed his eye and jerked the boot hard enough to burn his foot. He yanked the other one off as well and tossed them at the ferryman's feet. "Is that all?"

"Get up," the ferryman answered as the prow of the boat ground on the rocky shore. "Get up, Kit Marlowe." His eyes flashed blue, amused.

Kit shuddered.

"Get up. Go in."

Socks on his feet, hands reddened and weeping, mouth split with fiery kisses, Kit stood and turned in the ferry and did as he was bid.

Act III, scene xviii

Let me excuse thee: ah! my love well knows
Her pretty looks have been mine enemies;
And therefore from my face she turns my foes,
That they elsewhere might dart their injuries:
Yet do not so; but since I am near slain,
Kill me outright with looks, and rid my pain.

—WILLIAM SHAKESPEARE, Sonnet 139

Lucifer's own long hands steadied Will down from the white mare; Will staggered as someone stroked brands of fire up his thighs, and Lucifer caught him. :Pained by the ride?:

"Excessively." Will forced his body to straighten and limped away. "By my troth, if I never set arse in a saddle again, it will be sooner than I like."

The white mare regarded him expressively from under fringed eyelashes. He bowed a pained apology, spongy pine needles squishing under his feet. "No offense intended, madam."

Lucifer folded his wings tight against his doublet and slanted the identical look at Will. :None taken, I presume:

The angel patted her on the shoulder. She leaned against him briefly, smearing white horsehairs on the black velvet of his doublet,

and trotted away through the pines. Drifts of needles thicker than a
rush mat muffled her hoofbeats to a rainy sound, and then she was
gone, trailing the tinkling of bells behind her. Lucifer's black stud
followed.

Will closed his eyes and breathed deep of still. "A forest? In Hell?"

:They call it the Wood of Suicides:

Will turned quickly to catch Lucifer's expression, but the Devil's face remained placid. "It's so serene. I thought the trees—" Will
looked up at their soaring heights, at the greeny-gold light that filtered
through the needles. He heard the ridiculousness of his own unconsid-
ered words. *You're talking to the Father of Lies as if he were a familiar friend,
as if thou wert on a country outing.* "—would be sad."

:Why?: Lucifer's wings resettled. Will wondered whether the fidg-
eting reflected the angel's emotions. :They have what they wanted. I
imagine they are as content as such folk may ever be. Beside that, 'tis
oaks who hate and oaks who act. As thou well shouldst know by now:

"Oaks who   "

Lucifer smiled. :Surely thou knowst the rhyme. The Faerie trees:
Ellum grieve, and oak he hate—:

"Willow he walk, if yew travels late," Will finished, and sank down on
the ground with his head clutched in his fingers, his eyes shut so tight
they pained him. It didn't hurt enough to satisfy; Will ground the heels
of his palms into his eye. "The Faerie trees. Oh God. Oh Christ."

The angel crouched beside him, wings opening wide for balance,
or perhaps to shield Will's grief from the pitiless sky. He did not touch
Will, and Will was grateful for it. :I see: he said softly, :that thou didst
not understand how strongly some factions in Faerie oppose the Mebd,
and Gloriana, and anything that supports them. Master Shakespeare,
I must plead thine indulgence; it did not occur to me that thou hadst
not realized the connection:

"The Fae killed Hamnet," Will said, just to hear it given voice. So
calm and even. It must have been someone else, speaking the barb-
tipped words. *It was my fault. They did it to stop me writing. To break me and
drive me home.* "The Fae killed Hamnet. Because of me."

:Aye: Lucifer said. :Not all the Fae. But those who have no love for
Elizabeth and less love yet for the Daoine Sidhe:

Will's throat burned. His eyes were dry, somehow, although there was no strength in his arms or legs to lift him from the sweet-smelling carpet of needles. "It didn't work."

:Nor shall it now. Thy will is greater than it seems, Master Shakespeare: The wings spread, arched, sheltering.

Despite himself, Will laughed painfully at the pun. The smell of woodsmoke surrounded him, sweet and pungent, as if exhaled from Lucifer's feathers and skin.

"Someone will pay for this," Shakespeare said softly.

Lucifer patted him on the shoulder and offered him a hand. :Someone generally does. Come, Master Shakespeare, let me show you to your cottage, where you may begin your revenge:

Will wobbled when he stood, his hands trembling more than they had in Faerie, his arse and his inner thighs still aflame. He was thankful when Lucifer dropped his hand. The angel's touch was—not what Will would have expected. "A cottage and not a dungeon, Your Highness?"

:A poet with naught to poesy on but dungeons is of but little use: Lucifer walked ahead, arms swinging freely with his stride, wings luffing like sails. :Thou mayest go where thou list, and pass without fear. Here in Hell:

Will almost walked into a tree, unable to take his eyes from Lucifer. Lucifer did not return the regard. "I'm free?"

:Where couldst hide that Hell's master could not find thee, an I wish't? Ah. Here is thy home:

Home. The word had the sound of a hammer driving coffin nails. Will turned to regard a little cottage under the trees, a vegetable garden in a sunny glade beside it, a stone well with a yellow bucket resting on the lip. The smell of cool water and vegetable blossoms filled the air. "This?"

:Aye: Lucifer said. :I think thou wilt find what thou dost need within. Good morrow, Master Shakespeare—:

"Your Highness," Will said softly. *Don't leave me alone.* "What am I to do here?"

Lucifer, turning, looked over his shoulder and smiled. :Write poetry:

Will stood, mouth gaping. "A quiet cottage in the woods is *Hell,* Lord Lucifer?"

The angel smiled. :It shan't be quiet. Thou'lt have thy son and all thy many loves and failures to keep thee company, or I misjudge thee sorely:

Will shuddered. And Lucifer smiled, but it looked like sorrow. He dropped his eyes to the forest floor and drew a breath—Will saw it swell his wings. :I trust thou wilt find those adequate companions:

Will said not another word, but watched Lucifer vanish through the trees. He didn't turn to look at the homely cottage, its verdant garden, the warm coil of smoke rising from the chimney. He sat down on the arched sweep of a root and laid his chin in his hands.

"Oh, Annie," he said, miserably, what might have been hours later. "Oh, Hamnet. What have I done?"

Act III, scene xix

I'll frame me wings of wax like Icarus,
And o'er his ships will soar unto the Sun,
That they may melt and I fall in his arms.

—CHRISTOPHER MARLOWE, *Dido, Queen of Carthage*

A pleasant enough chamber, if a room walled with shadows and floored in cold stone—floating like a ship on a nothing sea—were one's ideal of pleasantry. Kit turned at its center as the ferry poled into oblivion, noticing spare furnishings, a master mason's hand in the angles where the stones turned down into the abyss. "Christ wept," he murmured.

:So he did: A voice like a fistful of velvet dragged across Kit's skin. Kit swallowed and turned toward his blind side. He might have raised his right hand to check if his jaw was hanging open, but didn't quite.

Father of Lies, Kit reminded himself, but nothing could have prepared him for the confounding beauty of the figure in black who faced him, a raptor's fanned wings glowing soft and pale as moonlight. Lucifer Morningstar tugged elegant fingers through tousled golden locks and smiled. :Sir Christofer: he said, furling his wings. :What an—unexpected—pleasure. May I offer you some refreshment?:

Kit licked dry lips with a tongue that failed to moisten them. He shook his head.

The Devil sauntered catlike toward him and shrugged as if to say—*suit yourself*. A casual gesture and a wineglass appeared in his hand, his fingers cupped around the bowl as if to a lover's cheek.

God help me.

:He looks in now and again: Lucifer commented, brow bent like a bow to dart that glance. :Thou dost interest me. Such eloquence in thee. And such pain:

As if pain were a thing to be savored.

The wings flipped and settled, and Kit's stomach flipped with them, in fear and something else. One white wing extended, a drift of snow glittering against the dark. Primaries trailed on dark stone as Lucifer paced in slow orbit. Deosil, sunwise, moving always to Kit's blind side and so forcing Kit to turn. Idly swirling that red wine in its glass, until a few drops scattered over the rim and splashed. :Thou hast a gift for the ages, Sir Christofer. Would that thou wouldst consider an allegiance with Hell:

Kit drew a breath. Feathers flicked the back of his calves. They carried a rich, earthy musk he knew. He wasn't sure where he found the humor he put into his voice, but he managed it. "I've come to bargain, not offer allegiance."

:I could make it very pleasant for thee. Thou hast a fascination with power—:

"Get thee behind me, Satan."

A wink broke the horse-trader's appraisal in the Devil's gaudy eyes. :The thought had occurred:

"Are angels equipped for such roguery?"

:Like man, made in God's image—:

"—So God has an arsehole?"

:Yes. He calls him Michael: Lucifer laughed in such merriment that Kit smiled, despite the trembling knot in his belly. :Surely, thou hast heard of *l'osculum infame*:

"The infamous kiss. Your kiss. The one that bestows power of witchcraft. 'Tis not a kiss on the mouth, I hear."

Lucifer only smiled.

"Rutting with devils is sorcery."

:So is rutting with boys. Of a kind with bestiality in thy human law books. It's all sodomy, dear poet:

"Only sodomy." Kit laughed. "Enough to burn on; but hanged for a lamb, hanged for a ewe—is that what you insinuate? What virtue lies in your kiss, then, Prince of Darkness?"

:No virtue at all. But power. Come, kiss me and discover—:

"Am I Faustus? Shall a man be confused with his creations?"

:Nay. Thou art Marley, who should know better, and come to bargain nonetheless:

The Prince of Darkness spread his wings as if stretching. Kit had never seen anything so white—swans nor snow, limestone nor linen. They gleamed as if sunlit from behind. Kit's fingers itched to stroke their arm-long primaries. Face burning, he forced his gaze to the well-masoned stones under his boots.

:Thou'rt fascinated:

". . . Yes." Kit folded his hands like a repentant schoolboy.

:Wouldst care to touch?:

"Touch?"

Lucifer smiled over the rim of his wineglass and flexed the trailing wing forward. Kit clenched fist in fist as the pinions breathed coolly across his cheek, trailed down his throat, bending where they brushed his doublet, a pressure like fingertips braced against his breast. :Touch:

Kit disentangled his fingers from each other *Lord how can he be so beautiful* and hesitantly raised his right hand *as if in oath* and laid it gently, gently on the leading edge of that vast white wing. Rapture swelled his breast; he half expected to yank his hand back, fingertips scorched, but the feathers were cool and firm and slick over buried warmth. Bone and muscle moved beneath strong flexing plumage, tiny barbs catching the ridges of his fingertips with a rasp more felt than heard. He let those fingers burrow through feathers, into down soft as blown thistleseeds, to the blood-hot membrane beneath. *And what has become of the burns on my hands?*

Lucifer shivered, a reflexive twitch of skin like a fly-bitten horse. Ravishing.

"Can you fly?"

The wing flicked from his fingers like snatched paper, snapped shut with a slapped drumhead sound. :If I care to: Lucifer set his glass aside—it vanished when it left his fingertips—and moved toward Kit, golden curls in disorder against the black velvet of his doublet. He raised sinewy fingers and pressed them curiously against Kit's forehead, hooking the strap of his eyepatch and dropping it to the floor. :Oh, thou art too lovely for this:

Kit thought he should step back, but the Devil's fingers were cool against his scar. "I should think to you, the damaged—vessel—might hold more appeal."

:Perfection in all things: Lucifer said.

He caressed Kit's sightless eye with rose-pale lips, the writhing shadows of his crown brushing Kit's face with a palpable touch. :There. Scars do not suit thee:

Kit blinked. And then gasped, because he *could* blink, and beyond blinking he could *see.*

Not as he would have seen before. Not as he would see with his left eye, even now. But—he looked for a word—but *otherwise.* The Devil still stood before him, close enough to kiss again, but on the right side Kit saw him as a vining of light and darkness, a twist of contradictions. Kit would have stepped back, but somehow those wings had crossed behind his back; he stood encircled by them and enfolded by the rich, heady pungency of sweat and good tobacco.

"I've dreamed of you," Kit said, wondering.

:And hast thy dream come true?:

"Not yet." But he wasn't sure it was truth as he said it.

:Now: Lucifer whispered, and his *breath* at least was as hot as Kit thought it should be. :Bargain with me:

Kit swallowed, shivered. The Devil's hands stayed slack and open by his sides; only the wings restrained Kit. Who raised his chin to meet eyes that twitched at the corner with an almost smile. "Will Shakespeare," he said. "I'm here to buy his life."

:The cost of *that* is dear:

"How dear?" *I could take his place—if I had to. But mayhap there's something else. . . .* "I could pay you with a song."

:Thine art might be enough to buy his freedom. Thy soul:

"Mine art. All of it?"

Just that smile. The wings parted, shifted, opened. Lucifer stepped

away—half lovely swan-winged man, half vortex of light and shadow—
and looked down, bowing his long aristocratic neck.

"What about my body?"

A gesture, as if the Devil reached out and pulled something from a
table, although there was no table near him. He wheeled about, wings
furled tight, their peaks reaching three foot or more over his head,
their primaries brushing the floor. Still silent, he tossed the black thing
that swung from his fingers at Kit. It sailed heavily though the air; Kit
got his hands up in time and caught it, barking his fingertips.

And almost dropped it, when he saw what he held.

Rough iron bands abraded his skin; if it were locked in place they
would go across the top of his skull, under the chin, around the sides.
Hinges made the thing to be opened. A padlock hung from the cheek-
piece. The bit or mouthpiece was flat and broad, the size of a small
woman's palm, scattered with blades that would score his tongue and
palate, worse if he was so foolish as to try to talk.

It weighed a great deal.

"A scold's bridle."

Lucifer smiled, and—as if the smile cast a shadow over him—
seemed to change and darken. Kit found himself looking further up,
into eyes he saw in his nightmares. *Richard Baines. God help me—*

"Holla," the image said, his lips moving gently, "ye pampered
Jades of Asia—"

Kit might have dropped the thing in his hands and run. But there
was only abyss to run to, and his right eye showed him that same
dancing twist of mocking light with the suggestion of wings behind it.
And Will was here. *Somewhere.*

"Father of Lies," Kit said.

White feathers settled. :Welcome to Hell, Christofer Marley. What
wilt thou sell me for the freedom of thy friend?:

"I—" He looked down at the instrument of torture in his hands,
and remembered something a Faerie Queen had said, about mortal
men and bindings. "If this is what it takes, Satan, I will do it. But I
think I have something you would value more than a little sport to my
torment."

An arched eyebrow rose. The Devil tilted his head politely, waiting for Kit to continue.

"My name," Kit said, and let the bridle fall. It vanished before it could clank on the stones. He wondered if it had ever existed. "I'll sell you my name, for Will's freedom."

He swallowed, but the Devil smiled. :Done: he answered promptly, leaving Kit to wonder if he had made a bad bargain indeed. :Thou art Christofer Marley no more. And more, I tell thee—it will be a long time indeed before thou art remembered for what thou hast been, and not what thine enemies proclaim thee. Thy trials are not over, in Faerie or the mortal realm:

"How bad will it be?"

:Bad. But all is illusion and memory. Thee, and me. God, and the world. Faerie and Hell:

Kit turned and walked to the edge of that vanishing tile of stone, floating in an infinite absence. "Where are the damned?" he asked, which was not what he had intended to ask at all.

The words seemed to surround Kit, floating on the air like the toll of the bell, the fumes of the snuffed candle that should accompany them. *Wherefore in the name of God the All-powerful, Father, Son, and Holy Ghost, of the Blessed Peter, Prince of the Apostles, and of all the saints, in virtue of the power which has been given us of binding and loosing in Heaven and on earth, we deprive Christofer Marley himself and all his accomplices and all his abettors of the Communion of the Body and Blood of Our Lord, we separate him from the society of all Christians, we exclude him from the bosom of our Holy Mother the Church in Heaven and on earth, we declare him excommunicated and anathematized and we judge him condemned to eternal fire with Satan and his angels and all the reprobate, so long as he will not burst the fetters of the demon, do penance, and satisfy the Church; we deliver him to Satan to mortify his body, that his soul may be saved on the day of judgment.*

:Is that what thou didst expect?: Satan asked. :Eternal fire, and the demons of Hell forking souls into furnaces like so much coke for burning?:

"I—" No. Ridiculous, on the face of it. But—

:The damned are all around thee:

"Those creatures on the glassy plain. Lost creatures, aye. But I saw—I see no souls in torment, Father of Lies."

:Seest thou not thyself? Seest thou not Satan and his angels, then?:

"Am I damned? I feel no fire upon my skin, or on my soul—"

:Fire cannot kiss thy soul, who was Christofer Marley. Such con-
ceits are for simpler hearts than thine. Thou art in Hell, and have been
every day of thy life since thy God abandoned thee in a little room
in France. And thou, brave soul, reconstructed Him into a God that
could love thee. But thou hast not the power to change God:

Kit closed his eyes, without turning. He felt the cup of a warm
wing against his shoulder, and knew Satan came to stand beside him.
"Haven't I?"

:Perhaps thou art more powerful than I: Lucifer admitted, and
Kit studied his profile. Leander. Adonis. Apollo. His body straight as
Circe's wand— Eyes as blue as Heaven looked on the darkness, un-
flinching, and then turned to regard Kit from beneath lashes frosted
in gold. :I have not succeeded. Is it not what children wish, a father's
acceptance? His love?:

"Yes," Kit said, into a hollowness that echoed. "If Hell is not torment," he asked, knowing the answer, "then what is Hell?" *If I fell, would
he come after me? On those white, white wings? Or would I fall forever, like*— Kit
stepped away from the abyss, retreated to the center. *—like him.*

:Sweet child: Lucifer said. And then said what Kit had always
known he would. :*Why this is hell: nor am I out of it. Thinkst thou that I
that saw the face of God, and tasted the eternal joys of heaven am not tormented
with ten thousand hells, In being deprived of everlasting bliss? O Faustus leave
these frivolous demands, which strikes a terror to my fainting soul*:

Kit's own words, given into the mouth of a seductive devil.
"Mephostophilis."

And again, the angel smiled. :*Hell hath no limits, nor is circumscribed
In one self place. But where we are is hell, And where hell is there must we ever be.
And to be short, when all the world dissolves, And every creature shall be purified,
All places shall be hell that is not heaven*:

That agony in his chest must be his inability to breathe, Kit
thought. The burning in his eyes, the taint of Hell.

:O child: Lucifer said into Kit's silence, :how canst thou deny what
thou thyself hast written, and known to be Truth as it was revealed to
thee?:

Kit scrubbed his hands on his breeches, as if to remove some rusty
stain. He tried to ignore the Devil circling, wings fallen into expan-

sion like a courting hawk's, but Lucifer caught his wrists and drew him close, nose to nose, mouth to mouth. :Hell: he said :is where God is not:

I am damned. His knees rattled. The Devil's strength held him up.

:Thou art as God made thee: Wry, startling humor. :As are we all:

"What could such as you want with such as me?"

:We have our reasons. Thou livest with demons that fright thee more than I do, and so for that which thou art as much as that which thou dost carry inside thee, as I have healed thy scars, I will give thee the power to destroy thine enemies:

"that which thou dost carry inside thee?" "Power. How?"

:Why: the Devil answered, his fingers dimpling Kit's skin, :Be thou a warlock, who was Christofer Marley. I shall make of thee a witch, as I have bewitched men before thee. As thou hast said . . . 'Tis only sodomy:

"Only." But he tasted something on the word. *Revenge.*

:Lover: the Devil whispered. :Brother. Thou givest me that only which is already mine:

Kit closed his eyes on the glorious eyes, the broad white wings, the twist of fire and purity that was the Prince of God's Angels, and whispered—*yes.*

Lucifer smiled, and this kiss—tasting of whiskey and smoke—began with Kit's lips and ended there—after an exploratory interval, during which clothing vanished by magic under the touch of caressing hands. Kit pressed both palms to the fallen angel's smooth-muscled back, clawing fingers digging for purchase against the base of those wings. Lucifer's forked tongue stopped his mouth as effectively as the scold's bridle would have, and Kit didn't care; the angel's arms clipped and embraced him, lifting him bodily, cradling him against the perfect strength of a chest that might have been carved of warm white marble by some Grecian master.

The angel knelt, never breaking the kiss, wings fanning wide for balance, their breeze pulling soft fingers through Kit's hair as Lucifer drew him down to straddle white thighs. Powerful shoulders, deep-rooted muscle nothing like a man's flexed under Kit's fingers, sliding beneath soft skin and slick feathers. Kit broke the breathlessness of the kiss to gasp sharply. With one hand he stroked the angel's belly, wrapped the silken member that dented the flesh of his thigh. The angel shuddered again, as he had when Kit touched his wing.

Lucifer drew back, glanced down, and smiled in intimate provocation. Kit's loins ached as if the regard were a caress.

:Come unto me:

The Devil's hands clenched on his flanks, lifting him without effort, indenting flesh and coaxing him open. Soft hands, strong. Kit winced in anticipation, wrapped his arms around Lucifer's neck to bear his weight, for all it seemed as nothing to the angel. *Witchcraft,* he thought, *how cunning, how quaint.* A silent chuckle shivered his belly, breath becoming an expectant whimper as Kit braced himself for a pain that never arrived. *If He hurts you, silly boy, it will not be out of carelessness —*

It came not as a thrust, or as the lingering accommodation that gentleness had almost seduced Kit into expecting. But one massive downsweep of those incredible wings hurled them upright — one, and then another, as the pale perfect mouth found Kit's again and Lucifer stood in a fluid arc, and Kit was pierced.

"Christ," Kit whispered, impassioned, hearing his own awe and fear, disbelief thick in his voice.

:'Tis not Christ thou wilt bear on thy back: Amusement, wryness. Wrathful irony, almost a lover's teasing. Lucifer's hair tumbled down around Kit's face, bearing his smoky, bitter, musky scent.

This is not real. This is not happening. There is no Devil. There is no Hell. God is love, and God judges not what is done in love — "Christ, Christ, Christ. . . ." *Rapt. Speaking in tongues. Possessed.*

Yes, possessed.

:God: Warm arms and wings supported him. :God judges. And He is not pleased with His creation, for it can never echo His perfection and His will. He does not wish thy love. He commands thine obedience and fear. The Lord thy God is a jealous God, and thou wilt have no Gods before him:

Bitterness? Sorrow? Oh, but that mouth on his throat, on his breast. The effortless puissance bearing him up. A decade and more of rationalization stripped away by that calm, gentle voice in his mind. Passion on him again, divine will, and remembering the agony that had come with the realization that whatever God had made of Christofer

Marley, that Marley was a thing whose love the God of the Church would never return. A calling. The craving they named *vocation*.

Put away now with other childish things.

Raped away from God, and *So this is what Leda felt*, which made him giggle. Kit leaned into the embrace, trusting himself to those powerful arms, body decisive while his heart struggled and tore itself in his breast.

:No Gods before Him. Not even Love. To love God completely, thou must set aside all others:

The Devil moved in Kit, and Kit wept and clung. *Christ the Redeemer —*

:God's Redeemer, perhaps:

Oh God, forgive me —

:First He would have to forgive Himself. And that, I assure thee, he will not:

Father of Lies. Oh, Christ, Christ, Christ —

Silent laughter. :Is that the name thou chooseth for me?: A lingering caress. :'Tis sweet, isn't it, child?:

Did you like it, puss? But even that pain was so far buried that Kit had no answer, no speech, no reason; was too far lost for anything more eloquent than whimpered sacrilege. *Died blaspheming,* he thought, and laughed out loud, and cursed again.

Act III, scene xx

The Prince of darkness is a Gentleman.

—WILLIAM SHAKESPEARE, *King Lear*

Will dug all ten fingers to the knuckles into friable loam, sand gritting under his nails, leaning the weight of his shoulders behind it. The earth was black as Faerie ink; he unearthed another turnip and rubbed crumbles between his hands. Neither the resin of pine needles nor the bittersweetness of the fertile earth soothed the ache in his breast, as sharp as it had ever been for all he'd carved the notches of too many winters to count at a glance on both doorposts of the cottage.

It seemed the ever-freshness of his grief was one of Hell's many charms. Or perhaps it was simply being left alone with it; no one to speak to but the self-murdering trees, no way to express his soul except through the quill and paper Lucifer had left him. The ink which stayed ever fresh in the horn, for all Will would not set a pen into it.

This is Hell, nor am I out of it. He thought perhaps he would have preferred the rack, the irons, to the slow wearing of days on his will like water on stone. *Irons indeed: then I must be an iron Will, and let me rust shut.* He stood, hands trembling now the work was done, and picked his turnips up. The irons.

Aye, which led him to think of Kit's smooth chest, and the mark etched there that Will's palm could just cover, if he angled it properly. The irons, indeed.

And the irony: when he troubled himself to count, fitting his shaking hands into the notches he had carved in the posts beside the peeling blue-gray door, Will knew that Annie must be gone by now, Susanna and Judith quite possibly grandmothers, Elizabeth cold in her grave and Mary Poley and Richard Burbage and *thank Christ* Robert Poley and Richard Baines and that thrice-cursed old bastard Edward de Vere as well. The years slipped by like seasons; the seasons slipped by like weeks; the weeks slipped by like water.

And still Will ate turnips and snared rabbits and lived (if it was living) among the quiet of the trees who had gotten what they wanted—and perhaps found it less than satisfying—and longed for someone to speak to. Someone to hold. *Somewhere,* he thought, carrying his turnips into the cottage, *somewhere Kit is alive. And Morgan.*

My gentle betrayers.

Oh, unkind, William. He laid the turnips on the low table, recalling the glow of banked embers, a young man's plea. *What do you take your Marley for?*

He had a knife and a hatchet; the rhythm of the words came to him as he worked, the thud of metal on a stump cut into a butcher's block, the verse cold and lovely as a winter freeze among his lonely pines. *That you were once unkind besuits me now—no, befriends. That you were once unkind befriends me now. Once unlike yourself, once untrue, once unfair—*

Unkind.

Aye. There under the pines, under the arching branches of dead souls slain by their own pettiness, their own spite, their own grief and helplessness and pain.

Pines.

How aptly named.

Oak, he hate—

He would not think on it. If he thought, he would think on vengeance. He would think on Kit, immortal, and on Annie, now surely dead.

If he thought, he would think on fifty years alone in a forest without end.

He would think on how Lucifer wanted him to write, and how he would not do what Lucifer willed of him. How he would not pay the price, even though he knew, somehow, if he did, his horizons would broaden. That the Devil would reward Will if Will gave up that piece of himself. Of his soul. If he served.

He would think on how there was someone left alive to take his vengeance for Hamnet on, someone in Faerie, and how poetry was the only tool he had to do it.

He would not think on it, because he would not think on any of those things.

His knife made cubes of the turnips, cubes of the rabbit. He browned them in the fat left from a pheasant and added an onion from the braid on the wall. Housewifely tasks; he'd learned them all well. *And for that sorrow, which I then did feel, / Needs must I under my transgression bow—*

The words came; he could not stop them. They chewed at his heart, another pain among many. They gnawed at his breast, bosom serpents, venomed worms.

He had no need to busy himself so; the pantry would fill on its own, the garden would unweed itself. Will himself had no need, it seemed, to eat unless the desire took him, although his hands did tremble with his illness when he had no task to set them to. *Idle hands are the Devil's playground.*

Idle hands had a tendency to stray to the well-appointed desk, to lift the white pen that was a twin to the one Kit had found under the covers of his bed. *Unless my nerves were brass or hammer'd steel. For if you were by my unkindness shaken—*

Perfect words.

Better than anything, Will knew, anything he had written before. *As I by yours, you've passed a hell of time; / And I, a tyrant, have no leisure taken / To weigh how once I suffered in your crime.* Kit was alive. Somewhere. In Faerie. And his crime was ever less than Will's; Kit had had no vow of marriage to forswear. Kit had made no promise of fidelity at all. Worse—worse. Kit had offered, and Will had refused him.

Only to react like a kicked whelp when he discovered that Kit had believed what Will had told him. Kit, who was alive. Kit who would always be alive. As alive as the Fae who had killed Will's only son.

Alive and grieving. *O! that our night of woe might have remembered / My deepest sense, how hard true sorrow hits, / And soon to you, as you to me, then tendered / The humble salve, which wounded bosoms fits!*

Will added well water to the stewpot, crumbled rosemary, stirred with a long peeled stick. Not pine; he'd learned the flavors of lingering resins in the wood the unpleasant way.

Oak. For all he would have liked to burn it.

Annie. I hope Kit found you. I hope he told you what became of me. He propped a plate across the lid of the stewpot, left a little gap, banked the coals about the iron bottom. He glanced at his desk, at the fine already-cut leaves of paper, at the elegant pens. At dust that covered all.

He glanced at the door, at the notches whittled bright and new in the posts, the oldest ones silvering to match the weathered texture of the beams. He closed his eyes and inhaled the savor of garlic and onions and rosemary bubbling over the fire. He turned in the center of the room, the soft light of evening slipping in through opened shutters, the dark streaks of loam on the thighs of his breeches, the strange incongruity of the clock on the rough-hewn mantel with its scroll-worked hands for seconds, minutes, days, months, years.

A Hell of time.

He dusted his hands again; black dirt made moons under his nail-beds. A bit of grease daubed the left one's back. He thought of turnips and swore. *If I called on Lucifer, would he come to me? Aye, and bid me write, and chide me for childishness.*

It had happened before.

Will blasphemed a little. It did nothing to ease the bitterness in his throat, the emptiness in his bowels. He picked up his greasy oak stick and his broom and crouched before the fireplace, upsetting the stewpot intentionally, spilling gravy and vegetables on the hearthstone and away from the fire. He burrowed in the embers like a badger, raked them from the fireplace, scorching his shoe, burning his hands.

The broom smoked as he swept the heaps of coals against the cottage walls; with the ash shovel he carried a smoking log outside and heaved it up onto the thatch. He caught his cloak from the peg by the door frame and settled under a pine tree, where he remained late into the warm autumn evening, watching the snug little cottage burn.

He slept smiling, rough on sponge-soft needles, savoring the pain of his blistered palms when he woke in the darkness before morning. When the sun rose in tawny and auburn, Will crunched across soft-rotted pine boughs and mounds of needles to wash soot from his face and bathe his hands in the well.

The cottage sat where it had always been, a thin ribbon of smoke and the smell of cooking bannock rising from the chimney. The door was propped open and had been repainted red; Will could see the unmarked, silvery doorpost from where he stood just under the roof-edge of the pines.

But that your trespass now becomes a fee; / Mine ransoms yours, and yours must ransom me.

He sighed, and went inside, and somehow, again, managed not to pick up the pen.

Will knelt in the sunlight over a bowl full of water, shaving himself as best he could. He kept his hair haggled to the shoulders with his dagger; the palsy made keeping his beard trimmed hard, but he was damned if he'd let himself turn into a wild man. Truth to tell, he was damned even if he wasn't pretty.

He laid the blade aside and dipped hands in the water, washing the trimmed hairs from his face. He sat back on his heels and blinked; a shadow fell over him and he startled, overbalanced, and fell on his ass as he began to rise.

:Master Shakespeare: Lucifer bent and extended a hand; Will took it reflexively, surprised that it felt . . . so much like a hand. :Still thou hast written not a word. Stubborn man:

"I am what I am."

:Stubborn enough: Lucifer said. :Come. Thou art released. Thou art no longer welcomed in Hell:

Will blinked, tilted his head to the side. "Released?"

:Aye: Lucifer chivvied him along with a guiding wing. Will might have glanced back at the little cottage, the glade in the pines. But Lucifer's wing blocked his vision, and he was half certain that if he turned the house would not be there.

"Your Highness, I do not understand."

:Thy lover has purchased thy freedom: The Devil smiled, his blue eyes glittering. :And lucky thou art to command such loyalty. And such a ferocious soul:

"My lover?" *I haven't one,* Will thought. *But I did. Once.* "Morgan?" *What would Morgan want with me again?*

:No: Lucifer said. :Not Morgan, gentle William. Ah, look. Already, here is the door:

Act III, scene xxi

His waxen wings did mount above his reach
And melting, heavens conspired his overthrow.

—CHRISTOPHER MARLOWE, *Faustus*

Will, thin and shivering in the red light of Hell, leaned against the yawning, gateless mouth of a dark stone stair. Eyebright as if with fever and clutching his doublet tight around him as if Hell had left not heat but deep cold in his marrow, he reminded Kit of a bony old cat. He would not look up, would not look Kit in the face. He didn't seem to notice the lack of scars or the missing eyepatch, but the light, in truth, was poor, and Kit could see Will shivering.

Kit thought to lay a hand on Will's sleeve. He was as helpless to bridge the gap between them as to thrust a hand through a brick wall.

Will touched *him* though, and Kit's mouth filled with the taste of whiskey, his nostrils with the scent of smoke. He stepped away more rudely than he could have. "Will. Don't—"

"Kit. Sweet Christofer—" Oh, strange, to hear the name said in a lover's voice and feel no shiver of recognition in its cadences. *'Tis no longer thy name, who was Christofer Marley.* "You came for me."

"I chose a side, Will. The side that would have me as God made me." The tone that should have been light and playful fell on his own ears like pebbles in a pool. *Plop, plop, plop.* Kit wondered if the ripples of what Lucifer had done would ever stop shaking the stillness of his soul.

"You came for me." Will said it again, and this time Kit heard the disbelief clearly.

"I love thee." He led Will to the stair.

"You love Morgan."

Oh. "No."

"Dammit, Kit, I saw the two of you together. Robin said—" Will swallowed, audibly. "And all the years I've been gone, have you not spent at her side? And now she needs me for something. Else why would it have taken you so long to come—"

Puck. Damn you, too. Ah, wait. I already did that. Kit bit his lip on a hysterical laugh. "Years, Will?"

"How much time has passed in the mortal realm?" Will asked wearily. "Who is King?"

"It's still Hallow's eve—or was when I rode out of Faerie. And Elizabeth reigns yet. Hours, not years." Kit knew he needed to turn and put his hand on Will's sleeve, to knot his fingers in Will's hair and hold him close. He knew it from Will's sidelong glances, and the careful, conscious way Will kept his hands at his sides. But all he could sense was the touch of Lucifer's hands on his body, those bright wings fanning over him, the taste of the angel's skin. "Damn. Faerie time. Time in Hell. How long was it, Will?"

Will would not return Kit's steady regard. "I lost my calendar."

"God. *Will*—" *I'm sorry.* Inadequate, and untrue. Kit shuddered. He wasn't sorry. He was *angry. God in Hell, Will, if you knew what you cost me— Pish. Kit. And if thou hadst gone to the teind as Morgan willed, wouldst have chosen differently what thou didst to Satan sell?* "Thou'rt safe now. My love."

Will flinched. "Mine other love sold thee to Hell. Whom thou didst love also."

" 'Tis not love," Kit said. "Morgan's Fae. Betrayal, 'tis . . . part of what she is. As for me—I'm sorry. I am *so* sorry, Will." And he was. And angry, still.

Will did not try to touch him again, but walked very near, without speaking, on Kit's left hand. Kit let the silence hold them, and hoped there was forgiveness in it. It was good for thinking, that silence, and he bent his mind to Lucifer, and Christ, and God, and Will.

Will, who turned and looked at him straight, finally, and let his eyebrows rise. "There's a revelation on your face."

Kit smiled. "More a bemusement. My plays, your plays—they *can* change the world. Hell, William. Here I am living the Orpheus I *wrote*, for Christ's sake. And Morgan told me she has changed and changed again, reflecting what the poets sing. So if Christ came to preach God's love and tolerance a thousand and a half years gone, and half the world is Christian, why is it that God himself has not become what Christ the Redeemer would have made him? The Morningstar told me—" Kit stopped, pierced by a vivid recollection of the circumstances of that conversation.

"You believe what the Devil says?"

"Thou needs must have spoken with him, in thy time in Hell. Did he ever lie to thee?" Will flinched; Kit leveled his voice. "Satan says that God loves not, nor forgives, as the New Testament would have it. God *judges*, Will. As fathers do."

"You *believe* what the Devil says?"

"No lie could have cut me so."

"Kit Marley." Climbing, Will favored him with a glance. "I've heard you dismiss Moses as a—what was the word—"

"Juggler."

"Juggler, aye. And Christ as a sodomite and fornicator—"

"Is fornication such a sin? Can not a man's words be holy though a man be but earth?" Their footsteps up the stair carried them from Stygian gloom to something like pale earthly moonlight. Kit ran fingers along the rough stone of the wall and did not look back. *Never look back. Never step off the path. Never trust the guardian.*

Oh, indeed.

"And now thou tellst me thou art shattered because the Devil says God does not love thee." Will turned dark blue eyes on him in a glare, and blinked. "Your face—"

"Satan," Kit said dryly, "healed me. When he agreed to release thee."

"What didst thou—"

"Don't," Kit said, shaking his head, feeling the movement of scrubbed curls against his neck, knowing no soap or simple could make him clean again. "Don't ever ask me. Just accept that what I did, I did in love for thee."

"Oh, Kit." But Will fell silent, and it was enough, and they ascended side by side for a time until Kit found his courage again.

" 'Tis the Church," he said quietly.

"What do you mean?"

"The reason God can't love us. The Church. All churches." He paused, hearing his own radical words. *True heresy, this.* "They speak to power and to money, and they teach a jealous and a wrathful God. Christ's God was not that. Christ's God is a God who can forgive. Who can love his creations. Mayhap there are two Gods, I don't know—or three. The Catholic God, the Protestant God, and the Promethean God. Three that are one."

"And the Puritan God. Ah. Kit? How long do you suppose it takes to climb out of Hell?"

"Three days," Kit guessed, and smiled to himself when Will's laugh forgot to be broken-edged. Kit stole a look: Will leaned on the wall, lifting each foot with painful concentration, but he kept up. *I'll carry him on my back if I have to.*

A calm voice, then, and one with a purpose in it. "Your Latin. I suppose you've forgotten it all. And your Greek—"

"No, I've kept it," Kit answered. "And learned some of the Hebrew, some Arabic and some Russian, too."

"Hebrew," Will said. "That *will* be useful."

"Useful to what purpose?"

"Well," he answered, as they came around a corner in the stair and the source of the pale reflected light revealed itself—a shaft in the ceiling, unguessably high, with a patch of blue at the top of it that Kit could have covered complete with his pinky nail, for perspective. "If I'm going to write a Bible, I need someone to translate it for me. And someone to push the pen. My hands are not what they were."

"You're serious."

Will sighed, filling his lungs with the sweeter air that fell down the shaft. He squared his shoulders and recommenced to climb. "I've had time to think on it. If you can suggest a simpler—and preferably shorter — plan for convincing people God loves them and forgives them, I would be overjoyed to hear it. I'm going back to England. Let's do something useful with Prometheus, shall we? It's there; it's got to be for something better than shoring up Princes and clothing upstart Earls in glory."

"If that's your plan," Kit answered, "it will have to be something on the order of a — liberal — translation. The world is not kindly to those who seek wisdom, Will. Look at the example of one Jesus of Nazareth —"

"You're the one who believes our circumstances would be improved if God took a personal interest," Will answered, and Kit was certain this time that he did not imagine the bitterness. "Personally, I think we'd be better off if we accepted some responsibility for our choices. But you're our translator. You'll be responsible for that."

"An atheistical warlock and a humanist conspiring on a Bible to free good Englishmen from the suzerainty of the Church."

"A warlock, eh?"

"So they assure me." Kit opened his palm at face level as they climbed. His right eye showed a spiral of possibilities hovering over it. He focused on them, and called forth — *"Light."* A thin blue flicker of Saint Elmo's Fire curled about his fingers. "Call me Faustus and I'll hit you. Although there's a degree of dramatic irony in this."

"Well," Will answered, toiling upward. "We're both somewhat prone to irony. I suppose it's appropriate. Ironic, but appropriate. Although I can't answer for mine actions should you summon up the shade of Helen."

"The furthest thing from my mind," Kit assured him, permitting the light to fail.

Act III, scene xxii

In loving thee thou know'st I am forsworn,
But thou art twice forsworn, to me love swearing;

—WILLIAM SHAKESPEARE, Sonnet 152

Will was never sure how they came to return to the Mebd's palace. One moment climbing tiredly, Kit's hand awkward and quickly withdrawn on the small of his back; the next the dry crunch of beech twigs under his feet, the scuff of grass. Will staggered as they came out of the trees. He turned to speak to Kit; Kit had fallen behind. Will stopped and retraced his steps.

Will found Kit leaning against a beech trunk, bent over as if he'd been punched. Head bowed, Kit stared at the backs of his hands, which were spaced widely on his half-flexed knees. He looked up as Will approached, the sunlight falling across his unblemished face. Wordlessly, Will studied Kit, realizing that he had almost forgotten what Kit had looked like before he was scarred. Will held out a hand; Kit nodded it away, sliding his back up the smooth bole of the tree.

A red bird such as Will had never seen sang in the branches overhead, a high chirruping whistle. Delicate bell-shaped flowers that almost seemed cast in wax poked through the leaf mold around Kit's unshod feet.

"Thou'rt not well," Will said.

"Overcome for a moment, is all."

Kit's right eye caught the green sunlight through the trees and blazed for a moment, yellow as citrine before it faded to match the other.

"Kit—" Will took Kit by the forearms and held him tight. Kit would not meet his eyes. Will couldn't find the words for the question he needed to ask and so he asked instead, "What hath become of thy shoes?"

"I sold them to a ferryman." Kit tugged ineffectually. "And my cloak to an ifrit, and my sword to a demon. I think they were all Lucifer."

Will released Kit's right hand; Kit braced it against Will's chest and pushed, but Will held him fast and caught his chin. They stood just within the embrace of the woods; the trees were half bare. Within the castle, observers could see them wrangle so. "Kit, what have I done to earn thine anger?"

Kit laughed, but there was no humor in it. Will held him fast when he leaned back, still tugging his wrist away like a restless horse fretting at its tie: absently, almost without intent. *My touch hurts him,* Will realized, and the thought might as well have been a dagger letting his bowels out a slit in his belly. He held fast nonetheless.

"Thou hast done nothing." Sweat beading on Kit's face. "And I everything to earn thine. I don't deserve thy forgiveness—"

"I forgive thee anyway."

"I went to Morgan because—"

"Because thou didst wish me hurt for leaving thee, and thyself hurt for not being what I wanted most." Will delivered the words coldly, a judgment pronounced. "And she took thee because it would influence me, and me because it should influence thee. Christofer. Christofer, *look* at me—Christofer, long I've had to consider this, and if thou needst forgiveness I forgive thee, although if anything 'tis I should beg thy dispensation. I cry thee mercy, my love."

He expected Kit to quit his fighting; indeed, he looked Will square in the eye now, but his wrist still twitched in Will's grip.

"I knew what would have driven me to it," Will said, softly, and made as if to kiss.

Kit stiffened in his hands, flexed like an eel, and shoved himself backward, out of Will's embrace. Kit fell gracelessly, sprawled in leaf litter, a rustling and crunching of twigs, a startled shout. "Will," Kit said, clambering to his feet. "Will, 'tis not thee."

"What *happened* down there?"

Kit checked. He lowered his hands and scrubbed them on his thighs. "I asked thee practice reticence—"

"Aye," Will said. "And I did not vow it. Kit, thy feet are bleeding." Spots of red showed on raveled silk stockings. Will knelt down among the twigs. "Thou hast walked thyself bloody. Come, let me help thee to the palace—"

Kit shied a step back, and Will desisted. " 'Tis not far," he said. "Methinks I can stagger a quarter mile downhill."

"On your head be it."

They went on.

Kit climbed the spiral stair like a clockwork, hauling himself up each step by clutching the rail, never looking at the Fae that flocked around, chattering questions. There were those that might have stopped them, and those that might have helped them, too. Will waved them all aside, servants and nobles, blocking them with his body when his voice wouldn't suffice.

They crowded, touching, prodding; Kit jerked away, keeping his eyes downcast, and Will interposed himself. Fingers tugged his doublet and hands outreached to touch his face. *You came back. He brought you back. How did you come back?*

Hope, Will realized, and wonder. He found himself stronger than he expected, and the Fae fell back from his glance and his hand upraised—after he shouldered a few aside quite physically. He chivvied Kit to the top of the stairs and toward their door, closing his eyes in a moment's relief at Robin Goodfellow barring the doorway, hands on his minuscule hips and his fool's bauble dangling from his fingers.

The Puck scattered the Fae with a gesture. When they were inside, he barred the door and jammed a chair under the handle, exchanging a look with Will. Kit turned and sat heavily on the bed. "How long have we been gone?"

"It's All Saints' Day," Puck said, and gestured out the window to the robust evening light. "Your horse came home with an empty saddle—"

"I sent him," Kit said, and lay back on the coverlet.

Will got up to check the fire and light a candle against the dimness that soon would fill the room.

"Don't trouble yourself," Kit said. Every wick in the room stirred to flame. "In a moment," he said, "I am going to get extremely drunk. You are both more than welcome to join me."

The Puck's voice was clipped. "Sir Christofer." He perched on the edge of the chair he'd wedged the door with, hooked his heels on the top rail, and leaned his elbows on his knees. "Was *that* what it took to buy William free?"

Will stood stupefied with exhaustion between them, wondering what Robin knew that he did not. Kit laid the back of his wrist across his eyes. "No."

Worry, now, and Puck's ears dipping and bobbing like buoys on a net. "Sir Christofer—"

"Don't call me that."

"Call you what?" Puck sucked his mobile lip. Will watched, blinking, shifting his gaze from poet to Faerie and back, struggling through the fatigue to understand.

"*Sir Christofer*. It signifies nothing," Kit replied. "It grates mine ears to hear such empty sound."

"As you wish it," Puck said, and leaned back. "The court has been in uproar."

"I noticed." Will felt pleasure at his self-possessed tone, but from the looks Kit and Robin shot him, it read not so much level as emotionless. Forcing his tingling feet to move, he crossed to the washstand and lifted the ewer and bowl in hands that shook enough to scatter droplets on the carpet. All his gardening had given him strength, at least; despite the palsy, he balanced the weight easily. "Come, Kit." He brought the water and knelt beside the bed. "Peel off thy stockings; let me work my will on thee."

Kit would not meet Will's smile. Instead, he sat stiffly as an old man, tucking his feet aside as Will reached for them. "I can pick the gravel from mine own wounds, Will."

Will grunted and heaved himself to his feet, sharing a sidelong glance with Robin as Kit peeled his shredded stockings from the lacerations on his feet. Puck watched with unsettling intensity. "When commenced you to study witchcraft, Sir—or rather, Kit?"

Kit tossed the garters on the bed. The stockings were rags. He hunched between his knees, using those rags to scrub the blood from his feet. The water in the basin grew pink, and so did the knot of knitted silk. "Since last night, Master Goodfellow."

"You've mastered a great deal."

"I had instruction."

Will's imagination, or did Kit's voice break on that word? Puck stood abruptly, sweeping the chair aside with a clatter. "I've just recalled, Master Marley. I've a package in my room 'tis thine: 'twas delivered this afternoon. Master Shakespeare?"

Will breathed again, in relief. "Can I be of service, Robin?" *Ask of me an errand, good Puck. Anything. Get me out of this room before I strike the man.*

"It is too heavy for me to carry—"

"Will?" Kit looked up, voice suddenly plaintive. "Robin, what sort of a package? Wilt be gone long?"

"Cloth, methinks." The Puck shrugged. "I opened it not."

"I'll return in a moment," Will said, and tugged open the door. "Robin's rooms are not far. Good Master Goodfellow, wilt ask for us that food be sent, and Morgan and the Queen apprised of our return?"

Will felt as much as heard Kit cease breathing.

"The Mebd knows," Robin said. " 'Twas she that sent me. And Morgan—"

"Morgan?" Kit, not Will, although he did not rise.

"Morgan is not currently welcomed at court," Puck said, and stepped through the door. He turned back over his shoulder. "Her Majesty was not pleased with the machinations that led to your brief absences from our company."

Brief, Will thought, as Kit made no protest and Puck closed the door. He laughed. "A hundred years if it were a day," he said, and Puck nodded.

" 'Tis as I expected. Was it very bad?" Puck set a good pace. Will fell in beside him.

"Bad enough. Robin—"

"Aye?"

"What's wrong with Kit?"

Silence, and one Will didn't like at all. They were nearly to Robin's door when the gnarled little man spoke again. "Do you know how witches get their powers, Will?"

Will chewed his nail and considered while Puck opened the door and slipped inside. A moment later, and Puck returned, lugging a linen-wrapped burden that completely filled his arms. Will took it and tucked it under his elbow, where it compressed softly. "Kit's thanks, I'm sure." He had to force his smile.

" 'Twas nothing."

There was a click as Robin shut the door. Will stood in the corridor for long moments, considering. *Another price I am not worthy of*, he thought, and shifted the bundle in his grip.

> *But how unseemly is it for my Sex,*
> *My discipline of arms and Chivalry,*
> *My nature and the terror of my name,*
> *To harbor thoughts effeminate and faint?*
> *Save only that in Beauties just applause,*
> *With whose instinct the soul of man is touched,*
> *And every warrior that is rapt with love*
> *Of fame, of valor, and of victory,*
> *Must needs have beauty beat on his conceits.*
> —CHRISTOPHER MARLOWE, *Tamburlaine the Great*

Kit limped to the window on linen-wrapped feet and shouldered the casement open, careful of the bowl of bloody water in his hands. He poured it down onto the garden at the base of the wall and set the bowl aside. Leaning over the window ledge, watching the stars shiver out in the crystalline blue-gray of the heavens, he swore. *If you cannot bear it, there's always the knife.*

Suicide, and back into Satan's hands.

He wished he didn't know the shiver that crept up his neck was desire, and not terror. *Back into his hands whenever he wants you. And you cannot pretend you did it for Will.*

No. The first thing he had done for Will. His name. His identity. His legacy. Little enough for his love's freedom and a chance at redemption.

The second thing he had done was for power. Like Faustus. And, like Faustus, he would make good his revenge ere the devil claimed him. *See if I don't.*

They called it soldier's heart. This weariness, this unsounded sorrow. Kit had felt it before, when he'd seen men who had called him friend hanged for treason. He'd felt it after Rheims: a mad, manic hollowness no prayer or drink or lover could fulfil.

The door opened behind him. He turned, sighed in half relief and half panic when he saw who stood framed in the opening. "Will. Distract me from my study; I am all black thoughts and foul humors tonight."

Will shut the door and shot the bolt. He held something white as angel wings wrapped in his arms; it gleamed while he leaned against the door, hugging it as a child hugs a doll.

"Will, what hast thee?" Kit tugged the window shut and limped toward Will, stopping a few feet away.

Will shrugged and dropped it on the chair that had settled kitty-corner, where Puck had left it. He stepped away, but not before Kit saw the shininess in the corners of his eyes. Will walked toward the sideboard where Kit kept wine and overturned cups. Kit came to the chair, picked at the wax and twine sealing the bundle; it fell open at his touch. "Oh."

A waterfall of rainbow colors spilled across Kit's hands, silks and satins and velvet and taffeta and lace. His cloak, in all its dozens of patches. And something more; someone's hands had sewn a collar on it, an upright blunt-cornered affair of soft black velvet that was the second-richest thing that Kit had ever touched. The stitches were as neat and tight as Kit's own hand—*I imagine Will sews a tight stitch too, growing up in a glover's house*—and he knew before he pressed it to his face that it would smell of smoke and strong liquor. He bundled it in his arms, walked across the carpet, and leaned against the bed. He closed his eyes and inhaled deeply, feeling the tears prick under his eyelids and hating himself for weakness as he did. "He sent my cloak back."

Will came back to him, carrying a cup. Kit slung the cloak across the coverlet, as if he meant to sleep beneath it. Accepted the wine. "I have a gift for thee as well," he said. "I meant to give it upon thy leaving."

"Kit, what could you—"

"Hush," he said, and turned to root in the box on the bedside stand. The ring was gold, cool and heavy in his hand, the flat face marked with Will's initials, which were both surmounted and linked by true-love's knots—a pair of them. "You'll need a signet, if you're to be a gentleman."

Will took it from his hand and stared down at it, a muscle twitching in his jaw.

"We should sleep early. As early as we can."

"Tomorrow—" Will dragged a stool over, crouched on it, and began to work on his boots. "I have to go home to Annie, Kit."

"Aye." Kit tossed back the wine, set his cup aside, and methodically began stripping his buttons from their holes. "I've decided not to get drunk after all. Wilt stay by me tonight?"

"Wilt flinch when I touch you?"

Kit couldn't look at Will, but he could imagine the expression on his face. *And what will I do for peace now, now that this is lost to me too?*

It seemed an ungrateful question, given what he had traded that chance of peace for. *Power.*

The ability to protect Will. And his children. The strength to do something about Richard Baines.

He tossed his doublet aside and stripped his shirt off over his head. And heard Will's sucked-in breath and remembered his own dramatic gesture with the candles and the brilliance of the lighting a moment too late.

"Kit, you've a bruise. . . ."

Kit reached up and over, felt down the sprung plane of his shoulder blade. His left arm with its old injury wouldn't flex so far; he reached with the right. Blood-gorged flesh heated his fingertips. He could feel, almost, the outline of each perfect tooth, the roughness of a seeking tongue. Right where someone might bite a lover taken from behind—

Right where a wing would take root, if he had wings.

His burn scars pained him suddenly, a low, sweet ache like the ache inside him. A longing that almost made him reach for the wine bottle again.

"It's a witch's mark," Kit said without turning, and pulled on his nightshirt with a grimace. "Lucifer's unclean brand. Come, Will. Get ready for bed."

"Kit."

"Will, no."

"Kit. What was it that thou didst in Hell?"

Kit read the play of emotions across Will's face: fear, grief, concern. *I don't want him to know. I want anything but for him to know. And if I pretend I do not understand what he's asking, I've lost not only a lover, but the trust of a friend.*

Kit swallowed. He doused the candles with a snap of his fingers, feeling the power move to his whim as if he tugged a dozen tiny threads. The room fell into near darkness; starlit from the window, a glow like the blue light of Hell except where it cast shadows. He reached up over his head and knotted his fingers in his hair, pulling; the pain felt good. Clean. Will's words, again: for them both, it always came back to the blasted words. *And I can teach thee, coz, to shame the devil by telling truth: tell truth and shame the devil —*

He smiled at Will, a smile no more thick than gilt on a page, and said, "I whored myself out to the Devil." And was surprised when it felt good to say it, another good pain like ripping a scab back from the wound. "I let — *God*. Don't touch me. Please. I can't —"

Will drew back the hand he had been about to lay on Kit's shoulder. "For me," he said softly, and jerked back in surprise when Kit shook his head.

"Nothing so noble," Kit answered. "I had thee back already by then." He turned and looked Will in the eyes. *I love him still, for all I can't so much as lay my damned hand on his arm.*

Aye. Damned indeed.

"Then what?"

Kit shrugged. "Baines. Poley."

"You could just outwait them. Outlive them." Placating. A pleading voice, and he hated to see Will beg.

"Elizabeth is over, Will. Walsingham and Burghley are gone.

Whatever happens next is ours. Ours, or De Vere's and Essex's.
Would you see that come to pass?" Kit smiled. Will drew back from
something: the fervor in his eyes, the glitter of his teeth. "And now
I can melt their Godsrotted eyes in their heads, if I'm lucky. Besides, it's too late now to give the gift back. I took the shilling, so to
speak."

"Up the arse."

"Christ, Will—"

"No," Will said, quietly. His blue eyes were black in the darkened
room. "Do you know what Lucifer told me?"

Kit shook his head; whatever he felt was too complex to speak
through. *Nor do I want to know.*

"He told me who killed Hamnet. And showed me how to use my
poetry to get vengeance on them."

"Oh."

"As long as I gave him mine allegiance."

"Will, I—"

"I didn't write a word," Will said. "Fifty years and more I spent in
his damned birdcage. Alone. Without books, without conversation. I
didn't write a word for all that time. And then something changed."

Kit nodded. Will wouldn't look away, for all Kit must have been
barely a shadow in the starlight. Kit could see *Will* perfectly well, out
of his right eye at least. Could see in the dark like a demon. "What
happened, then?"

Will smiled, and clapped Kit on the shoulder too quickly for Kit
to flinch away, stinging his flesh beneath the thin lawn of his shirt.
"My faith was rewarded," he said softly. "My savior came. Come to
bed, Kit; you don't have to armor yourself in nightshirts and dressing
gowns like a maiden."

Will turned away, moving through the darkness to their bed, peeling the covers back, leaving a trail of clothes like breadcrumbs behind
him on the floor. "Don't give up hope. I know for a fact that someday
your savior will come as well."

"How do you know it?" Kit ran a comb through his hair in the
darkness, scattering crushed beech leaves on the floor. He peeled the
nightshirt off again and slid into bed beside Will, tugging the cloak up

close to his chin and inhaling the complex scent saturating the petal-soft velvet collar.

"Because," Will said quietly, stretching against the far edge of the bed. "That's how all the best stories end."

Not Romeo and Juliet, Kit thought. But he couldn't bring himself to break the warm darkness to say so.

Intra-act: Chorus

Annie Shakespeare touched the breast of her bodice with two fingers, paper rustling between her chemise and her skin. Her second-floor sitting room was quiet and gleaming with sunset; her needle paused before her frame, glinting in the cold winter light. It had hovered so for minutes as she leaned forward in her chair and looked out the window, and now she sat back with a sigh, and pressed her bosom again. *He won't be here.*

He won't—

A clatter of hoofbeats on the road. Only one horse, and no creak of wheels. *A messenger, then, and not my Will.* She tucked the needle through the cloth and stood, stretching before the window with her hands against the small of her back, to see who came to her house too late to be sent along to the tavern for supper. She couldn't see his face for the broad wings of his cap, but he sat his horse as awkwardly as a sack of barley, and the animal shook his head in complaint.

He reined up before the gates of the New Place and tilted his head back, looking up at the facade and the five gables. Annie pressed her hand against the glass: if Will had described the ramshackle century-old dwelling he'd bought for her—that she'd bought under his signature, to be truthful—the messenger was unlikely to recognize it, whitewashed and gracious now as a bride in her mother's remade wedding dress.

The rider pushed his hat back on his forehead, looking up from the shadow of the roadway into the light that still gleamed on the wall, and Annie's hand on the window rose to her mouth. She turned, tripped on her hem, knocked the embroidery frame sideways with her hip and dove down the stairs pell-mell, calling for Susanna and for Judith and for Cook.

Will went to put the girls to bed with a story—a little child's treat, and perhaps not fitting for young women nearly old enough to go into service or off to wed—and Annie turned the mattress and the feather-bed and tucked the covers straight. Will found her, she guessed, as much by the spill of candlelight into the hall as by knowing where the bedroom lay.

"The house has changed, wife," he said. He shut the door behind and, trembling softly with his palsy, set his own candlestand on the shelf beside it. " 'Tis much improved—"

"As it was uninhabitable when we bought it, I should hope. 'Tis empty, though—" *without a man*. Annie bit her lip, and tugged the coverlet down. And bit it harder when Will came up behind her and stroked both hands down her hips, laced his fingers across her belly and tugged her into his embrace.

"Will, don't tease—"

His mouth on her neck, tracing the line of her hair, the dints along her spine. "I should not attempt such cruelty." He strung something about her throat, the soft, lingering touch of his fingers, a stroke as of satin. "I have confessions, Annie. And promises to make."

"Confessions?"

"Aye—" He was knotting a silken ribbon, a braid of red and black and green. Something that weighed like an acorn hung upon it; she slipped her hand beneath. A silken pouch no bigger than her thumb. "Annie, I have loved thee."

She held her breath. "And now do not?"

He turned her in his arms and looked into her eyes. Curious, she reached up to touch the golden earring that adorned him. He smiled at the touch. "And love thee more than ever I could have told thee. I, Will, love thee to wordlessness."

"Never hast thou been wordless," she answered, and kissed his nose to make him smile like that again.

"Annie, hush," he said. And she obeyed, and he continued. "I promised I'd love no other but thee—whatever sins my flesh was heir to. And I've broken that promise, my love."

She'd been lulled by the moment. By the spell of him, the gentleness, the kisses she'd almost forgotten the sweetness of. She closed her eyes and stepped away, acid burning in her throat. "A mistress—"

"No," Will said, and pulled her close. And kissed her on the mouth. "A man."

She wanted to jerk away, retreat to the corner between the clothespress and the bed. But his hands were on her wrists, and he held her tight, with a strength she didn't remember in him. "A—man."

"Aye," he said. "I won't—won't lie to thee. I loved him, and I love him still. And more—"

She steeled herself to stand motionless in his embrace, wondering if he could feel the thunder of her heart. *So there's a reason for his fevered kisses. Will, I'd not have thought thee so capably cruel. . . .*

"—the man I love is no mortal, but an Elf-knight, a warlock. A creature of the Fae. And under a geas, that I may never touch him. No, nor any other, until his curse be lifted—"

Anne blinked, not understanding. "Thou'rt leaving me for a man thou canst not touch?" *Oh, why not? He cannot touch thee either, sister—*

"No," Will said. He stepped back and touched the silk hung at the hollow of her throat. "No, I tell thee so thou wilt understand what he has given me. This man. This knight—"

She reached up and caught his wrist. "What? He's bought thee from me for a bit of silk?"

"No, Annie." He kissed the fingers that bound his trembling forearm. Kissed her wrist and the tenderness inside her elbow and bowed his head there, inhaling her scent. "Annie, he's given thee back to me. How long has it been?"

"Judith is nearly fourteen," she said softly. "What canst thy meaning be?"

He pushed her nightgown down over her shoulders as he kissed her again, without restraint this time. Despite her confusion, she gave herself up to the kiss, buried her fingers in his hair, tasted mutton and onions on his tongue. "Witches have spells for causing barrenness, my love."

Author's Note (brief version)

This is the first of two tightly linked novels, a duology collectively known as *The Stratford Man*. The second book, *Hell and Earth*, will be published in August 2008.

A complete Author's Note and Acknowledgements—enumerating this narrative's extensive historical and linguistic malfeasances and encompassing a semi-exhaustive list of who may be assessed for the same—may be found at the end of the second book.

About the Author

Originally from Vermont and Connecticut, **Elizabeth Bear** spent six years in the Mojave Desert and currently lives in southern New England. She attended the University of Connecticut, where she studied anthropology and literature. She was awarded the 2005 Campbell Award for Best New Writer.